CARVE

THE

MARK

ASSEMBLY SHIP

CURRENTSTREAM BARRIER · CURRENTSTREAM BARRIER

OGRA

TEFES

KOLLANDE

ESSANDER

TRELLA

SUN

OTHYR

ZOLD

PIITHA

PIIO4

THUVHE

THE BRIM

CARVE

THE

MARK

VERONICA
ROTH

KATHERINE TEGEN BOOKS
An Imprint of HarperCollins Publishers

BOOKS BY
VERONICA ROTH

Divergent

Insurgent

Allegiant

Four: A Divergent Collection

Katherine Tegen Books is an imprint of HarperCollins Publishers.

Library of Congress Control Number: 2016949683
ISBN 978-0-06-234863-0

Typography by Joel Tippie
16 17 18 19 20 PC/LSCH 10 9 8 7 6 5 4 3 2 1
❖
First Edition

To Ingrid and Karl—
because there is no version of you I don't love

CHAPTER 1 | AKOS

HUSHFLOWERS ALWAYS BLOOMED WHEN the night was longest. The whole city celebrated the day the bundle of petals peeled apart into rich red—partly because hushflowers were their nation's lifeblood, and partly, Akos thought, to keep them all from going crazy in the cold.

That evening, on the day of the Blooming ritual, he was sweating into his coat as he waited for the rest of the family to be ready, so he went out to the courtyard to cool off. The Kereseth house was built in a circle around a furnace, all the outermost and innermost walls curved. For luck, supposedly.

Frozen air stung his eyes when he opened the door. He yanked his goggles down, and the heat from his skin fogged up the glass right away. He fumbled for the metal poker with his gloved hand and stuck it under the furnace hood. The burnstones under it just looked like black lumps before friction lit them, and then they sparked in different colors, depending on what they were dusted with.

The burnstones scraped together and lit up bright red as blood. They weren't out here to warm anything, or light anything—they were just supposed to be a reminder of the current. As if the hum in Akos's body wasn't enough of a reminder. The current flowed through every living thing, and showed itself in the sky in all different colors. Like the burnstones. Like the lights of the floaters that zoomed overhead on their way to town proper. Off-worlders who thought their planet was blank with snow had never actually set foot on it.

Akos's older brother, Eijeh, poked his head out. "Eager to freeze, are you? Come on, Mom's nearly ready."

It always took their mom longer to get ready when they were going to the temple. After all, she was the oracle. Everybody would be staring right at her.

Akos put the poker down and stepped inside, popping the goggles off his eyes and pulling his face shield down to his throat.

His dad and his older sister, Cisi, were standing by the front door, stuffed into their warmest coats. They were all made of the same material—kutyah fur, which didn't take dye, so it was always white gray—and hooded.

"All ready then, Akos? Good." His mom was fastening her own coat closed. She eyed their dad's old boots. "Somewhere out there, your father's ashes are collectively shuddering at how dirty your shoes are, Aoseh."

"I know, that's why I fussed about dirtying them up," their dad said with a grin at their mom.

"Good," she said. Almost chirped it, in fact. "*I* like them this way."

"You like anything my father didn't like."

"That's because he didn't like anything."

"Can we get into the floater while it's still warm?" Eijeh said, a little bit of a whine in his voice. "Ori's waiting for us by the memorial."

Their mom finished with her coat, and put on her face shield. Down the heated front walk they bobbed, all fur and goggle and mitten. A squat, round ship waited for them, hovering at knee height just above the snowbank. The door opened at their mom's touch and they piled in. Cisi and Eijeh had to yank Akos in by both arms because he was too small to climb on his own. Nobody bothered with safety belts.

"To the temple!" their dad cried, his fist in the air. He always said that when they went to the temple. Sort of like cheering for a boring lecture or a long line on voting day.

"If only we could bottle that excitement and sell it to all of Thuvhe. Most of them I see just once a year, and then only because there's food and drink waiting for them," their mom drawled with a faint smile.

"There's your solution, then," Eijeh said. "Entice them with food all season long."

"The wisdom of children," their mom said, poking the ignition button with her thumb.

The floater jerked them up and forward, so they all fell into each other. Eijeh punched Akos away from him, laughing.

The lights of Hessa twinkled up ahead. Their city wrapped around a hill, the military base at the bottom, the temple at the top, and all the other buildings in between. The temple, where they were headed, was a big stone structure with a dome—made of hundreds of panes of colored glass—right in the middle of it. When the sun shone on it, Hessa's peak glowed orange red. Which meant it almost never glowed.

The floater eased up the hill, drifting over stony Hessa, as old as their nation-planet—Thuvhe, as everyone but their enemies called it, a word so slippery off-worlders tended to choke on it. Half the narrow houses were buried in snowdrifts. Nearly all of them were empty. Everybody who was anybody was going to the temple tonight.

"See anything interesting today?" their dad asked their mom as he steered the floater away from a particularly tall windmeter poking up into the sky. It was spinning in circles.

Akos knew by the tone of his dad's voice that he was asking their mom about her visions. Every planet in the galaxy had three oracles: one rising; one sitting, like their mother; and one falling. Akos didn't quite understand what it meant, except that the current whispered the future in his mom's ears, and half the people they came across were in awe of her.

"I may have spotted your sister the other day—" their mom started. "Doubt she'd want to know, though."

"She just feels the future ought to be handled with the appropriate respect for its weight."

Their mom's eyes swept over Akos, Eijeh, and Cisi in turn.

"This is what I get for marrying into a military family, I guess," she said eventually. "You want everything to be regulated, even my currentgift."

"You'll notice that *I* flew in the face of family expectation and chose to be a farmer, not a military captain," their dad said. "And my sister doesn't mean anything by it, she just gets nervous, that's all."

"Hmm," their mom said, like that wasn't all.

Cisi started humming, a melody Akos had heard before, but

couldn't say from where. His sister was looking out the window, not paying attention to the bickering. And a few ticks later, his parents' bickering stopped, and the sound of her hum was all that was left. Cisi had a way about her, their dad liked to say. An ease.

The temple was lit up, inside and out, strings of lanterns no bigger than Akos's fist hanging over the arched entrance. There were floaters everywhere, strips of colored light wrapped around their fat bellies, parked in clusters on the hillside or swarming around the domed roof in search of a space to touch down. Their mom knew all the secret places around the temple, so she pointed their dad toward a shadowed nook next to the refectory, and led them in a sprint to a side door that she had to pry open with both hands.

They went down a dark stone hallway, over rugs so worn you could see right through them, and past the low, candlelit memorial for the Thuvhesits who had died in the Shotet invasion, before Akos was born.

He slowed to look at the flickering candles as he passed the memorial. Eijeh grabbed his shoulders from behind, making Akos gasp, startled. He blushed as soon as he realized who it was, and Eijeh poked his cheek, laughing, "I can tell how red you are even in the dark!"

"Shut up!" Akos said.

"Eijeh," their mom chided. "Don't tease."

She had to say it all the time. Akos felt like he was always blushing about *something*.

"It was just a *joke*. . . ."

They found their way to the middle of the building, where a crowd had formed outside the Hall of Prophecy. Everyone was stomping their way out of their outer boots, shrugging off coats, fluffing hair that had been flattened by hoods, breathing warm air on frozen fingers. The Kereseths piled their coats, goggles, mittens, boots, and face coverings in a dark alcove, right under a purple window with the Thuvhesit character for the current etched into it. Just as they were turning back to the Hall of Prophecy, Akos heard a familiar voice.

"Eij!" Ori Rednalis, Eijeh's best friend, came barreling down the hallway. She was gangly and clumsy-looking, all knees and elbows and stray hair. Akos had never seen her in a dress before, but she was in one now, made of heavy purple-red fabric and buttoned at the shoulder like a formal military uniform.

Ori's knuckles were red with cold. She jumped to a stop in front of Eijeh. "There you are. I've had to listen to two of my aunt's rants about the Assembly already and I'm about to explode." Akos had heard one of Ori's aunt's rants before, about the Assembly—the governing body of the galaxy—valuing Thuvhe only for its iceflower production, and downplaying the Shotet attacks, calling them "civil disputes." She had a point, but Akos always felt squirmy around ranting adults. He never knew what to say.

Ori continued, "Hello, Aoseh, Sifa, Cisi, Akos. Happy Blooming. Come on, let's go, Eij." She said all this in one go, hardly taking the time to breathe.

Eijeh looked to their dad, who flapped his hand. "Go on, then. We'll see you later."

"And if we catch you with a pipe in your mouth, as we did last year," their mom said, "we will make you eat what's inside it."

Eijeh quirked his eyebrows. He never got embarrassed about anything, never flushed. Not even when the kids at school teased him for his voice—higher than most boys'—or for being rich, not something that made a person popular here in Hessa. He didn't snap back, either. Just had a gift for shutting things out and letting them back in only when he wanted to.

He grabbed Akos by the elbow and pulled him after Ori. Cisi stayed behind, with their parents, like always. Eijeh and Akos chased Ori's heels all the way into the Hall of Prophecy.

Ori gasped, and when Akos saw inside the hall, he almost echoed her. Somebody had strung hundreds of lanterns—each one dusted with hushflower to make it red—from the apex of the dome down to the outermost walls, in every direction, so a canopy of light hung over them. Even Eijeh's teeth glowed red, when he grinned at Akos. In the middle of the room, which was usually empty, was a sheet of ice about as wide as a man was tall. Growing inside it were dozens of closed-up hushflowers on the verge of blooming.

More burnstone lanterns, about as big as Akos's thumb, lined the sheet of ice where the hushflowers waited to bloom. These glowed white, probably so everyone could see the hushflowers' true color, a richer red than any lantern. As rich as blood, some said.

There were a lot of people milling about, dressed in their finery: loose gowns that covered all but the hands and head, fastened with elaborate glass buttons in all different colors; knee-length waistcoats lined with supple elte skin, and twice-wrapped scarves. All in dark, rich colors, anything but gray or white, in contrast to their coats. Akos's jacket was dark green, one of Eijeh's old ones, still too big in the shoulders for him, and Eijeh's was brown.

Ori led the way straight to the food. Her sour-faced aunt was there, offering plates to passersby, but she didn't look at Ori. Akos got the feeling Ori didn't like her aunt and uncle, which was why she pretty much lived at the Kereseth house, but he didn't know what had happened to her parents.

Eijeh stuffed a roll in his mouth, practically choking on the crumbs.

"Careful," Akos said to him. "Death by bread isn't a dignified way to go."

"At least I'll die doing what I love," Eijeh said, around all the bread.

Akos laughed.

Ori hooked her elbow around Eijeh's neck, tugging his head in close. "Don't look now. Stares coming in from the left."

"So?" Eijeh said, spraying crumbs. But Akos already felt heat creeping into his neck. He chanced a look over at Eijeh's left. A little group of adults stood there, quiet, eyes following them.

"You'd think you'd be a little more used to it, Akos," Eijeh said to him. "Happens all the time, after all."

"You'd think *they* would be used to *us*," Akos said. "We've lived here all our lives, and we've had fates all our lives, what's there to stare at?"

Everyone had a future, but not everyone had a fate—at least, that was what their mom liked to say. Only parts of certain "favored" families got fates, witnessed at the moment of their births by every oracle on every planet. In unison. When those visions came, their mom said, they could wake her from a sound sleep, they were so forceful.

Eijeh, Cisi, and Akos had fates. Only they didn't know what they were, even though their mom was one of the people who had

Seen them. She always said she didn't need to tell them; the world would do it for her.

The fates were supposed to determine the movements of the worlds. If Akos thought about that too long, he got nauseous.

Ori shrugged. "My aunt says the Assembly's been critical of the oracles on the news feed lately, so it's probably just on everyone's minds."

"Critical?" Akos said. "Why?"

Eijeh ignored them both. "Come on, let's find a good spot."

Ori brightened. "Yeah, let's. I don't want to get stuck staring at other people's butts like last year."

"I think you've grown past butt height this year," Eijeh said. "Now you're at mid-back, maybe."

"Oh good, because I definitely put on this dress for my aunt so I could stare at a bunch of backs." Ori rolled her eyes.

This time Akos slipped into the crowd in the Hall of Prophecy first, ducking under glasses of wine and swooping gestures until he got to the front, right by the ice sheet and the closed-up hushflowers. They were right on time, too—their mom was up by the ice sheet, and she had taken off her shoes, though it was chilly in here. She said she was better at being an oracle when she was closer to the ground.

A few ticks ago he'd been laughing with Eijeh, but as the crowd went quiet, everything in Akos went quiet, too.

Eijeh leaned in close to him and whispered in his ear, "Do you feel that? The current's humming like crazy in here. It's like my chest is vibrating."

Akos hadn't noticed it, but Eijeh was right—he did feel like his chest was vibrating, like his blood was singing. Before he could

answer, though, their mom started talking. Not loud, but she
didn't have to be, because they all knew the words by heart.

"The current flows through every planet in the galaxy, giving
us its light as a reminder of its power." As if on cue, they all looked
up at the currentstream, its light showing in the sky through the
red glass of the dome. At this time of year, it was almost always
dark red, just like the hushflowers, like the glass itself. The currentstream was the visible sign of the current that flowed through
all of them, and every living thing. It wound across the galaxy,
binding all the planets together like beads on a single string.

"The current flows through everything that has life," Sifa went
on, "creating a space for it to thrive. The current flows through
every person who breathes breath, and emerges differently
through each mind's sieve. The current flows through every flower
that blooms in the ice."

They scrunched together—not just Akos and Eijeh and Ori,
but everyone in the whole room, standing shoulder to shoulder,
so they could all see what was happening to the hushflowers in the
ice sheet.

"The current flows through every flower that blooms in the
ice," Sifa repeated, "giving them the strength to bloom in the deep-
est dark. The current gives the most strength to the hushflower,
our marker of time, our death-giving and peace-giving blossom."

For a while there was silence, and it didn't feel odd, like it
should have. It was as if they were all hum-buzz-singing together,
feeling the strange force that powered their universe, just like friction between particles powered the burnstones.

And then—movement. A shifting petal. A creaking stem.
A shudder went through the small field of hushflowers growing

among them. No one made a sound.

Akos glanced up at the red glass, the canopy of lanterns, just once, and he almost missed it—all the flowers bursting open. Red petals unfurling all at once, showing their bright centers, draping over their stems. The ice sheet teemed with color.

Everyone gasped, and applauded. Akos clapped with the rest of them, until his palms itched. Their dad came up to take their mom's hands and plant a kiss on her. To everyone else she was untouchable: Sifa Kereseth, the *oracle*, the one whose currentgift gave her visions of the future. But their dad was always touching her, pressing the tip of his finger into her dimple when she smiled, tucking strays back into the knot she wore her hair in, leaving yellow flour fingerprints on her shoulders when he was done kneading the bread.

Their dad couldn't see the future, but he could mend things with his fingers, like broken plates or the crack in the wall screen or the frayed hem of an old shirt. Sometimes he made you feel like he could put people back together, too, if they got themselves into trouble. So when he walked over to Akos, swung him into his arms, Akos didn't even get embarrassed.

"Smallest Child!" his dad cried, tossing Akos over his shoulder. "Ooh—not so small, actually. Almost can't do this anymore."

"That's not because I'm big, it's because you're old," Akos replied.

"Such words! From my own *son*," his dad said. "What punishment does a sharp tongue like that deserve, I wonder?"

"Don't—"

But it was too late; his dad had already pitched him back and let him slide so he was holding both of Akos's ankles. Hanging upside down, Akos pressed his shirt and jacket to his body, but he couldn't help laughing. Aoseh lowered him down, only letting go when Akos was safe on the ground.

"Let that be a lesson to you about sass," his dad said, leaning over him.

"Sass causes all the blood to rush to your head?" Akos said, blinking innocently up at him.

"Precisely." Aoseh grinned. "Happy Blooming."

Akos returned the grin. "You too."

That night they all stayed up so late Eijeh and Ori both fell asleep upright at the kitchen table. Their mom carried Ori to the living room couch, where she spent a good half of her nights these days, and their dad roused Eijeh. Everybody went one way or another after that, except Akos and his mom. They were always the last two up.

His mom switched the screen on, so the Assembly news feed played at a murmur. There were nine nation-planets in the Assembly, all the biggest or most important ones. Technically each nation-planet was independent, but the Assembly regulated trade, weapons, treaties, and travel, and enforced the laws in unregulated space. The Assembly feed went through one nation-planet after another: water shortage on Tepes, new medical innovation on Othyr, pirates boarded a ship in Pitha's orbit.

His mom was popping open cans of dried herbs. At first Akos thought she was going to make a calming tonic, to help them both rest, but then she went into the hall closet to get the jar of hushflower, stored on the top shelf, out of the way.

"I thought we'd make tonight's lesson a special one," Sifa said. He thought of her that way—by her given name, and not as

"Mom"—when she taught him about iceflowers. She'd taken to calling these late-night brewing sessions "lessons" as a joke two seasons ago, but now she sounded serious to Akos. Hard to say, with a mom like his.

"Get out a cutting board and cut some harva root for me," she said, and she pulled on a pair of gloves. "We've used hushflower before, right?"

"In sleeping elixir," Akos said, and he did as she said, standing on her left with cutting board and knife and dirt-dusted harva root. It was sickly white and covered in a fine layer of fuzz.

"And that recreational concoction," she added. "I believe I told you it would be useful at parties someday. *When you're older*."

"You did," Akos said. "You said 'when you're older' then, too."

Her mouth slanted into her cheek. Most of the time that was the best you could get out of his mom.

"The same ingredients an *older* version of you might use for recreation, you can also use for poison," she said, looking grave. "As long as you double the hushflower and halve the harva root. Understand?"

"Why—"Akos started to ask her, but she was already changing the subject.

"So," she said as she tipped a hushflower petal onto her own cutting board. It was still red, but shriveled, about the length of her thumb. "What is keeping your mind busy tonight?"

"Nothing," Akos said. "People staring at us at the Blooming, maybe."

"They are so fascinated by the fate-favored. I would love to tell you they will stop staring someday," she said with a sigh, "but I'm afraid that you . . . *you* will always be stared at."

He wanted to ask her about that pointed "you," but he was careful around his mom during their lessons. Ask her the wrong question and she ended the lesson all of a sudden. Ask the right one, and he could find out things he wasn't supposed to know.

"How about you?" he asked her. "What's keeping your mind busy, I mean?"

"Ah." His mom's chopping was so smooth, the knife *tap tap* tapping on the board. His was getting better, though he still carved chunks where he didn't mean to. "Tonight I am plagued by thoughts about the family Noavek."

Her feet were bare, toes curled under from the cold. The feet of an oracle.

"They are the ruling family of Shotet," she said. "The land of our enemies."

The Shotet were a people, not a nation-planet, and they were known to be fierce, brutal. They stained lines into their arms for every life they had taken, and trained even their children in the art of war. And they lived on Thuvhe, the same planet as Akos and his family—though the Shotet didn't call this planet "Thuvhe," or themselves "Thuvhesits"—across a huge stretch of feathergrass. The same feathergrass that scratched at the windows of Akos's family's house.

His grandmother—his dad's mom—had died in one of the Shotet invasions, armed only with a bread knife, or so his dad's stories said. And the city of Hessa still wore the scars of Shotet violence, the names of the lost carved into low stone walls, broken windows patched up instead of replaced, so you could still see the cracks.

Just across the feathergrass. Sometimes they felt close enough to touch.

"The Noavek family is fate-favored, did you know that? Just like you and your siblings are," Sifa went on. "The oracles didn't always see fates in that family line, it happened only within my lifetime. And when it did, it gave the Noaveks leverage over the Shotet government, to seize control, which has been in their hands ever since."

"I didn't know that could happen. A new family suddenly getting fates, I mean."

"Well, those of us who are gifted in seeing the future don't control who gets a fate," his mom said. "We see hundreds of *futures*, of possibilities. But a fate is something that happens to a particular person in every single version of the future we see, which is very rare. And those fates determine who the fate-favored families are—not the other way around."

He'd never thought about it that way. People always talked about the oracles doling out fates like presents to special, important people, but to hear his mom tell it, that was all backward. Fates *made* certain families important.

"So you've seen their fates. The fates of the Noaveks."

She nodded. "Just the son and the daughter. Ryzek and Cyra. He's older; she's your age."

He'd heard their names before, along with some ridiculous rumors. Stories about them frothing at the mouth, or keeping enemies' eyeballs in jars, or lines of kill marks from wrist to shoulder. Maybe that one didn't sound so ridiculous.

"Sometimes it is easy to see why people become what they are," his mom said softly. "Ryzek and Cyra, children of a tyrant. Their father, Lazmet, child of a woman who murdered her own brothers and sisters. The violence infects each generation." She bobbed her head, and her body went with it, rocking back and forth. "And I see it. I see all of it."

Akos grabbed her hand and held on.

"I'm sorry, Akos," she said, and he wasn't sure if she was saying sorry for saying too much, or for something else, but it didn't really matter.

They both stood there for a while, listening to the mutter of the news feed, the darkest night somehow even darker than before.

CHAPTER 2 | AKOS

"HAPPENED IN THE MIDDLE of the night," Osno said, puffing up his chest. "I had this scrape on my knee, and it started burning. By the time I threw the blankets back, it was gone."

The classroom had one curved wall and two straight ones. A large furnace packed with burnstones stood in the center, and their teacher always paced around it as she taught, her boots squeaking on the floor. Sometimes Akos counted how many circles she made during one class. It was never a small number.

Around the furnace were metal chairs with glass screens fixed in front of them at an angle, like tabletops. They glowed, ready to show the day's lesson. But their teacher wasn't there yet.

"Show us, then," another classmate, Riha, said. She always wore scarves stitched with maps of Thuvhe, a true patriot, and she never trusted anyone at their word. When someone made a claim, she scrunched up her freckled nose until they proved it.

Osno held a small pocket blade over his thumb and dug in. Blood bubbled from the wound, and even Akos could see, sitting across the room from everyone, that his skin was already starting to close up like a zipper.

Everybody got a currentgift when they got older, after their bodies changed—which meant, judging by how small Akos still was at fourteen seasons old, he wouldn't be getting his for awhile yet. Sometimes gifts ran in families, and sometimes they didn't. Sometimes they were useful, and sometimes they weren't. Osno's was useful.

"Amazing," Riha said. "I can't wait for mine to come. Did you have any idea what it would be?"

Osno was the tallest boy in their class, and he stood close to you when he talked to you so you knew it. The last time he'd talked to Akos had been a season ago, and Osno's mother had said as she walked away, "For a fate-favored son, he's not much, is he?"

Osno had said, "He's nice enough."

But Akos wasn't "nice"; that was just what people said about quiet people.

Osno slung his arm over the back of his chair, and flicked his dark hair out of his eyes. "My dad says the better you know yourself, the less surprised you'll be by your gift."

Riha's head bobbed in agreement, her braid sliding up and down her back. Akos made a bet with himself that Riha and Osno would be dating by season's end.

And then the screen fixed next to the door flickered and switched off. All the lights in the room switched off, too, and the ones that glowed under the door, in the hallway. Whatever Riha had been about to say froze on her lips. Akos heard a loud voice coming from the hall. And the squeal of his own chair as he scooted back.

"Kereseth . . . !" Osno whispered in warning. But Akos wasn't sure what was scary about peeking in the hallway. Not like something was going to jump out and bite him.

He opened the door wide enough to let his body through, and leaned into the narrow hallway just outside. The building was circular, like a lot of the buildings in Hessa, with teachers' offices in the center, classrooms around the circumference, and a hallway separating the two. When the lights were off, it was so dark in the hall he could see only by the emergency lights burning orange at the top of every staircase.

"What's happening?" He recognized that voice—it was Ori. She moved into the pool of orange light by the east stairwell. Standing in front of her was her aunt Badha, looking more disheveled than he'd ever seen her, pieces of hair hanging around her face, escaped from its knot, and her sweater buttons done up all wrong.

"You are in danger," Badha said. "It is time for us to do as we have practiced."

"Why?" Ori demanded. "You come in here, you drag me out of class, you want me to leave everything, everyone—"

"All the fate-favored are in danger, understand? You are exposed. You must go."

"What about the Kereseths? Aren't they in danger, too?"

"Not as much as you." Badha grabbed Ori's elbow and steered her toward the landing of the east stairwell. Ori's face was shaded, so Akos couldn't see her expression. But just before she went around a corner, she turned, hair falling across her face, sweater slipping off her shoulder so he could see her collarbone.

He was pretty sure her eyes found his then, wide and fearful. But it was hard to say. And then someone called Akos's name.

Cisi was hustling out of one of the center offices. She was in her heavy gray dress, with black boots, and her mouth was taut.

"Come on," she said. "We've been called to the headmaster's office. Dad is coming for us now, we can wait there."

"What—" Akos began, but as always, he talked too softly for most people to pay attention.

"Come on." Cisi pushed through the door she had just closed. Akos's mind was going in all different directions. Ori was fate-favored. All the lights were off. Their dad was coming to get them. Ori was in danger. *He* was in danger.

Cisi led the way down the dark hallway. Then: an open door, a lit lantern, Eijeh turning toward them.

The headmaster sat across from him. Akos didn't know his name; they just called him "Headmaster," and saw him only when he was giving an announcement or on his way someplace else. Akos didn't pay him any mind.

"What's going on?" he asked Eijeh.

"Nobody will say," Eijeh said, eyes flicking over to the headmaster.

"It is the policy of this school to leave this sort of situation to the parents' discretion," the headmaster said. Sometimes kids joked that the headmaster had machine parts instead of flesh, that if you cut him open, wires would come tumbling out. He talked like it, anyway.

"And you can't say what sort of situation it *is*?" Eijeh said to him, in much the way their mom would have, if she'd been there. *Where is Mom, anyway?* Akos thought. Their dad was coming for them, but nobody had said anything about their mom.

"Eijeh," Cisi said, and her whispered voice steadied Akos, too. It was almost like she spoke into the hum of the current inside him, leveling it just enough. The spell lasted awhile, the headmaster, Eijeh, Cisi, and Akos quiet, waiting.

"It's getting cold," Eijeh said eventually, and there was a draft creeping under the door, chilling Akos's ankles.

"I know. I had to shut off the power," the headmaster said. "I intend to wait until you are safely on your way before turning it back on."

"You shut off the power for us? Why?" Cisi said sweetly. The same wheedling voice she used when she wanted to stay up later or have an extra candy for dessert. It didn't work on their parents, but the headmaster melted like a candle. Akos half expected there to be a puddle of wax spreading under his desk.

"The only way the screens can be turned off during emergency alerts from the Assembly," the headmaster said softly, "is if the power is shut down."

"So there was an emergency alert," Cisi said, still wheedling.

"Yes. It was issued by the Assembly Leader just this morning."

Eijeh and Akos traded looks. Cisi was smiling, calm, her hands folded over her knees. In this light, with her curly hair framing her face, she was Aoseh's daughter, pure and simple. Their dad could get what he wanted, too, with smiles and laughs, always soothing people, hearts, situations.

A heavy fist pounded on the headmaster's door, sparing the wax man from melting further. Akos knew it was his dad because the doorknob fell out at the last knock, the plate that held it fast to the wood cracking right down the middle. He couldn't control his temper, and his currentgift made that pretty clear. Their dad was always fixing things, but half the time it was because he himself had broken them.

"Sorry," Aoseh mumbled when he came into the room. He shoved the doorknob back in place and traced the crack with his fingertip. The plate came together a little jagged, but mostly good as new. Their mom insisted he didn't always fix things right, and they had the uneven dinner plates and jagged mug handles to prove it.

"Mr. Kereseth," the headmaster began.

"Thank you, Headmaster, for reacting so quickly," their dad said to him. He wasn't smiling even a little. More than the dark hallways or Ori's shouting aunt or Cisi's pressed-line mouth, his serious face scared Akos. Their dad was always smiling, even when the situation didn't call for it. Their mom called it his very best armor.

"Come on, Small Child, Smaller Child, Smallest Child," Aoseh said halfheartedly. "Let's go home."

They were up on their feet and marching toward the school entrance as soon as he said "home." They went straight to the coatracks to search the identical gray furballs for the ones with their names stitched into the collars: *Kereseth, Kereseth, Kereseth.* Cisi and Akos confused theirs for a tick and had to switch, Akos's just a little too small for her arms, hers just a little too long for his short frame.

The floater waited just outside, the door still thrown open. It was a little bigger than most, still squat and circular, the dark metal outsides streaked with dirt. The news feed, usually playing in a stream of words around the inside of the floater, wasn't on. The nav screen wasn't on, either, so it was just Aoseh poking at buttons and levers and controls without the floater telling them what he was doing. They didn't buckle themselves in; Akos felt like it was stupid to waste the time.

"Dad," Eijeh started.

"The Assembly took it upon itself to announce the fates of the favored lines this morning," their dad said. "The oracles shared the fates with the Assembly seasons ago, in confidence, as a gesture of trust. Usually a person's fate isn't made public until after they die, known only to them and their families, but now . . ." His eyes raked over each of them in turn. "Now everyone knows your fates."

"What are they?" Akos asked in a whisper, just as Cisi asked, "Why is that dangerous?"

Dad answered her, not him. "It's not dangerous for everyone with a fate. But some are more . . . revealing than others."

Akos thought of Ori's aunt dragging her by the elbow to the stairwell. *You are exposed. You must go.*

Ori had a fate—a dangerous one. But as far as Akos could remember, there wasn't any "Rednalis" family in the list of favored lines. It must not have been her real name.

"What are our fates?" Eijeh asked, and Akos envied him for his loud, clear voice. Sometimes when they stayed up later than they were supposed to, Eijeh tried to whisper, but one of their parents always ended up at their door to shush them before long. Not like Akos; he kept secrets closer than his own skin, which was why he wasn't telling the others about Ori just yet.

The floater zoomed over the iceflower fields their dad managed. They stretched out for miles in every direction, divided by low wire fences: yellow jealousy flowers, white purities, green harva vines, brown sendes leaves, and last, protected by a cage of wire with current running through it, red hushflower. Before they put up the wire cage, people used to take their lives by running straight into the hushflower fields and dying there among the bright petals, the poison putting them to sleepy death in a few breaths. It didn't seem like a bad way to go, really, Akos thought. Drifting off with flowers all around you and the white sky above.

"I'll tell you when we're safe and sound," their dad said, trying to sound cheery.

"Where's Mom?" Akos said, and this time, Aoseh heard him.

"Your mother . . ." Aoseh clenched his teeth, and a huge gash opened up in the seat under him, like the top of a loaf of bread splitting in the oven. He swore, and ran his hand over it to mend it. Akos blinked at him, afraid. What had gotten him so angry?

"I don't know where your mother is," he finished. "I'm sure she's fine."

"She didn't warn you about this?" Akos said.

"Maybe she didn't know," Cisi whispered.

But they all knew how wrong that was. Sifa always, *always* knew.

"Your mother has her reasons for everything she does. Sometimes we don't get to know them," Aoseh said, a little calmer now. "But we have to trust her, even when it's difficult."

Akos wasn't sure their dad believed it. Like maybe he was just saying it to remind himself.

Aoseh guided the floater down in their front lawn, crushing the tufts and speckled stalks of feathergrass under them. Behind their house, the feathergrass went on as far as Akos could see. Strange things sometimes happened to people in the grasses. They heard whispers, or they saw dark shapes among the stems; they waded through the snow, away from the path, and were swallowed by the earth. Every so often they heard stories about it, or someone spotted a full skeleton from their floater. Living as close to the tall grass as Akos did, he'd gotten used to ignoring the faces that surged toward him from all directions, whispering his name. Sometimes they were crisp enough to identify: dead grandparents; his mom or dad with warped, corpse faces; kids who were mean to him at school, taunting.

But when Akos got out of the floater and reached up to touch the tufts above him, he realized, with a start, that he wasn't seeing or hearing anything anymore.

He stopped, and hunted the grasses for a sign of the hallucinations anywhere. But there weren't any.

"Akos!" Eijeh hissed.

Strange.

He chased Eijeh's heels to the front door. Aoseh unlocked it, and they all piled into the foyer to take off their coats. As he breathed the inside air, though, Akos realized something didn't smell right. Their house always smelled spicy, like the breakfast bread their dad liked to make in the colder months, but now it smelled like engine grease and sweat. Akos's insides were a rope, twisting tight.

"Dad," he said as Aoseh turned on the lights with the touch of a button.

Eijeh yelled. Cisi choked. And Akos went stock-still.

There were three men standing in their living room. One was tall and slim, one taller and broad, and the third, short and thick. All three wore armor that shone in the yellowish burnstone light, so dark it almost looked black, except it was actually dark, dark blue. They held currentblades, the metal clasped in their fists and the black tendrils of current wrapping around their hands, binding the weapons to them. Akos had seen blades like that before, but only in the hands of the soldiers that patrolled Hessa. They had no need of currentblades in their house, the house of a farmer and an oracle.

Akos knew it without really knowing it: These men were Shotet. Enemies of Thuvhe, enemies of *theirs*. People like this were responsible for every candle lit in the memorial of the Shotet invasion; they had scarred Hessa's buildings, busted its glass so it showed fractured images; they had culled the bravest, the strongest, the fiercest, and left their families to weeping. Akos's grandmother and her bread knife among them, so said their dad.

"What are you doing here?" Aoseh said, tense. The living room looked untouched, the cushions still arranged around the low table, the fur blanket curled by the fire where Cisi had left it when she was reading. The fire was embers, still glowing, and the air was cold. Their dad took a wider stance, so his body covered all three of them.

"No woman," one of the men said to one of the others. "Wonder where she is?"

"Oracle," one of the others replied. "Not an easy one to catch."

"I know you speak our language," Aoseh said, sterner this time. "Stop jabbering away like you don't understand me."

Akos frowned. Hadn't his dad heard them talking about their mom?

"He is quite demanding, this one," the tallest one said. He had golden eyes, Akos noticed, like melted metal. "What is the name again?"

"Aoseh," the shortest one said. He had scars all over his face, little slashes going every direction. The skin around the longest one, next to his eye, was puckered. Their dad's name sounded clumsy in his mouth.

"Aoseh Kereseth," the golden-eyed one said, and this time he sounded . . . different. Like he was suddenly speaking with a thick accent. Only he hadn't had one before, so how could that be? "My name is Vas Kuzar."

"I know who you are," Aoseh said. "I don't live with my head in a hole."

"Grab him," the man called Vas said, and the shortest one lunged at their dad. Cisi and Akos jumped back as their dad and the Shotet soldier scuffled, their arms locked together. Aoseh's teeth gritted. The mirror in the living room shattered, the pieces flying everywhere, and then the picture frame on the mantel, the one from their parents' wedding day, cracked in half. But still the Shotet soldier got a hold on Aoseh, wrestling him into the living room and leaving the three of them, Eijeh, Cisi, and Akos, exposed.

The shortest soldier forced their dad to his knees, and pointed a currentblade at his throat.

"Make sure the children don't leave," Vas said to the slim one. Just then Akos remembered the door behind him. He seized the knob, twisted it. But by the time he was pulling it, a rough hand had closed around his shoulder, and the Shotet lifted him up with one arm. Akos's shoulder ached; he kicked the man hard in the leg. The Shotet just laughed.

"Little thin-skinned boy," the soldier spat. "You, as well as the rest of your pathetic kind, would do better to surrender now."

"We are not pathetic!" Akos said. It was a stupid thing to say— something a little kid said when he didn't know how to win an argument. But for some reason, it stopped everyone in their tracks. Not just the man with his hand clamped around Akos's arm, but Cisi and Eijeh and Aoseh, too. Everyone stared at Akos, and—*damn it all*—heat was rushing into his face, the most ill-timed blush he had ever felt in all his life, which was saying something.

Then Vas Kuzar laughed.

"Your youngest child, I presume," Vas said to Aoseh. "Did you know he speaks Shotet?"

"I don't speak Shotet," Akos said weakly.

"You just did," Vas said. "So how did the family Kereseth find itself with a Shotet-blooded son, I wonder?"

"Akos," Eijeh whispered wonderingly. Like he was asking Akos a question.

"I do not have Shotet blood!" Akos snapped, and all three of the Shotet soldiers laughed at once. It was only then that Akos heard it—he heard the words coming out of his mouth, with their sure meaning, and he also heard harsh syllables, with sudden stops and closed vowels. He heard Shotet, a language he had never learned. So unlike graceful Thuvhesit, which was like wind catching snow-flakes in its updraft.

He was speaking Shotet. He sounded just like the soldiers. But how—*how* could he speak a language he had never learned?

"Where is your wife, Aoseh?" Vas said, turning his attention back to their dad. He turned the currentblade in his fist, so the black tendrils shifted over his skin. "We could ask her if she had a dalliance with a Shotet man, or if she shares our fine ancestry and never saw fit to tell you about it. Surely the oracle knows how her youngest son came to be fluent in the revelatory tongue."

"She's not here," Aoseh said, terse. "As you may have observed."

"The Thuvhesit thinks he is clever?" Vas said. "I think that cleverness with enemies gets a man killed."

"I'm sure you think many foolish things," Aoseh said, and

somehow, he stared Vas down, despite being on the ground at his feet. "Servant of the Noaveks. You're like the dirt I remove from under my fingernails."

Vas swung at their dad, striking his face so hard he fell to the side. Eijeh yelled, fighting to get closer but intercepted by the Shotet who still held Akos's arm. Held both brothers without effort, in fact, like it cost him nothing at all, though Eijeh, at sixteen seasons, was almost man-size.

The low table in the living room cracked right down the middle, from end to end, splitting in half and falling to each side. All the little things that had been on top of it—an old mug, a book, a few scraps of wood from their dad's whittling—scattered across the floor.

"If I were you," Vas said, low, "I would keep that currentgift under control, Aoseh."

Aoseh clutched his face for a tick, and then dove, grabbing the wrist of the short, scarred Shotet soldier standing off to the side and twisting, hard, so his grip faltered. Aoseh grabbed the blade by the handle and wrenched it free, then turned it back on its owner, his eyebrows raised.

"Go ahead and kill him," Vas said. "There are dozens more where he came from, but you have a limited number of sons."

Aoseh's lip was swollen and bleeding, but he licked the blood away with the tip of his tongue and looked over his shoulder at Vas.

"I don't know where she is," Aoseh said. "You should have checked the temple. This is the last place she would come, if she knew you were on your way here."

Vas smiled down at the blade in his hand.

"It is just as well, I suppose," he said in Shotet, looking at the soldier who held Akos with one hand and was pressing Eijeh to the wall with the other. "Our priority is the child."

"We know which one is youngest," the soldier replied in the same language, jerking Akos by the arm again. "But which of the other two is the second-born?"

"Dad," Akos said desperately. "They want to know about the Smaller Child. They want to know which one of them is younger—"

The soldier released Akos, but only to swing the back of his hand at him, hitting him right in the cheekbone. Akos stumbled, slamming into the wall, and Cisi choked on a sob, bending over him, her fingers stroking her brother's face.

Aoseh screamed through his teeth, and lunged, plunging the stolen currentblade deep into Vas's body, right under the armor.

Vas didn't even flinch. He just smiled, crookedly, wrapped his hand around the blade's handle, and tugged the knife free. Aoseh was too stunned to stop him. Blood poured from the wound, soaking Vas's dark trousers.

"You know my name, but you don't know my gift?" Vas said softly. "I don't feel pain, remember?"

He grabbed Aoseh's elbow again, and pulled his arm out from his side. He plunged the knife into the fleshy part of their dad's arm and dragged down, making him groan like Akos had never heard before. Blood spattered on the floor. Eijeh screamed again, and thrashed, and Cisi's face contorted, but she didn't make a sound.

Akos couldn't stand the sight. It had him on his feet, though his face still ached, though there was no purpose to moving and nothing he could do.

"Eijeh," he said, quiet. "Run."

And he threw his body at Vas, meaning to dig his fingers into the wound in the man's side, deeper and deeper, until he could tear out his bones, tear out his heart.

Scuffling, shouting, sobbing. All the voices combined in Akos's ears, full of horror. He punched, uselessly, at the armor that covered Vas's side. The blow made his hand throb. The scarred soldier came at him, and threw him to the floor like a sack of flour. He put his boot on Akos's face and pressed down. He felt the grit of dirt on his skin.

"Dad!" Eijeh was screaming. "Dad!"

Akos couldn't move his head, but when he lifted his eyes, he saw his dad on the ground, halfway between the wall and the doorway, his elbow bent back at a strange angle. Blood spread like a halo around his head. Cisi crouched at Aoseh's side, her shaking hands hovering over the wound in his throat. Vas stood over her with a bloody knife.

Akos went limp.

"Let him up, Suzao," Vas said.

Suzao—the one with his boot digging into Akos's face—lifted his foot and dragged Akos to his feet. He couldn't take his eyes off his dad's body, how his skin had broken open like the table in the living room, how much blood surrounded him—*how can a person have that much blood?*—and the color of it, the dark orange-red-brown.

Vas still held the bloodstained knife out from his side. His hands were wet.

"All clear, Kalmev?" Vas said to the tall Shotet. He grunted in reply. He had grabbed Eijeh and put a metal cuff around his wrists. If Eijeh had resisted, at first, he was finished now, staring dully at their dad, slumped on the living room floor.

"Thank you for answering my question about which of your siblings we are looking for," Vas said to Akos. "It seems you will both be coming with us, by virtue of your fates."

Suzao and Vas flanked Akos, and pushed him forward. At the last second he broke away, falling to his knees at his dad's side and touching his face. Aoseh felt warm and clammy. His eyes were still open, but losing life by the second, like water going down a drain. They skipped to Eijeh, who was halfway out the front door, pressed forward by the Shotet soldiers.

"I'll bring him home," Akos said, jostling his dad's head a little so he would look at him. "I will."

Akos wasn't there when the life finally left his dad. Akos was in the feathergrass, in the hands of his enemies.

CHAPTER 3 | CYRA

I WAS ONLY SIX seasons old when I went on my first sojourn.

When I stepped outside, I expected it to be into sunlight. Instead, I walked into the shadow of the sojourn ship, covering the city of Voa—the capital of Shotet—like a massive cloud. It was longer than it was wide, its nose coming to a gentle point with panes of unbreakable glass above it. Its metal-plated belly was battered by over a decade of space travel, but some of the overlapping sheets were polished where they had been replaced. Soon we would be standing inside it, like masticated food inside the stomach of a great beast. Near the rear jets was the open terminal where we would soon board.

Most Shotet children were permitted to go on their first sojourn—our most significant rite—when they were eight seasons old. But as a child of the sovereign, Lazmet Noavek, I was prepared for my first journey through the galaxy two seasons earlier. We would follow the currentstream around the galaxy's edge until it turned darkest blue, and then descend to a planet's surface to scavenge, the second part of the rite.

It was traditional for the sovereign and his or her family to enter the sojourn ship first. Or at least, it had been traditional since my grandmother, the first Noavek leader of Shotet, had declared it to be so.

"My hair itches," I said to my mother, tapping at the tight braids on the side of my head with my fingertip. There were only a few, pulled back and twisted together so my hair wouldn't fall in my face. "What was wrong with my regular hair?"

My mother smiled at me. She wore a dress made of feather-grass, the stalks crossed over the bodice and extending to frame her face. Otega—my tutor, among other things—had taught me that the Shotet had planted an ocean of feathergrass between us and our enemies, the Thuvhesit, to keep them from invading our land. My mother commemorated that clever act now, with her dress. By design, everything my mother did echoed our history.

"Today," she told me, "is the first day that most Shotet will lay eyes on you, not to mention the rest of the galaxy. The last thing we want is for them to fixate on your hair. By fixing it up, we make it invisible. Understand?"

I didn't, but I didn't press the issue. I was looking at my mother's hair. It was dark, like mine, but a different texture—hers was so curly it trapped fingers, and mine was just straight enough to escape them.

"The rest of the galaxy?" Technically, I knew how vast the galaxy was, that it held nine significant planets and countless other fringe ones, as well as stations nestled in the unfeeling rock of broken moons, and orbiting ships so large they were like nation-planets unto themselves. But to me, planets still seemed about as large as the house where I had spent most of my life, and no larger.

"Your father authorized the Procession footage to be sent to the general news feed, the one accessed by all Assembly planets," my mother replied. "Anyone who is curious about our rituals will be watching."

Even at that age I did not assume that other planets were like ours. I knew we were unique in our pursuit of the current across the galaxy, that our detachment from places and possessions was singular. Of course the other planets were curious about us. Maybe even envious.

The Shotet had been going on the sojourn once a season for as long as our people had existed. Otega had told me once that the sojourn was about tradition, and the scavenge, which came afterward, was about renewal—the past and the future, all in one ritual. But I had heard my father say, bitterly, that we "survived on other planets' garbage." My father had a way of stripping things of their beauty.

My father, Lazmet Noavek, walked ahead of us. He was the first to pass through the great gates that separated Noavek manor from the streets of Voa, his hand lifted in greeting. Cheers erupted at the sight of him from the huge, pulsing crowd that had gathered outside our house, so dense I couldn't see light between the shoulders of the people before us, or hear my own thoughts through the cacophony of cheers. Here in the center of the city of Voa, just streets away from the amphitheater where the arena challenges were held, the streets were clean, the stones under my feet intact. The buildings here were a patchwork of old and new, plain stonework and tall, narrow doors mixed with intricate metalwork and glass. It was an eclectic mixture that was as natural to me as my own body. We knew how to hold the beauty of old things against the beauty of the new, losing nothing from either.

It was my mother, not my father, who drew the loudest cry from the sea of her subjects. She extended her hands to the people who reached for her, brushing their fingertips with her own and smiling. I watched, confused, as eyes teared up at the sight of her alone, as crooning voices sang her name. *Ylira, Ylira, Ylira.* She plucked a feathergrass stalk from the bottom of her skirt and tucked it behind a little girl's ear. *Ylira, Ylira, Ylira.*

I ran ahead to catch up to my brother, Ryzek, who was a full ten seasons older than I was. He wore mock armor—he had not yet earned the armor made from the skin of a slain Armored One, which was a status symbol among our people—and it made him look bulkier than usual, which I suspected was on purpose. My brother was tall, but lean as a ladder.

"Why do they say her name?" I asked Ryzek, stumbling to keep up with him.

"Because they love her," Ryz said. "Just as we do."

"But they don't *know* her," I said.

"True," he acknowledged. "But they believe they do, and sometimes that's enough."

My mother's fingers were stained with paint from touching so many outstretched, decorated hands. I didn't think I would like to touch so many people at once.

We were flanked by armored soldiers who carved a narrow path for us in the bodies. But really, I didn't think we needed them—the crowd parted for my father like he was a knife slicing through them. They may not have shouted his name, but they bent their heads to him, guided their eyes away from him. I saw, for the first time, how thin the line was between fear and love, between reverence and adoration. It was drawn between my parents.

"Cyra," my father said, and I stiffened, almost going still as he turned toward me. He reached for my hand, and I gave it to him, though I didn't want to. My father was the sort of man a person just *obeyed*.

Then he swung me into his arms, quick and strong, startling a laugh from me. He held me against his armored side with one arm, like I was weightless. His face was close to mine, smelling of herbs and burnt things, his cheek rough with a beard. My father, Lazmet Noavek, sovereign of Shotet. My mother called him "Laz" when she didn't think anyone could hear her, and spoke to him in Shotet poetry.

"I thought you might want to see your people," my father said to me, bouncing me a little as he shifted my weight to the crook of his elbow. His other arm, returning to his side, was marked from shoulder to wrist with scars, stained dark to stand out. He had told me, once, that they were a record of lives, but I didn't know what that meant. My mother had a few, too, though not half as many as my father.

"These people long for strength," my father said. "And your mother, brother, and I are going to give it to them. Someday, so shall you. Yes?"

"Yes," I said quietly, though I had no idea how I would do that.

"Good," he said. "Now wave."

Trembling a little, I extended my hand, mimicking my father. I stared, stunned, as the crowd responded in kind.

"Ryzek," my father said.

"Come on, little Noavek," Ryzek said. He didn't need to be asked to take me from my father's arms; he saw it in the man's posture, as surely as I felt it in the restless shift of his weight. I put my arms around Ryzek's neck, and climbed onto his back, hitching my legs on the straps of his armor.

I looked down at his pimple-spotted cheek, dimpled with a smile.

"Ready to run?" he said to me, raising his voice so I could hear him over the crowd.

"Run?" I said, squeezing tighter.

In answer, he held my knees tight against his sides, and jogged down the pathway the soldiers had cleared, laughing. His bouncing steps jostled a giggle from me, and then the crowd—our people, my people—joined in, my eyeline full of smiles.

I saw a hand up ahead, stretching toward me, and I brushed it with my fingers, just like my mother would. My skin came away damp with sweat. I found that I didn't mind it as much as I expected. My heart was full.

CHAPTER 4 | CYRA

THERE WERE HIDDEN HALLWAYS in the walls of Noavek manor, built for the servants to travel through without disturbing us and our guests. I often walked them, learning the codes that the servants used to navigate, carved into the corners of the walls and the tops of entrances and exits. Otega sometimes scolded me for coming to her lessons covered in cobwebs and grime, but mostly, no one cared how I spent my free time as long as I didn't disturb my father.

When I was newly seven seasons old, my wanderings took me to the walls behind my father's office. I had followed a clattering sound there, but when I heard my father's voice, raised in anger, I stopped and crouched.

For a moment, I toyed with the idea of turning back, running the same way I had come so that I could be safe in my own room. Nothing good came of my father's raised voice, and it never had. The only one who could calm him was my mother, but even she couldn't control him.

"Tell me," my father said. I pushed my ear to the wall to better hear him. "Tell me *exactly* what you told him."

"I—I thought . . ." Ryz's voice wobbled like he was on the verge of tears. That wasn't good, either. My father hated tears. "I thought, because he is training to be my steward, that he would be trustworthy—"

"Tell me what you told him!"

"I told him . . . I told him that my fate, as declared by the oracles, was—was to fall to the family Benesit. That they are one of the two Thuvhesit families. That's all."

I pulled away from the wall. A cobweb caught on my ear. I hadn't heard Ryzek's fate before. I knew my parents had shared it with him when most fated children found out their fates: when they developed a currentgift. I would find out my own in a handful of seasons. But to know Ryzek's—to know that Ryzek's was to *fall* to the family Benesit, which had kept itself hidden for so many seasons we didn't even know their aliases or their planet of residence—was a rare gift. Or a burden.

"Imbecile. That's 'all'?" my father said, scornful. "You think that you can afford trust, with a coward fate like yours? You must keep it hidden! Or else perish under your own weakness!"

"I'm sorry." Ryz cleared his throat. "I won't forget. I will never do it again."

"You are correct. You will not." My father's voice was deeper now, and flat. That was almost worse than yelling. "We will just have to work harder to find a way out of it, won't we? Of the hundreds of futures that exist, we will find the one in which you are not a waste of time. And in the meantime, you will work hard to appear as strong as possible, even to your closest associates. Understand?"

"Yes, sir."

"Good."

I stayed crouched there, listening to their muffled voices, until the dust in the tunnel made me want to sneeze. I wondered about my fate, if it would raise me up to power or cut me down. But now it felt more frightening than before. All my father wanted was to conquer Thuvhe, and Ryzek was destined to failure, fated to let my father down.

Dangerous, to anger my father with something you could not change.

I ached for Ryz, there in the tunnel, as I fumbled my way back to my bedroom. I ached, before I knew better.

CHAPTER 5 | CYRA

A SEASON LATER, WHEN I was eight, my brother barged into my bedroom, breathless and soaked through with rain. I had just finished setting up the last of my figurines on the carpet in front of my bed. They were scavenged from the sojourn to Othyr the year before, where they had a fondness for small, useless objects. He knocked some of them over when he marched across the room. I cried out in protest—he had ruined the army formation.

"Cyra," he said, crouching beside me. He was eighteen seasons old, his arms and legs too long, with spots on his forehead, but terror made him look younger. I put my hand on his shoulder.

"What is it?" I asked, squeezing.

"Has Father ever brought you somewhere just to . . . show you something?"

"No." Lazmet Noavek never took me anywhere; he barely looked at me when we were in the same room together. It didn't bother me. Even then, I knew that being the target of Father's gaze was not a good thing. "Never."

"That's not exactly fair, is it?" Ryz said eagerly. "You and I are both his children, we ought to be treated the same. Don't you think?"

"I . . . I suppose," I said. "Ryz, what is—"

But Ryz just placed his palm on my cheek.

My bedroom, with its rich blue curtains and dark wood paneling, disappeared.

"Today, Ryzek," my father's voice said, "you will give the order."

I was in a small dark room, with stone walls and a huge window in front of me. My father stood at my left shoulder, but he seemed smaller than he usually was—I only came up to his chest in reality, but in that room I stared right at his face. My hands were clenched in front of me. My fingers were long and thin.

"You want . . ." My breaths came shallow and fast. "You want me to . . ."

"Get yourself together," my father growled, grabbing the front of my armor and jerking me toward the window.

Through it I saw an older man, creased and gray haired. He was gaunt and dead in the eyes, with his hands cuffed together. At Father's nod, the guards in the next room approached the prisoner. One of them held his shoulders to keep him still, and the other wrapped a cord around his throat, knotting it tightly at the back of his head. The prisoner didn't put up any protest; his limbs seemed heavier than they were supposed to be, like he had lead for blood.

I shuddered, and kept shuddering.

"This man is a traitor," my father said. "He conspires against our family. He spreads lies about us stealing foreign aid from the hungry and the sick of Shotet. People who speak ill of our family can't simply be killed— they have to be killed slowly. And you have to be ready to order it. You must even be ready to do it yourself, though that lesson will come later."

Dread coiled in my stomach like a worm.

My father made a frustrated noise in the back of his throat, and shoved something into my hand. It was a vial sealed with wax.

"If you can't calm yourself down, this will do it for you," he said. "But one way or another, you will do as I say."

I fumbled for the edge of the wax, peeled it off, and poured the vial's contents into my mouth. The calming tonic burned my throat, but it took only moments for my heartbeat to slow and the edges of my panic to soften.

I nodded to my father, who flipped the switch for the amplifiers in the next room. It took me a moment to find the words in the haze that had filled my mind.

"Execute him," I said, in an unfamiliar voice.

One of the guards stepped back and pulled on the end of the cord, which ran through a metal loop in the ceiling like a thread through the eye of a needle. He pulled until the prisoner's toes just barely brushed the floor. I watched as the man's face turned red, then purple. He thrashed. I wanted to look away, but I couldn't.

"Not everything that is effective must be done in public," Father said casually as he flipped the switch to turn the amplifiers off again. "The guards will whisper of what you are willing to do to those who speak out against you, and the ones they whisper to will whisper also, and then your strength and power will be known all throughout Shotet."

A scream was building inside me, and I held it in my throat like a piece of food that was too big to swallow.

The small dark room faded.

I stood on a bright street teeming with people. I was at my mother's hip, my arm wrapped around her leg. Dust rose into the air around us—in the capital city of the nation-planet Zold, the dully named Zoldia City, which we had visited on my first sojourn, everything was coated in a fine layer of gray dust at that time of year. It came not from rock or earth, as I had assumed, but from a vast field of flowers that grew east of here and disintegrated in the strong seasonal wind.

I knew this place, this moment. It was one of my favorite memories of my mother and me.

My mother bent her head to the man who had met her in the street, her hand skimming my hair.

"Thank you, Your Grace, for hosting our scavenge so graciously," my mother said to him. "I will do my best to ensure that we take only what you no longer need."

"I would appreciate that. There were reports during the last scavenge of Shotet soldiers looting. Hospitals, no less," the man responded gruffly. His skin was bright with the dust, and almost seemed to sparkle in the sunlight. I stared up at him with wonder. He wore a long gray robe, almost like he wanted to resemble a statue.

"The conduct of those soldiers was appalling, and punished severely," my mother said firmly. She turned to me. "Cyra, my dear, this is the leader of the capital city of Zold. Your Grace, this is my daughter, Cyra."

"I like your dust," I said. "Does it get in your eyes?"

The man seemed to soften a little as he replied, "Constantly. When we are not hosting visitors, we wear goggles."

He took a pair from his pocket and offered them to me. They were big, with pale green glass for lenses. I tried them on, and they dropped straight from my face to my neck, so I had to hold them up with one hand. My mother laughed—light, easy—and the man joined in.

"We will do our best to honor your tradition," the man said to my mother. "Though I confess we do not understand it."

"Well, we seek renewal above all else," she said. "And we find what is to be made new in what has been discarded. Nothing worthwhile should ever be wasted. Surely we can agree on that."

And then her words were playing backward, and the goggles

were lifting up to my eyes, then over my head, and into the man's hand again. It was my first scavenge, and it was unwinding, unraveling in my mind. After the memory played backward, it was gone.

I was back in my bedroom, with the figurines surrounding me, and I knew that I had *had* a first sojourn, and that we had met the leader of Zoldia City, but I could no longer bring the images to mind. In their place was the prisoner with the cord around his throat, and Father's low tones in my ear.

Ryz had traded one of his memories for one of mine.

I had seen him do it before, once to Vas, his friend and steward, and once to my mother. Each time he had come back from a meeting with my father looking like he had been shredded to pieces. Then he had put a hand on his oldest friend, or on our mother, and a moment later, he had straightened, dry-eyed, looking stronger than before. And they had looked . . . emptier, somehow. Like they had lost something.

"Cyra," Ryz said. Tears stained his cheeks. "It's only fair. It's only fair that we should share this burden."

He reached for me again. Something deep inside me burned. As his hand found my cheek, dark, inky veins spread beneath my skin like many-legged insects, like webs of shadow. They moved, crawling up my arms, bringing heat to my face. And pain.

I screamed, louder than I had ever screamed in my life, and Ryz's voice joined mine, almost in harmony. The dark veins had brought pain; the darkness *was* pain, and I was made of it, I was pain itself.

He yanked his hand away, but the skin-shadows and the agony stayed, my currentgift beckoned forward too soon.

My mother ran into the room, her shirt only half buttoned,

her face dripping from washing without drying. She saw the black stains on my skin and ran to me, setting her hands on my arms for just a moment before yanking them back, flinching. She had felt the pain, too. I screamed again, and clawed at the black webs with my fingernails.

My mother had to drug me to calm me down.

Never one to bear pain well, Ryz didn't lay a hand on me again, not if he could help it. And neither did anyone else.

CHAPTER 6 | CYRA

"WHERE ARE WE GOING?"

I chased my mother through the polished hallways, the floors gleaming with my dark-streaked reflection. Ahead of me, she was holding her skirts, her spine straight. She always looked elegant, my mother. She wore dresses with plates from an Armored One built into the bodices, draped with fabric so they still looked light as air. She knew how to draw a perfect line on her eyelid that made it look like she had long eyelashes at each corner. I had tried to do that once, but I hadn't been able to keep my hand steady long enough to draw the line, and I had to stop every few seconds to gasp through pain. Now I favored simplicity over elegance, loose shifts and shoes without laces, pants that didn't require buttoning and sweaters that covered most of my skin. I was almost nine seasons old, and already stripped of frivolities.

The pain was just part of life now. Simple tasks took twice as long because I had to pause for breath. People no longer touched me, so I had to do everything myself. I tried feeble medicines and potions from other planets in the vain hope they would suppress my gift, and they always made me sick.

"Quiet," my mother said, touching her finger to her lips. She opened a door, and we walked onto the landing pad on the roof of Noavek manor. There was a transport vessel perched there like a bird resting midflight, its loading doors open for us. She looked around once, then grabbed my shoulder—covered with fabric, so I didn't hurt her—and pulled me toward the ship.

Once we were inside, she sat me down in one of the flight seats and pulled the straps tight across my lap and chest.

"We're going to see someone who might be able to help you," she said.

The sign on the specialist's door said *Dr. Dax Fadlan*, but he told me to call him Dax. I called him Dr. Fadlan. My parents had raised me to show respect to people who had power over me.

My mother was tall, with a long neck that tilted forward, like she was always bowing. Right now the tendons stood out from her throat, and I could see her pulse there, fluttering just at the surface of her skin.

Dr. Fadlan's eyes kept drifting to my mother's arm. She had her kill marks exposed, and even they looked beautiful, not brutal, each line straight, all at even intervals. I didn't think Dr. Fadlan, an Othyrian, saw many Shotet in his offices.

It was an odd place. When I arrived, they put me in a room with a bunch of unfamiliar toys, and I played with some of the small figurines the way Ryzek and I had at home, when we still played together: I lined them up like an army, and marched them into battle against the giant, squashy animal in the corner of the room. After about an hour Dr. Fadlan had told me to come out, that he had finished his assessment. Only I hadn't done anything yet.

"Eight seasons is a little young, of course, but Cyra isn't the youngest child I've seen develop a gift," Dr. Fadlan said to my mother. The pain surged, and I tried to breathe through it as they told Shotet soldiers to when they had to get a wound stitched and there was no time for a numbing agent. I had seen recordings of it. "Usually it happens in extreme circumstances, as a protective measure. Do you have any idea what those circumstances might have been? They may give us an insight into why this particular gift developed."

"I told you," my mother said. "I don't know."

She was lying. I had told her what Ryzek did to me, but I knew better than to contradict her now. When my mother lied, it was always for a good reason.

"Well, I'm sorry to tell you that Cyra is not simply growing into her gift," Dr. Fadlan said. "This appears to be its full manifestation. And the implications of that are somewhat disturbing."

"What do you mean?" I didn't think my mother could sit up any straighter, and then she did.

"The current flows through every one of us," Dr. Fadlan said gently. "And like liquid metal flowing into a mold, it takes a different shape in each of us, showing itself in a different way. As a person develops, those changes can alter the mold the current flows through, so the gift can also shift—but people don't generally change on such a fundamental level."

Dr. Fadlan had an unmarked arm, and he did not speak the revelatory tongue. There were deep lines around his mouth and eyes, and they grew even deeper as he looked at me. His skin was the same shade as my mother's, however, suggesting a common

lineage. Many Shotet had mixed blood, so it wasn't surprising—
my own skin was a medium brown, almost golden in certain lights.

"That your daughter's gift causes her to invite pain into herself, and project pain into others, suggests something about what's
going on inside her," Dr. Fadlan said. "It would take further study
to know exactly what that is. But a cursory assessment says that on
some level, she feels she deserves it. And she feels others deserve
it as well."

"You're saying this gift is my daughter's fault?" The pulse in
my mother's throat moved faster. "That she wants to be this way?"

Dr. Fadlan leaned forward and looked directly at me. "Cyra,
the gift comes from you. If you change, the gift will, too."

My mother stood. "She is a child. This is not her fault, and it's
not what she wants for herself. I'm sorry that we wasted our time
here. Cyra."

She held out her gloved hand, and wincing, I took it. I wasn't
used to seeing her so agitated. It made all the shadows under my
skin move faster.

"As you can see," Dr. Fadlan said, "it gets worse when she's
emotional."

"Quiet," my mother snapped. "I won't have you poisoning her
mind any more than you already have."

"With a family like yours, my fear is that she has already seen
too much for her mind to be saved," he retorted as we left the
room.

My mother rushed us through the hallways to the loading bay.
By the time we reached the landing pad, there were Othyrian soldiers surrounding our vessel. Their weapons looked feeble to me,
slim rods with dark current wrapped around them, set to stun

instead of kill. Their armor, too, was pathetic, made of pillowed synthetic material that left their sides exposed.

My mother ordered me into the ship, and paused to speak with one of them. I dawdled on my way to the door to hear what they said.

"We are here to escort you off-world," the soldier said.

"I am the wife of the sovereign of Shotet. You should address me as 'my lady,'" my mother snapped.

"My apologies, ma'am, but the Assembly of Nine Planets recognizes no Shotet nation, and therefore no sovereign. If you leave the planet immediately, we will cause you no trouble."

"No Shotet nation." My mother laughed a little. "A time will come when you will wish you hadn't said that."

She clutched her skirts to lift them, and marched into the ship. I scrambled inside and found my seat, and she sat beside me. The door closed behind us, and ahead of us, the pilot gave the signal for liftoff. This time I pulled the straps across my own chest and lap, because my mother's hands were shaking too badly to do it for me.

I didn't know it at the time, of course, but that was the last season I had with her. She passed away after the next sojourn, when I was nine.

We burned a pyre for her in the center of the city of Voa, but the sojourn ship carried her ashes into space. As our family grieved, the people of Shotet grieved along with us.

Ylira Noavek will sojourn forever after the current, the priest said as the ashes launched behind us. *It will carry her on a path of wonder.*

For seasons afterward, I couldn't even speak her name. After all, it was my fault she was gone.

CHAPTER 7 | CYRA

THE FIRST TIME I saw the Kereseth brothers, it was from the servants' passageway that ran alongside the Weapons Hall. I was several seasons older, fast approaching adulthood.

My father had joined my mother in the afterlife just a few seasons prior, killed in an attack during a sojourn. My brother, Ryzek, was now walking the path our father had set for him, the path toward Shotet legitimacy. Maybe even Shotet dominance.

My former tutor, Otega, had been the first to tell me about the Kereseths, because the servants in our house were whispering the story over the pots and pans in the kitchen, and she always told me of the servants' whispers.

"They were taken by your brother's steward, Vas," she said to me as she checked my essay for grammatical errors. She still taught me literature and science, but I had outstripped her in my other subjects, and now studied on my own as she returned to managing our kitchens.

"I thought Ryzek sent soldiers to capture the oracle. The old one," I said.

"He did," Otega said. "But the oracle took her life in the struggle, to avoid capture. In any case, Vas and his men were tasked to go after the Kereseth brothers instead. Vas dragged them across the Divide kicking and screaming, to hear the others tell of it. But the younger one—Akos—escaped his bonds somehow, stole a blade, and turned it against one of Vas's soldiers. Killed him."

"Which one?" I asked. I knew the men Vas traveled with. Knew how one liked candy, another had a weak left shoulder, and yet another had trained a pet bird to eat treats from his mouth. It was good to know such things about people. Just in case.

"Kalmev Radix."

The candy lover, then.

I raised my eyebrows. Kalmev Radix, one of my brother's trusted elite, had been killed by a Thuvhesit boy? That was not an honorable death.

"Why were the brothers taken?" I asked her.

"Their fates." Otega waggled her eyebrows. "Or so the story goes. And since their fates are, evidently, unknown by all but Ryzek, it is quite the story."

I didn't know the fates of the Kereseth boys, or any but mine and Ryzek's, though they had been broadcast a few days ago on the Assembly news feed. Ryzek had cut the news feed within moments of the Assembly Leader coming on screen. The Assembly Leader had given the announcement in Othyrian, and though the speaking and learning of all languages but Shotet had been banned in our country for over ten seasons, it was still better to be safe.

My father had told me my own fate after my currentgift manifested, with little ceremony: *The second child of the family Noavek will cross the Divide.* A strange fate for a favored daughter, but only because it was so dull.

I didn't wander the servants' passages that often anymore—there were things happening in this house I didn't want to see—but to catch a glimpse of the kidnapped Kereseths . . . well. I had to make an exception.

All I knew about the Thuvhesit people—apart from the fact that they were our enemies—was they had thin skin, easy to pierce with a blade, and they overindulged in iceflowers, the lifeblood of their economy. I had learned their language at my mother's insistence—the Shotet elite were exempt from my father's prohibitions against language learning, of course—and it was hard on my tongue, which was used to harsh, strong Shotet sounds instead of the hushed, quick Thuvhesit ones.

I knew Ryzek would have the Kereseths taken to the Weapons Hall, so I crouched in the shadows and slid the wall panel back, leaving myself just a crack to see through, when I heard footsteps.

The room was like all the others in Noavek manor, the walls and floor made of dark wood so polished it looked like it was coated in a film of ice. Dangling from the distant ceiling was an elaborate chandelier made of glass globes and twisted metal. Tiny fenzu insects fluttered inside it, casting an eerie, shifting light over the room. The space was almost empty, all the floor cushions—balanced on low wooden stands, for comfort—gathering dust, so their cream color turned gray. My parents had hosted parties in here, but Ryzek used it only for people he meant to intimidate.

I saw Vas, my brother's steward, before anyone else. The long side of his hair was greasy and limp, the shaved side red with razor burn. Beside him shuffled a boy, much smaller than I was, his skin a patchwork of bruises. He was narrow through the shoulders, spare and short. He had fair skin, and a kind of wary tension in his body, like he was bracing himself.

Muffled sobs came from behind him, where a second boy, with dense, curly hair, stumbled along. He was taller and broader than the first Kereseth, but cowering, so he almost appeared smaller.

These were the Kereseth brothers, the fate-favored children of their generation. Not an impressive sight.

My brother waited for them across the room, his long body draped over the steps that led to a raised platform. His chest was covered with armor, but his arms were bare, displaying a line of kill marks that went all the way up the back of his forearm. They had been deaths ordered by my father, to counteract any rumors about my brother's weakness that might have spread among the lower classes. He held a small currentblade in his right hand, and every few seconds he spun it in his palm, always catching it by the handle. In the bluish light, his skin was so pale he looked almost like a corpse.

He smiled when he saw his Thuvhesit captives, his teeth showing. He could be handsome when he smiled, my brother, even if it meant he was about to kill you.

He leaned back, balancing on his elbows, and cocked his head.

"My, my," he said. His voice was deep and scratchy, like he had just spent the night screaming at the top of his lungs.

"*This* is the one I've heard so many stories about?" Ryzek nodded to the bruised Kereseth boy. He spoke Thuvhesit crisply. "The Thuvhesit boy who earned a mark before we even got him on a ship?" He laughed.

I squinted at the bruised one's arm. There was a deep cut on the outside of his arm next to the elbow, and a streak of blood that had run between his knuckles and dried there. A kill mark, unfinished. A very new one, belonging, if the rumors were true, to Kalmev Radix. This was Akos, then, and the snuffling one was Eijeh.

"Akos Kereseth, the third child of the family Kereseth." Ryzek stood, spinning his knife on his palm, and walked down the steps. He dwarfed even Vas. He was like a regular-size man stretched taller and thinner than he was supposed to be, his shoulders and hips too narrow to bear his own height.

I was tall, too, but that was where my physical similarities with my brother ended. It wasn't uncommon for Shotet siblings to look dissimilar, given how blended our blood was, but we were more distinct than most.

The boy—Akos—lifted his eyes to Ryzek's. I had first seen the name "Akos" in a Shotet history book. It had belonged to a religious leader, a cleric who had taken his life rather than dishonor the current by holding a currentblade. So this Thuvhesit boy had a Shotet name. Had his parents simply forgotten its origins? Or did they want to honor some long-forgotten Shotet blood?

"Why are we here?" Akos said hoarsely, in Shotet.

Ryzek only smiled further and responded in the same language. "I see the rumors are true—you can speak the revelatory tongue. How fascinating. I wonder how you came by your Shotet blood?" He prodded the corner of Akos's eye, at the bruise there, making him wince. "You received quite a punishment for your murder of one of my soldiers, I see. I take it your rib cage is suffering damage."

Ryzek flinched a little as he spoke. Only someone who had known him as long as I had could have seen it, I was certain. Ryzek hated to watch pain, not out of empathy for the person suffering it, but because he didn't like to be reminded that pain existed, that he was as vulnerable to it as anyone else.

"Almost had to carry him here," Vas said. "Definitely had to carry him onto the ship."

"Usually you would not survive a defiant gesture like killing one of my soldiers," Ryzek said, speaking down to Akos like he was a child. "But your fate is to die serving the family Noavek, to die serving *me*, and I'd rather get a few seasons out of you first, you see."

Akos had been tense since I laid eyes on him. As I watched, it was as if all the hardness in him melted away, leaving him looking as vulnerable as a small child. His fingers were curled, but not into fists. Passively, like he was sleeping.

I guess he hadn't known his fate.

"That isn't true," Akos said, like he was waiting for Ryzek to soothe away the fear. I pressed a sharp pain from my stomach with a palm.

"Oh, I assure you that it is. Would you like me to read from the transcript of the announcement?" Ryzek took a square of paper from his back pocket—he had come to this meeting prepared to wreak emotional havoc, apparently—and unfolded it. Akos was trembling.

"'The third child of the family Kereseth,'" Ryzek read, in Othyrian, the most commonly spoken language in the galaxy. Somehow hearing the fate in the language in which it had been announced made it sound more real to me. I wondered if Akos, shuddering at each syllable, felt the same. "'Will die in service to the family Noavek.'"

Ryzek let the paper drop to the floor. Akos grabbed it so roughly it almost tore. He stayed crouched as he read the words—again and again—as if rereading them would change them. As if his death, and his service to our family, were not preordained.

"It won't happen," Akos said, harder this time, as he stood. "I would rather . . . I would rather *die* than—"

"Oh, I don't think that's true," Ryzek said, lowering his voice to a near whisper. He bent close to Akos's face. Akos's fingers tore holes in the paper, though he was otherwise still. "I know what people look like when they want to die. I've brought many of them to that point myself. And you are still very much desperate to survive."

Akos took a breath, and his eyes found my brother's with new steadiness. "My brother has nothing to do with you. You have no claim to him. Let him go, and I . . . I won't give you any trouble."

"You seem to have made several incorrect assumptions about what you and your brother are doing here," Ryzek said. "We did not, as you have assumed, cross the Divide just to speed along your fate. Your brother is not collateral damage; *you* are. We went in search of him."

"*You* didn't cross the Divide," Akos snapped. "You just sat here and let your lackeys do it all for you."

Ryzek turned and climbed to the top of the platform. The wall above it was covered with weapons of all shapes and sizes, most of them currentblades as long as my arm. He selected a large, thick knife with a sturdy handle, like a meat cleaver.

"Your brother has a particular destiny," Ryzek said, looking the knife over. "I assume, since you did not know your own fate, that you don't know his, either?"

Ryzek grinned the way he always did when he knew something other people didn't.

"'To see the future of the galaxy,'" Ryzek quoted, in Shotet this time. "In other words, to be this planet's next oracle."

Akos was silent.

I sat back from the crack in the wall, closing my eyes against the line of light so I could think.

For my brother and my father, every sojourn since Ryzek was young had been a search for an oracle, and every search had turned up empty. Likely because it was nearly impossible to catch someone who knew you were coming. Or someone who might lay on a blade to avoid capture, as the elder oracle had in the same invasion that had brought the Kereseths here.

But finally, it seemed Ryzek had found a solution: he had gone after two oracles at once. One had avoided being taken by dying. And the other—this Eijeh Kereseth—didn't know what he was. He was still soft and pliable enough to be shaped by Noavek cruelty.

I sat forward again to hear Eijeh speak, his curly head tipped forward.

"Akos, what is he saying?" Eijeh asked in slippery Thuvhesit, wiping his nose with the back of his hand.

"He's saying they didn't come to Thuvhe for me," Akos said, without looking back. It was strange to hear someone speak two languages so perfectly, without an accent. I envied him the ability. "They came for you."

"For me?" Eijeh's eyes were pale green. An unusual color, like iridescent insect wings, or the currentstream after the Deadening time. Against his light brown skin, so like the milky earth of the planet Zold, they almost glowed. "Why?"

"Because you are the next oracle of this planet," Ryzek said to Eijeh in the boy's mother tongue, stepping down from the platform with the knife in hand. "You will see the future, in all its many, many varieties. And there is one variety in particular that I wish to know about."

A shadow darted across the back of my hand like an insect, my currentgift making my knuckles ache like they were breaking. I stifled a groan. I knew what future Ryzek wanted: to rule Thuvhe, as well as Shotet, to conquer our enemies, to be recognized as a legitimate world leader by the Assembly. But his fate hung over him as heavily as Akos's likely now hung over him, saying that Ryzek would fall to our enemies instead of reign over them. He needed an oracle if he wanted to avoid that failure. And now he had one.

I wanted Shotet to be recognized as a nation instead of a collection of rebellious upstarts just as much as my brother did. So why was the pain of my currentgift—ever-present—mounting by the second?

"I . . ." Eijeh was watching the knife in Ryzek's hand. "I'm not an oracle, I've never had a vision, I can't . . . I can't possibly . . ."

I pressed against my stomach again.

Ryzek balanced the knife on his palm and flicked it to turn it. It wobbled, moving in a slow circle. *No, no, no,* I found myself thinking, unsure why.

Akos shifted into the path between Ryzek and Eijeh, as if he could stop my brother with the meat of his body alone.

Ryzek watched his knife turn as he moved toward Eijeh.

"Then you must learn to see the future quickly," Ryzek said. "Because I want you to find me the version of the future I need, and tell me what it is I must do to get to it. Why don't we start with a version of the future in which Shotet, not Thuvhe, controls this planet—hmm?"

He nodded to Vas, who forced Eijeh to his knees. Ryzek caught the blade by its handle and touched the edge of it to Eijeh's head, right under his ear. Eijeh whimpered.

"I can't—" Eijeh said. "I don't know how to summon visions, I don't—"

And then Akos barreled into my brother from the side. He wasn't big enough to topple Ryzek, but he had caught him off guard, and Ryzek stumbled. Akos pulled his elbow back to punch—stupid, I thought to myself—but Ryzek was too fast. He kicked up from the ground, hitting Akos in the stomach, then stood. He grabbed Akos by the hair, wrenching his head up, and sliced along Akos's jawline, ear to chin. Akos screamed.

It was one of Ryzek's preferred places for cutting people. When he decided to give a person a scar, he wanted it to be visible. Unavoidable.

"Please," Eijeh said. "Please, I don't know how to do what you ask, please don't hurt him, don't hurt me, please—"

Ryzek stared down at Akos, who was clutching his face, his neck streaked with blood.

"I do not know this Thuvhesit word, 'please,'" Ryzek said.

Later that night I heard a scream echoing in the quiet hallways of Noavek manor. I knew it didn't belong to Akos—he had been sent to our cousin Vakrez, "to grow thicker skin," as Ryzek put it. Instead I recognized the scream as Eijeh's voice raised in acknowledgment of pain, as my brother tried to pry the future from his head.

I dreamt of it for a long time thereafter.

CHAPTER 8 | CYRA

I WOKE WITH A groan. Someone was knocking.

My bedroom looked like a guest room, no personal touches, all the clothes and beloved objects hidden in drawers or behind cabinet doors. This drafty house, with its polished wood floors and grand candelabras, held bad memories like too much dinner. Last night one of those memories—of Akos Kereseth's blood trailing down his throat, two seasons earlier—had come into my dreams.

I didn't want to take root in this place.

I sat up and dragged the heels of my hands over my cheeks to smear the tears away. To call it crying would have been inaccurate; it was more an involuntary oozing, brought on by particularly strong surges of pain, often while I slept. I raked my fingers through my hair and stumbled to the door, greeting Vas with a grunt.

"What?" I said, pacing away. Sometimes it helped to pace the room—it was soothing, like being rocked.

"I see I've found you in a good mood," Vas said. "Were you sleeping? You do realize it's well into the afternoon?"

"I don't expect you to understand," I said. After all, Vas didn't feel pain. That meant he was the only person I had encountered since I had developed my currentgift who could touch me with bare hands, and he liked to make sure I remembered that. *When you get older*, he sometimes said to me when Ryzek couldn't hear him, *you may see value in my touch, little Cyra*. And I always told him I would rather die alone. It was true.

That he couldn't feel pain also meant he didn't know about the gray space just beneath consciousness that made it more bearable.

"Ah," Vas said. "Well, your presence has been requested in the dining room this evening for a meal with Ryzek's closest supporters. Dress nicely."

"I'm not really feeling up for a social engagement right now," I said, teeth gritted. "Send my regrets."

"I said 'requested,' but maybe I should have chosen my words more carefully," Vas said. "'Required' was the word your brother used."

I closed my eyes, stalling in my pacing for a moment. Whenever Ryzek demanded my attendance, it was to intimidate, even when he was dining with his own friends. There was a Shotet saying—*a good soldier does not even dine with friends unarmed*. And I armed him.

"I came prepared." Vas held out a small brown bottle, corked with wax. It wasn't labeled, but I knew what it was anyway: the only painkiller strong enough to make me fit for polite company. Or fit enough, anyway.

"How am I supposed to eat dinner while I'm on that stuff? I'll throw up on the guests." It might improve some of them.

"Don't eat." Vas shrugged. "But you can't really function without it, can you?"

I snatched the bottle from his hand, and nudged the door closed with my heel.

§

I spent a good part of the afternoon crouched in the bathroom, under a stream of warm water, willing the tension from my muscles. It didn't help.

And so I uncorked the bottle and drank.

As revenge, I wore one of my mother's dresses to the dining room that evening. It was light blue and fell straight to my feet, its bodice embroidered with a small geometric pattern that reminded me of feathers layered over each other. I knew it would hurt my brother to see me in it—to see me in anything she had ever worn—but he wouldn't be able to say anything about it. I was, after all, dressed nicely. As instructed.

It had taken me ten minutes to fasten it closed, my fingertips were so numb from the painkiller. And as I walked the halls, I kept one hand on the wall to steady myself. Everything tipped and swayed and spun. I carried my shoes in my other hand—I would put them on right before I entered the room, so I wouldn't slip on the polished wood floors.

The shadows spread down my bare arms from shoulder to wrist, then wrapped around my fingers, pooling beneath my fingernails. Pain seared me wherever they went, dulled by drugs but not eliminated. I shook my head at the guard outside the dining room doors to stop him from opening them, and stepped into my shoes.

"Okay, go ahead," I said, and he pulled the handles apart.

The dining room was grand but warm, lit by lanterns that glowed on the long table and the fire along the back wall. Ryzek stood, bathed in light, with a drink in his hand and Yma Zetsyvis at his right. Yma was married to a close friend of my mother's,

Uzul Zetsyvis. Though she was relatively young—younger than
Uzul, at least—her hair was bright white, her eyes a shocking
blue. She was always smiling.

I knew the names of everyone else gathered around them: Vas,
of course, at my brother's left. His cousin, Suzao Kuzar, eagerly
laughing at something Ryzek had said a moment before; our cousin
Vakrez, who trained the soldiers, and his husband, Malan, swallowing the rest of his drink in one gulp; Uzul, and his and Yma's
grown daughter, Lety, with the long bright braid; and last, Zeg
Radix, who I had last seen at his brother Kalmev's funeral. The
funeral of the man Akos Kereseth had killed.

"Ah, there she is," Ryzek said, gesturing toward me. "You all
remember my sister, Cyra."

"Wearing her mother's clothes," Yma remarked. "How lovely."

"My brother told me to dress nicely," I said, working to enun-
ciate though my lips were numb. "And no one knew the art of
dressing nicely like our mother."

Ryzek's eyes glittered with malice. He lifted his glass. "To Ylira
Noavek," he said. "The current will carry her on a path of wonder."

Everyone else raised their glasses and drank. I refused the glass
offered to me by a silent servant—my throat was too tight for me
to swallow. Ryzek's toast was a repetition of what the priest had
said at my mother's funeral. Ryzek wanted to remind me of it.

"Come here, little Cyra, and let me have a look at you," Yma
Zetsyvis said. "Not so little anymore, I suppose. How old are you?"

"I've sojourned ten times," I said, using the traditional time
reference—marking what I had survived rather than how long I
had existed. Then I clarified, "I began early, though—I'll be sixteen seasons in a few days."

"Oh, to be young and think in days!" Yma laughed. "So, still a child, then, tall as you are."

Yma had a gift for elegant insults. Calling me a child was one of her mildest ones, I was sure. I stepped into the firelight with a small smile.

"Lety, you've met Cyra, haven't you?" Yma said to her daughter. Lety Zetsyvis was a head smaller than I was, though several seasons older, and a charm hung in the hollow of her throat, a fenzu trapped in glass. It still glowed, though dead.

"No, I haven't," Lety said. "I would shake your hand, Cyra, but . . ."

She shrugged. My shadows, as if responding to her call, darted across my chest and throat. I stifled a groan.

"Let's hope you never earn the privilege," I said coolly. Lety's eyes widened, and everyone went quiet. Too late, I realized that I was only playing into Ryzek's hands; he wanted them to fear me, even though they followed him devoutly, and I was making it so.

"Your sister has sharp teeth," Yma said to Ryzek. "Bad for those who would oppose you."

"But no better for my friends, it seems," Ryzek said. "I haven't yet taught her when not to bite."

I scowled at him. But before I could bite again—so to speak—the conversation moved on.

"How is our recent batch of recruits?" Vas asked my cousin Vakrez. He was tall, handsome, but old enough that there were creases at the corners of his eyes even when he wasn't smiling. A deep scar, shaped like a half circle, was etched in the center of his cheek.

"Fair," Vakrez said. "Better, now they're through the first round."

"Is that why you're back for a visit?" Yma asked him. The army trained closer to the Divide, outside Voa, so it had been a few hours' journey for Vakrez to make it here.

"No. Had to deliver Kereseth," Vakrez said, nodding to Ryzek. "The younger Kereseth, that is."

"His skin any thicker than when you first got him?" Suzao asked. He was a short man, but he was tough as armor skin, crisscrossed with scars. "When we took him, it was touch him and—wham!— he bruises."

The others laughed. I remembered how Akos Kereseth had looked when he was first dragged into this house, his sobbing brother at his heels, blood still dried on his hand from his first kill mark. He had not seemed weak to me.

"Not so thin-skinned," Zeg Radix said gruffly. "Unless you're suggesting that my brother Kalmev died so easily?"

Suzao looked away.

"I am sure," Ryzek said smoothly, "that no one means to insult Kalmev, Zeg. My father was killed by someone who was unworthy of him, too." He sipped his drink. "Now, before we eat, I have arranged for some entertainment for us."

I tensed as the doors opened, sure that whatever Ryzek called "entertainment" was much worse than it sounded. But it was just a woman, dressed throat to ankle in tight, dark fabric that showed every muscle, every bony joint. Her eyes and lips were traced with some kind of pale chalk, garish.

"My sisters and I, of the planet Ogra, offer the Shotet our greetings," the woman said, her voice raspy. "And we present to you a dance."

At her last word, she brought her hands together in a sharp

clap. All at once, the fire in the fireplace and the shifting glow from the fenzu disappeared, leaving us in darkness. Ogra, a planet wreathed in shadow, was a mystery to most in our galaxy. Ograns did not allow many visitors, and even the most sophisticated surveillance technology couldn't penetrate their atmosphere. The most anyone knew about them was from observation of spectacles like these. For once, I was grateful for how freely Ryzek indulged in the offerings of other planets, while restricting the rest of Shotet from doing the same. Without that hypocrisy I would never have gotten to see this.

Eager, I tilted forward on my toes and waited. Tendrils of light wrapped around the Ogran dancer's clasped hands, weaving between her fingers. When she pulled her palms apart, the orange tongues of fire from the fireplace stayed in one palm and the blueish orbs of fenzu glow stayed hovering in the other. The faint light made the chalk around her eyes and mouth stand out, and when she smiled, her teeth were fangs in the dark.

Two other dancers filed into the room behind her. They were still for a few long moments, and movement came slowly, when it did. The dancer farthest to the left tapped her breastbone, lightly, but it wasn't the sound of skin on skin that came from the motion—it was the sound of a full-bellied drum. The next dancer moved to that off-kilter rhythm, her stomach contracting and her back rounding as her shoulders hunched. Her body found a curved shape, and then light shuddered through her skeleton, making her spine glow, every vertebra visible for a few faltering seconds.

I gasped, along with several others.

The light-handler twisted her hands, bending firelight around fenzu light like she was weaving a tapestry from them. Their glow revealed complex, almost mechanical movements in her fingers and wrists. As the rhythm from the chest-drummer changed, the light-handler joined the third, the one with glowing bones, in a lurching, stumbling dance. I tensed, watching them, not sure if I should be disturbed or amazed. Every other moment I felt like they were going to lose their balance and hit the floor, but they caught each other every time, swinging and tilting, lifting and twisting, all flashing with multicolored light.

I was breathless when the performance ended. Ryzek led us in our applause, which I joined reluctantly, feeling it unequal to what I had just seen. The light-handler sent the flames back into our fire and the glow back into our fenzu lights. The three women clasped hands and bowed for us, smiling with closed lips.

I wanted to speak to them—though I didn't know what I could possibly say—but they were already filing out. As the third dancer made her way to the door, though, she pinched the fabric of my skirt between her thumb and forefinger. Her "sisters" stopped with her. The force of all their eyes on me at once was overwhelming— their irises were pitch-black, and took up more space than usual, I was certain. I wanted to shrivel before them.

"She is herself a small Ogra," the third dancer said, and the bones in her fingers flickered with light, just as shadows wound around my arms like bracelets. "All clothed in darkness."

"It is a gift," the light-handler said.

"It is a gift," the chest-drummer echoed.

I did not agree.

The fire in the dining room was just embers. My plate was full of half-eaten food—the shreds of roasted deadbird, pickled saltfruit, and some kind of leafy concoction dusted with spices—and my head was throbbing. I nibbled the corner of a piece of bread and listened to Uzul Zetsyvis brag about his investments.

The Zetsyvis family had been charged with the breeding and harvesting of fenzu from the forests north of Voa for almost one hundred seasons. In Shotet we used the bioluminescent insects for light more often than current-channeling devices, unlike the rest of the galaxy. It was a relic of our religious history, now waning—only the truly religious didn't use the current casually.

Maybe because of the Zetsyvis family industry, Uzul, Yma, and Lety were highly religious, refusing to take hushflower even in medicine, which meant eschewing most medicine. They said any substance that altered a person's "natural state," even anesthesia, defied the current. They also wouldn't travel by current-powered engines. They considered them to be a too-frivolous use of the current's energy—except for the sojourn ship, of course, which they defined as a religious rite. Their glasses were all full of water instead of fermented feathergrass.

"Of course, it's been a difficult season," Uzul said. "At this point in our planet's rotation, the air doesn't get warm enough to foster fenzu growth properly, so we have to introduce roving heat systems—"

Meanwhile, on my right, Suzao and Vakrez were having some kind of tense discussion about weaponry.

"All I'm saying is—regardless of what our ancestors believed—currentblades aren't sufficient for all forms of combat. Long-range or in-space combat, for example—"

"Any idiot can fire a currentblast," Suzao snapped. "You want us to put our currentblades down and turn soft and doughy year by year, like the Assembly nation-planets?"

"They're not so doughy," Vakrez said. "Malan translates Othyrian for the Shotet news feed; he's showed me the reports." Most of the people in this room, being Shotet elite, spoke more than one language. Outside of this room, that was prohibited. "Things are getting tense between the oracles and the Assembly, and there are whispers the planets are choosing sides. In some cases getting ready for a greater conflict than we've ever seen. And who knows what kind of weapons tech they'll have by the time that conflict happens? Do you really want us to be left behind?"

"Whispers," Suzao scoffed. "You put too much stock in gossip, Vakrez, and always have."

"There is a reason Ryzek wants an alliance with the Pithar, and it isn't because he likes the ocean views," Vakrez said. "They've got something we can *use*."

"We're doing just fine with Shotet mettle alone, is my point."

"Go ahead and tell Ryzek that. I'm sure he'll listen to you."

Across from me, Lety's eyes were focused on the webs of dark color that stained my skin, surging into new places every few seconds—the crook of my elbow, the rise of my collarbone, the corner of my jaw.

"What do they feel like to you?" she asked me when she caught my eye.

"I don't know, what does any gift feel like?" I said irritably.

"Well, I just remember things. Everything. Vividly," she said. "So my gift feels like anyone else's. . . . Like ringing in my ears, like energy."

"Energy." Or agony. "That sounds right."

I swallowed some of the fermented feathergrass in my glass.

Her face was a steady pinhole with everything spinning around it; I fought to focus on her, spilling some of the drink on my chin.

"I find your fasci—" I paused. *Fascination* was a difficult word to say with so much painkiller coursing through my veins. "Your *curiosity* about my gift a little strange."

"People are so afraid of you," Lety said. "I simply want to know if I should be, too."

I was about to answer, when Ryzek stood at the end of the table, his long fingers framing his empty plate. His rise was a signal for everyone to leave, and they trickled out, Suzao first, then Zeg, then Vakrez and Malan.

But when Uzul began to move toward the door, Ryzek stopped him with a hand.

"I'd like to speak with you and your family, Uzul," Ryzek said.

I struggled to my feet, using the table to balance. Behind me, Vas pushed a bar across the door handles, locking us in. Locking *me* in.

"Oh, Uzul," Ryzek said with a faint smile. "I'm afraid tonight is going to be very difficult for you. You see, your wife told me something interesting."

Uzul looked to Yma. Her ever-present smile was finally gone, and now she looked equal parts accusatory and afraid. I was sure she wasn't afraid of Uzul. Even his appearance was harmless—he had a round stomach, a sign of his wealth, and feet that turned out a little when he walked, giving his gait a slight hobble.

"Yma?" Uzul said to his wife weakly.

"I didn't have a choice," Yma said. "I was looking for a network address, and I saw your contact history. I saw coordinates there, and I remembered you talking about the exile colony—"

The exile colony. When I was young, it was just a joke that people told, that a lot of Shotet who had met with my father's displeasure had set up a home on another planet where they couldn't be discovered. As I grew older, the joke became a rumor, and a serious one. Even now, the mention of it made Ryzek work his jaw like he was trying to tear off a bite of old meat. He considered the exiles, as enemies of my father and even my grandmother, to be one of the highest threats to his sovereignty that existed. Every Shotet had to be under his control, or he would never feel secure. If Uzul had contacted them, it was treason.

Ryzek pulled a chair from the table, and gestured to it. "Sit."

Uzul did as he was told.

"Cyra," Ryzek said to me. "Come here."

At first I just stood by my place at the table, clutching the glass of fermented feathergrass. I clenched my jaw as my body filled with shadows, like black blood from broken vessels.

"Cyra," Ryzek said quietly.

He didn't need to threaten me. I would set my glass down and walk over to him and do whatever he told me. I would always do that, for as long as we both lived, or Ryzek would tell everyone what I had done to our mother. That knowledge was a stone in my stomach.

I put my glass down. I walked over to him. And when Ryzek told me to put my hands on Uzul Zetsyvis until he gave whatever information Ryzek needed to know, I did.

I felt the connection form between Uzul and me, and the temptation to force all the shadow into him, to stain him black as space and end my own agony. I could kill him if I wanted to, with just my touch. I had done it before. I wanted to do it again, to escape this, the horrible force that chewed through my nerves like acid.

Yma and Lety were clutched together, weeping, Yma holding Lety back when she tried to lunge at me. Our eyes met as I pushed the pain and the inky darkness into her father's body, and all I saw in her was hate.

Uzul screamed. He screamed for so long I grew numb to the sound.

"Stop!" he wailed eventually, and at Ryzek's nod, I took my hands from his head. I stumbled back, seeing spots, and Vas's hands pressed to my shoulders, steadying me.

"I tried to find the exiles," Uzul said. His face was slick with sweat. "I wanted to flee Shotet, have a life free from this . . . tyranny. I heard they were on Zold, but the contact I found there fell through. They had nothing. So I gave up, I gave up."

Lety was sobbing, but Yma Zetsyvis was still, her arm wrapped across her daughter's chest.

"I believe you," Ryzek said softly. "Your honesty is noted. Cyra will now administer your punishment."

I willed the shadows in my body to drain out like water from a wrung rag. I willed the current to leave me and never return—blasphemy. But there was a limit to my will. At Ryzek's stare the currentshadows spread, like he controlled them more than I did. And maybe he did.

I didn't wait for his threats. I touched my skin to Uzul Zetsyvis's until his screams filled all the empty spaces in my body, until Ryzek said to stop.

CHAPTER 9 | CYRA

I SAW WHERE I was only dimly, the smooth step beneath my foot—bare now, I must have lost a shoe in the dining room—and the shifting fenzu light reflected in the floorboards and the webs of black coursing up and down my arms. My fingers looked crooked, like I had broken them, but it was just the angle at which they were all bent, digging into the air as they sometimes dug into my own palms.

I heard a muffled scream coming from somewhere in the belly of Noavek manor, and my first thought was of Eijeh Kereseth, though I had not heard his voice in months.

I had seen Eijeh only once since his arrival. It had been in passing, in a corridor near Ryzek's office. He had been thin, and dead in the eyes. As a soldier muscled him past me, I had stared at the hollows above his collarbone, deep trenches now empty of flesh. Either Eijeh Kereseth had an iron will, or he really didn't know how to wield his currentgift, just as he claimed. If I had to bet on one or the other, it would be the latter.

"Send for him," Ryzek snapped at Vas. "This is what he's for, after all."

The top of my foot skimmed the dark wood. Vas, the only one who could touch me, was half carrying me back to my room.

"Send for who?" I mumbled, but I didn't listen to the answer. A wave of agony enveloped me, and I thrashed in Vas's grip as if that would help me escape it.

It didn't work. Obviously.

He peeled his fingers away from my arms, letting me slide to the floor. I braced myself on hands and knees in my bedroom. A drop of sweat—or tears, it was hard to say—fell from my nose.

"Who—" I rasped. "Who was screaming?"

"Uzul Zetsyvis. Your gift has a lingering effect, evidently," Vas replied.

I touched my forehead to the cool floor.

Uzul Zetsyvis had collected fenzu shells. He had showed me, once, the more colorful ones, pinned to a board in his office, labeled by harvest year. They were iridescent, multicolored, as if they held strands of the currentstream itself. He had touched them like they were the finest things in his house, which was bursting at the seams with wealth. A gentle man, and I . . . I had made him scream.

A while later—I didn't know how long—the door opened again, and I saw Ryzek's shoes, black and clean. I tried to sit up, but my arms and legs shook, so I had to settle for just turning my head to look at him. Hesitating in the hallway behind him was someone I recognized distantly, as if from a dream.

He was *tall*—almost as tall as my brother. And he stood like a soldier, straight-backed, like he knew himself. Despite that soldier's posture, however, he was thin—gaunt, really, little shadows pooling under his cheekbones—and his face was again dappled with old bruises and cuts. There was a thin scar running along his jaw, ear to chin, and a white bandage wrapped around his right arm. A fresh mark, if I had to guess, still healing.

He lifted his gray eyes to mine. It was their wariness—*his* wariness—that made me remember who he was. Akos Kereseth, third child of the family Kereseth, now almost a grown man.

All the pain that had been building in me came rushing back at once, and I seized my head with both hands, stifling a cry. I could hardly see my brother through the haze of tears, but I tried to focus on his face, which was pale as a corpse.

There were rumors about me all throughout Shotet and Thuvhe, encouraged by Ryzek—and maybe those rumors had traveled all throughout the galaxy, since all mouths loved to chatter about the favored lines. They spoke of the agony my hands could bring, of an arm littered with kill marks from wrist to shoulder and back again, and of my mind, addled to the point of insanity. I was feared and loathed at the same time. But this version of me—this collapsing, whimpering girl—was not that person of rumor.

My face burned hot, from something other than pain: humiliation. No one was supposed to see me like this. How could Ryzek bring him here when he knew how I always felt, after . . . well, afterward?

I tried to choke back my anger so Ryzek wouldn't hear it in my voice. "Why have you brought him here?"

"Let's not delay this," Ryzek said, and he beckoned Akos forward. They both drew closer to me, Akos's right arm pulled close to his body, like he was trying to stay as far away from my brother as possible without disobeying him.

"Cyra, this is Akos Kereseth. Third child of the family Kereseth. Our"—Ryzek smirked—"*faithful* servant."

He was referring, of course, to Akos's fate, to die for our family. To die *in service*, as the Assembly feed had proclaimed two seasons ago. Akos's mouth twisted at the reminder.

"Akos has a peculiar currentgift that I think will interest you," Ryzek said.

He nodded to Akos, who crouched beside me, then extended his hand, palm up, for me to take.

I stared at it. I almost didn't know what he meant by it, at first. Did he want me to hurt him? Why?

"Trust me," Ryzek said. "You'll like it."

As I reached for Akos, the darkness spread beneath my skin like spilled ink. I touched my hand to his, and waited for his scream.

Instead, all the currentshadows ran backward and disappeared. And with them went my pain.

It was not like the remedy that I had swallowed earlier, which made me sick, at worst, and dulled all sensation, at best. It was like returning to the way I had been before my gift developed; no, even that had never been as quiet and as still as I felt now, with my hand on his.

"What is this?" I said to him.

His skin was rough and dry, like a pebble not quite smoothed by the tide. Yet there was some warmth in it. I stared at our joined hands.

"I interrupt the current." His voice was surprisingly deep, but it cracked like it was supposed to at his age. "No matter what it does."

"My sister's gift is substantial, Kereseth," Ryzek said. "But lately it has lost most of its usefulness because of how it incapacitates her. It seems to me that *this* is how you can best fulfill your fate." He bent closer to Akos's ear. "Of course, you should never forget who really runs this house."

Akos didn't move, though a look of revulsion passed over his face.

I sat back on my heels, careful to keep my palm on Akos's, though I couldn't look him in the eye. It was as if he had walked in on me while I was changing; he had seen more than I ever let people see.

When I stood, he stood with me. Though I was tall myself, I only came up to his nose.

"What are we supposed to do, hold hands everywhere we go?" I said. "What will people think?"

"They will think he is a servant," Ryzek said. "Because that is what he is."

Ryzek stepped toward me, lifting his hand. I recoiled, yanking my hand from Akos's grasp, and flushing with black tendrils all over again.

"Do I detect ingratitude?" Ryzek asked. "Do you not appreciate the efforts I have made to ensure your comfort, what I am giving up by offering you our fated servant as a constant companion?"

"I do." I had to be careful not to provoke him. The last thing I wanted was more of Ryzek's memories replacing my own. "Thank you, Ryzek."

"Of course." Ryzek smiled. "Anything to keep my best general in prime condition."

But he didn't think of me as a general; I knew that. The soldiers called me "Ryzek's Scourge," the instrument of torment in his hand, and indeed, the way he looked at me was the same way he looked at an impressive weapon. I was just a blade to him.

§

I stayed still until Ryzek left, and then, when Akos and I were alone, I started pacing, from the desk to the foot of the bed, to the closed cabinets that held my clothes, back to the bed again. Only my family—and Vas—had been in this room. I didn't like how Akos stared at everything, like he was leaving little fingerprints everywhere.

He frowned at me. "How long have you been living this way?"

"What way?" I said, more harshly than I meant to. All I could think about was how I must have looked when he saw me, cowering on the floor, streaked with tears and soaked with sweat, like some kind of wild animal.

His voice softened with pity. "Like this, keeping your suffering a secret."

Pity, I knew, was just disrespect wrapped in kindness. I had to address it early, or it would grow unwieldy in time. My father had taught me that.

"I came into my gift when I had only lived eight seasons. To the great delight of my brother and father. We agreed that I would keep my pain private, for the good of the Noavek family. For the good of Shotet."

Akos let out a little snort. Well, at least he was done with pity. That hadn't taken long.

"Hold out your hand," I said quietly. My mother had always talked quietly when she was angry. She said it made people listen. I didn't have her light touch; I had all the subtlety of a fist to the face. But still, he listened, stretching out his hand with a resigned sigh, palm up, like he meant to relieve my pain.

I brought my right wrist to the inside of his, grabbed him under his shoulder with my left hand, and turned, sharply. It was like a dance—a shifted hand, a transfer of weight, and I was behind him, twisting his arm hard, forcing him to bend.

"I may be in pain, but I am not weak," I whispered. He stayed still in my grasp, but I could feel the tension in his back and his arm. "You are convenient, but you are not necessary. Understand?"

I didn't wait for a response. I released him, stepping back, my currentshadows returning with stinging pain that made my eyes water.

"Next door there's a room with a bed in it," I said. "Get out."

After I heard him leave, I leaned into the bed frame, eyes closed. I didn't want this; I didn't want this at all.

CHAPTER 10 | CYRA

I DIDN'T EXPECT AKOS Kereseth to return, not without being dragged. But he was at my door the next morning, a guard lingering a few paces behind him, and he had a large vial of purple-red liquid in hand.

"*My lady*," he said, mocking. "I thought, since neither of us wants to maintain constant physical contact, you might try this. It's the last of my stores."

I straightened. When the pain was at its worst, I was just a collection of body parts, ankle and knee and elbow and spine, each working to pull me up straight. I pushed my tangled hair over one shoulder, suddenly aware of how strange I must look, still in my nightgown at noonday, a sleeve of armor around my left forearm.

"A painkiller?" I asked. "I've tried those. They either don't work or they're worse than the pain."

"You've tried painkillers made from hushflower? In a country that doesn't like to use it?" he asked me, eyebrows raised.

"Yes," I replied, terse. "Othyrian medicines, the best available."

"Othyrian medicines." He clicked his tongue. "They may be the best for most people, but your problem isn't what 'most people' need help with."

"Pain is pain is pain."

Still, he tapped my arm with the vial. "Try it. It may not get rid of your pain entirely, but it will take the edge off and it won't have as many side effects."

I narrowed one eye at him, then called for the guard standing in the hallway. She came at my urging, bobbing her head to me when she arrived in the doorway.

"Taste this, would you?" I said, pointing to the vial.

"You think I'm trying to poison you?" Akos said to me.

"I think it's one of many possibilities."

The guard took the vial, her eyes wide with fear.

"It's fine, it's not poison," Akos said to her.

The guard swallowed some of the painkiller, wiping her mouth with the back of her hand. We all stood for a few seconds, waiting for something, anything, to happen. When she didn't collapse, I took the vial from her, currentshadows surging to my fingers so they prickled and stung. She walked away as soon as I did, recoiling from me as she would have an Armored One.

The painkiller smelled malty and rotten. I gulped it down all at once, sure it would taste as disgusting as these potions usually did, but the flavor was floral and spicy. It coated my throat and pooled in my stomach, heavy.

"Should take a few minutes to set in," he said. "You wear that thing to sleep?" He gestured to the sheath of armor around my arm. It covered me from wrist to elbow, made from the skin of an Armored One. It was scratched in places from the swipes of sharpened blades. I took it off only to bathe. "Were you expecting an attack?"

"No." I thrust the empty vial back into his hands.

"It covers your kill marks." He furrowed his brow. "Why would Ryzek's Scourge want to hide her marks?"

"Don't call me that." I felt pressure inside my head, like someone was pushing my temples from both sides. "Never call me that."

A cold feeling was spreading through my body, out from my center, like my blood was turning to ice. At first I thought it was just anger, but it was too *physical* for that—too . . . painless. When I looked at my arms, the shadow-stains were still there, under my skin, but they were languid.

"The painkiller worked, didn't it," he said.

The pain was still there, aching and burning wherever the currentshadows traveled, but it was easier to ignore. And though I was starting to feel a little drowsy, too, I didn't mind it. Maybe I would finally get a good night's sleep.

"Somewhat," I admitted.

"Good," he said. "Because I have a deal to offer you, and it relies on the painkiller being useful to you."

"A deal?" I said. "You think you're in a position to make deals with me?"

"Yeah, I do," he said. "As much as you insist you don't need my help with your pain, you want it, I know you do. And you can either try to batter me into submission to get it, or you can treat me like a *person,* listen to what I have to say, and maybe get my help easily. Your choice, of course, *my lady.*"

It was easier to think when his eyes weren't bearing down on mine, so I stared at the lines of light coming through the window coverings, showing the city in strips. Beyond the fence that kept Noavek manor separate, people would be out walking the streets, enjoying the warmth, dust floating all around them because the earthen streets were dry.

I had begun my acquaintance with Akos in a position of weakness—literally, huddled on the floor at his feet. And I had tried to force my way back to a place of strength, but it wasn't working; I couldn't erase what was so obvious to anyone who looked at me: I was covered in currentshadows, and the longer I suffered because of them, the more difficult it was for me to live a life that was worth anything to me. Maybe this was my best option.

"I'll listen," I said.

"Okay." He brought a hand to his head, touching his hair. It was brown, and clearly thick, judging by how his fingers knotted in it. "Last night, that . . . *maneuver* you did. You know how to fight."

"That," I said, "is an understatement."

"Would you teach me, if I asked you?"

"Why? So you can keep insulting me? So you can try—and fail—to kill my brother?"

"You just assume I want to kill him?"

"Don't you?"

He paused. "I want to get my brother home." He spoke each word with care. "And in order to do that, in order to survive here, I have to be able to fight."

I didn't know what it was to love a brother that much, not anymore. And from what I had seen of Eijeh—a flimsy wreck of a person—he didn't seem worthy of the effort. But Akos, with his soldier's posture and his still hands, seemed certain.

"You don't know how to fight already?" I said. "Why did Ryzek send you to my cousin Vakrez for two seasons, if not to teach you competency?"

"I'm competent. I want to be *good.*"

I crossed my arms. "You haven't gotten to the part of this deal that benefits me."

"In exchange for your instruction, I could teach you to make that painkiller you just drank," he said. "You wouldn't have to rely on me. Or anyone else."

It was like he knew me, knew the one thing he could say that would tempt me the most. It wasn't relief from pain that I wanted above all, but self-reliance. And he was offering it to me in a glass vial, in a hushflower potion.

"All right," I said. "I'll do it."

Soon after that I led him down the hall, to a small room at the end with a locked door. This wing of Noavek manor wasn't updated; the locks still took keys instead of opening at a touch or the prick of a finger, like the gene locks that opened the rooms where Ryzek spent most of his time. I fished the key out of my pocket—I had put on real clothes, loose pants and a sweater.

The room held a long countertop with shelves above and below it, packed with vials, beakers, knives, spoons, and cutting boards, and a long line of white jars marked with the Shotet symbols for iceflowers—we kept a small store of them, even hushflower, though Thuvhe had not exported any goods to Shotet in over twenty seasons, so we had to import it illegally using a third party—as well as other ingredients scavenged from across the galaxy. Pots, all a shade of warm orange-red metal, hung from a rack above the burners on the right, the largest bigger than my head and the smallest, the size of my hand.

Akos took one of the larger pots down and set it on a burner.

"Why did you learn to fight, if you could hurt with a touch?"

he said. He filled a beaker with water from the spout in the wall, and dumped it in the pot. Then he lit the burner beneath it and took out a cutting board and a knife.

"It's part of every Shotet education. We begin as children." I hesitated for a moment before adding, "But I continued because I enjoyed it."

"You have hushflower here?" he said, scanning the jars with his finger.

"Top right," I said.

"But the Shotet don't use it."

"'The Shotet' don't," I said stiffly. "We're the exception. We have everything here. Gloves are under the burners."

He snorted a little. "Well, *Exceptional One*, you should find a way to get more. We'll be needing it."

"All right." I waited a beat before asking, "No one in army training taught you to read?"

I had assumed that my cousin Vakrez had taught him more than competent fighting skills. Written language, for example. The "revelatory tongue" referred only to spoken language, not written—we all had to learn Shotet characters.

"They didn't care about things like that," he said. "They said 'go' and I went. They said 'stop' and I did. That was all."

"A soft Thuvhesit boy shouldn't complain about being made into a hard Shotet man," I said.

"I can't change into a Shotet," he said. "I am Thuvhesit, and will always be."

"That you are speaking to me in Shotet right now suggests otherwise."

"That I'm speaking Shotet right now is a quirk of genetics," he snapped. "Nothing more."

I didn't bother to argue with him. I felt certain he would change his mind, in time.

Akos reached into the jar of hushflower and took one of the blossoms out with his bare fingers. He broke a piece off one of the petals and put it in his mouth. I was too stunned to move. That amount of iceflower at that level of potency should have knocked him out instantly. He swallowed, closed his eyes for a moment, then turned back to the cutting board.

"You're immune to them, too," I said. "Like my currentgift."

"No," he said. "But their effect is not as strong, for me."

I wondered how he had discovered that.

He turned the hushflower blossom over and pressed the flat of the blade to the place where all the petals joined. The flower broke apart, separating petal by petal. He ran the tip of the knife down the center of each petal, and they uncurled, one by one, flattening. It was like magic.

I watched him as the potion bubbled, first red with hushflower, then orange when he added the honeyed saltfruit, and brown when the sendes stalks went in, stalks only, no leaves. A dusting of jealousy powder and the whole concoction turned red again, which was nonsense, impossible. He moved the mixture to the next burner to cool, and turned toward me.

"It's a complex art," he said, waving a hand to encompass the vials, beakers, iceflowers, pots, everything. "Particularly the painkiller, because it uses hushflower. Prepare one element incorrectly and you could poison yourself. I hope you know how to be precise as well as brutal."

He felt the side of the pot with the tip of his finger, just a light touch. I could not help but admire his quick movement, jerking his hand back right when the heat became too much, muscles coiling. I could already tell what school of combat he had trained in: zivatahak, school of the heart.

"You assume I'm brutal because that's what you've heard," I said. "Well, what about what I've heard about you? Are you thin-skinned, a coward, a fool?"

"You're a Noavek," he said stubbornly, folding his arms. "Brutality is in your blood."

"I didn't choose the blood that runs in my veins," I replied. "Any more than you chose your fate. You and I, we've become what we were made to become."

I knocked the back of my wrist against the door frame, so armor hit wood, as I left.

The next morning I woke when the painkiller wore off, just after sunrise, when the light was pale. I got out of bed the way I usually did, in fits and starts, pausing to take deep breaths like an old woman. I dressed in my training clothes, which were made of synthetic fabric from Tepes, light but loose. No one knew how to keep the body cool like the Tepessar people, whose planet was so hot no person had ever walked its surface bare-skinned.

I leaned my forehead against a wall as I braided my hair, eyes shut, fingers feeling for every strand. I didn't brush my thick dark hair anymore, at least not the way I had as a child, so meticulous, hoping each stroke of the bristles would coax it into perfect curls. Pain had stripped me of such indulgences.

When I finished, I took a small currentblade—turned off, so the dark tendrils of current wouldn't wrap around the sharpened metal—into the apothecary chamber down the hall where Akos had moved his bed, stood over him, and pressed the blade to his throat.

His eyes opened, then widened. He thrashed, but when I pushed harder into his skin, he went still. I smirked at him.

"Are you insane?" he said, his voice husky from sleep.

"Come now, you must have heard the rumors!" I said cheerfully. "More importantly, though: Are *you* insane? Here you are, sleeping heavily without even bothering to bar your door, a hallway away from one of your enemies? That is either insanity or stupidity. Pick one."

He brought his knee up sharply, aiming at my side. I bent my arm to block the strike with my elbow, pointing the blade instead at his stomach.

"You lost before you woke," I said. "First lesson: The best way to win a fight is to avoid having one. If your enemy is a heavy sleeper, cut his throat before he wakes. If he's softhearted, appeal to his compassion. If he's thirsty, poison his drink. Get it?"

"So, throw honor out the window."

"Honor," I said with a snort. "Honor has no place in survival."

The phrase, quoted from an Ogran book I had once read—translated into Shotet, of course; who could read Ogran?—appeared to scatter the sleep from his eyes in a way that even my attack had not been able to manage.

"Now get up," I said. I straightened, sheathed the knife at the small of my back, and left the room so he could change.

By the time we finished breakfast, the sun had risen and I could hear the servants in the walls, carrying clean sheets and towels to the bedrooms, through the passages that ran parallel to every east-west corridor. The house had been built to exclude the ones who ran it, just like Voa itself, with Noavek manor at the center, surrounded by the wealthy and powerful, and the rest around the edge, fighting to get in.

The gym, down the hall from my bedroom, was bright and spacious, a wall of windows on one side, a wall of mirrors on the other. A gilded chandelier dangled from the ceiling, its delicate beauty contrasting with the black synthetic floor and the stacks of pads and practice weapons along the far wall. It was the only room in the house my mother had allowed to be modernized while she lived; she had otherwise insisted on preserving the house's "historical integrity," down to the pipes that sometimes smelled like rot, and the tarnished doorknobs.

I liked to practice—not because it made me a stronger fighter, though that was a welcome side benefit—but because I liked how it felt. The heat building, the pounding heart, the productive ache of tired muscles. The pain I *chose*, instead of the pain that had chosen me. I once tried to spar against the training soldiers, like Ryzek had as he was learning, but the current's ink, coursing through every part of my body, caused them too much pain, so after that I was left to my own devices.

For the past year I had been reading Shotet texts about our long-forgotten form of combat, the school of the mind, elmetahak. Like so many things in our culture, it was scavenged, taking some of Ogran ferocity and Othyrian logic and our own resourcefulness and melding them until they were inextricable. When Akos and I went to the training room, I crouched over the book I had left near the wall the day before, *Principles of Elmetahak: Underlying Philosophy and Practical Exercises.* I was on the chapter "Opponent-Centered Strategy."

"So in the army, you trained in zivatahak," I said, to begin.

When he gave me a blank look, I continued.

"Altetahak—school of the arm. Zivatahak—school of the heart. Elmetahak—school of the mind," I said. "The ones who trained you didn't tell you in what school you were trained?"

"They didn't care about teaching me the names for things," Akos replied. "As I already told you."

"Well, you trained in zivatahak, I can tell by the way you move."

This seemed to surprise him. "The way I move," he repeated. "How do I move?"

"I suppose I shouldn't be surprised that a Thuvhesit hardly knows himself," I said.

"Knowing how you fight isn't knowing yourself," he retorted. "Fighting isn't important if the people you live with aren't violent."

"Oh? And what mythical people are those? Or are they imaginary?" I shook my head. "All people are violent. Some resist the impulse, and some don't. Better to acknowledge it, to use it as a point of access to the rest of your being, than to lie to yourself about it."

"I'm not *lying to mysel*—" He paused, and sighed. "Whatever. Point of access, you were saying?"

"You, for example." I could tell he didn't agree with me, but at least he was willing to listen. Progress. "You're quick, and not particularly strong. You're reactive, anticipating attacks from anyone, everyone. That means zivatahak, school of the heart—speed." I tapped my chest. "Speed requires endurance. Heart endurance. We took that one from the warrior-ascetics of Zold. The school of the arm, altetahak, means 'strength.' Adapted from the style of fringe mercenaries. The last, elmetahak, means 'strategy.' Most Shotet don't know it anymore. It's a patchwork of styles, of places."

"And which one did you study in?"

"I'm a student of all," I said. "Of anything." I straightened, moving away from the book. "Let's begin."

I opened a drawer in the far wall. It squeaked as old wood scraped against old wood, and the tarnished handle was loose, but inside the drawer were practice blades made of a new, synthetic material, hard but also flexible. They would bruise a person, if used effectively, but they wouldn't break skin. I tossed one to Akos, and took one for myself, holding it out from my side.

He mirrored me. I could see him adjusting, putting a bend in his knees and shifting his weight so he looked more like me. It was strange to be observed by someone so thirsty to learn, someone who knew that his survival depended on how much he took in. It made me feel useful.

This time I made the first move, swiping at his head. I pulled back before I actually made contact, and snapped, "Is there something fascinating about your hands?"

"What? No."

"Then stop staring at them and look at your opponent."

He raised his hand, fist to cheek, then swung at me from the side with the practice blade. I stepped away and turned, fast, smacking him in the ear with the flat of the knife handle. Wincing, he twisted around, trying to stab me when he was off balance. I caught his fist and held on tight, stalling him.

"I already know how to beat you," I said. "Because you know that I'm better than you are, but you're still standing right *here*." I waved my hand, gesturing to the area right in front of my body. "This area is the part of me that has the most potential to hurt you, the part where all my strikes will have the greatest impact and focus. You need to keep me moving so you can attack *outside* of this area. Step outside of my right elbow so it's hard for me to block you. Don't just stand there, letting me cut you open."

Instead of making a snide comment back to me, he nodded, and put his hands up again. This time, when I moved to "cut" him, he shuffled out of the way, dodging me. And I smiled a little.

We moved that way for a while, turning circles around each other. And when I noticed that he was breathless, I called him off.

"So tell me about your marks," I said. My book was still open to the chapter on "Opponent-Centered Strategy," after all. There was no opponent quite like one you had marked on your arm.

"Why?" He clasped his left wrist. The bandage was gone today, displaying an old kill mark near his elbow—the same one I had seen seasons ago in the Weapons Hall, but it was finished now, stained the color of the marking ritual, a blue so dark it was almost black. There was another mark beside it, still healing. Two slashes on a Thuvhesit boy's arm. A unique sight.

"Because knowing your enemies is the beginning of strategy," I said. "And apparently you have already faced some of your enemies, twice-marked as you are."

He turned his arm away from his body so he could frown at the dashes, and said, like it was a recitation, "The first was one of the men who invaded my home. I killed him while they were dragging my brother and me through the feathergrass."

"Kalmev," I said. Kalmev Radix had been one of my brother's chosen elite, a sojourn captain and a news feed translator—he had spoken four languages, including Thuvhesit.

"You knew him?" Akos said, face contorting a little.

"Yes," I said. "He was a friend of my parents. I met him when I was a child, and watched his wife cry at the memorial dinner after you killed him." I cocked my head at the memory. Kalmev had been a hard man, but he kept candies in his pockets. I had watched him sneak them into his mouth during fancy dinners. But I hadn't mourned his death—he was not, after all, mine to mourn. "What about the second mark?"

"The second . . ."

He swallowed hard. I had rattled him. Good.

". . . was the Armored One whose skin I stole for my own status."

I had earned my own armor three seasons ago. I had crouched in the low grasses near the army camp until the daylight waned, then hunted one of the creatures in the night. I had crawled beneath it as it slept, and arched up to stab the soft place where its leg joined its body. It had taken hours to bleed to death, and its horrible moans had given me nightmares. But I had never thought to carve the death of the Armored One into my skin, the way he had.

"The kill marks are for people," I said.

"The Armored One may as well have been a person," he said in a low voice. "I was looking into its eyes. It knew what I was. I fed it poison, and it fell asleep at my touch. I grieved for it more than I grieved the loss of a man who robbed my sister of two brothers and a father."

He had a sister. I had almost forgotten, though I had heard her fate from Ryzek: *The first child of the family Kereseth will succumb to the blade.* It was almost as grim a fate as my brother's. Or Akos's.

"You should put a hash through your second mark," I said. "Diagonal, through the top. That's what people do for losses that aren't kills. Miscarried babies, spouses taken by sickness. Runaways who never return. Any . . . significant grief."

He just looked at me, curious, and still with that ferocity.

"So my father . . ."

"Your father is recorded on Vas's arm," I said. "A loss can't be marked twice."

"It's a *kill* that's marked." His brow furrowed. "A murder."

"No, it isn't," I said. "'Kill mark' is a misnomer. They are always records of loss. Not triumph."

Without meaning to, I brought my right hand across my body to grip my forearm guard, hooking my fingers in its straps. "Regardless of what some foolish Shotet will tell you."

The hushflower petals on the board in front of me were curled tightly into themselves. I dragged the knife down the center of the first petal, fumbling a little with the gloves on—gloves weren't necessary for *him*, but we weren't all hushflower-resistant.

The petal didn't flatten.

"You have to hit the vein right in the center," he said. "Look for the darker red streak."

"It all just looks *red* to me. Are you sure you're not seeing things?"

"Try again."

That was how he responded every time I lost my patience—he just quietly said, "Try again." It made me want to punch him.

Every evening for the past few weeks, we had stood at this apothecary counter, and he taught me about iceflowers. It was warm and quiet in Akos's room, the only sound the bubbling of water set to boil and the *chop chop chop* of his knife. His bed was always made, the dingy sheets pulled taut across the mattress, and he often slept without a pillow, tossing it instead in the corner, where it gathered dust.

Each iceflower had to be cut with the right technique: the hushflowers needed to be coaxed into lying flat, the jealousy flowers had to be sliced in just such a way that they didn't burst into clouds of powder, and the hard, indigestible vein of the harva leaf had to be first loosened and then tugged by its base—*Not too hard. But harder than that*, Akos had said as I glared.

I was handy with the knife, but had no patience for subtlety with it, and my nose was nearly useless as a tool. In our combat training, the situation was reversed. Akos grew frustrated if we dwelled too long on theory or philosophy, which I considered to be the fundamentals. He was quick, and effective when he managed to make contact, but careless, with little aptitude for reading his opponent. But it was easier for me to deal with the pain of my gift when I was teaching him, or when he was teaching me.

I touched the point of a knife to another one of the hushflower petals, and dragged it in a straight line. This time, the petal unfurled at my touch, flattening on the board. I grinned. Our shoulders brushed, and I twitched away—touch was not something I was used to. I doubted I would ever be used to it again.

"Good," Akos said, and he swept a pile of dried harva leaves into the water. "Now do that about a hundred more times and it will start to feel easy."

"Only one hundred? Here I thought this was going to be time-consuming," I said with a sideways glance at him. Instead of rolling his eyes at me, or snapping, he smiled a little.

"I'll trade you a hundred hushflower slices for a hundred of the push-ups you're making me do," he said.

I pointed the hushflower-stained knife at him. "One day you'll thank me."

"Me, thank a Noavek? Never."

It was supposed to be a joke, but it was also a reminder. I was a Noavek, and he was a Kereseth. I was nobility, and he was a captive. Whatever ease we found together was built on ignoring the facts. Both our smiles faded, and we returned to our respective tasks in silence.

A while later, when I had done four petals—only ninety-six left!—I heard footsteps in the hallway. Quick, purposeful ones, not the movements of a wandering guard doing the rounds. I set my knife down and took off the gloves.

"What is it?" Akos asked.

"Someone's coming. Don't let on what we're really doing in here," I said.

He didn't have time to ask why. The door to the apothecary chamber opened, and Vas came in, a young man at his heels. I recognized him as Jorek Kuzar, son of Suzao Kuzar, Vas's second cousin. He was short and slim, with warm brown skin and a patch of hair on his chin. I hardly knew him—Jorek had chosen not to follow in his father's path as a soldier and translator, and was regarded as both a disappointment and a danger to my brother as a result. Anyone who did not enthusiastically enter Ryzek's service was suspect.

Jorek bobbed his head to me. I, flush with currentshadows at the sight of Vas, could hardly nod in return. Vas clasped his hands behind his back and looked with amusement at the little room, at Akos's green-stained fingers and the bubbling pot on the burner.

"What brings you to the manor, Kuzar?" I asked Jorek, before Vas could comment. "Surely it's not visiting Vas. I can't imagine anyone would do that for pleasure."

Jorek looked from Vas glaring at me, to me smiling back, to Akos staring determinedly at his hands, which gripped the edge of the counter. I hadn't noticed, at first, how tense Akos had become the moment Vas appeared. I could see the muscles in his shoulders bunching where his shirt stretched tight across them.

"My father is meeting with the sovereign," Jorek said. "And he thought Vas could talk some sense into me in the meantime."

I laughed. "Did he?"

"Cyra has many qualities that are useful to the sovereign, but 'sense' is not one of them; I would not take her opinion of me too seriously," Vas said.

"While I do love our little chats, Vas," I said, "why don't you just tell me what you want?"

"What are you brewing? A painkiller?" Vas smirked. "I thought groping Kereseth was your painkiller."

"What," I repeated, terse this time, "do you want?"

"I'm sure you've realized that the Sojourn Festival begins tomorrow. Ryz wanted to know if you would be attending the arena challenges at his side. He wanted to remind you, before you answer, that part of giving Kereseth's service to you was to get you on your feet, so you can attend events like these, in public."

The arena challenges. I had not watched them in seasons, claiming pain as my excuse, but really, I just didn't want to watch people killing each other for social status, or revenge, or money. It was a legal practice—even a celebrated one, these days—but that didn't mean I needed to add those images to the violent ones that already existed in my mind. Uzul Zetsyvis's melting scowl among them.

"Well, I'm not quite 'on my feet' yet," I said. "Send my regrets."

"Very well." Vas shrugged. "You might want to teach Kereseth to unspool a little, or he'll pull a muscle every time he sees me."

I glanced back at Akos, at his shoulders rounded over the countertop. "I'll take it under advisement."

Later that day, when the news feed cycled through the planets in turn, the report on our planet included the comment: "Prominent Shotet fenzu producer Uzul Zetsyvis found dead in his house. Preliminary investigations suggest cause of death is suicide by hanging." The Shotet subtitles read: *Shotet mourns the loss of beloved fenzu caretaker Uzul Zetsyvis. Investigation of his death suggests a Thuvhesit assassination, aiming to eliminate essential Shotet power source.* Of course. The translations were always lies, and only people Ryzek already trusted knew enough languages to be the wiser. Of course he would blame Uzul's death on Thuvhe, rather than himself.

Or me.

I received a message, delivered by the hallway guard, later that day. It read:

> *Record my father's loss. It belongs to you.*
> —Lety Zetsyvis

Ryzek may have blamed Uzul's death on Thuvhe, but Uzul's daughter knew where it really belonged. On me, on my skin.

My currentgift, when experienced for long periods, stayed in the body for a long time even after I took my hands away. And the longer I touched someone, the longer it lingered—unless, of course, they drowned it in hushflower. But the Zetsyvis family didn't believe in taking hushflower. Some people, when faced with the choice between death or pain, chose death. Uzul Zetsyvis was one of those. Religious to the point of self-destruction.

I did carve Uzul's mark on my arm, right before burning Lety's message to ash. I painted the fresh wound with feathergrass root extract, which stung so badly it brought tears to my eyes, and I whispered his name, not daring to say the rest of the ritual words because they were a prayer. And I dreamt of him that night. I heard his screams and saw his bulging, bloodshot eyes. He chased me through a dark forest lit by the fenzu glow. He chased me into a cave where Ryzek waited for me, his teeth like knifepoints.

I woke, sweat-soaked and screaming, with Akos's hand on my shoulder. His face was close to mine, his hair and shirt rumpled from sleep. His eyes were serious and wary, and they asked me a question.

"I heard you," was all he said.

I felt the warmth of his hand through my shirt. His fingertips reached over the collar, brushing my bare throat, and even that light touch was enough to extinguish my currentgift and relieve my pain. When his fingers slipped away, I almost cried out, too tired for things like dignity and pride, but he was only finding my hand.

"Come on," he said. "I'll teach you to get rid of your dreams."

In that moment, with our fingers laced together and his calm voice in my ear, I would have done whatever he suggested. I nodded, and pulled my legs free from the twisted sheets.

He lit the fixtures in his room, and we stood side by side at the counter, the jars, marked now in Thuvhesit letters, stacked above us.

"Like almost everything," he said, "this blend starts with hush-flower."

CHAPTER 11 | CYRA

THE SOJOURN FESTIVAL BEGAN every season with the pounding of drums at sunrise. The first sounds came from the amphitheater in the middle of the city, and radiated outward as faithful participants joined in. The drumbeats were supposed to symbolize our beginnings—the first beats of our hearts, the first stirrings of life that had led us to the might we possessed today. For a week we would celebrate our beginnings, and then all our able-bodied would pile into the sojourn ship to chase the current across the galaxy. We would follow its path until the currentstream turned blue, and then we would descend on a planet to scavenge, and return home.

I had always loved the sound of the drums, because they meant we would leave soon. I always felt freer in space. But with Uzul Zetsyvis still in my dreams, this season I heard the drums as his slowing heartbeat.

Akos had appeared in my doorway, his short brown hair sticking out in all directions, leaning into the wood.

"What," he said, eyes wide, "is that sound?"

In spite of the current's pain shooting through me, I laughed. I had never seen him this disheveled before. His drawstring pants were twisted halfway around, and his cheek bore the red imprint of creased sheets.

"It's just the start of the Sojourn Festival," I said. "Relax. Untwist your pants."

His cheeks turned faintly pink, and he righted the waistband of his pants.

"Well, how was I supposed to know that?" he replied irritably. "Next time, when something that sounds remarkably like war drums is going to wake me at dawn, could you maybe warn me?"

"You're determined to deprive me of fun."

"That's because apparently, your version of 'fun' is making me believe I'm in mortal peril."

Smiling a little, I went to the window. The streets were flooded with people. I watched them kicking up dust as they charged toward the center of Voa to participate in the festivities. They were all dressed in blue, our favorite color, and purple, and green; armored and armed; faces painted, necks and wrists draped with fake jewels or crowns of fragile flowers. Flowers here, along the planet's equator, didn't have to be as hardy as iceflowers to survive. They turned to mush between a person's fingers, and smelled sweet.

The festival would feature public challenges in the amphitheater, visitors from other planets, and reenactments of significant moments in Shotet history, all while the crew of the sojourn ship worked on cleaning and repairs. On the last day, Ryzek and I would process from Noavek manor to the transport vessel, which would take us to the sojourn ship as its first official passengers. Everyone else would board after us. It was a rhythm I knew well, and even loved, though my parents were no longer here to guide me through it.

"My family's rule is relatively recent, you know," I said, tilting my head. "By the time I was born, Shotet had already changed, under the reign of my father. Or so I've read."

"You read a lot?" he asked me.

"Yes." I liked to pace and read. It helped me distract myself. "I think this is when we get closest to how things were before. The festival. The sojourn ship." There were children running along our fence line, hands linked, laughing. Other faces, blurry at this distance, turned toward Noavek manor. "We were wanderers, once, not—"

"Murderers and thieves?"

I grasped my left arm, and the armor dug into my palm.

"If you enjoy the festival so much, why don't you go?" he asked me.

I snorted. "And stand at Ryzek's side all day? No."

He stood beside me, looking through the glass. An old woman shuffled down the middle of the street, wrapping a bright scarf around her head—it had come undone in the chaos, and her fingers were clumsy. As we watched her, a young man carrying an armful of flower crowns placed one on her head, atop the scarf.

"I don't understand the wandering, the scavenge," Akos said. "How do you decide where to go?"

The drums were still pounding out the Shotet heartbeat. Beneath them was a dull roar in the distance, and music, layered over itself.

"I can show you, if you want," I said. "They should be starting soon."

§

A little while later we ducked into the hidden passageways of the Noavek home, through the secret door in my bedroom wall. Ahead, a globe of fenzu light gave us something to walk toward, but still I stepped carefully—some of the boards were loose here, the nails jutting out at odd angles from the support beams. I paused where the tunnel split off, and felt the beam for the telltale notches. One notch on the left beam meant it led to the first floor. I reached back for Akos, finding the front of his shirt, and tugged him behind me as I followed the left path.

He touched my wrist, guiding my hand into his, so we walked with fingers clasped. I hoped the sound of creaking floorboards disguised the sound of my breaths.

We walked the tunnels to the room where the Examiners worked, near the Weapons Hall, where I had first seen Akos and Eijeh. I pressed the panel forward, then slid it just enough to let us slip out. The room was so dark the Examiners didn't notice us—they stood among the holograms in the center of the room, measuring distances with fine beams of white light, or checking their wrist screens, calling out coordinates. Still, my pride drove me to step away from him, releasing his hand.

They were calibrating the galaxy model. After they verified the model's accuracy, they would begin their analysis of the current. Its ebb and flow told them where the next scavenge would be.

"The galaxy model," I said softly.

"Galaxy," Akos repeated. "But it shows only our solar system."

"The Shotet are wanderers," I reminded him. "We have gone far beyond the boundaries of our system, and found only stars, no other planets. As far as we are concerned, this solar system is alone in the galaxy."

The model was a hologram that filled the room from corner to corner, glowing sun in the center and broken moon fragments drifting around the edges. The holograms looked solid until an Examiner walked through them to measure something else, and then they shifted like they were exhaling. Our planet passed in front of me as I watched, by far the whitest of all the simulated planets, like a sphere of vapor. Floating nearest to the sun was the Assembly station, a ship even larger than our sojourn ship, the hub of our galaxy's government.

"All calibrated once you get Othyr distal to the sun," one of the Examiners said. He was tall, with rounded shoulders, like he was curling them in to protect his heart. "An izit or two."

An "izit" was slang for IZ, a measurement about the width of my smallest finger. In fact, sometimes I used my fingers to measure things when I didn't have a beamer on hand.

"Really precise measuring there," another overseer responded, this one short, a small paunch bubbling over the top of his pants. "'An izit or two,' honestly. That's like saying 'a planet or two.'"

"1.467IZ," the first overseer said. "Like it'll make a difference to the current."

"You've never really embraced the subtlety of this art," a woman said, striding through the sun to measure its distance from Othyr, one of the closer planets to the galaxy's center. Everything about her was strict, from the line of her short hair across her jaw to the starched shoulders of her jacket. For a moment she was encased in yellow-white light, standing in the middle of the sun. "And an art it is, though some would call it a science. Miss

Noavek, how honored we are to have you with us. And your . . . companion?"

She didn't look at me as she spoke, just bent to point the beam of light at the band of Othyr's equator. The other Examiners jumped at the sight of me, and in unison backed up a step, though they were already across the room. If they had known how much effort it was taking me to stand in one place without fidgeting and crying, they might not have worried.

"He's a servant," I said. "Carry on, I'm just observing."

They did, in a way, but their careless chatter was gone. I put my hands in fists and wedged them between my back and the wall, squeezing so tightly my fingernails bit my palms. But I forgot about the pain when the Examiners activated the hologram of the current; it wove its way through the simulated planets like a snake, but formless, ethereal. It touched every planet in the galaxy, Assembly-governed and brim alike, and then formed a strong band around the edge of the room like a strap holding the planets in. Its light shifted always, so rich in some places it hurt my eyes to stare at it, and so dim in others it was only a wisp.

Otega had taken me here as a child, to teach me how the scavenge worked. These Examiners would spend days observing the flow of the current.

"The current's light and color is always strongest over our planet," I said to Akos in a low voice. "Wrapped three times around it, Shotet legend says—which is why our Shotet ancestors chose to settle here. But its intensity fluctuates around the other planets, anointing one after another, with no discernible pattern. Every season we follow its leading, then we land, and scavenge."

"Why?" Akos murmured back.

We cull each planet's wisdom and take it for our own, Otega had said, crouched down beside me at one of our lessons. *And when we do that, we show them what about them is worthy of their appreciation. We reveal them to themselves.*

As if in response to the memory, the currentshadows moved faster beneath my skin, surging and receding, the pain following wherever they went.

"Renewal," I said. "The scavenge is about renewal." I didn't know how else to explain. I had never had to before. "We find things that other planets have discarded, and we give them a new life. It's . . . what we believe in."

"Seeing activity around P1104," the first Examiner said, hunching even lower over one of the hunks of rock near the edge of the galaxy. His body looked almost like a dead insect, curled into a husk. He touched a section of the current where the color—green now, with hints of yellow—swirled darker.

"Like a wave about to hit shore," the sharp-edged woman purred. "It may build or fizzle, depending. Mark it for observation. But right now my guess for the best scavenge planet is still Ogra."

The scavenge is a kindness, Otega had whispered in my child-ear. *To them as well as to us. The scavenge is one of the current's purposes for us.*

"Much good your guessing will do," the first overseer said. "Didn't you say His Highness specifically requested information about current activity over Pitha? Barely a wisp there, but I doubt that matters to him."

"His Highness has his own reasons for requesting information, and they are not ours to question," the woman said, glancing at me.

Pitha. There were rumors about that place. That buried deep

under the water planet's oceans, where the currents were not as strong, were advanced weapons, unlike anything we had seen. And with Ryzek determined to claim not just Shotet's nationhood, but control over the entire planet, weapons would surely be useful.

Pain was building behind my eyes. That was how it started, when my currentgift was about to hit me harder than usual. And it had been hitting me harder than usual whenever I thought about Ryzek waging war in earnest, as I stood passive at his side.

"We should go," I said to Akos. I turned to the Examiners. "Best wishes on your observations." Then, on a whim, I added, "Don't lead us astray."

Akos was quiet as we walked back through the passages. Akos was always quiet, I realized, unless he was asking questions. I didn't know that I could have been so curious about someone I hated, though maybe that was the point: he was trying to decide if he hated me.

Outside, the drumbeats petered out, as they always did. But the silence seemed to signal something to Akos—he stopped under one of the fenzu lights. Only one insect still drifted in the glass orb above us, glowing palest blue, a sign that it was close to death. There was a pile of dead shells beneath it, insects with their legs bent in the air.

"Let's go to the festival," he said. He was too thin, I thought. There were shadows under his cheekbones where flesh should have been, in a face so young. "No Ryzek. Just you and me."

I stared down at his upturned palm. He offered touch to me so freely, without realizing how rare it was. How rare *he* was, to a person like me.

"Why?" I said.

"What?"

"You've been nice to me recently." I furrowed my brow. "You're being nice to me now. Why? What's in it for you?"

"Growing up here really has warped you, hasn't it?"

"Growing up here," I clarified, "has made me see the truth about people."

He sighed, like he disagreed with me but didn't want to bother to argue. He sighed that way a lot. "We spend a lot of time together, Cyra. Being nice is a matter of survival."

"I'll be recognized. The currentshadows are memorable, even if my face is not."

"You won't have any currentshadows. You'll be with me." He cocked his head to the side. "Or are you really that uncomfortable with touching me?"

It was a challenge. And maybe a manipulation. But I imagined my skin being neutral in a dense crowd, people brushing up against me without feeling pain, smelling the sweat in the air, letting myself disappear among them. The last time I had been close to a crowd like that had been before my first sojourn, when my father hoisted me in the air. Even if Akos did have ulterior motives, maybe it was worth the risk, if I got to leave.

I put my hand in his.

A little while later we were back in the passages again, dressed in festival clothes. I wore a purple dress—not my mother's finery this time, but something cheap that I didn't mind ruining—and I had painted my face to disguise it, with a thick diagonal stripe that covered all of one eye and most of the other. I had bound my hair back tightly, painting it blue to keep it in place. Without the currentshadows, I wouldn't look like the Cyra Noavek that the city of Voa knew.

Akos was dressed in black and green, but since he wasn't recognizable, he hadn't bothered with any disguise.

When he saw me, he stared. For a long time.

I knew how I looked. My face was not a relief to the eyes, the way the faces of uncomplicated people were; it was a challenge, like the blinding color of the currentstream. How I looked wasn't important, particularly as my appearance was always obscured by the shifting veins of the current. But it was strange to see him notice at all.

"Put your eyes back in your head, Kereseth," I said. "You're embarrassing yourself."

Our arms clasped hand-to-elbow, I led him along the east edge of the house and down the stairs. I felt the beams for the carved circles that warned of secret exits. Like the one near the kitchens.

Feathergrass grew right up to the house there, and we had to push through it to reach the gate, which was locked with a code. I knew it. It was my mother's birthday. All of Ryzek's codes were related to my mother in some way—the day of her birth, the day of her death, my parents' wedding day, her favorite numbers— except closest to his rooms, where the doors were locked with Noavek blood. I didn't go near there, didn't spend more time with him than I had to.

I felt Akos's eyes on my hand as I typed in the code. But it was only the back gate.

We walked down a narrow alley that opened up to one of the main thoroughfares of Voa. My body clenched, for a moment, as a man's eyes lingered on my face. And a woman's. And a child's. Everywhere eyes caught mine and then shifted away.

I grabbed Akos's arm, and pulled him in to whisper, "They're staring. They know who I am."

"No," he said. "They're staring because you've got bright blue paint all over your face."

I touched my cheek, lightly, where the paint had dried. My skin felt rough and scaly. It hadn't occurred to me that today it meant nothing if people stared at me.

"You're kind of paranoid, you know that?" he said to me.

"And you're starting to sound kind of cocky, for someone I routinely beat up."

He laughed. "So where do we go?"

"I know a place," I said. "Come on."

I led him down a less crowded street on the left, away from the city's center. The air was full of dust, but soon the sojourn ship would launch, and we would have our storm. It would wash the city clean, stain it blue.

The official, government-sanctioned festival activities took place in and around the amphitheater in the center of Voa, but that wasn't the only place where people celebrated. As we dodged elbows on a narrow street where the buildings fell together like lovers, there were people dancing, singing. A woman adorned with fake jewels stopped me with a hand, a luxury I had never enjoyed; it almost made me shiver. She set a crown of fenzu flowers— named so because they were the same color as the insects' wings, blue gray—on my head, grinning.

We turned into a crowded marketplace. Everywhere there were low tents or booths with worn awnings, people arguing and young women touching their fingers to necklaces they couldn't afford. Weaving through the crowd were Shotet soldiers, their armor shining in the daylight. I smelled cooked meat and smoke, and turned to smile at Akos.

His expression was strange. Confused, almost, like this was not a Shotet he had ever imagined.

We walked hand in hand down the aisle between the booths. I paused at a table of plain knives—their blades weren't made of channeling material, so the current wouldn't flow around them— with carved handles.

"Does the lady know how to handle a plain knife?" the old man at the booth asked me in Shotet. He wore the heavy gray robes of a Zoldan religious leader, with long, loose sleeves. Religious Zoldans used plain knives because they believed currentblades were a frivolous use of the current, which deserved more respect—the same basic belief as the most religious Shotet. But unlike a Shotet religious leader, this man would not find his religious practice in the everyday, reworking the world around him. He was likely an ascetic; he withdrew, instead.

"Better than you," I said to him in Zoldan. I spoke Zoldan poorly—a generous way of putting it—but I was happy to practice.

"That right?" He laughed. "Your accent is horrible."

"Hey!" A Shotet soldier approached us, and tapped the tip of his currentblade against the old man's table. The Zoldan man regarded the weapon with disgust. "Shotet language only. If she talks back in your tongue . . ." The soldier grunted a little. "It would not turn out well for her."

I ducked my head so the soldier wouldn't look too carefully at my face.

The Zoldan man said in clumsy Shotet, "I'm sorry. The fault was mine."

The soldier held his knife there for a moment, puffing up his chest like he was displaying mating feathers. Then he sheathed his weapon, and kept walking through the crowd.

The old man turned back to me, his tone now more business-like: "These are the best weighted ones you'll find in the square—"

He talked to me about how the knives were made—from metal forged in the northern pole of Zold, and reclaimed wood from old houses in Zoldia City—and part of me was listening, but the other part was with Akos as he stared out at the square.

I bought a dagger from the old man, a sturdy one with a dark blade and a handle built for long fingers. I offered it to Akos.

"From Zold," I said. "It's a strange place, half covered in gray dust from fields of flowers. Takes some getting used to. But the metal is strangely flexible, despite being so strong . . . what? What is it?"

"All of this stuff," he said, gesturing to the square itself. "It's from other planets?"

"Yeah." My palm was sweaty where it pressed against his. "Extraplanetary vendors are allowed to sell in Voa during the Sojourn Festival. Some of it is scavenged, of course—or we wouldn't be Shotet. Repurposing the discarded, and all that."

He had stopped in the middle of everything and turned toward me.

"Do you know where it's all from just by looking at it? Have you been to all these places?" he said.

I scanned the market, once. Some of the vendors were covered head to toe in fabric, some bright and some dull; some wore tall headpieces to draw attention to themselves, or spoke in loud, chattering Shotet I hardly understood, because of the accents. Lights erupted from a booth at the end, showering the air in sparks that disappeared as quickly as they came. The woman standing behind it almost glowed for all the fair skin she showed. Another stand was surrounded by a cloud of insects so dense I could hardly see the man sitting at it. What use did anyone have for a swarm of insects, I wondered.

"All nine Assembly nation-planets," I said with a nod. "But no, I can't tell where it's all from. Some of it, though, is obvious. Look at this—"

Standing on a nearby counter was a delicate instrument. It was an abstract shape, different from every angle, composed of tiny panes of an iridescent material that felt like something between glass and stone.

"Synthetic," I said. "Everything from Pitha is, since it's covered in water. They import materials from their neighbors and combine them. . . ."

I tapped one of the tiny panes, and a sound like thunder came from the belly of the instrument. I ran my fingers over the rest, and they left music in their wake like waves. The melody was light, like my touch had been, but when I flicked one of the glass panels, drums sounded. Each panel seemed to glow with some kind of internal light.

"It's supposed to simulate the sound of water for homesick travelers," I said.

When I looked at him again, he was smiling at me hesitantly.

"You love them," he said. "All these places, all these things."

"Yeah," I said. I had never thought of it that way. "I guess I do."

"What about Thuvhe?" he said. "Do you love it, too?"

When he said the name of his home, comfortable with the slippery syllables that I would have stumbled over, it was easier to remember that though he spoke Shotet fluently, he was not one of us, not really. He had grown up encased in frost, his house lit by burnstones. He probably still dreamt in Thuvhesit.

"Thuvhe," I repeated. I had never been to the frozen country in the north, but I had studied their language and culture. I had seen pictures and footage. "Iceflowers and buildings made of leaded glass." They were people who loved intricate, geometric patterns, and bright colors that stood out in the snow. "Floating cities and endless white. Yes, there are things I love about Thuvhe."

He looked suddenly stricken. I wondered if I had made him homesick.

He took the dagger that I had offered him and looked it over, testing the blade with his fingertip and wrapping his hand around the handle.

"You handed over this weapon so easily," he said. "But I could use this against you, Cyra."

"You could *try* to use it against me," I corrected him quietly. "But I don't think you will."

"I think you might be lying to yourself about what I am."

He was right. Sometimes it was too easy to forget that he was a prisoner in my house, and that when I was with him, I was serving as a kind of warden.

But if I let him escape right now, to try to get his brother home, as he wanted, I would be resigning myself to a lifetime of agony again. Even as I thought it, I couldn't bear it. It was too many seasons, too many Uzul Zetsyvises, too many veiled threats from Ryzek and half-drunk evenings at his side.

I started down the aisle again. "Time to visit the Storyteller."

While my father had been busy shaping Ryzek into a monster, my education had been in Otega's hands. Every so often she had dressed me head to toe in heavy fabric, to disguise the shadows that burned me, and taken me to parts of the city my parents would never have allowed me to go.

This place was one of them. It was deep in one of the poorer areas of Voa, where half the buildings were caving in and the others looked like they were about to. There were markets here, too, but they were more temporary, just rows of things arranged on blankets, so they could be gathered and carried away at a moment's notice.

Akos drew me in by my elbow as we walked past one of them, a purple blanket with white bottles on it. They had glue from peeled-off labels still on them, attracting purple fuzz.

"Is that medicine?" he asked me. "Those look like they're from Othyr."

I nodded, not trusting myself to speak.

"For what ailment?" he asked.

"Q900X," I replied. "Known more colloquially as 'chills and spills.' You know, because it affects balance."

He frowned at me. We paused there in the alley, the festival sounds far off. "That disease is preventable. You don't inoculate against it?"

"You understand that we are a poor country, right?" I frowned back at him. "We have no real exports, and hardly enough natural resources to sustain ourselves independently. Some other planets send aid—Othyr, among them—but that aid falls into the wrong hands, and is distributed based on status rather than need."

"I never . . ." He paused. "I've never thought about it before."

"Why would you?" I said. "It's not high on Thuvhe's list of concerns."

"I grew up wealthy in a poor place, too," he said. "That's something we have in common."

He seemed surprised that we would have anything in common at all.

"There's nothing you can do for these people?" he said, gesturing to the buildings around us. "You're Ryzek's sister, can't you—"

"He doesn't listen to me," I said, defensive.

"You've tried?"

"You say that like it's easy." My face felt warm. "Just have a meeting with my brother and tell him to rearrange his whole system and he'll do it."

"I didn't say it was *easy*—"

"High-status Shotet are my brother's insulation against an uprising," I said, even more heated now. "And in exchange for their loyalty, he gives them medicine, food, and the trappings of wealth that the others don't get. Without them as his insulation, he will die. And with my Noavek blood, I die with him. So no . . . no, I have not embarked on some grand mission to save the sick and the poor of Shotet!"

I sounded angry, but inside I was shriveling from the shame of it. I had almost thrown up the first time Otega brought me here, from the smell of a starved body in one of the alleys. She had covered my eyes as we walked past it, so I couldn't get a close look. That was me: Ryzek's Scourge, combat virtuoso, driven to vomit by the sight of death alone.

"I shouldn't have brought it up," he said, his hand gentle on my arm. "Let's go. Let's go visit this . . . storyteller."

I nodded, and we kept walking.

Buried deep in the maze of narrow alleys was a low doorway painted with intricate blue patterns. I knocked, and it creaked open, just enough to emit a tendril of white smoke that smelled like burnt sugar.

This place felt like an exhale; it felt sacred. In a sense, maybe it was. This was where Otega had first taken me to learn our history, many seasons ago, on the first day of the Sojourn Festival.

A tall, pale man opened the door, his hair shaved so close his scalp shone. He lifted his hands and smiled.

"Ah, Little Noavek," he said. "I didn't think I would see you again. And who have you brought me?"

"This is Akos," I said. "Akos, this is the Storyteller. At least, that's what he prefers to be called."

"Hello," Akos said. I could tell he was nervous by the way his posture changed, the soldier in him disappearing. The Storyteller's smile spread, and he beckoned us in.

We stepped down into the Storyteller's living room. Akos hunched to fit under the curved ceiling, which arched to a globe of bright fenzu at its apex. There was a rusted stove with an exhaust pipe stretching to the room's only window, to let out smoke. I knew the floors were made of hard-packed dirt because I had peeked under the bland, woven rugs as a child to see what was beneath them. The hard fibers had made my legs itch.

The Storyteller directed us to a pile of cushions, where we settled, a little awkwardly, our hands gripped between us. I let go of Akos to wipe my palm on my dress, and as the currentshadows flushed back into my body, the Storyteller smiled again.

"There they are," he said. "I almost didn't recognize you without them, Little Noavek."

He set a metal pot on the table before us—really two footstools bolted together, one metal and one wood—and a pair of mismatched, glazed mugs. I poured the tea for us. It was pale purple, almost pink, and accounted for the sweet smell in the air.

The Storyteller sat across from us. The white paint on the wall above his head was flaking, revealing yellow paint beneath it, from another time. Yet even here was the ever-present news screen, fixed crookedly on the wall next to the stove. This place was full to bursting with scavenged objects, the dark metal teapot clearly Tepessar, the stove grate made of Pithar flooring, and the Storyteller's clothing itself silky as any of Othyr's wealthy. In the corner there was a chair, its origin unfamiliar to me, that the Storyteller was in the middle of repairing.

"Your companion—Akos, was it?—smells of hushflower," the Storyteller said, for the first time furrowing his brow.

"He is Thuvhesit," I said. "He means no disrespect."

"Disrespect?" Akos said.

"Yes, I do not permit people who have recently ingested hushflower, or any other current-altering substance, into my home," the Storyteller said. "Though they are welcome to return once it has passed through their system. I am not in the habit of rejecting visitors outright, after all."

"The Storyteller is a Shotet religious leader," I said to Akos. "We call them clerics."

"He is a Thuvhesit, truly?" The Storyteller frowned, and closed his eyes. "Surely you are mistaken, sir. You speak our sacred language like a native."

"I think I know my own home," Akos replied testily. "My own identity."

"I meant no offense," the Storyteller said. "But your name is Akos, which is a Shotet name, so you can see why I am confused.

Thuvhesit parents would not give their child a name with such a hard sound in it without purpose. What are your siblings' names, for example?"

"Eijeh," Akos said breathily. Obviously he hadn't thought about this before. "And Cisi."

His hand tightened around mine. I didn't think he was aware of it.

"Well, no matter," the Storyteller said. "Obviously you have come here with a purpose, and you don't have much time before the storm for it to be accomplished, so we will move on. Little Noavek, to what do I owe this visit?"

"I thought you could tell Akos the story you told me as a child," I said. "I'm not good at telling stories, myself."

"Yes, I can see that being the case." The Storyteller picked up his own mug from the floor by his feet, which were bare. The air had been crisp outside, but in here it was warm, almost stifling. "As to the story, it doesn't really have a beginning. We didn't realize our language was revelatory, carried in the blood, because we were always together, moving as one through the galaxy as wanderers. We had no home, no permanence. We followed the current around the galaxy, wherever it saw fit to lead us. This, we believed, was our obligation, our mission."

The Storyteller sipped his tea, set it down, and wiggled his fingers in the air. When I had first seen him do it, I had giggled, thinking he was acting strange. But now I knew what to expect: faint, hazy shapes appeared in front of him. They were smoky, not lit up like the hologram of the galaxy we had seen earlier, but the image was the same: planets arranged around a sun, a line of white current wrapping around them.

Akos's gray eyes—the same color as most of the smoke—widened.

"Then one of the oracles had a vision, that our ruling family would lead us to a permanent home. And they did—to an uninhabited, cold planet we called 'Urek,' because it means 'empty.'"

"Urek," Akos said. "That's the Shotet name for our planet?"

"Well, you didn't expect us to call the whole thing 'Thuvhe' the way your people do, did you?" I snorted. "Thuvhe" was the official, Assembly-recognized name for our planet, which contained Thuvhesit and Shotet people both. But that didn't mean *we* had to call it that.

The Storyteller's illusion changed, focusing on a single orb of dense smoke.

"The current was stronger there than anywhere we had ever been. But we didn't want to forget our history, our impermanence, our reclaiming of broken objects, so we began to go on the sojourn. Every season, all of us who were able would return to the ship that had carried us around the galaxy for so long, and follow the current again."

If I had not been holding Akos's hand, I would have been able to feel the current humming in my body. I didn't always think about it, because along with that hum came pain, but it was what I had in common with every person across the galaxy. Well, every person but the one beside me.

I wondered if he ever missed it, if he remembered what it felt like.

The Storyteller's voice became low, and dark, as he continued, "But during one of the sojourns, those who had settled north of Voa to harvest the iceflowers, who called themselves the Thuvhesit, ventured too far south. They came into our city, and saw that we had left many of our children here, to await their parents' return from the sojourn. And they took our children from their beds, from their kitchen tables, from their streets. They stole our young ones, and brought them north as captives and servants."

His fingers painted a flat street, a rough figure of a person running down it, chased by a rolling cloud. At the end of the street, the running person was subsumed by the cloud.

"When our sojourners came home to find their children missing, they waged war for their return. But they were not trained for battle, only for scavenging and for wandering, and they were killed in large numbers. And so we believed those children lost forever," he said. "But a generation later, on a sojourn, one of our number ventured alone on the planet Othyr, and there—among those who did not know our tongue—a child spoke to him in Shotet. She was a child of a Thuvhesit captive, collecting something for her masters, and she didn't even realize that she had traded one language for another. The child was Reclaimed, brought back to us."

He tilted his head.

"And then," he said, "we rose, and became soldiers, so we would never be overcome again."

As he whispered, as the smoke of his illusions disappeared, drums from the city's center pounded louder and louder, and drums all throughout the poor sector joined in. They thudded and rumbled, and I looked to the Storyteller, mouth drifting open.

"It is the storm," he said. "Which is all the better, because my story is done."

"Thank you," I said. "I'm sorry to—"

"Go, Little Noavek," the Storyteller said with a crooked smile. "Don't miss it."

I grabbed Akos's arm and pulled him to his feet. He was

scowling at the Storyteller. He had not touched the cup of sweet purple tea that I had poured for him. I tugged hard to get him to follow me up the steps of the Storyteller's house and into the alley. Even from here, I could see the ship drifting toward Voa from far off. I knew its shape the way I had known my mother's silhouette, even from a distance. How it bowed out at the belly and tapered at the nose. I knew which scavenges had yielded its uneven plates by how worn they were, or by their tints, orange and blue and black. Our patchwork craft, large enough to cast all of Voa in shadow.

All around us, all throughout the city, I heard cheers.

Out of habit, I raised my free hand up to the sky. A loud, sharp sound like the crack of a whip came from somewhere near the loading bay door of the ship, and veins of dark blue color spread from it in every direction, wrapping around the clouds themselves, or forming new ones. It was like ink dropped into water, separate at first and then mixing, blending together until the city was covered in a blanket of dark blue mist. The ship's gift to us.

Then—as it had every season of my life—it started to rain blue.

Keeping one hand firmly in Akos's, I turned my other palm to catch some of the blue. It was dark, and wherever it rolled across my skin, it left a faint stain. The people at the end of the alley were laughing and smiling and singing and swaying. Akos's chin was tipped back. He gazed at the ship's belly, and then at his hand, at the blue rolling over his knuckles. His eyes met mine. I was laughing.

"Blue is our favorite color," I said. "The color of the current-stream when we scavenge."

"When I was a child," he replied wonderingly, "it was my

favorite color, too, though all of Thuvhe hates it."

I took the palmful of blue water I had collected, and smeared it into his cheek, staining it darker. Akos spluttered, spitting some of it on the ground. I raised my eyebrows, waiting for his reaction. He stuck out his hand, catching a stream of water rolling off a building's roof, and lunged at me.

I sprinted down the alley, not fast enough to avoid the cold water rolling down my back, with a childlike shriek. I caught his arm by the elbow, and we ran together, through the singing crowd, past swaying elders, men and women dancing too close, irritable off-planet visitors trying to cover up their wares in the market. We splashed through bright blue puddles, soaking our clothes. And we were both, for once, laughing.

CHAPTER 12 | CYRA

THAT NIGHT I SCRUBBED the blue stain from my skin and hair, then joined Akos at the apothecary counter to make the painkiller so I could sleep. I didn't ask him what he thought of the Storyteller's account of Shotet history, which blamed Thuvhe, not Shotet, for the hostility between our people. He didn't offer his reaction. When the painkiller was done, I carried it back to my room and sat on the edge of my bed to drink it. And that was the last thing I remembered.

When I woke, I was slumped sideways on the bed, on top of the blankets. Beside me, the half-empty mug of painkiller had turned on its side, and the sheets were stained purple where it had spilled. Sunrise was just beginning, judging by the pale light coming through the curtains.

My body aching, I pushed myself up. "Akos?"

The tea had knocked me unconscious. I pressed the heel of my hand to my forehead. But I had helped him make it; had I made it too strong? I stumbled down the hallway and knocked on his door. No, I couldn't have made it too strong; I had only prepared the sendes stalks for it. He had done the rest.

He had drugged me.

There was no answer at his door. I pushed it open. Akos's room was empty, drawers open, clothes missing, dagger gone.

I had been suspicious of his kindness as he coaxed me into leaving the house. And I had been right to be.

I yanked my hair back and tied it away from my face. I went back to my room, shoving my feet into my boots. I didn't bother with the laces.

He had *drugged* me.

I wheeled around and searched the far wall for the panel we had pushed through yesterday to slip out of the house. There was a small gap between it and the rest of the wall. I gritted my teeth against pain. He had wanted me to leave the house with him so I would show him how to get out. And I had armed him with that Zoldan knife, I had trusted him with my potion, and now . . . now I would suffer for it.

I think you're lying to yourself about what I am, he had said.

Honor has no place in survival, I had taught him.

I charged into the hallway. There was already a guard walking toward me. I braced myself against the door. What was he coming to say? I didn't know what to hope for, Akos's escape or his capture.

The guard stopped just shy of my door, and bent his head to me. He was one of the shorter, younger ones—baby-faced and carrying a blade. One of the ones who still stared wide-eyed at my arms when the dark lines spread over them.

"What?" I demanded, gritting my teeth. The pain was back, almost as bad as it had been after I tortured Uzul Zetsyvis. "What is it?"

"The sovereign's steward, Vas Kuzar, sends word that your

servant was discovered trying to flee the grounds with his brother last night," the guard said. "He is currently confined, awaiting the sovereign's assigned punishment. Vas requests your presence at the private hearing, in two hours, in the Weapons Hall."

With his brother. That meant Akos had found a way to get Eijeh out, too. I remembered Eijeh's screams after he first arrived here, and shuddered.

I went to the "private hearing" fully armed, dressed as a soldier. Ryzek had left the curtains down in the Weapons Hall, so it was as dark as night, lit by the wavering light of the fenzu above. He stood on the platform, hands behind his back, staring at the wall of weapons above him. No one else was in the room. Yet.

"This was our mother's favorite," he said as the door closed behind me. He touched the currentstick, suspended on a diagonal from the wall. It was a long, narrow pole with blades at either end. Each of the blades contained a channeling rod, so if the weapon touched skin, dark shadows of current wrapped around the whole thing, from end to end. It was nearly as long as I was tall.

"An elegant choice," he said, still without turning around. "More for show than anything; did you know our mother was not particularly proficient in combat? Father told me. But she was clever, strategic. She found ways to avoid physical altercations, acknowledging her weakness."

He turned. He wore a smug smile.

"You should be more like her, sister," he said. "You are an excellent fighter. But up here . . ." He tapped the side of his head. "Well, it's not your strength."

The shadows traveled faster beneath my skin, spurred on by my anger. But I kept my mouth closed.

"You gave Kereseth a weapon? You took him through the tunnels?" Ryzek shook his head. "You slept through his escape?"

"He drugged me," I said tersely.

"Oh? And how did he do that?" Ryzek said lightly, still smirking. "Pinned you down and poured the potion into your mouth? I don't think so. I think you drank it, trustingly. Drank a powerful drug prepared by your enemy."

"Ryzek—" I started.

"You almost cost us our *oracle*," Ryzek snapped. "And why? Because you're foolish enough to let your heart flutter for the first painkiller who comes around?"

I didn't argue. He had spent a long time searching the galaxy for an oracle, with my father and without. In one night, that oracle had almost escaped. My doing. And maybe he was right. Maybe whatever small trust I had felt for Akos, whatever appeal he had held, had come because he offered me relief. Because I was so grateful for the reprieve from pain—and from isolation—that my heart had softened. I had been stupid.

"You can't blame him for wanting to rescue his brother, or for wanting to get out of here," I said, my voice quaking with fear.

"You really don't get it, do you?" Ryzek said, laughing a little. "People will always want things that will destroy us, Cyra. That doesn't mean we just let them act on what they want."

Ryzek pointed to the side of the room.

"Stand over there and don't say a word," he said. "I brought you here to watch what happens when you don't keep your servants under control."

I was shivering, burning, and I looked like I was standing under a canopy of vines, marked by their shadows. I stumbled to the side of the room, my arms clutched tightly around me. I heard Ryzek's order to enter.

The huge doors at the other end of the room opened. Vas walked in first, armored, his shoulders back. Behind him, flanked by soldiers, was the sagging, stumbling form of Akos Kereseth. Half his face was covered in blood, coming from a gash in his eyebrow. His face was swollen, his lip split. Beaten already, but then, he had gotten good at taking a beating.

Behind him walked Eijeh—also bleeding and beaten, but more than that . . . vacant. His face was rough with a patchy beard, and he was gaunt, a shred of the young man I had seen from my hidden vantage point two seasons ago.

I could hear Akos breathing from where I stood, sputtering. But he straightened at the sight of my brother.

"My, my, aren't you a sight," Ryzek said, descending the steps slowly. "How far did he get, Vas? Past the fence?"

"Not even," Vas said. "Got him in the kitchens, coming out of the tunnels."

"Well, let me clarify your miscalculation, for future reference, Kereseth," Ryzek said. "Just because my late mother enjoyed the old-fashioned appearance of this house doesn't mean that I didn't outfit my home with the most advanced security measures possible after her passing. Including motion sensors around secure rooms, such as your brother's."

"Why are you keeping him here?" Akos said through gritted teeth. "Does he even *have* a currentgift? Or have you starved it out of him?"

Vas—casually, lazily—backhanded Akos. Akos crumpled, clutching his cheek.

"Akos," Eijeh said. His voice was like a light touch. "Don't."

"Why don't you tell him, Eijeh?" Ryzek said. "Have you developed a currentgift?"

Akos peered past his fingers at his brother. Eijeh closed his eyes for a moment, and when he opened them again, nodded.

"Rising oracle," Akos murmured in Shotet. At first I didn't know what he meant—it was not a phrase we used. But Thuvhesit had different words for all three oracles—one falling, close to retiring; one sitting, prophesying from the temple; and one rising, coming into the fullness of his or her power.

"You would be correct in assuming that I have not been able to make him use his gift for my benefit," Ryzek said. "So instead, I intend to take it."

"Take it?" Akos said, echoing my own thoughts.

Ryzek stepped closer to Akos and crouched in front of him, his elbows balanced on his knees.

"Do you know what *my* currentgift is?" he said lightly.

Akos didn't answer.

"Tell him about it, Cyra dear," Ryzek said, jerking his head toward me. "You are intimately acquainted with it."

Akos, bracing himself with one hand, lifted his eyes to mine. There were tears mixed with the blood on his face.

"My brother can trade memories," I said. I sounded empty. Felt like it, too. "He gives you one of his, and takes one of yours in return."

Akos went still.

"A person's gift proceeds from who they are," Ryzek said. "And who they are is what their pasts have made them. Take a person's memories, and you take the things that formed them. You take their gift. And at last . . ." Ryzek ran his finger down the side of Akos's face, collecting blood. He rubbed it between his thumb and forefinger, examining it. "At last, I will not have to rely on another to tell me the future."

Akos threw himself at Ryzek, moving fast to give the soldiers the slip, his hands outstretched. He pressed his thumb hard into the side of Ryzek's throat, pinning his right arm with the other, teeth bared. Animal.

Vas was on top of him in seconds, yanking him by the back of his shirt and punching him hard in the ribs. When Akos was flat on his back, Vas pressed a shoe to his throat, and raised his eyebrows.

"One of my soldiers did this to you once," Vas said. "Before I killed your father. It seemed to be effective then. Stay still or I will crush your trachea."

Akos twitched, but stopped thrashing. Ryzek picked himself up, massaging his throat and brushing dust from his pants and checking the straps of his armor. Then he approached Eijeh. The soldiers who had walked in with Akos were now flanking Eijeh, each one with a firm grip on one of his arms. As if it was necessary. Eijeh looked so dazed I was surprised he was still awake.

Ryzek lifted both hands, and touched them to Eijeh's head, his eyes focused and hungry. Hungry for escape.

It was not much to watch. Just Ryzek and Eijeh, joined by Ryzek's hands, stares locked, for a long time.

When I first watched Ryzek do this, I was too much of a child to understand what was going on, but I did remember that it had taken only a moment for him to trade one memory. Memories happened in flashes, not as drawn-out as reality, and it seemed strange that something so important, so essential to a person, could disappear so quickly.

Breathless, all I could do now was watch.

When Ryzek released Eijeh, it was with a strange, bewildered look. He stepped back, and looked around like he wasn't sure where he was. Felt his body like he wasn't sure who he was. I wondered if he had thought about what trading his memories away would cost him, or if he had just assumed that he was so potent a personality there was more than enough of him to go around.

Eijeh, meanwhile, looked at the Weapons Hall like he had only just recognized it. Was I just imagining the familiarity in his eyes as they followed the steps up to the platform?

Ryzek nodded to Vas to take his foot from Akos's throat. Vas did. Akos lay still, staring at Ryzek, who crouched beside him again.

"Do you still blush so easily?" Ryzek said softly. "Or was that something you grew out of, eventually?"

Akos's face contorted.

"You will never disrespect me with silly escape plans again," Ryzek said. "And your punishment for this first and only attempt is that I will keep your brother around, taking piece after piece from him until he is no longer someone you wish to rescue."

Akos pressed his forehead to the ground, and closed his eyes.

And no wonder. Eijeh Kereseth was as good as gone.

CHAPTER 13 | CYRA

THAT NIGHT I DIDN'T take a painkiller. I couldn't rely on Akos to make it anymore, after all, and I didn't really trust myself to make it alone yet.

When I returned to my room I found the dagger I had given Akos on my pillow. Left there as a warning, by Ryzek, I assumed. I locked Akos's room from the outside.

It was hard to say whether he wasn't speaking to me, or I wasn't speaking to him. In any case, we didn't exchange words. The Sojourn Festival carried on all around us, and I was called to stand at my brother's side, dark-streaked and silent, at some of the festivities. Akos was always at my back, his occasional touch compulsory, his gaze distant. Every time his skin grazed mine to bring relief, I twitched away at first, all trust gone.

Most of the time I spent at the arena, presiding over challenges at Ryzek's side. Arena challenges—one-on-one, public fights— were a long-standing Shotet tradition, originally intended as a sport to hone our combat skills in the days when we had been weak and abused by almost everyone in the galaxy. Now, during the week of the Sojourn Festival, it was legal to challenge almost anyone you had a grievance with to fight, either until one person surrendered, or until death.

However, a person couldn't challenge someone whose social status—arbitrarily decided by Ryzek, or someone he appointed— exceeded their own. As a result, people often chose to provoke their true enemies by targeting the people around them, friends and loved ones, until the other extended the challenge. As the festival advanced, the fights became bloodier and more deadly.

So I dreamt of death, and death filled my days.

The day after I turned sixteen, the day before we boarded the sojourn ship, and five days after Ryzek began trading memories with Eijeh, Akos Kereseth received the armor he had earned long ago, at the soldier camp.

I had just finished running sprints in the gym, so I was pacing back and forth in my bedroom, catching my breath, sweat dripping down the back of my neck. Vas knocked on the doorframe, a polished armor vest dangling from one of his hands.

"Where's Kereseth?" Vas said.

I took him down the hallway, and unlocked Akos's door. Akos was sitting on his bed, and judging by his unfocused gaze, he was drugged by hushflower, which he now consumed petal by petal, raw. He stashed them in his pockets.

Vas tossed the armor at Akos, who caught it with both hands. He handled it like it might shatter, turning it over and running his fingers over each dark-blue panel.

"It is as much as you earned, I'm told, under Vakrez's teaching last season," Vas said.

"How is my brother?" Akos said, throaty.

"He no longer needs a lock to stay in his room," Vas said. "He stays of his own free will."

"That's not true. It can't be."

"Vas," I said. "Go."

I knew rising tension when I felt it. And I didn't really want to watch whatever happened when it broke.

Vas tilted his head as he regarded me, then bowed slightly, and left.

Akos held the armor up to the light. It was built for him—with adjustable straps to accommodate his inevitable growth, flexibility through the rib cage, extra padding over his stomach, which he always forgot to protect when we trained. There was a sheath built into the right shoulder so he could draw over his head with his left hand. It was a high honor, to wear this kind of armor, especially at such a young age.

"I'm going to lock you in again now," I said.

"Is there any way to undo what Ryzek does?" Akos asked, like he hadn't heard me. He looked like he had lost the strength to stand. I thought of refusing to answer him.

"Short of asking Ryzek nicely to trade the memories back and hoping he's in a giving mood, no."

Akos stood and dropped the armor over his head. When he tried to tighten the first strap over his rib cage, he winced, shaking out his hand. The straps were made of the same material as the rest of it, and they were hard to maneuver. I pinched the strap between my fingers, tugging him toward me. My own fingers were already callused.

I pulled at the strap, working it back and forth until it was pulled tight around his side.

"I didn't mean to involve you," Akos said quietly.

"Oh, don't patronize me," I said tersely. "Manipulating me was a crucial part of your plan. And it's exactly what I expected."

I finished with the straps, and stepped back. *Oh*, I thought. He was tall—so tall—and strong and armored, the dark blue skin of the creature he had hunted still rich with color. He looked like a Shotet soldier, like someone I could have wanted, if we had found a way to trust each other.

"Fine," Akos said, again in that quiet voice. "I meant to involve you. But I didn't expect to feel bad about it."

I felt choked. I didn't know why. I ignored it.

"And now you want me to help you feel less bad, is that it?" I said. Before he could answer, I walked out, bringing the door closed behind me.

Before Akos and me were the dusty streets of Voa, behind a tall metal fence. A large, shrill crowd waited for us beyond it. Ryzek stepped out of the house with his long, pale arm raised to greet them, and they let out a dissonant cry.

The Sojourn Festival was almost over. Today all the able-bodied and of-age Shotet would board the sojourn ship, and soon after that, we would leave this planet behind.

Vas followed Ryzek out the door, and then, dressed in a clean white shirt and looking more present than I had ever seen him: Eijeh. His shoulders were back, his steps wider, as if for a taller man, his mouth curled at one corner. Eijeh's eyes passed over his brother and scanned the street beyond Noavek manor.

"Eijeh," Akos said, his voice breaking.

Eijeh's face betrayed some recognition, as if he had spotted his brother from a great distance. I turned toward Akos.

"Later," I said harshly, grabbing the front of his armor. I couldn't have him breaking down with all these people watching us. "Not here, not now. Okay?"

As I pulled away, released him, I watched his throat work to swallow. He had a freckle under his jaw, near his ear; I had never seen it before.

His eyes still on Eijeh, Akos nodded.

Ryzek descended the steps, and we all followed him. The sojourn ship shaded us, casting Voa in shadow. Decades of the sojourn had produced the city that surrounded us, a patchwork of old stone structures reinforced with clay and new technology scavenged from other cultures and lands: low buildings with glass spires built on top of them, reflecting images of other planets; dusty, dirt-packed streets with sleek reflective ships gliding above them; street carts selling current-channeling talismans next to carts selling screen implants that could be wedged beneath a person's skin.

That morning, between surges of pain, I had traced and shaded my dark eyes with blue powder, and braided my thick hair. I wore the armor I had earned at the edge of the Divide when I was younger, and the guard around my left forearm.

I looked back at Akos. He was armored, too, of course, with new black boots and a long-sleeved gray shirt that pulled too tight around his forearms. He looked afraid. He had told me that morning, as we walked to the entrance of the manor, that he had never been off-planet before. And then there was Eijeh, changed, walking right in front of us. There was plenty to fear.

As we passed through the gate, I nodded to him, and he released my arm. It was time for my eleventh Procession, and I wanted to make it to the transport vessel on my own strength.

The walk passed in a haze. Shouting, applauding, Ryzek's fingers finding outstretched hands and squeezing. His laugh, my breaths, Akos's trembling hands. Dust in the air, and smoke from cooked food.

I finally made it inside the transport vessel, where Eijeh and Vas were already waiting. Eijeh was adjusting his own straps with the ease of someone who had done it a dozen times before. I pulled Akos toward a seat in the back, wanting to keep him separate from his brother. A great roar sounded from the crowd as Ryzek waved from the doorway.

Just after the hatch closed, Eijeh fell into the straps holding him in his seat, his eyes wide but also blank, like he was staring at something none of the rest of us could see. Ryzek, who had been fastening his own restraints, undid them and sat forward, his face inches from Eijeh's.

"What is it?" Ryzek said.

"A vision of trouble," Eijeh said. "An act of defiance. Public."

"Preventable?" It was almost as if they had had this exact conversation before. Maybe they had.

"Yes, but in this case, you should let it come," Eijeh said, now focusing on Ryzek. "You can use it to your advantage. I have a plan."

Ryzek narrowed his eyes. "Tell me."

"I would, but we have an audience." Eijeh jerked his head toward the back of the vessel, where Akos sat across from me.

"Yes, your brother is an inconvenience, isn't he?" Ryzek clicked his tongue.

Eijeh didn't disagree. He leaned back in his seat, and closed his eyes as we launched.

The loading dock of the sojourn ship was one of my favorite places, vast and open, a maze of metal. Before us was a fleet of transport vessels ready to take us to a planet's surface—polished to perfection now, but soon to return streaked with dirt and smoke and rain and stardust, badges of where they had been.

They were not round and squat like passenger floaters, or jagged and hulking like the sojourn ship. Instead, they were smooth and sleek, like birds caught mid-dive, with their wings folded back. Each one was multicolored, formed from different metals, and big enough to hold at least six passengers, though some were larger.

Mechanics in dark blue jumpsuits swarmed our vessel when it landed. Ryzek got off first, jumping down before the steps had even descended from the hatch.

Akos had come to his feet, his hands squeezed into fists so tight I could see tendons standing out from knuckle bone.

"Are you still in there?" Akos asked Eijeh, quiet.

Eijeh sighed, and dragged one fingernail under another. I watched him carefully. Ryzek was obsessed with clean fingernails, and would sooner have broken one off than allow dirt beneath it. Was this gesture, Eijeh scraping fingernails clean, something that belonged to him, too, or was it Ryzek's, a sign of Eijeh's transformation? How much of my brother now pulsed inside of Eijeh Kereseth?

He answered, "I don't know what you mean."

"Yes, you do." Akos pressed a hand to his brother's chest and pushed him back against the metal wall of the vessel—not violently, but urgently, leaning in close. "Do you remember me? Cisi? Dad?"

"I remember . . ." Eijeh blinked slowly, like he was just waking. "I remember your secrets." He scowled at Akos. "The time you stole with our mother after the rest of us went to sleep. How you followed me around all the time because you couldn't manage on your own. Is that what you mean?"

Tears shone in Akos's eyes.

"That isn't all of it," Akos said. "That isn't all I am to you. You have to know that. You—"

"Enough." Vas walked to the back of the ship. "Your brother is coming with me, Kereseth."

Akos's hands twitched at his sides, itching to strangle. He was Vas's height now, so their eyes met on the same plane, but he had half the other man's bulk. Vas was a war machine, a man of muscle. I couldn't even imagine the two fighting; all I could see was Akos on the ground, limp.

Akos lunged, and so did I. His hand was just reaching for Vas's throat when I got to them, one hand on each chest, pressing them apart. It was surprise, not strength, that made this effective; they both moved backward, and I wedged myself between them.

"Come with me," I said to Akos. "Now."

Vas laughed. "Better listen to her, Kereseth. Those aren't little heart tattoos she hides under that arm guard."

Then he took Eijeh's arm, and together they left the ship. I waited until I could no longer hear their footsteps before backing off.

"He's one of the best soldiers in Shotet," I said to Akos. "Don't be an idiot."

"You have no idea," Akos snapped. "Have you ever even cared about someone enough to hate the person who took them from you, Cyra?"

An image of my mother came to mind, a vein in her forehead bulging, like it always did when she was angry. She was scolding Otega for taking me to dangerous parts of the city during our lessons, or for cutting my hair to my chin, I couldn't remember which. I had loved her even in those moments, because I knew she was paying attention, unlike my father, who didn't even look me in the eye.

I said, "Lashing out at Vas because of what happened to Eijeh will only get you injured and me aggravated. So take some hushflower and get ahold of yourself before I shove you out the loading bay doors."

For a moment it looked like he might refuse, but then, shaking, he slid a hand into his pocket and took out one of the raw hushflower petals he kept there. He pressed it into his cheek.

"Good," I said. "Time to go."

I stuck out my elbow, and he put his hand around it. Together we walked through the empty hallways of the sojourn ship, which were polished metal, loud with echoes of distant feet and voices.

My quarters on the warship looked nothing like my wing of Noavek manor—the latter had dark, polished floors and clean white walls, impersonal, but the former was packed with objects from other worlds. Exotic plants suspended in resin and hanging from the ceiling like a chandelier. Mechanical, glowing insects buzzing in circles around them. Lengths of fabric that changed color depending on the time of day. A stain-spattered stove and a metal coldbox, so I didn't have to go to the cafeteria.

Along the far wall, past the little table where I ate my meals, were hundreds of old discs that held holograms of dancing, fighting, sports in other places. I loved to mimic the staggering, collapsing techniques of Ogra dancers or the stiff, structured ritual dances of Tepes. It helped me focus through the pain. There were history lessons among the discs, too, and films from other planets: old news broadcasts; long, dry documentaries about science and language; recordings of concerts. I had watched them all.

My bed was in the corner, under a porthole and a net of tiny burnstone lanterns, the blankets still rumpled from the last time I had slept in it. I didn't allow anyone into my quarters on the sojourn ship, not even to clean.

Dangling from a hole in the ceiling, between the preserved plants, was a length of rope; it led to the room above, which I used for training, among other things.

I cleared my throat. "You'll be staying through here," I said, crossing the crowded space. I waved my hand over the sensor next to a closed door; it slid open to reveal another room, also with a single porthole to the outside. "It used to be an obscenely large closet. These were my mother's private quarters, before she died." I was babbling. I didn't know how to talk to him anymore, now that he had drugged me and taken advantage of my kindness, now that he had lost the thing he had been fighting for and I hadn't done anything to stop it. Which was my pattern: stand by while Ryzek wreaks havoc.

Akos had paused next to the door to look at the armor that decorated the wall. It was nothing like Shotet armor, bulky or unnecessarily decorated, but some of it was beautiful, made of gleaming orange metal or draped with durable black fabric. He made his way into the next room slowly.

It looked a lot like the one he had left behind in Noavek manor: all the supplies and equipment necessary to brew poisons and potions were along one wall, arranged the way he liked it. In the week before his betrayal, I had sent a picture of his setup ahead of us to be copied exactly. There was a bed with dark gray sheets—most Shotet fabric was blue, so the sheets had been hard to find. The burnstones in the lanterns above the bed had been dusted with jealousy powder, so they burned yellow. There were books on elmetahak and Shotet culture on the low bookcase next to the bed. I pressed a button next to the door, and a huge, holographic map of our location sprawled over the ceiling—right now it displayed Voa, since we were still hovering above it, but it would show our path through the galaxy as we traveled.

"I know quarters are close here," I said. "But space on the ship is limited. I tried to make it livable for us both."

"*You* made this place?" he said, turning toward me. I couldn't read his expression. I nodded.

"Unfortunately, we'll have to share a bathroom." Still babbling. "But it's not for long."

"Cyra," he interrupted. "Nothing is blue. Not even the clothes. And the iceflowers are labeled in Thuvhesit."

"Your people think blue is cursed. And you can't read Shotet," I said quietly. My currentshadows started to move faster, sprawling under my skin and pooling beneath my cheeks. My head pounded so hard I had to blink away tears. "The books on elmetahak are in Shotet, unfortunately, but there's a translation device next to them. Just place it over the page, and—"

"But after what I did to you . . ." he began.

"I sent the instructions before that," I replied.

Akos sat down on the edge of the bed.

"Thank you," he said. "I'm sorry, about . . . everything. I just wanted to get him out. It was all I could think about."

His brow was a straight, low line above his eyes that made it too easy to see his sadness as anger. He had cut his chin shaving.

There was a rumble in his whisper: "He was the last thing I had left."

"I know," I replied, but I didn't know, not really. I had watched Ryzek do things that made my stomach turn. But it was different for me than it was for Akos. I at least knew that I was capable of similar horrors. He had no way of understanding what Eijeh had become.

"How do you keep doing this?" he said. "Keep going, when everything is so horrible?"

Horrible. Was that what life was? I had never put a word to it. Pain had a way of breaking time down. I thought about the next minute, the next hour. There wasn't enough space in my mind to put all those pieces together, to find words to summarize the whole of it. But the "keep going" part, I knew the words for.

"Find another reason to go on," I said. "It doesn't have to be a good one, or a noble one. It just has to be a reason."

I knew mine: There was a hunger inside me, and there always had been. That hunger was stronger than pain, stronger than horror. It gnawed even after everything else inside me had given up. It was not hope; it did not soar; it slithered, clawed, and dragged, and it would not let me stop.

And when I finally named it, I found it was something very simple: the desire to live.

§

That night was the last night of the Sojourn Festival, when the last few transport vessels landed in the loading bay and we all feasted on the sojourn ship together. The people we brought with us were supposed to be energetic by now, their confidence and determination bolstered by the celebratory events of the past week, and it seemed to me that they were. The crowd that carried Akos and me on their tide toward the loading bay was buoyant and loud. I was careful to keep my bare skin away from them; I didn't want to draw attention to myself by causing people pain.

I walked to the platform where Ryzek stood braced against the railing, Eijeh at his right. Where was Vas?

I wore my Shotet armor, polished to perfection, over a long, sleeveless black dress. The fabric brushed the toes of my boots as I moved.

Ryzek's kill marks were on full display; he kept his arm flexed to show them at their best. Someday he would begin a second row, like my father. When I arrived, he flashed a smile at me, which made me shudder.

I took my place on his left at the railing. I was supposed to display my currentgift at times like these, to remind all the people around us that despite Ryzek's charm, we were not to be trifled with. I tried to accept the pain, absorb it like I did the cold wind when I had forgotten to wear the right coat, but I found it difficult to focus. In front of me, the waiting crowd wavered and swam. I wasn't supposed to wince; I wouldn't, I wouldn't. . . .

I let out a relieved exhale when the last two transport vessels drifted through the open loading bay hatch. Everyone applauded when the ships' doors opened, and the last group of Shotet spilled in. Ryzek held up both of his hands to quiet the crowd. It was time for his welcoming speech.

But just as Ryzek opened his mouth, a young woman stepped forward from the group that had just left the transport vessel. She had a long blond braid and wore, not the bright colors of the more common Shotet in the crowd below, but subtle blue-gray finery to match her eyes. It was a popular color among Shotet's wealthy.

She was Lety Zetsyvis, Uzul's daughter. She held a current-blade high in the air, and the dark tendrils wrapped around her hand like strings, binding the blade to her body.

"The first child of the family Noavek," she shouted, "will fall to the family Benesit!"

It was my brother's fate, spoken plainly.

"That is your fate, Ryzek Noavek!" Lety shouted. "To fail us, and to fall!"

Vas, who had pushed through the crowd, now seized her wrist with the certainty of a well-trained warrior. He bent over her, pressing her hand back so she was forced to her knees. Her cur-rentblade clattered to the floor.

"Lety Zetsyvis," Ryzek said, lilting. It was so quiet in the room that he didn't even need to raise his voice. He was smiling as she struggled against Vas's grip, her fingers turning white under the pressure.

"That fate . . . is a lie told by the people who want to destroy us," he began. Beside him, Eijeh bobbed his head a little, like Ryzek's voice was a song he knew by heart. Maybe that was why Ryzek didn't look surprised to see Lety on her knees below us—because Eijeh had seen it coming. Thanks to his oracle, Ryzek already knew what to say, what to do.

"They are people who fear us for our strength and seek to

undermine us: the Assembly. Thuvhe," Ryzek continued. "Who taught you to believe such lies, Lety? I wonder why it is that you espouse the same views as the people who came to your house to murder your father?"

So that was how Ryzek was twisting things. Now, instead of Lety declaring my brother's fate, a crusader for the truth, she was spouting the same lies that our Thuvhesit enemies supposedly told. She was a traitor, possibly even one who had allowed assassins to penetrate her family's home so they could kill her father. Ridiculous, really, but sometimes people just believed what they were told. It was easier to survive that way.

"My father was not murdered," Lety said in a low voice. "He took his own life, because you tortured him, you tortured him with that *thing* you call a sister, and the pain was driving him mad."

Ryzek smiled at her as if she was the mad one, spewing nonsense. He cast his gaze all around him at the people who waited with bated breath to hear his response.

"This," he said, gesturing to Lety. "*This* is the poison our enemies wish to use to destroy us—from within, not without. They tell lies to turn us against each other, to turn us against our own families and friends. That is why we must protect ourselves against not only their potential threats to our lives, but also their words. We are a people who has been weak before. We must not become so again."

I felt it, the shiver that went through the crowd at his words. We had just spent a week remembering how far our ancestors had come, battered across the galaxy, our children taken from us, our beliefs about scavenging and renewal universally derided. We had learned to fight back, season by season. Even though I knew that Ryzek's true intentions were not to protect Shotet, but rather *himself* and the Noavek dynasty, I was still almost taken in by the emotion in his voice, and the power he offered us like an out-stretched hand.

"And there is no more effective blow than to strike against me, the leader of our great people." He shook his head. "This poison cannot be allowed to spread through our society. It must be drained, drop by drop, until it poses no more harm."

Lety's eyes were full of hate.

"Because you are the daughter of one of our most beloved families, and because you are clearly in pain after the loss of your father, I will give you a chance to fight for your life in the arena instead of simply losing it. And since you assign some of this supposed blame to my sister, it is she who will face you there," Ryzek said. "I hope you see this as the mercy it is."

I was too stunned to protest—and too aware of what the consequences would be: Ryzek's wrath. Looking like a coward in front of all these people. Losing my reputation as someone to fear, which was my only leverage. And then, of course, the truth about my mother, which always loomed over Ryzek and me.

I remembered the way people chanted my mother's name as we walked the streets of Voa during my first Procession. Her people had loved her, the way she held strength and mercy in tension. If they knew that I was responsible for her passing, they would destroy me.

Veins of dark stained my skin as I stared down at Lety. She gritted her teeth, and stared back. I could tell she would take my life with pleasure.

As Vas jerked Lety to her feet, people in the crowd shouted at her: "Traitor!" "Liar!" I felt nothing, not even fear. Not even Akos's hand, catching my arm to soothe me.

"You okay?" Akos asked me.

I shook my head.

We stood in the anteroom just outside the arena. It was dim but for the glow of our city through the porthole, reflecting sunlight for a few hours yet. The room was adorned with portraits of the Noavek family over the door: my grandmother, Lasma Noavek, who had murdered all her brothers and sisters to ensure that her own bloodline was fate-favored; my father, Lazmet Noavek, who had tormented the goodness from my brother because of his weak fate; and Ryzek Noavek, pale and young, the product of two vicious generations. My darker skin and sturdier build meant I took after my mother's family, a branch of the Radix line, distant relation to the first man Akos had killed. All the portraits wore the same mild smiles, bound by their dark wooden frames and fine clothing.

Ryzek and every Shotet soldier who could fit in the hall waited outside. I could hear their chatter through the walls. Challenges weren't permitted during the sojourn, but there was an arena in the ship anyway, for practice matches and the occasional performance. My brother had declared that the challenge would take place just after his welcome speech, but before the feast. Nothing like a good fight to the death to make Shotet soldiers hungry, after all.

"Was it true, what that woman said?" Akos said. "Did you do that to her father?"

"Yes," I said, because I thought it was better not to lie. But it wasn't better; it didn't feel better that way.

"What is Ryzek holding over you?" Akos said. "To make you do things you can barely stand to admit to?"

The door opened, and I shuddered, thinking the time had come. But Ryzek closed the door behind him, standing beneath his own portrait. It didn't look quite like him anymore, the face in it too round and spotted.

"What do you want?" I said to him. "Aside from the execution you commanded without even consulting me, that is."

"What would I have gained by consulting you?" Ryzek said. "I would have had to hear your irritating protestations first, and then, when I reminded you of how foolish you were to trust this one"— here he nodded toward Akos—"how that foolishness nearly lost me my *oracle*, when I offered this arena challenge to you as a way to make it up to me, you would agree to do it."

I closed my eyes, briefly.

"I came to tell you that you are to leave your knife behind," Ryzek said.

"No *knife?*" Akos demanded. "She could get stabbed before she ever has a chance to lay a hand on that woman! Do you want her to die?"

No, I answered in my own head. He wanted me to kill. Just not with a knife.

"She knows what I want," Ryzek said. "And she knows what will happen if I don't get it. Best of luck, little sister."

He swept out of the room. He was right: I knew, I always knew. He wanted everyone to see that the shadows that traveled under my skin were good for more than just pain, they also made me lethal. Not just Ryzek's Scourge. Time for my promotion to Ryzek's Executioner.

"Help me take my armor off," I mumbled.

"What? What are you talking about?"

"Don't question me," I snapped. "Help me take my armor off."

"You don't want your armor?" Akos said. "Are you just going to let her kill you?"

I started on the first strap. My fingers were callused, but the straps were pulled so tight they still stung my fingertips. I forced them back and forth in small increments, my movements jerky and frantic. Akos covered my hand with his own.

"No," I said. "I don't need armor. I don't need a knife."

Twisting around my knuckles were the shadows, dense and dark as paint.

I had taken great pains to ensure that no one else discovered what had happened to my mother—what I had done to her. But it was better that Akos knew, before he suffered for knowing me, more than he already had. Better that he never look at me with sympathy again than that he believe a lie.

"How do you think my mother died?" I laughed. "I touched her, and I pushed all the light and all the pain into her, all because I was angry about having to go to some other doctor for some other ineffective treatment for my currentgift. All she wanted to do was help me, but I threw a tantrum, and it killed her." I tugged my forearm guard down just enough to reveal a crooked scar carved just below my elbow, on the outside of my arm. My first kill mark. "My father carved the mark. He hated me for it, but he was also . . . *proud*."

I choked on the word.

"You want to know what Ryzek is holding over me?" I laughed again, this time through tears. I tugged the last strap of my chest armor loose, yanked it over my head, and hurled it at the wall with both hands. When it collided with the metal, the sound was deafening in the small anteroom.

The armor dropped to the floor, unharmed. It hadn't even lost its shape.

"My mother. My beloved, revered mother was taken from him, from Shotet," I spat at him. Loud, my voice was loud. "I took her. I took her from myself."

It would have been easier if he had looked at me with loathing or disgust. He didn't. He reached for me, his hands carrying relief, and I walked out of the anteroom and into the arena. I didn't want relief. I had earned this pain.

The crowd roared when I walked out. The black floor of the arena shone like glass; it had likely just been polished for the occasion. I saw my boots reflected in it, the buckles undone. Rising up all around me were rows of metal benches, packed with observers, their faces too dark to see clearly. Lety was already there, dressed in her Shotet armor, wearing heavy shoes with metal toes, shaking out her hands.

I assessed her right away, according to the teachings of elmetahak: she was a head shorter than I was, but muscular. Her blond hair was tied in a tight knot at the back of her head to keep it out of the way. She was a student of zivatahak, so she would be fast, nimble, in the seconds before she lost.

"Didn't even bother to put on your armor?" Lety sneered at me. "This will be easy."

Yes, it would.

She drew her currentblade, her hand wrapped in dark current—like my currentshadows in color, but not in form. For her, though they wrapped around her wrist, they never touched her skin. But my current was buried inside me. She paused, waiting for me to draw.

"Go on," I said, and I beckoned to her.

The crowd roared again, and then I couldn't hear them anymore. I was focused on Lety, the way she was inching toward me, trying to read strategy into my actions. But I was just standing there, my arms limp at my sides, letting my currentgift's strength build along with my fear.

Finally she decided to make her first move. I saw it in her arms and legs before she budged, and stepped aside when she lunged, arching away from her like an Ogra dancer. The move startled her; she stumbled forward, catching herself on the arena wall.

My currentshadows were so dense now, so painful, that I could hardly see straight. Pain roared through me, and I welcomed it. I remembered Uzul Zetsyvis's contorted face between my stained hands, and I saw him in his daughter, her brow furrowed with concentration.

She lunged again, this time driving her blade toward my ribs, and I batted her aside with my forearm, then reached over her to grab her wrist. I twisted, hard, and forced her head down. I kneed her in the face. Blood spilled over her lips, and she screamed. But not from the wound. From my touch.

The currentblade fell between us. Keeping my hand on one of her arms, I pushed her to her knees with the other, and moved to stand behind her. I found Ryzek in the crowd, sitting on the raised platform with his legs crossed, like he was watching a lecture or a speech instead of a murder.

I waited until his eyes found mine, and then I pushed. I pushed all the shadow, all the pain, into Lety Zetsyvis's body, keeping none of it for myself. It was easy, so easy, and quick. I closed my eyes as she screamed and shuddered, and then she was gone.

For a moment, everything was dim. I released her limp body, then turned to walk into the anteroom again. The entire crowd was silent. As I passed through the doorway to the anteroom, I was, for once, clear of shadows. It was only temporary. They would return soon.

Just out of sight, Akos reached for me, pulling me against him. He pressed me to his chest in something like an embrace, and said something to me in the language of my enemies.

"It's over," he said, in whispered Thuvhesit. "It's over now."

Later that night, I barred the door to my quarters so no one could come in. Akos sterilized a knife over the burners in his room, and cooled it with water from the faucet. I rested my arm on the table, then undid the fasteners on my forearm guard, one by one, beginning at the wrist and ending at the elbow. The guard was stiff and hard, and despite its lining, made my skin moist with sweat by the end of the day.

Akos sat across from me, sterilized knife in hand, and watched me peel the edges of the wrist guard back to reveal the bare skin beneath. I didn't ask him what he imagined. He had probably assumed, like most people, that the guard covered row after row of kill marks. That I had chosen to cover them because, somehow, fostering the mystery around them made me more menacing. I had never discouraged that rumor. The truth was so much worse.

There *were* marks up and down my arm, from elbow to wrist, row after row. Little dark lines, perfectly spaced, each one the same length. And through each one, a small diagonal hash mark, negating it under Shotet law.

Akos's brow furrowed, and he took my arm in both hands, holding me with just his fingertips. He turned my arm over, running his fingers down one of the rows. When he reached the end, he touched his index finger to one of the hashes, turning his arm to compare it to his own. I shivered to see our skin side by side, mine tawny and his pale.

"These aren't kills," he said quietly.

"I only marked my mother's passing," I said, just as quietly. "Make no mistake, I am responsible for more deaths, but I stopped recording them after her. Until Zetsyvis, anyway."

"And instead, you record . . . what?" He squeezed my arm. "What are all these marks for?"

"Death is a mercy compared to the agony I have caused. So I keep a record of pain, not kills. Each mark is someone I have hurt because Ryzek told me to." I had counted the marks, at first, always sure of their number. I had not known, then, exactly how long Ryzek would put me to use as his interrogator. Over time, though, I had just stopped keeping track. Knowing the number only made it worse.

"How old were you, when he first asked you to do this?"

I didn't understand the tone of his voice, with all its softness. I had just shown him proof of my own monstrousness, and still his eyes fixed on mine with sympathy instead of judgment. He couldn't possibly understand what I was telling him, to look at me like that. Or he thought I was lying, or exaggerating.

"Old enough to know it was wrong," I snapped.

"Cyra." Soft again. "How old?"

I sat back in my chair. "Ten," I admitted. "And it was my father, not Ryzek, who first asked."

His head bobbed. He touched the point of the knife to the table and spun the handle in quick circles, marking the wood.

Finally, he said, "When I was ten, I didn't know my fate yet. So I wanted to be a Hessa soldier, like the ones that patrolled my father's iceflower fields. He was a farmer." Akos balanced his chin on a hand as he looked me over. "But one day criminals went into the fields while he was working, to steal some of the harvest, and Dad tried to stop them before the soldiers got there. He came home with this huge gash across his cheek. Mom just started screaming at him." He laughed a little. "Doesn't make much sense, does it, yelling at someone for getting hurt?"

"Well, she was afraid for him," I said.

"Yeah. I was scared, too, I guess, because that night I decided I never wanted to be a soldier, if my job would be to get cut up like that."

I couldn't help but laugh a little.

"I know," he said, his lip curling at the corner. "Little did I know how I would be spending my days now."

He tapped the table, and I noticed, for the first time, how jagged his nails were, and all the cuts along his cuticles. I would have to break him of the habit of chewing on his own hands.

"My point is," he continued, "that when I was ten I was so scared of even *seeing* pain that I could hardly stand it. Meanwhile, when you were ten, you were being told to cause it, over and over again, by someone much more powerful than you were. Someone who was supposed to be taking care of you."

For a moment I ached at the thought. But only for a moment.

"Don't try to absolve me of guilt." I meant to sound sharp, like

I was scolding him, but instead I sounded like I was pleading with him. I cleared my throat. "Okay? It doesn't make it better."

"Okay," he said.

"You were taught this ritual?" I asked him.

He nodded.

"Carve the mark," I said, my throat tight.

I extended my arm, pointing to a square of bare skin on the back of my wrist, beneath the knobby bone. He touched the knifepoint there, adjusted it so it was at the same interval as the other marks, then dug in. Not too deep, but enough that the feathergrass extract could settle.

Tears came to my eyes, unwelcome, and blood bubbled up from the wound. It dripped down the side of my arm as I fumbled in one of the kitchen drawers for the right bottle. He took out the cork, and I dipped the little brush I kept with it. I spoke Lety Zetsyvis's name as I painted the line he had carved with dark fluid.

It burned. Every time, I thought I would be used to how much it burned, and every time, I was wrong. It was supposed to burn, supposed to remind you that it was no trifling thing, to take a life, to carve a loss.

"You don't say the other words?" Akos said. He was referring to the prayer, the end of the ritual. I shook my head.

"I don't either," he said.

As the burning subsided, Akos wrapped the bandage around my arm, once, twice, three times, and secured it with a piece of tape. Neither of us bothered to clean up the blood on the table. It would probably dry there, and I would have to scrape it off with a knife later, but I didn't care.

I climbed the rope to the room above us, past the plants

preserved in resin and the mechanical beetles perched among them, recharging for the moment. Akos followed me.

The sojourn ship was shuddering, its engines preparing to launch into the atmosphere. The ceiling of the room above us was covered with screens that showed whatever was above us—in this case, the Shotet sky. Pipes and vents crowded the space from all sides—it was only big enough for one person to move around in, really, but along the back wall were emergency jump seats, folded into the wall. I pulled them out, and Akos and I sat.

I helped him fasten the straps across his chest and legs that would keep him steady during launch, and handed him a paper bag in case the ship's movement made him sick. Then I strapped myself in. All through the ship, the rest of the Shotet would be doing the same thing, gathering in the hallways to pull jump seats from the walls and buckling each other in.

Together we waited for the ship to launch, listening to the countdown on the intercom. When the voice reached "ten," Akos reached for my hand, and I squeezed, hard, until the voice said "one."

The Shotet clouds rushed past us, and the force bore down on us, crushing us into our seats. Akos groaned, but I just watched as the clouds moved away and the blue atmosphere faded into the blackness of space. All around us was the starry sky.

"See?" I said, lacing my fingers with his. "It's beautiful."

CHAPTER 14 | CYRA

A KNOCK CAME AT my door that night as I was lying in bed in my sojourn ship quarters, face buried in a pillow. I dragged myself up one limb at a time to answer it. There were two soldiers waiting in the hallway, one male and one female, both slim. Sometimes a person's school of combat was obvious just from a glance—these were students of zivatahak, fast and deadly. And they were afraid of me. No wonder.

Akos stumbled into the kitchen to stand beside me. The two soldiers exchanged a knowing look, and I remembered what Otega had said about Shotet mouths loving to chatter. There was no avoiding it: Akos and I lived in close proximity, so there was bound to be talk about what we were, and what we did behind closed doors. I didn't care enough to discourage it. Better to be talked about for that than for murdering and torturing, anyway.

"We are sorry to disturb you, Miss Noavek. The sovereign needs to speak to you right away," the woman said. "Alone."

Ryzek's office on the sojourn ship was like his office in Voa, in miniature. The dark wood that comprised the floor and wall panels, polished to perfection, was native to Shotet—it grew in dense forests across our planet's equator, dividing us from the Thuvhesits who had invaded the north centuries ago. In the wild, the fenzu we now kept trapped in the orb chandelier hummed in the treetops, but because most older Shotet houses used them for light, the Zetsyvis family—now helmed by Yma alone—ensured that farmed fenzu were available in large numbers for those willing to pay the high price for them. And Ryzek was—he insisted their glow was more pleasant than burnstones, though I didn't see much of a difference.

When I walked in, Ryzek was standing in front of a large screen he usually kept hidden behind a sliding panel. It displayed a dense paragraph of text; it took me a few beats to realize that he was reading a transcript of the Assembly Leader's announcement of the fates. Nine lines of nine families, spread across the galaxy, their members' paths predetermined and unalterable. Ryzek usually avoided all references to his "weakness," as my father had called it, the fate that had haunted him since his birth: that he would fall to the family Benesit. It was illegal in Shotet to speak of it or to read it, punishable by imprisonment or even execution.

If he was reading the fates, he was not in a good mood, and most of the time, that meant I should tread lightly. But tonight, I wondered why I should bother.

Ryzek folded his arms, and tilted his head, and spoke.

"You don't know how lucky you are, that your fate is so ambiguous," he said. "'The second child of the family Noavek will cross the Divide.' For what purpose will you cross the Divide to Thuvhe?" He lifted a shoulder. "No one knows or cares. Lucky, lucky."

I laughed. "Am I?"

"That is why it's so important that you help me," Ryzek went on, like he hadn't heard me. "You can afford to. You don't need to fight so hard against what the world expects from you."

Ryzek had been weighing his life against mine since I was a child. That I was in constant pain, that I could not get close to anyone, that I had experienced deep loss just as he had, didn't seem to register in his mind. All he saw was that our father had ignored me rather than subjecting me to horrors, and that my fate didn't make the Shotet doubt my strength. To him, I was the lucky child, and there was no point in arguing about it.

"What happened, Ryzek?"

"You mean aside from all of Shotet being reminded of my ridiculous fate by Lety Zetsyvis?"

At the mention of her, I shuddered involuntarily, remembering how warm her skin had been as she died. I clasped my hands in front of me to keep them from trembling. Akos's painkiller didn't suppress the shadows completely; they moved, sluggish now, beneath my skin, bringing with them a sharp ache.

"But you were ready for that," I said, fixing my eyes on his chin. "No one would dare repeat what she said now."

"It's not just that," Ryzek said, and I heard in his voice a reminder of what he had sounded like when he was younger, before my father sank in his teeth. "I followed the trail from Uzul Zetsyvis's confession to an actual source. There is a colony of exiles somewhere out there. Maybe more than one. And they have contacts among us."

I felt a thrill in my chest. So the rumor of the exile colony had been confirmed. For the first time, the colony represented to me not a threat, but something like . . . hope.

"One display of strength is good, but we need more. We need there to be no doubt that I am in command, and that we will return from this sojourn even more powerful than before." He let his hand hover over my shoulder. "I will need your help now more than ever, Cyra."

I know what you want, I thought. He wanted to root out every doubt and every whisper against him and crush them. And I was supposed to be the tool he used to do that. Ryzek's Scourge.

I closed my eyes briefly as memories of Lety came to me. I stifled them.

"Please, sit." He gestured to one of the chairs set up near the screen. They were old, with stitched upholstery. I recognized them from my father's old office. The rug beneath them was Shotet-made, of rough woven grasses. In fact, nothing in the room was scavenged——my father had hated the practice, said it made us weak and needed to be gradually abandoned, and Ryzek seemed to agree. I was the only one left with an affinity for other people's garbage.

I sat on the edge of the chair, the fates of the favored lines glowing next to my head. Ryzek didn't sit across from me. Instead, he stood behind the other chair, braced against its high back. He had rolled up the sleeve on his left arm, displaying the marks.

He tapped his crooked index finger against one of the fates on the screen, so the words grew larger.

The fates of the family Benesit are as follows:

The first child of the family Benesit will raise her double to power.

The second child of the family Benesit will reign over Thuvhe.

"I have heard mutterings that this second child"—he tapped the second fate, his knuckle brushing the word *reign*—"will soon declare herself, and that she is Thuvhesit-born," Ryzek said. "I can't ignore the fates any longer—whoever this Benesit child is, the fates say she will be the ruler of Thuvhe, and responsible for my undoing." I hadn't quite put the pieces together before. Ryzek's fate was to fall to the family Benesit, and the family Benesit was fated to rule Thuvhe. Of course he was fixating on them, now that he had his oracle.

"My intention," he added, "is to kill her before that happens, with the help of our new oracle."

I stared at the fate written on the screen. All my life I had been taught that every fate would be fulfilled, no matter what anyone tried to do to stop it. But that was exactly what he was proposing: he wanted to thwart his own fate by killing the one who was supposed to bring it about. And he had Eijeh to tell him how.

"That's . . . that's impossible," I said, before I could stop myself.

"Impossible?" He raised his eyebrows. "Why? Because no one has managed to do it?" His hands clenched around the chair back. "You think that I, of all the people in the galaxy, can't be the first to defy his fate?"

"That's not what I meant," I said, trying to stay controlled in the face of his anger. "All I meant was that I've never heard of it happening, that's all."

"You soon will," he snapped, his face twisting into a scowl. "And you're going to help me."

I thought, suddenly, of Akos thanking me for the way I arranged his room, when we got to the sojourn ship. His calm expression as he took in my marked arm. The way he laughed when we chased each other through the blue sojourn rain. Those were the first moments of relief I had experienced since my mother died. And I wanted more of them. And less of . . . this.

"No," I said. "I won't."

His old threat—that if I didn't do as he said, he would tell the Shotet what I had done to my beloved mother—no longer frightened me. This time, he had made a mistake: he had confessed to needing my help.

I crossed one leg over another, and folded my hands over my knee.

"Before you threaten me, let me say this: I don't think that you would risk losing me right now," I said. "Not after trying so hard to make sure that they are terrified of me."

That was what the challenge with Lety had been, after all: a demonstration of power. *His* power.

But that power actually belonged to me.

Ryzek had been learning to imitate our father ever since he was a child, and my father had been excellent at hiding his reactions. He had believed that any uncontrolled expression made him vulnerable; he had been aware that he was always being watched, no matter where he was. Ryzek had gotten better at this skill since his youth, but he was still not a master of it. As I stared at him, unblinking, his face contorted. Angry. And afraid.

"I don't need you, Cyra," he said, quiet.

"That isn't true," I said, coming to my feet. "But even if it was true . . . you should remember what would happen if I decided to lay a hand on you."

I showed him my palm, willing my currentgift to surface. For once, it came at my call, rippling across my body and—for a moment—wrapping around each of my fingers like black threads. Ryzek's eyes were drawn to it, seemingly without permission.

"I will continue to play the part of your loyal sister, of this fearsome thing," I said. "But I will not cause pain for you anymore."

With that, I turned. I moved toward the door, my heart pounding, hard.

"Careful," Ryzek said as I walked away. "You may regret this moment."

"I doubt it," I said, without turning around. "After all, I'm not the one who's afraid of pain."

"I am not," he said tersely, "afraid of pain."

"Oh?" I turned back. "Come over here and take my hand, then."

I offered it to him, palm up and shadow-stained, my face twitching from the pain that still lingered. Ryzek didn't budge.

"Thought so," I said, and I left.

When I returned to my room, Akos sat on the bed with the book on elmetahak on his lap, the translator glowing over one of the pages. He looked up at me with furrowed eyebrows. The scar along his jaw was still dark in color, its line perfectly straight as it followed his jaw. It would pale, in time, fading into his skin.

I walked into the bathroom to splash water on my face.

"What did he do to you?" Akos said as he slumped against the bathroom wall, next to the sink.

I splashed my face again, then leaned over the sink. Water rolled down my cheeks and over my eyelids and dripped into the basin beneath me. I stared at my reflection, eyes wild, jaw tensed.

"He didn't do anything," I said, grabbing a cloth from the rack next to the sink and dragging it over my face. My smile was almost a grimace of fear. "He didn't do anything, because I didn't let him. He threatened me, and I . . . I threatened him back."

The webs of dark color were dense on my hands and arms, like splatters of black paint. I sat in one of the kitchen chairs and laughed. I laughed from my belly, laughed until I felt warm all over. I had never stood up to Ryzek before. The cord of shame curled up in my belly unspooled a little. I was not quite as complicit anymore.

Akos sat across from me.

"What . . . what does this mean?" he said.

"It means he leaves us alone," I said. "I . . ." My hands trembled. "I don't know why I'm so . . ."

Akos covered my hands with his own. "You just threatened the most powerful person in the country. I think it's okay to be a little shaken."

His hands weren't much larger than mine, though thicker through the knuckles, with tendons that stood out all the way to his wrists. I could see blue-green veins through his skin, which was much paler than my own. Almost like those rumors about Thuvhesits having thin skin were true, except that whatever Akos was, it wasn't weak.

I slipped my hands out of his.

Now, with Ryzek out of the way, and Akos here, I wondered how we would both fill our days. I was used to spending sojourns alone. There was still something splattered on the side of the stove from the last sojourn, when I had cooked for myself every night, experimenting with ingredients from different planets—unsuccessfully, most of the time, since I had no talent for cooking. I had spent my nights watching footage from other places, imagining lives other than my own.

He crossed the room to get a glass from the cupboard and fill it with water from the faucet. I tilted my head back to look at the plants that hung above our heads, shining in their resin cages. Some of them glowed when the lights were out; others would decay, even in resin, withering into bright colors. I had been watching them for three sojourns already.

Akos wiped his mouth and set the glass down.

"I figured it out," he said. "A reason to keep going, I mean."

He flexed his left arm, where his first kill mark was etched.

"Oh?"

"Yeah." His head bobbed. "Something Ryzek said kept bothering me . . . that he would make Eijeh into someone I didn't want to rescue. Well, I decided that's impossible." Days ago he had looked empty to me, and now full, an overflowing cup. "There's no version of Eijeh that I don't want to rescue from him."

This was the cost of the same softness that had made him look at me with sympathy earlier that day instead of disgust: madness. To continue to love someone so far beyond help, beyond redemption, was madness.

"You don't make any sense to me," I said to him. "It's like the more terrible things you find out about a person, or the more terrible a person is to you, the kinder you are to them. It's masochism."

"Says the person who's been scarring herself for things she was coerced into doing," he said wryly.

It wasn't funny, what either of us was saying. And then it was. I grinned, and after a moment, so did he. A new grin—not the one that told me he was proud of himself, or the one that he forced when he felt like he needed to be polite, but a thirsty, crazed kind of smile.

"You really don't hate me for this," I said, lifting up my left arm.

"No, I don't."

I had experienced only a few different reactions to what I was, what I could do. Hatred, from those who had suffered at my hand; fear, from those who hadn't but might; and glee, from those capable of using me for it. I had never seen this before. It was almost like he understood.

"You don't hate me at all," I said in almost a whisper, afraid to hear the answer.

But his answer came steadily, like it was obvious to him: "No."

I found, then, that I wasn't angry anymore about what he had done to me, to get Eijeh out. He had done it because of the same quality, in him, that made him so accepting of me now. How could I fault him for it?

"All right." I sighed. "Be up early tomorrow, because we'll need to train harder if you expect to get your brother out of here."

His water glass was marked with fingerprints around the base. I took it from him.

He frowned at me. "You'll help me? Even after what I did to you?"

"Yeah." I drained the water glass, and set it back down. "I guess I will."

3

CHAPTER 15 | AKOS

AKOS RAN THROUGH THE memory of his almost-escape with Eijeh over and over again:

He'd run through the corridors in the walls of the Noavek house, stopping where the walls joined to peek through cracks and figure out where he was. He had spent a long time in the dark, gulping dust and catching splinters in his fingers.

Finally he got to the room where Eijeh was kept—triggering some sensor without meaning to, as Ryzek told him later. But at the time he hadn't known. He had just stuck his fingers in the lock that held Eijeh's door shut. Most doors these days were locked by the current, and his touch could unlock them. Wrist cuffs, too. That was how he had gotten free to kill Kalmev Radix in the feathergrass.

Eijeh had stood by a barred window, high over the manor's back gate. There was feathergrass there, too, tufts swaying in the wind. Akos wondered what Eijeh saw there—their dad? He didn't know how feathergrass worked for other people, since it didn't do anything to him anymore.

Eijeh had turned to him, taking him in bit by bit. It had only been two seasons since they had seen each other, but they had both changed—Akos was taller, thicker, and Eijeh had gone ashen and thin, curly hair matted in places. He wobbled a little, and Akos caught him by the elbows.

"Akos," Eijeh had whispered. "I don't know what to do, I don't—"

"It's okay," Akos said. "It's okay, I'll get us out of here, you don't need to do anything."

"You . . . you killed that man, that man who was in our house—"

"Yeah." Akos knew the man's name: Kalmev Radix, now just a scar on his arm.

"Why did this happen?" Eijeh's voice broke. Akos's heart broke. "Why didn't Mom see it coming?"

Akos didn't remind him that she probably had. No point to it, really.

"Don't know," he had said. "But I'm getting you out if it kills me."

Akos put his arm around his brother, holding him mostly upright as they walked out of the room together. His hand found the top of Eijeh's head as they ducked into the passage, to keep him from hitting it. Eijeh had heavy footsteps, and Akos had been sure that someone would hear them through the walls.

"It's s'posed to be me saving you," Eijeh whispered at one point. Or the closest to a whisper as he could get; he'd always been terrible at sneaking.

"Who says? Some kind of manual on brotherly conduct?"

Eijeh had laughed. "You didn't read yours? Typical."

Also laughing, Akos had pushed open the door at the end of the passage. Waiting for them in the kitchens, cracking his knuckles, was Vas Kuzar.

§

A week after the sojourn ship launched and sailed for the current-stream, Akos went to the public training room to practice. He could have used the empty room above Cyra's quarters, but lately she'd taken to watching footage up there. Mostly it was of people from other planets fighting, but a week ago he caught her imitating an Othyrian dancer, all pointed toes and fingers fluttering. She'd gotten so grouchy with him after that, he didn't want to risk it again.

He didn't even need to check the crumpled map Cyra had drawn for him on their second night. The training room was dim and near empty, just a few others lifting weights at the far end. *Good*, he thought. People knew him in Shotet as the kidnapped Thuvhesit, the one who Ryzek's Scourge couldn't hurt. Nobody gave him any grief—probably because they were afraid of Cyra— but he didn't enjoy the staring.

It made his face red.

He was trying to touch his toes—emphasis on *trying*—when he figured out someone was watching him. He couldn't say how, just that when he looked up, Jorek Kuzar was standing there.

Jorek Kuzar, son of Suzao Kuzar.

They had met only once, when Vas brought Jorek to Cyra's part of Noavek manor. His skinny brown arms were bare. Akos had taken to checking for marks whenever he met somebody, and Jorek had none. When he caught Akos staring, he rubbed at the side of his neck, leaving red streaks from his fingernails behind.

"Need something?" Akos said, like there would be trouble if Jorek did.

"Someone to spar with?" Jorek held up two practice knives just like the ones Cyra had, hard and synthetic.

Akos looked him over. Did he really expect Akos to just . . . train with him? Him, the son of the man who had once pushed a boot sole into Akos's face?

"I was just leaving," Akos said.

Jorek cocked an eyebrow. "I know all of *this*"—he waved a hand over his slim torso—"is downright terrifying, but it's just for practice, Kereseth."

Akos didn't buy that all Jorek really wanted was "someone to spar with," but he might as well figure out what the truth was. Besides, a person didn't choose their own blood.

"Fine," Akos said.

They walked to one of the practice arenas. A circle of paint defined the space, reflective, peeling off in places. The air was warm, thanks to the hot water moving through the pipes above, so Akos was already sweating. He took the knife Jorek held out to him.

"I've never seen a person so wary of a fake fight," Jorek said, but Akos wasn't sparing any time for banter. He swiped, testing his opponent's speed, and Jorek jumped back, startled.

Akos slipped under Jorek's first jab, and elbowed him in the back. Jorek stumbled forward, catching himself with his fingertips, and turned to strike again. This time Akos caught him by the elbow and dragged him sideways, heaving him to the ground, though not for long.

Jorek bent low, catching Akos's stomach with the tip of the practice knife.

"Not a good place to aim, Kuzar," Akos said. "In a real fight, I'd be wearing armor."

"I go by 'Jorek,' not 'Kuzar.' You've earned armor?"

"Yeah." Akos used his distraction against him, smacking the front of Jorek's throat with the flat of the weapon. Jorek choked, clapping his hands over his neck.

"All right, all right," he gasped, showing a palm. "That answers that question."

Akos backed up to the edge of the arena to put some space between them. "What question? About my armor?"

"No. Damn, that *sucked*." He massaged his throat. "I came here wondering how good you'd gotten, training with Cyra. My father said you didn't know hand from foot when he first met you."

Akos's anger was slow to come, like water turning to ice, but it had some heft to it, when it did. Like right then.

"Your father—" he started, but Jorek interrupted.

"Is the worst kind of man, yes. That's what I want to talk to you about."

Akos flipped the practice knife in his hand, again and again, waiting for the right response to come, or for Jorek to keep going. Whatever he had to say, though, it didn't seem to come easy. Akos watched the ones lifting weights on the other end of the room. They weren't looking, didn't seem to be listening.

"I know what my father did to you, and your family," Jorek said. "I also know what you did to one of the other men who was there." He nodded to Akos's marked arm. "And I want to ask you for something."

As far as Akos knew, Jorek was a big disappointment to his family. Born to an elite Shotet name and working in maintenance. He was grease-streaked even then.

"What, exactly?" Akos said. Another flip of the knife.

"I want you to kill my father," Jorek said plainly.

The knife clattered to the ground.

The memory of Jorek's father was as close to him as two threads in a tapestry. Suzao Kuzar had been there when his dad's blood seeped into the living room floor. He had slapped the cuffs on Akos's wrists.

"I'm not a fool, no matter what you people think of the Thuvhesit," Akos snapped, his cheeks going ruddy as he picked up the practice blade. "You think I'm going to just let you set me up for a fall?"

"I'm as much at risk as you are," Jorek replied. "For all I know you could go whisper in Cyra Noavek's ear about what I just asked you, and it could get back to Ryzek, or my father. But I'm choosing to trust in your hatred. As you should trust in mine."

"Trust in your hatred. For your own father," Akos said. "Why—why would you want this?"

Jorek was a head shorter than Akos, and not even as wide. Smaller than his age. But his eyes were steady.

"My mother is in danger," Jorek said. "Probably my sister, too. And as you've seen, I'm not skilled enough to fight him off myself."

"So you, what? Leap straight to killing him? What is it with you Shotet?" Akos said in a low voice. "If your family really is in danger, can't you just find a way to get your mom and sister out of here? You work in maintenance, and there are hundreds of floaters in the loading bay."

"They wouldn't go. Besides, as long as he's alive, he's a danger to them. I don't want them to have to live that way, on the run, always scared," Jorek said, firm. "I'm not taking any unnecessary risks."

"And there's no one else who can help you."

"No one can force Suzao Kuzar to do anything he doesn't want to do." Jorek laughed. "Except Ryzek, and I'll give you one guess what the sovereign of Shotet would say to that request."

Akos rubbed at the marks by his elbow, and thought of the savagery of them. *He doesn't look like much*, Osno's mother had said about him. *He's nice enough*, Osno had replied. Well, neither of them had known what he could do with a knife, had they?

"You want me to kill a man," Akos said, if only to test it out in his own mind.

"A man who aided in your kidnapping. Yes."

"What, out of the goodness of my heart?" Akos shook his head and held out the practice knife handle-first for Jorek to take. "No."

"In return," Jorek said, "I can offer you your freedom. As you said, there are hundreds of floaters in the loading bay. It would be a simple thing, to help you take one. To open the doors for you. To make sure someone on the nav deck was looking the other way."

Freedom. He offered it like someone who didn't know what it meant, someone who had never had it taken away. Only, it didn't exist for Akos anymore, and hadn't since the day he found out his fate. Maybe even since he promised his dad he would get Eijeh home.

So Akos shook his head again. "No deal."

"You don't want to go home?"

"I have unfinished business here. And I really should get back to it, so . . ."

Jorek still wasn't taking the practice knife, so Akos let it fall between them and started toward the door. He felt for Jorek's mother, maybe even for Jorek himself, but he had enough family trouble of his own, and these marks weren't getting any easier to bear.

"Then what about that brother of yours?" Jorek said. "The one who inhales when Ryzek exhales?"

Akos stopped, grinding his teeth. *It's your own fault,* he told himself. *You're the one who hinted at "unfinished business."* Somehow knowing that didn't make it any easier.

"I can get him out," Jorek said. "Get him home, where they can fix whatever's addled his brain."

He thought of the almost-escape again, of Eijeh's broken voice asking him, *"Why did this happen?"* His sunken cheeks, his sallow skin. He was disappearing, day by day, season by season. Soon there wouldn't be much left to rescue.

"Okay." It came out like a whisper, not how he meant it.

"Okay?" Jorek sounded a little breathless. "You mean you'll do it?"

Akos forced out the word. "Yes."

For Eijeh, the answer was always yes.

They didn't grip hands, like two Thuvhesits might have, to settle a deal. Here, just saying the words in the language the Shotet held sacred was enough.

That there was a guard stationed at the end of Cyra's hallway didn't make much sense to Akos. No one got the better of Cyra in a fight. Even the guard seemed to agree—he didn't so much as check Akos for weapons when he walked past.

Cyra was hunched in front of the stove, a pot at her feet and water pooled on the floor. There were curved dents in her palms—fingernail marks, from too-tight fists—and dark current-streaks everywhere Akos could see. He ran to her, slipping a little on the wet floor.

Akos took up her wrists, and the streaks disappeared, like a river flowing backward to its source. He felt nothing, as always. He often heard people talking about the hum of the current, the places and times it waned, but that was just a memory for him. Not even a clear one.

Her skin felt hot in his hands. Her eyes lifted to his. Akos had figured out early that she didn't look "upset" the way other people did—she either looked angry or she didn't. But now that he knew her better, he could see the sadness showing through the cracks in the armor.

"Thinking about Lety?" he said, shifting his grip a little so he held her hands instead, first two fingers fitting into the cleft of her thumb.

"I just dropped it." She nodded to the pot. "That's all."

That's never "all," he thought, but he didn't press. On an impulse he ran a hand over her hair, smoothing it down. It was thick, and curled, sometimes tempting him to twist it around his fingers for no particular reason.

The light touch brought a stab of guilt along with it. He wasn't supposed to do things like that—wasn't supposed to march toward his own fate instead of being dragged. Back in Thuvhe, all who met eyes with him now would see a traitor. He couldn't let them be right.

Sometimes, though, he felt Cyra's pain like it was his own, and he couldn't help but dull it for the both of them.

Cyra turned her hand in his, so her fingertips rested on his palm. Her touch was soft, curious. Then she pressed him back. Away.

"You're early," she said, and she grabbed a cloth to dry the floor. The water was starting to seep through the soles of Akos's shoes. She was shadowy again, and flinching from the pain of it, but if she didn't want his help, he wasn't going to force it on her.

"Yeah," he said. "I ran into Jorek Kuzar."

"What did he want?" She stepped on the cloth to soak up more water.

"Cyra?"

She tossed the wet cloth into the sink. "Yes?"

"How would I go about killing Suzao Kuzar?"

Cyra puckered her lips, the way she always did when she was thinking something over. It was unsettling, for him to ask that question like it was normal. For her to react like it was.

He was very, very far from home.

"It would have to be in the arena to be legal, as you know," she said. "And you would want it to be legal, or you would end up dead. Arena challenges are banned from when the ship leaves the atmosphere until after the scavenge, which means you have to wait until after. Another part of our religious legacy." She quirked her eyebrows. "But you don't have the status to challenge Suzao even then, so you have to provoke him to challenge you, instead."

It was almost like she'd thought about it before, only he knew she hadn't. It was times like this that he understood why everybody was scared of her. Or why they ought to be, even without her currentgift.

"Could I beat him once we were in the arena?"

"He's a good fighter, but not excellent," she said. "You could probably master him with skill alone, but your true advantage is that he still thinks of you as the child you once were."

Akos nodded. "So. I should let him think I'm still that way."

"Yes."

She put the now-empty pot under the faucet to fill it again. Akos was wary of Cyra's cooking; she almost always burned food when she tried, filling the little room with smoke.

"Make sure this is really what you want to do," she said. "I don't want to see you become like me."

She didn't say it like she wanted him to comfort her, or debate her. She said it with absolute conviction, like her belief in her own monstrousness was a religion, and maybe it was the closest thing to religion she had.

"You think I go sour that easy?" Akos said, trying out the low-class Shotet diction he'd heard in the soldiers' camp. It didn't sound half bad.

She pulled her hair back and tied it with the string she wore around her bare wrist. Her eyes found his again. "I think everyone goes 'sour that easy.'"

Akos almost laughed at how awkward it sounded when she said it.

"You know," he said, "the condition of sourness—or monstrousness, as you might call it—doesn't have to be permanent."

She looked like she was chewing on the idea. Had it ever even occurred to her before?

"Let me cook, okay?" He took the pot from her. The water sloshed, spilling on his shoes. "I guarantee I won't set anything on fire."

"That happened *one time*," she said. "I'm not a walking, talking hazard."

Like so much of what she said about herself, it was both a joke and not a joke.

"I know you're not," he said seriously. Then he added, "That's why you're going to chop the saltfruit for me."

She looked thoughtful still—a weird expression for a face that frowned so easily—as she took the saltfruit from the coldbox in the corner and settled herself at the counter to cut it up.

CHAPTER 16 | CYRA

My QUARTERS WERE FAR away from everything except the engine rooms, by design, so it was a long walk from Ryzek's office. He had called me in to give me my sojourn itinerary: I would join him and some of the other elites of Shotet in a pre-scavenge social gathering, to help him politick with the leaders of Pitha. I agreed to the plan because it required only my ability to pretend, not my currentgift.

As the cynical Examiner had predicted when Akos and I visited the room of planets, Ryzek had set our sojourn destination as Pitha, the water planet, known for its innovative technologies in weather resistance. If the rumors about Pitha's secret store of advanced weaponry were true, Eijeh Kereseth had surely confirmed them, now that he was warped by Ryzek's memories. And if Eijeh helped Ryzek find some of the Assembly's most powerful weapons, it would be simple for my brother to wage war against Thuvhe, to conquer our planet, as he had always intended.

I was still only halfway to my rooms when all the lights went out. Everything was dark. The distant hum from the ship's power control center was gone.

I heard a tapping sound, in a pattern. One, three, one. One, three, one.

I turned, my back to the wall.

One, three, one.

The currentshadows raced up my arms and over my shoulders. As the strips of emergency light at my feet began to glow, I saw a body hurtling toward me, and I bent, driving my elbow at whatever flesh it could find. I swore as my elbow hit armor, and turned on light feet, the dances I had practiced for enjoyment shifting into instinct. I drew my currentblade, then slammed into my attacker, pressing her to the wall with my blade to her throat. Her own knife clattered to the floor between her feet.

She wore a mask with one eye stitched closed. It covered her face from forehead to chin. A hood, made of a heavy material, shrouded her head. She was a head shorter than I was, and her armor was earned, made from the skin of an Armored One.

She was whimpering at my touch.

"Who are you?" I said.

The backup announcer on the ship crackled to life as soon as I finished the question. It was old, a relic from our early sojourns, and it made voices sound tinny and warped.

"The first child of the family Noavek will fall to the family Benesit," it said. "The truth can be suppressed, but it can never be erased."

I waited for the voice to continue, but the crackling went dead, the announcer switching off. The ship began to hum again. The woman whose throat was captive to my arm and my blade moaned softly.

"I should arrest you," I whispered. "Arrest you, and bring you in for questioning." I tilted my head. "Do you know how my brother interrogates people? He uses me. He uses *this*." I pushed more of the shadows toward her, so they collected around my forearm. She screamed.

For a moment, she sounded just like Lety Zetsyvis.

I released her, pulling away from the wall.

The lights on the floor had come to life, making us both glow from beneath. I could see a single bright eye in her head, fixed on me. The overhead lights clicked on, and she sprinted down the hallway, disappearing around a corner.

I had let her go.

I put my hands in fists to keep them from trembling. I couldn't believe what I had just done. If Ryzek ever found out . . .

I picked up her knife—if it could be called that; it was a jagged metal rod, sharpened by hand, with tape wrapped around the bottom to make a handle—and I started to walk. I wasn't sure what direction I was going, just that I needed to keep moving. I had no injuries, no evidence that the attack had ever occurred. Hopefully it had been too dark for the security footage to show that I had just let a renegade go free.

What have you done?

I ran through the ship's hallways, my footsteps echoing for just a few seconds before I dove into a crowd, into chaos. Everything was loud and hurried, like my heart. I stuffed my hands into my sleeves so I wouldn't touch anyone by accident. I wasn't going to my quarters. I needed to see Ryzek before anyone else did—I needed to make sure he believed I had not been a part of this. It was one thing to refuse to torture people, but it was another to participate in a revolt. I put the renegade's knife in my pocket, out of sight.

The soldiers stepped back for me when I reached Ryzek's rooms on the far side of the ship, the one closest to the current-stream. They directed me to his office, and when I reached the door I wasn't sure that he would let me in, but he shouted the command right away.

Ryzek stood barefoot in his office, facing the wall. He was alone, a mug of diluted hushflower extract—I recognized it on sight, these days—clutched in one hand. He wasn't wearing his armor, and when he looked at me, there was chaos in his eyes.

"What do you want?" he demanded.

"I . . ." I paused. I didn't know what I wanted, except to cover myself. "I just came to find out if you were all right."

"Of course I'm all right," he said. "Vas killed the two renegades who tried to enter this part of the ship before they could even scream." He tugged one of the curtains back from the porthole—larger than most, it was almost as tall as he was—and stared out at the currentstream, which had turned dark green. Almost blue, almost time for the invasion, the scavenging, the tradition of our ancestors. "You think the childish actions of a few renegades can harm me?"

I stepped toward him, careful, like he was a wild animal. "Ryzek, it's all right to be a little rattled when people are attacking you."

"I am not rattled!" He shouted every word, slamming his mug down on a nearby table. The hushflower blend spilled everywhere, staining his white cuff red.

As I stared at him, I was struck by the memory of his quick, sure hands, fastening the buckles across my lap before my first sojourn, and how he had smiled as he teased me about being nervous. It wasn't his fault that he had turned out this way, so ter-rified and so creative with his cruelty. Our father had conditioned him to become this person. The greatest gift Lazmet Noavek had ever given me, even greater than life itself, had been leaving me alone.

I had come at Ryzek with threats, with anger, with disdain, with fear. I had never tried kindness. While my father had relied on well-aimed threats and intimidating silence as his weapons, my mother had always wielded kindness with the deftness of a blade. After all this time, I was still more Lazmet than Ylira, but that could change.

"I'm your sister. You don't have to be this way with me," I said, as gently as I could.

Ryzek was staring at the stain on his cuff. He didn't respond, which I decided was a good sign.

"Do you remember how we used to play with those little fig-urines in my room?" I said. "How you taught me to hold a knife? I kept making that tight fist and cutting off circulation to my finger-tips, and you taught me how to fix it."

He frowned. I wondered if he did remember—or was that one of the memories he had traded for one of Eijeh's? Still, maybe he had taken in some of Eijeh's gentleness when he traded away his pain.

"We weren't always like this, you and I," I said.

In his pause, I let myself hope—for a quiet shift in the way he regarded me, for the slow and steady change that our relationship could undergo, if he would just let go of his fear. His gaze found mine and it was almost there, I could see it, I could almost hear it. We could be as we once were.

"Then you killed our mother," he said quietly. "And now, this is all that we can be."

I shouldn't have been surprised, shouldn't have marveled at the way words could hit me like a hard punch to the stomach. But hope had made me a fool.

I spent all night awake, dreading what he would do about the attack.

The answer came the next morning, when his calm, self-assured voice came from the news screen on the far wall. I rolled out of bed and crossed the room so I could turn on the video. My brother filled the screen, pale and skeletal. His armor caught the light, casting an eerie glow across his face.

"Yesterday, we experienced a . . . disruption—" His lip curled, like he thought it was amusing. It made sense—Ryzek knew not to show fear, to minimize the renegades' actions as much as possible. "Childish though it was, the perpetrators of this stunt compromised the security of the ship by stalling its flight, which means they must be found and rooted out." His tone had turned sinister. "People of any age will be selected at random from the ship's database and brought in for questioning, beginning today. There will be a shipwide curfew, from the twentieth hour to the sixth hour, imposed on all of the ship's occupants except those essential to its functioning, until such time as we have eradicated this problem. The sojourn will also be delayed until we have ensured the ship's safety."

"Questioning," Akos said from behind me. "Is that code for 'interrogation involving torture'?"

I nodded.

"If you know anything about the identities of the individuals involved in this prank, it is in your best interest to come forward," Ryzek said. "Those who are discovered to have withheld information or lie during questioning will also be punished, for the good of the Shotet people. Rest assured, the safety of the sojourn ship, and all the people in it, is my highest concern."

Akos snorted.

"If you have nothing to hide, you have nothing to fear," Ryzek said. "Let us continue to prepare to show the other planets in this galaxy our might and our unity."

His head remained on the screen for a few moments longer, and then the news feed returned, this time in Othyrian, which I knew passably well. There was a water shortage on Tepes, in the western continent. The Shotet subtitles were accurate. For once.

"Showing our might and our unity," I said, quoting Ryzek, more to myself than to Akos. "Is that what the sojourn is for now?"

"What else is it for?"

The Assembly was debating further requirements for the oracles on each planet, to be voted on in forty days. Shotet subtitles: "Assembly attempts to assert tyrannical control over oracles through another predatory measure, to be enacted at the end of the forty day cycle." Accurate, but biased.

Some notorious band of space pirates had just been sentenced to fifteen seasons in prison. Shotet subtitles: "Band of Zoldan traditionalists sentenced to fifteen seasons in prison for speaking out against unnecessarily restrictive Assembly regulations." Not so accurate.

"The sojourn is supposed to be an acknowledgment of our reliance on the current and the one who masters it," I said quietly. "A religious rite, and a way of honoring those who came before us."

"The Shotet you describe is not the one that I've seen," Akos said.

I glanced back at him. "Maybe you see what you want to see."

"Maybe we both do," Akos said. "You look worried. Do you think Ryzek will stop leaving you alone?"

"If things get bad enough."

"And if you refuse to help him again? What's the worst he can do?"

I sighed. "I don't think you understand. My mother was beloved. A deity among mortals. When she died, all of Shotet mourned. It was like the world had come apart." I closed my eyes, briefly, letting an image of her face pass through my mind. "If they find out what I did to her, they will tear me limb from limb. Ryzek knows that, and he'll use it if he gets too desperate."

Akos frowned. Not for the first time, I wondered how he would feel if I died. Not because I thought he hated me, but because I knew that his fate echoed in his head whenever he looked at me. I might be the Noavek he would one day die for, given how much time we spent together. And I could not believe that I was worth that, worth his life.

"Well," he said. "Let's hope he doesn't, then."

He was angled toward me. There were only a few inches separating us. We were often close together, when sparring, when training, when making our breakfasts, and he had to touch me to keep my pain at bay. So it should not have felt strange that his hip was so close to my stomach, that I could see ropy muscle standing out from his arm.

But it did.

"How is your friend Suzao?" I said as I stepped back.

"I gave some sleeping potion to Jorek to slip into the medicine he takes in the morning," Akos said.

"Jorek's going to drug his own father?" I said. "Interesting."

"Yeah, well, we'll see if Suzao actually collapses into his lunch. Might make him angry enough to challenge me to the arena."

"I'd do it a few more times before you reveal yourself," I said. "He needs to be afraid, as well as angry."

"Hard to think of a man like that being afraid."

"Yeah, well, we're all afraid." I sighed. "The angry more than most, I think."

The currentstream made the slow transition from green to blue, and still we didn't descend on Pitha, still Ryzek delayed the sojourn. We coasted along the edge of the galaxy, out of the Assembly's reach. Impatience was like a humid cloud that had settled over the ship; I breathed it in whenever I left my isolated quarters. And these days, I rarely left my quarters.

Ryzek couldn't delay our descent forever—he couldn't forgo the sojourn altogether, or he would be the first sovereign to ignore our traditions in over one hundred seasons.

I had promised him that I would keep up appearances, which was why I found myself at a gathering of his closest associates again, on the observation deck several days after the attack. The first thing I saw upon entering was the darkness of space through the windows, open to us like we were soaring into a huge crea-ture's mouth. Then I saw Vas, clutching a mug of tea with bleeding knuckles. When he noticed the blood, he dabbed at it with a hand-kerchief and stuffed it back into his pocket.

"I know you can't feel pain, Vas, but there is some value in taking care of your own body," I said to him.

He raised his eyebrows at me, then set his mug down. The others were gathered on the opposite end of the room, holding glasses, standing in small groups. Most had collected around Ryzek like debris around a drain hole. Yma Zetsyvis—white hair almost glowing against the dark backdrop of space—was among them, her body stiff with obvious tension.

Otherwise the room was empty, the black floors polished, the walls just curved windows. I half expected us all to float away.

"You know so little about my gift, for all the time we've known each other," Vas said. "Do you know I have to set alarms to eat and drink? And check myself constantly for broken bones and bruises?"

I had never thought about what else Vas had lost when he lost the ability to feel pain.

"That's why I let the little wounds slide," Vas said. "It's exhausting, paying this much attention to your own body."

"Hmm," I said. "I think I might know something about that."

Not for the first time, I marveled at how opposite we were—and how similar that made us, both our lives revolving around pain, in one way or another, both spending an exorbitant amount of energy on the physical. It made me curious if we had anything else in common.

"When did you develop it?" I said. "What was happening at the time?"

"I was ten." He leaned against the wall and ran his hand over his head. His hair was shaved close to his scalp. Near his ear, there were a few cuts from the razor—he probably hadn't noticed them.

"Before I was accepted into your brother's service, I attended a regular school. I was scrawny then, an easy target. Some of the bigger children were attacking me." He smiled. "Once I realized I couldn't feel pain, I beat one of them half to death. They didn't come after me again."

He had been in danger, and his body had responded. His *mind* had responded. His story was the same as mine.

"You think of me the way I think of Kereseth," Vas said. "You think I'm Ryzek's little pet, just like Akos is yours."

"I think we all serve my brother," I said. "You. Me. Kereseth. We're all the same." I glanced at the crowd gathered around Ryzek. "Why is Yma here?"

"You mean, after she was disgraced by both husband and child?" Vas said. "She's rumored to have gotten on hands and knees, begging for forgiveness for their transgressions. That may be a slight exaggeration, of course."

I slipped past him, edging closer to the others. Yma's hand was on Ryzek's arm, sliding down to his elbow. I expected him to pull away; he nearly always did when people tried to touch him. But he permitted the caress, even leaned into it, maybe.

How could she stand to look at him, after he ordered the deaths of her daughter and husband, let alone touch him? I watched her laugh at something Ryzek had said. Her eyebrows drew in like she was in pain. *Or desperate*, I thought. The expressions were often the same.

"Cyra!" Yma said, drawing everyone's attention to me. I tried to make myself look her in the eye, but it was difficult, given what I had done to Lety. I dreamt of Yma when I dreamt of her daughter, sometimes, imagined her hunched over Lety's corpse, screaming at the top of her lungs. "It's been a while. What have you been up to?"

I met Ryzek's eyes, just for a moment.

"Cyra has been on a special assignment from me," Ryzek said easily. "To stay close to Kereseth."

He was taunting me.

"Is the younger Kereseth so valuable?" Yma asked me. She wore that peculiar smile.

"That remains to be seen," I said. "But he is Thuvhesit-born, after all. He knows things about our enemies that we do not."

"Ah," Yma said lightly. "I just thought you might have made yourself useful during these interrogations, Cyra, in the way you have made yourself useful before."

I felt like I might be sick.

"Unfortunately, the interrogations require a clever tongue and a mind skilled at the detection of subtleties," Ryzek said. "Two things my sister has always lacked."

Stung, I couldn't think of a response. Maybe he was right about my tongue not being clever.

So I just let the currentshadows sprawl, and when the conversation had turned to another topic, I walked to the edge of the room to look out at the dark that enfolded us.

We were on the edge of the galaxy, so the only planets—or pieces of planets—left to see were not populous enough to participate in the Assembly. We called them "peripheral planets," or just "the brim," more casually. My mother had urged the Shotet to regard them as our brothers and sisters in the same struggle for legitimacy. My father had privately scoffed at that idea, saying that Shotet was greater than any brim spawn.

I saw one of those planets from this vantage point, just a spot of light ahead, too big to be one of our stars. A bright thread of the currentstream stretched toward it and wrapped around it like a belt.

"P1104," Yma Zetsyvis said to me, sipping from her mug. "That's the planet you're looking at."

"Have you been there?" I was tense, standing beside her, but I tried to keep my voice light. Behind us the others erupted into laughter at something cousin Vakrez had said.

"Of course not," Yma said. "The last two sovereigns of Shotet have not permitted travel to brim planets. They—rightfully—want to put distance between us and them in the eyes of the Assembly. We can't be associated with such rough company if we want to be taken seriously."

Spoken like a Noavek loyalist. Or more accurately, a Noavek apologist. She knew the script well.

"Right," I said. "So . . . I take it the interrogations haven't yielded any results."

"Some low-level renegades, yes, but none of the key players. And unfortunately, we are running out of time."

We? I thought. She so confidently included herself as one of my brother's close associates. Maybe she really had begged him for forgiveness. Maybe she had found another way to ingratiate herself to him.

I shuddered at the thought.

"I know. The currentstream is almost blue. Changing by the day," I said.

"Indeed. So your brother needs to find someone. Make it public. Show strength before the sojourn. Strategy is, of course, important for unstable times like these."

"And what's the strategy if he doesn't find someone in time?"

Yma turned her strange smile on me. "I would think you already know the strategy. Hasn't your brother been filling you in, despite your *special assignment?*"

I got the sense we both knew that my "special assignment" was a lie.

"Of course," I said dryly. "But you know, with a mind as dull as mine, I forget things like this all the time. I probably forgot to turn off my stove this morning."

"I sense it will not be difficult for your brother to find a suspect in time for the scavenge," Yma said. "All they have to do is *look* the part of a renegade, right?"

"He's going to frame someone?" I said.

I felt cold at the thought of an innocent person dying because Ryzek needed a scapegoat, and I wasn't sure why. Months ago—even weeks ago—this would not have troubled me as much. But something Akos had said was working its way through me: that the thing I was did not have to be permanent.

Maybe I could change. Maybe I *was* changing, just by believing I could.

I thought of the one-eyed woman I had let go, the day of the attack. Her small frame, her distinct movements. If I wanted to, I could find her, I was sure of it.

"A small sacrifice for the good of your brother's regime." Yma bobbed her head. "We must all make sacrifices for our own good."

I turned to her. "What kind of sacrifices have you made?"

She seized my wrist and squeezed it hard. Harder than I

thought her capable of. Though I knew my currentgift must be burning into her, she didn't let go, drawing me closer to her, so I could smell her breath.

"I have denied myself the pleasure of watching you bleed to death," she whispered.

She released me and moved back toward the group, sashaying as she went. Her long pale hair hung to the middle of her back, perfectly straight. She was like a pillar of white from behind, even her dress such a light blue it almost matched.

I rubbed my wrist, my skin red from her grasp. I would bruise, I was sure of it.

The clatter of pans stopped when I walked into the kitchens. A smaller selection of our staff worked on the sojourn ship than in Noavek manor, but I recognized some of the faces. And the gifts, too—one of the scrubbers was making the pots float, suds dripping on the backs of his hands, and one of the choppers was doing the task with her eyes closed, the knife strokes clean and even.

Otega had her head in the coldbox. When silence fell, she straightened, and wiped her hands off on her apron.

"Ah, Cyra," she said. "No one makes a room quiet like you."

The other staff stared openly at her for her familiarity, but I only laughed a little. Even when I hadn't seen her in a while—I had surpassed her capacity to teach me last season; now we saw each other only rarely, in passing—she fell back into our old rhythms without trouble.

"It's a unique talent," I replied. "Can I speak with you in private, please?"

"You phrase it like a question when it's really an order," Otega said, waggling her eyebrows. "Follow me. I trust you don't mind chatting in the garbage closet."

"Mind? I've always *wanted* to spend time in a garbage closet," I said, wry, and followed her through the narrow galley to a door in the back.

The stink in the closet was so powerful it made my eyes water. From what I could tell, it came from rotten fruit skins and old meat rinds dusted with herbs. There was only enough space for two of us, standing close together. Beside us was the huge door that opened to a trash incinerator; it was hot, which only made the stench worse.

I breathed through my mouth, aware, suddenly, of how soft-palmed I looked to her, how spoiled. My fingernails always clean, my white shirt still bright. And Otega, covered in food splatter, with the look of a woman who was supposed to be stockier but hadn't gotten enough food to become so.

"What can I do for you, Cyra?"

"How do you feel about doing me a favor?"

"Depends on the favor."

"It would involve lying to my brother if he ever asks you about it."

Otega crossed her arms. "What could you want that would involve lying to Ryzek?"

I sighed. I took the renegade's knife from my pocket and held it out to her.

"During the renegade attack," I said, "an attempt was made against my life in an isolated hallway. I overpowered her, but then I . . . let her go."

"Why the hell did you do that?" she said. "As the current flows, girl, even your mother wasn't that kind."

"I don't—it doesn't matter." I turned the knife in my hand. The tape that made up the handle was light and springy, bent according to its owner's fingers. She had a much smaller hand than I did. "But I want to find her. She dropped this, and I knew you could use it to find her."

Otega's currentgift was one of the most mysterious I had encountered. Given an object, she could trace the person who owned it. My parents had asked her to find the owners of weapons that way. Once she had even located someone who tried to poison my father. Sometimes the trails were difficult to read, she said, like when two or three different owners called an object theirs, but she was adept at interpreting them. If anyone could find my renegade, it was her.

"And you don't want your brother to know about it," she said.

"You know what my brother would do to her," I said. "And the execution would be the kindest part."

Otega pursed her lips. I thought of her deft fingers in my hair, pulling it into braids under my mother's supervision before my first Procession. The snap of my bloody sheets as she pulled them from my mattress, the day my cycles began and my mother was not alive to help me.

"You aren't going to tell me why you want to find her, are you."

"No," I said.

"Does it involve seeking your own revenge?"

"See, answering that would be a form of telling you why I want to find her, which I just said I wouldn't do." I smiled. "Come on, Otega. You know I can take care of myself. I'm just not as harsh as my brother."

"Fine, fine." She took the knife from me. "I'll need to spend a little time with it. Come back here right before curfew tomorrow, I'll take you to its owner then."

"Thank you."

She guided a loose strand of hair behind my ear, and smiled a little, to disguise her wince at touching me.

"You're not so scary, girl," she said. "Don't worry. I won't tell my staff."

CHAPTER 17 | AKOS

NOT MANY STARS WERE out on the edge of the galaxy. Cyra loved it, he could tell by how calm the currentshadows were when she stared out the window. It made him shiver, all that space, all that dark. But they were getting close to the edge of the current-stream, so there was a little purple at the corner of the hologram in the ceiling.

Pitha wasn't the planet the current had led them to. Cyra and Akos had seen that, the day they went to see the Examiners—who had been thinking of Ogra, or even P1104. But apparently Ryzek saw the ruling of the Examiners as a formality only. He'd picked the planet that offered him the most useful alliance, Cyra said.

She had a distinct knock, four light taps. He knew it was her in the doorway without looking up.

"We should hurry, or we'll miss it," she said.

"You realize you're being intentionally vague, right?" Akos said with a smile. "You still haven't told me what 'it' is."

"I do realize that, yes." She returned the smile.

She was wearing a muted blue dress with sleeves that stopped just above the elbow, so when Akos's hand swung forward to grab her arm, he made sure his grip settled where the fabric stopped. The color of the dress didn't really suit her, he thought. She'd looked more like herself in purple during the Sojourn Festival, or in dark training clothes. But then again, there wasn't much Cyra Noavek could do to take away from her looks, and he was pretty sure she knew that.

No point in denying the obvious, after all.

They walked fast through the hallways, taking a different path than Akos had ever walked before. The signs, fixed to the walls wherever the hallways broke apart, said they were going to the nav deck. They climbed some narrow stairs, and Cyra stuck her hand in a slot in the wall at the top. Two heavy doors opened. A wall of glass greeted him.

And beyond it: space. Stars. Planets.

And the currentstream, getting bigger and brighter by the second.

Dozens of people worked at rows of screens just in front of the glass. Their uniforms were clean and looked a little like Shotet armor: darkest blue, bulky through the shoulders, but with flexible fabric instead of hard Armored One skin. One of the older men spotted Cyra and bowed to her.

"Miss Noavek," he said. "I was beginning to think I wouldn't see you this time."

"I wouldn't miss it, Navigator Zyvo," Cyra said. To Akos, she added, "I've been coming here since I was a child. Zyvo, this is Akos Kereseth."

"Ah yes," the older man said. "I've heard one or two stories about you, Kereseth."

Judging by his tone, Akos was sure he meant much more than "one or two" stories, and it made him nervous enough to flush.

"Shotet mouths love chatter," Cyra said to him. "Especially about the fate-favored."

"Right," Akos managed to say. Fate-favored—he was that, wasn't he? It sounded stupid to him now.

"You can take your usual place, Miss Noavek," Zyvo said, throwing out a hand toward the wall of glass. It dwarfed them easily, curving over their heads with the roof of the ship.

Cyra led the way to a spot in front of all the screens. All around them the crew was shouting directions or numbers at each other. Akos had no idea what to make of any of it. Cyra sat right on the ground, her arms wrapped around her knees.

"What are we here for, anyway?"

"Soon the ship will pass through the currentstream," she said, grinning. "You've never seen anything like it, I promise you. Ryzek will be on the observation deck with his closest supporters, but I get to come here, instead, so I don't scream in front of his guests. It can get kind of . . . intense. You'll see."

From this distance, the currentstream looked like a thunderhead, swollen with color instead of rain. Everybody in the galaxy agreed it existed—pretty hard to deny something that was plainly visible from every single planet's surface—but it meant different things to different people. Akos's parents had talked about it like it was a spiritual guide they didn't fully understand, but he knew a lot of the Shotet worshipped it, or something higher that directed it, depending on the sect. Some people thought it was just a natural phenomenon, nothing spiritual about it at all. Akos had never asked Cyra what she thought.

He was about to when somebody called out, "Prepare your-selves!"

All around him people grabbed whatever they could hang on to. The thunderhead of currentstream filled the glass in front of him, and then, almost as one, everybody but Akos gasped. Every inch of Cyra's skin went black as space. Her teeth, which looked white against her currentgift, were gritted, but it almost looked like she was smiling. Akos reached for her, but she shook her head.

Swirls of rich blue filled the glass. There were veins of lighter color, too, and almost-purple, and deep navy. The currentstream was huge and bright and everywhere, everywhere. Like being wrapped up in the arms of a god.

Some people had their hands stretched out in worship; others were on their knees; still others, clutching their chests, or stom-achs. One man's hands glowed as blue as the currentstream itself; small orbs, like fenzu, swam around a woman's head. Currentgifts run amok.

Akos thought of the Blooming. Thuvhesits weren't as . . . *expressive* as the Shotet during their rites, but the sense of it was the same. Gathering to celebrate something that happened only to them, of all people in the galaxy, and only at a certain time. The reverence they had for it, for its particular sort of beauty.

Everybody knew the Shotet followed the currentstream around space as an act of faith, but until then, Akos hadn't under-stood why, except maybe that they felt like they had to. But once you saw this up close, he thought, it was impossible to imagine a life without seeing it again.

He felt separate, though—not just because he was Thuvhesit and they were Shotet, but because they could feel the hum-buzz of the current and he couldn't. The current didn't go through him. It was like he wasn't as real as they were, like he wasn't as *alive*.

Just as he was thinking it, Cyra held out her hand. He took it, to relieve her of the shadows, and he was startled to see tears in her eyes—from the pain or from the wonder, it was hard to say.

And then she said something strange. Breathlessly, and with reverence: "You feel like silence."

The Assembly news feed was playing on the screen in Cyra's quarters when they returned. Cyra must have left it on by mistake, Akos thought, and while Cyra made her way to the bathroom, he moved to turn it off. Before he could flip the switch, however, he noticed the headline at the bottom of the screen: *Oracles Gather on Tepes*.

Akos sank down to the edge of Cyra's bed.

He might see his mom.

Half the time he tried to tell himself that she and Cisi were gone. It was easier than remembering they weren't, and that he wouldn't see them again, his fate being what it was. But he couldn't make himself believe a lie. They were right there, right across the feathergrass.

The news feed sights swooped in on Tepes. Tepes was the planet closest to the sun, the fire planet to their ice planet. You had to wear a special suit to walk around there, Akos knew, sort of like you couldn't walk outside in the Deadening time in Hessa without freezing to death. He couldn't imagine it—couldn't imagine his body burning in that way.

"The oracles prohibit outside intervention in their sessions, but this footage was submitted by a local child as the last ships arrived," a voice-over said in Othyrian. Most of the Assembly broadcasts were in Othyrian, since most people outside Shotet understood it. "Inside sources suggest that the oracles will be discussing another set of legal restrictions imposed by the Assembly last week, as the Assembly moves closer to requiring all oracle discussions be publicized."

It was an old complaint of his mother's, that the Assembly was always trying to interfere with the oracles, that they couldn't stand that there was one thing left in the galaxy they couldn't regulate. And no trifling thing, he knew, the fates of the favored families, the futures of the planets in their endless variety. *Maybe a little regulation wouldn't hurt the oracles,* Akos thought, and it felt like a betrayal.

Akos couldn't read most of the Shotet characters at the bottom of the screen, translating the voice-over. Just the ones for *oracle* and *Assembly*. Cyra said that something about the Shotet character for *Assembly* expressed Shotet bitterness at not being acknowledged by the Assembly. Decisions about the planet Thuvhe and Shotet shared—about trade, or aid, or travel—were made by Thuvhe and Thuvhe alone, leaving Shotet at the mercy of their enemies. They had reason enough to be bitter, Akos supposed.

He heard water running. Cyra was showering.

The Tepes footage showed two ships. The first one clearly wasn't a Thuvhesit ship—too sleek for that, all swooping shapes and perfect plates. But the other one looked like it could have been a Thuvhesit vessel, its fuel burners armed for cold instead of heat with a system of vents. Like gills, he'd always thought.

The hatch on that ship opened, and a spry woman in a reflective suit hopped down. When no others joined her, he knew it had to be the Thuvhesit ship. Every nation-planet had three oracles, after all, except Thuvhe. With Eijeh in captivity and the falling oracle dying in the Shotet invasion, only Akos's mother was left.

The sun on Tepes filled the sky like the whole planet was on fire, full and rich with color. Heat came off the planet's surface in ripples. He knew his mom's gait as she led the way to the monastery where the oracles were meeting. Then she disappeared behind a door and the footage cut off, the feed moving to a famine on one of the outer moons.

He didn't know how to feel. It was his first real glimpse of home in a long time. But it was also a glimpse of the woman who hadn't so much as warned her own family about what she knew was coming to them. Who hadn't shown up for it, even. She had let her husband die, let the falling oracle sacrifice herself, let a son—now Ryzek's very best weapon—be kidnapped, instead of offering herself in his place. *Fates be damned*, Akos thought. She was supposed to be their mother.

Cyra opened the bathroom door to let out the steam, and pulled her hair over one shoulder. She was dressed, this time in dark training clothes.

"What is it?" she asked. She followed his gaze to the screen. "Oh, you—you saw her?"

"I think so," Akos replied.

"I'm sorry," she said. "I know you try to avoid feeling homesick."

Homesick was the wrong word. *Lost* was the right one—lost out in the nothingness, among people he didn't understand, with no hope of getting his brother home except murdering Suzao Kuzar as soon as it was legal again.

Instead of telling her all that, he said, "How do you know that?"

"We never speak Thuvhesit, even though you know I could." She lifted a shoulder. "It's the same reason I don't keep any likenesses of my mother around. Better, sometimes, to just . . . keep moving forward."

Cyra ducked back into the bathroom. He watched her lean close to the mirror to poke at a pimple on her chin. Dab water from her forehead and neck. The same thing she always did, only now he noticed—noticed that he knew it, that was; knew her routines, knew *her*.

And liked her.

CHAPTER 18 | CYRA

"FOLLOW ME," OTEGA SAID when I met her outside the kitchens that evening. Clutched in her fist was the renegade's knife, the white tape showing between her fingers. She had found my renegade.

I put up my hood, and walked in her footsteps. I was well covered—pants tucked into boots, jacket sleeves covering my hands, hood shading my face—so that I wouldn't be recognized. Not every Shotet knew what I looked like, since my face was not plastered in every public building and important room the way Ryzek's was, but once they saw a currentshadow pool in my cheek or the crook of my arm, they knew me. Today I did not want to be known.

We walked from the Noavek wing, past the public practice arenas and the swimming pool—there so younger Shotet could learn to swim in preparation for sojourns to the water planet—past a cafeteria that smelled of burnt bread, and several janitor's closets. By the time Otega's walk slowed and her grip tightened on the renegade's knife, we had walked all the way to the engine deck.

It was so loud from the proximity to the engines that if we had tried to speak to each other, we would have had to shout to be heard. Everything smelled like oil.

Otega took me away from the noise somewhat to the technicians' living quarters, near the loading bay. What faced us was a long, narrow hallway with a doorway every few feet on either side, marked with a name. Some were decorated with strings of fenzu lights or little burnstone lanterns in all different colors, or collages of comic sketches drawn on engine schematic pages, or grainy pictures of family or friends. I felt like I had entered another world, one completely separate from what I knew to be Shotet. I wished Akos was here to see it. He would have liked it here.

Otega stopped at a sparsely decorated door near the end. Above the name "Surukta" was a bundle of dried feathergrass pinned in place with a metal charm. There were a few pages of what looked like a technical manual, written in another language. Pithar, if I had to guess. They were contraband—the possession of documents in another language for any purpose other than government-approved translation was illegal. But down here, I was sure no one bothered to enforce things like that. There was freedom in being unimportant to Ryzek Noavek.

"She lives here," Otega said, tapping the door with the knifepoint. "Though she isn't here now. I followed her here this morning."

"Then I will wait for her," I said. "Thank you for your help, Otega."

"It's my pleasure. We see each other too rarely, I think."

"So come to see me, then."

Otega shook her head. "The line dividing your world from

mine is thick." She offered me the knife. "Be careful."

I smiled at her as she walked away, and when she disappeared around the corner at the end of the corridor, I tried to open the renegade's door. It wasn't locked—I doubted she would be gone for long.

Inside was one of the smallest living spaces I had ever stood in. A sink was wedged into one corner, and a bed on stilts stood in the other. Beneath the bed was an overturned crate covered in wires and switches and screws. A magnetic strip pasted to the wall held tools so small I doubted I could ever use them. And beside the bed was a picture.

I leaned in close to see it. In it, a young girl with long blond hair had her arms wrapped around a woman with hair so silver it looked like a coin. Beside them was a young boy making a face, his tongue sticking out the side of his mouth. In the background were a few other people—mostly pale haired, like the rest—too blurry to make out.

Surukta. Was that name familiar, or was I just fooling myself?

The door opened behind me.

She was small and slim, just as I remembered. Her baggy, one-piece uniform was unbuttoned to the waist, with a sleeveless shirt beneath it. She had bright blond hair tied back from her face, and she was wearing an eye patch.

"What—"

Her fingers spread out, taut, at her sides. There was something in her back pocket—some kind of tool. I watched her hand move toward it, slowly, trying to hide the movement from me.

"Go ahead and draw your screwdriver or whatever it is," I said. "I'm happy to beat you a second time."

Her eye patch was black, and ill-fitting, too large for her face. But her remaining eye was the same rich blue I remembered from the attack.

"It's not a screwdriver; it's a wrench," she said. "What is Cyra Noavek doing in my humble living space?"

I had never heard my name spoken with such venom before. Which was saying something.

She had a look of practiced confusion on her face. It would have fooled me if I hadn't been so convinced that I had found her. Despite what Ryzek insisted, I was capable of detecting subtleties.

"Your name?" I said.

"You're the one who broke into my home, and you need me to give you a name?" She stepped in farther, and closed the door behind her.

She was a head shorter than me, but her movements were strong and purposeful. I didn't doubt that she was a talented fighter, which was probably why the renegades had sent her after me that night. I wondered if they had wanted her to kill me. It didn't really matter anymore.

"It'll be faster if you give me your name."

"Teka Surukta, then."

"Okay, Teka Surukta." I put her makeshift knife down on the edge of the sink. "I think that belongs to you. I came to return it."

"I . . . don't know what you're talking about."

"I didn't turn you in that night, so what makes you think I'm going to turn you in now?" I tried to slouch, like she was, but the position felt unnatural to me. My mother and father had taught me to stand up straight, knees together, hands folded when I wasn't using them. There was no such thing as casual conversation when you were a Noavek, so I had never learned the art of it.

She didn't look confused anymore.

"You know, you might have better luck carrying around some of your tools over there as weapons instead of the tape . . . thing," I said, gesturing to the delicate instruments magnetized to the wall. "They look sharp as needles."

"They're too valuable," Teka replied. "What do you want from me?"

"I suppose that depends on what sort of people you and your renegade cohort are." All around me was the sound of dripping water and creaking pipes. Everything smelled moldy and dank, like a tomb. "If the interrogations don't yield actual results within the next few days, my brother is going to frame someone and execute them. They will likely be innocent. He doesn't care."

"I'm shocked that you do," Teka said. "I thought you were supposed to be some kind of sadist."

I felt a sharp pain as a currentshadow darted across my cheek and spread over my temple. I saw it in my periphery, and suppressed the urge to wince at the pain it brought, a sharp ache in my sinuses.

"Presumably you all knew the potential consequences of your actions when you signed up for your cause, whatever it is," I said, ignoring her comment. "Whoever my brother selects to take the fall will not have made that calculated risk. They will die because you wanted to pull a prank on Ryzek Noavek."

"A prank?" Teka said. "Is that what you call acknowledging the truth? Destabilizing your brother's regime? Showing that we can control the movement of the ship itself?"

"For our purposes, yes," I said. Currentshadows traveled up my arm and curled around my shoulder, showing through my white shirt. Teka's eye followed them. I flinched, and continued, "If you care about the death of an innocent person, I suggest you come up with a real name to give me by the end of the day. If you don't care, I will just let Ryzek pick his target. It's entirely up to you—for me it's the same either way."

She uncrossed her arms and turned, so both shoulders were against the door.

"Well, shit," she said.

A few minutes later I was following Teka Surukta down the maintenance tunnel, toward the loading bay. I jumped at every noise, every creak, which in this part of the ship meant I jumped more often than not. It was loud down here, though we were far from most of the ship's population.

We were on a raised metal platform, wide enough for two slim people to pass each other with stomachs held in, hanging above all the machinery and water tanks and furnaces and current engines that kept the ship running and habitable. If I had gotten lost among the gears and pipes, I would never have found my way out.

"You know," I said, "if your plan is to get me far away from most people so that you can kill me, you might find it's more difficult than you imagine."

"I'd like to see what you're about first," Teka said. "You're not quite what I expected."

"Who is?" I said grimly. "I suppose it would be a waste of time for me to ask you how you managed to disable the ship's lights."

"No, that's easy." Teka stopped, and touched her palm to the wall. She closed her eye, and the light just above us, trapped in a metal cage to protect it, flickered. Once, then three times. The same rhythm I had heard tapped out when she attacked me.

"Anything that runs on current, I can mess with," Teka said. "That's why I'm a technician. Sadly that 'light' trick only works on the sojourn ship—all the lights in Voa are fenzu or burnstone, and there's not much I can do to those."

"You must like the sojourn ship best, then."

"In a manner of speaking," she said. "But it's a little claustrophobic on this ship when you live in a room the size of a closet."

We reached an open area, a grate above one of the oxygen converters, which were three times my height, and twice again as wide around. They processed the carbon dioxide we emitted, drawn in by the ship's vents, and converted it through a complex process I didn't understand. I had tried to read a book about it on the last sojourn, but the language was too technical for me. There were only so many things I could master.

"Stay here," she said. "I'm going to get someone."

"Stay here?" I said, but she was already gone.

As I stood on the grate, beads of sweat collected at the small of my back. I could hear her footsteps, but because of the echoes, couldn't tell which direction they were going. Would she bring back a horde of renegades to finish the work she had begun during the attack? Or was she sincere in saying that she no longer wanted to kill me? I had walked into this situation with so little regard for my own safety, and I wasn't even sure why, except that I didn't want to watch the execution of an innocent when there were so many guilty hidden away.

When I heard the scrape-scrape-scrape of feet on metal stairs, I turned to see a tall, lean older woman loping toward me. Her long hair shone like the side of a transport floater. I recognized her from the picture next to Teka's bed.

"Hello, Miss Noavek," she said. "My name is Zosita Surukta."

Zosita wore the same clothes as her daughter, the pant legs rolled up to expose her ankles. There were deep lines in her forehead from a lifetime of scowling. Something about her reminded me of my own mother, poised and elegant and dangerous. It wasn't easy to intimidate me, but Zosita did. My shadows traveled faster than usual, like breath, like blood.

"Do I know you from somewhere?" I said. "Your name sounds familiar."

Zosita cocked her head like a bird. "I'm not sure how I could manage to make the acquaintance of Cyra Noavek before now."

I didn't quite believe her. There was something about her smile.

"Teka told you why I'm here?" I said.

"Yes," Zosita said. "Though she doesn't yet know what I will do next, which is to turn myself in."

"When I asked her for a name," I said, swallowing hard, "I didn't think it would be her mother's—"

"We are all prepared to face the consequences of our actions," Zosita said. "I will take full responsibility for the attack, and it will be believable, since I am a Shotet exile. I used to teach Shotet children how to speak Othyrian."

Some of the older Shotet still knew other languages, from before it was illegal to speak them. There was nothing my father or Ryzek could do about that—you couldn't force a person to unlearn something. I knew some of them taught classes, and that doing so could earn a person exile, but I had never thought I would meet one.

She tilted her head, to the other side this time.

"It was, of course, my voice that spoke over the intercom," Zosita added.

"You . . ." I cleared my throat. "You know Ryzek's going to execute you. Publicly."

"I am aware of that, Miss Noavek."

"Okay." I winced as the currentshadows spread. "Are you prepared to endure an interrogation?"

"I assumed he wouldn't need to interrogate me if I came of my own accord." She raised her eyebrows.

"He's concerned about the exile colony. He'll want to get whatever information he can out of you before he . . ." The word *execute* stuck in my throat.

"Kills me," Zosita said. "My, my, Miss Noavek. You can't even say the words? Are you so soft?"

Her eyes shifted to the armor that covered my marked arm.

"No," I snapped.

"It's not an insult," Zosita said, a little more gently. "Soft hearts make the universe worth living in."

Unexpectedly, I thought of Akos, whispering an apology in Thuvhesit, instinctively, when he brushed past me in the kitchen. I had played his gentle words over and over in my mind that night, like it was music I couldn't get out of my head. It came to me just as easily now.

"I know what it's like to lose a mother," I said. "I don't wish it on anyone, even renegades I hardly know."

Zosita let out a little laugh, shaking her head.

"What?" I said, defensive.

"I . . . celebrated your mother's passing," she said. I went cold. "As I celebrated your father's, and would have celebrated your brother's. Even yours, perhaps." She ran her fingers over the metal railing beside her. I imagined her daughter's fingerprints, pressed there earlier minutes ago, now wiped clean by her touch. "It is a strange thing to realize that your worst enemies can be loved by their families."

You didn't know my mother, I wanted to snarl. As if it mattered, now or ever, what this woman thought of Ylira Noavek. But Zosita was already half faded in my mind, like her own shadow. Marching, in this moment, toward her own doom. And for what? For a well-aimed blow against my brother? Two renegades had fallen to Vas in that attack. Had it been worth *their* lives?

"Is it really worth it?" I said, frowning. "Losing your life for this?"

She was still smiling that strange smile.

"After I fled Shotet, your brother summoned what remained of my family to his home," she said. "I had meant to send for my children when I reached a safe place, but he got to them first. He killed my eldest son, and he took my daughter's eye, for crimes they had no part in." She laughed again. "And you see, you aren't even shocked. You have seen him do worse, no doubt, and his father before him. Yes, it is worth it. And it was worth it to the two who died trying to take down your brother's steward. I don't imagine you can understand."

For a long time we stood, with just the hum of the pipes and distant footsteps to break the silence. I was too confused, too tired, to hide the wincing and flinching as my currentgift did its work.

"To answer your question, yes, I can endure an interrogation," Zosita said. "Can you tell lies?" She smirked again. "I suppose that's a silly question. *Will* you tell lies?"

I hesitated.

When had I become the sort of person who helped renegades? She had just told me that she would have celebrated my death. At least Ryzek wanted to keep me alive—what would the renegades do to me, if they managed to overthrow my brother?

Somehow, I didn't care.

"'I tell lies better than I tell truths,'" I said. It was a quote from some poetry I had read on the side of a building with Otega on one of our excursions. *I am a Shotet. I am sharp as broken glass, and just as fragile. I tell lies better than I tell truths. I see all of the galaxy and never catch a glimpse of it.*

"Let us go tell some, then," Zosita said.

CHAPTER 19 | AKOS

AKOS BENT OVER THE pot, resting on a burner in his little room on the sojourn ship, and breathed in some of the yellow fumes. Everything in front of him blurred, and his head dropped, heavy, toward the countertop. Just for a tick, before he caught himself.

Strong enough, then, he thought. *Good.*

He'd had to ask Cyra to get him some sendes leaf to strengthen the drug, so it would work faster. And it had worked—he had tested it the night before, dropping asleep so soon after swallowing it that the book he was reading slid right out of his hands.

He turned off the flames to let the elixir cool, then jerked to attention at the sound of a knock. He checked the clock. In Thuvhe, he'd been more aware of the world's rhythms, dark in the Deadening time and bright in the Awakening, the way the day closed like a shutting eye. Here, without the sunset and sunrise to guide him, he was always checking. It was the seventeenth hour. Time for Jorek.

The corridor guard was there when he opened the door, looking critical. Jorek was behind him.

"Kereseth," the guard said. "This one says he's here to see you?"

"Yes," Akos said.

"Didn't think you could receive visitors," the guard said with a sneer. "Not your quarters, are they?"

"My name is Jorek *Kuzar*," Jorek said, leaning hard into his surname. "So. Get out of his face."

The guard looked over Jorek's mechanic uniform, eyebrows raised.

"Go easy on him, *Kuzar*," Akos said. "He's got the world's most boring job: protecting Cyra Noavek."

Akos went back to his narrow room, which was giving off a leafy, malty smell. Medicinal. Akos dipped a finger in the mixture to test its heat. Still warm, but now cool enough to put in a vial. He wiped the potion off on his pants, not wanting it to absorb through his skin. He searched the drawers for a clean vessel.

Jorek was standing just inside the doorway. Staring. His hand hanging off the back of his neck, like always.

"What?" Akos said. He got out a dropper and touched it to the potion.

"Nothing, it's just . . . this isn't what I expected Cyra Noavek's room to look like," Jorek said.

Akos grunted a little—it wasn't what he'd expected, either— as he squeezed the yellow elixir from the dropper into the vial.

"You really *don't* sleep in the same bed," Jorek said.

Cheeks hot, Akos scowled at him. "No. Why?"

"Rumors." Jorek shrugged. "I mean, you do live together. Touch each other."

"I help her with her pain," Akos said.

"And you're fated to die for the Noaveks."

"Thanks for the reminder; I'd almost forgotten," Akos snapped. "Did you want my help, or not?"

"Yeah. Sorry." Jorek cleared his throat. "So, same plan for this one?"

They had already done this once. Jorek had dosed Suzao with a sleeping potion so he would collapse in the middle of breakfast. Now Suzao was on edge, and searching for whoever had drugged him and embarrassed him in front of everybody. Akos figured it wouldn't take much to make Suzao angry enough to challenge him to fight to the death—Suzao wasn't exactly a reasonable man— but he didn't want to take chances, so he was having Jorek drug his dad again, just to be sure. Hopefully this would send Suzao on a rampage, and after the scavenge, Akos could confess to being behind all the drugging, and fight him in the arena.

"Two days before the scavenge, slip it into his medicine," Akos said. "Leave the door to his quarters cracked so it looks like some- one came in from outside, or else he might suspect you."

"Right." Jorek took the vial from Akos, testing the cork with his thumb. "And after that . . ."

"It's under control," Akos said. "After the scavenge, I'll tell him I'm the one who's been drugging him, he'll challenge me, and I'll . . . end it. The first day arena challenges are legal again. Okay?"

"Okay." Jorek bit down hard on his lip. "Good."

"Your mom okay?"

"Um . . ." Jorek looked away, at Cyra's rumpled sheets and the burnstone lanterns strung together over the bed. "She'll make it, yeah."

"Good," Akos said. "You'd better go."

Jorek put the vial in his pocket. It seemed to Akos like he

didn't really want to go—he dawdled by the end of the counter, skimming it with a fingertip that likely came away sticky. Neither Akos nor Cyra cared all that much for scrubbing.

When Jorek finally opened the door, Eijeh and Vas were in the hallway, about to come in.

Eijeh's hair was long enough now to be tied back, and his face was bony—and *old*, like he was ten seasons Akos's senior instead of two. At the sight of him Akos felt a powerful urge to grab him and run. No plan for what he might do after that, of course, because they were on a city-size spaceship on the galaxy's edge, but he wanted to anyway. Wanted a lot of things he would never get, these days.

"Jorek," Vas said. "How interesting, running into you here. What's your business?"

"Akos and I have been sparring together," Jorek said, without hesitating. He was a good liar—Akos figured he had to be, growing up in his family, with all *these* people around. "Just checking if he would go for another round."

"Sparring." Vas laughed a little. "With Kereseth? Really?"

"Everyone needs hobbies," Akos said, like it didn't matter. "Maybe tomorrow, Jorek. Brewing something."

Jorek waved, and walked away. Fast. Akos waited until he turned the corner before turning back to Eijeh and Vas.

"Did Mother teach you to do that?" Eijeh said, nodding to the yellow fumes still wafting from the burner.

"Yes." Akos was already flushed and shaking, though he had no reason to be scared of his own brother. "*Mom* taught me." Eijeh had never called her "Mother" in his life. That was a word for snotty Shissa kids, or for the Shotet—not for children of Hessa.

"So kind of her to prepare you for what awaited you. It's a shame she didn't feel the need to do that with me." Eijeh stepped into Akos's room, running his fingers over the taut sheets, the even stack of books. Marking them in a way that wouldn't erase. He drew the knife at his side, and spun it on his palm, catching it with his thumb. It would have struck Akos as menacing if he hadn't seen Ryzek do it so many times.

"Maybe she didn't think this future would come to be." He didn't believe it. But he didn't know what else to say.

"She did. I know she did. I saw her speak of it in a vision."

Eijeh had never talked about his visions with Akos, had never gotten the chance. Akos couldn't imagine it. The future intruding on his present. So many possibilities it was dizzying. Seeing his family but not knowing if the images would come to be. Not being able to speak to them.

Not that it seemed to matter to Eijeh anymore.

"Well," he said. "We should go home and ask her about it."

"I'm doing just fine here," Eijeh said. "I suspect you are, too, judging by these . . . accommodations."

"You talk like him now," Akos said. "You realize that, right? You talk like *Ryzek Noavek*, the man who killed Dad. Hate Mom if you want, but you can't possibly hate Dad."

Eijeh's eyes went hazy. Not quite blank, but far, far away, instead. "I don't— He was always at work. Never at home."

"He was home all the time." Akos spat out the words like they had rotted. "He made dinner. He checked our homework. He told stories. You don't remember?"

But he knew the answer to his own question. It was in Eijeh's blank eyes. Of course, *of course* Ryzek had taken Eijeh's memories of their dad—he had to have been so horrified by his own father that he'd stolen theirs instead.

Suddenly Akos's hands were in fists in Eijeh's shirt, and he was shoving his brother against the wall, knocking over a row of vials. He looked so small between Akos's hands; he was so light it was easy to lift him. It was that, more than his slack surprise, that made Akos let go as quick as he'd grabbed him.

When did I *get so big?* he thought, staring at his thick knuckles. Long fingers, like his dad's, but thicker. Good for hurting people.

"She's taught you her brutality." Eijeh straightened his shirt. "If I don't remember something, do you think you can shake it out of me?"

"If I could, I'd have tried it already." Akos stepped back. "I would do anything to make you remember him." He turned away, running his hand over the back of his neck like Jorek always did. He couldn't look at Eijeh anymore, couldn't look at either of the men standing in his quarters. "Why did you come here? Did you want something?"

"We came here with two purposes," Eijeh said. "First, there is an iceflower blend that promotes clear thinking. I need it to crystallize some of my visions. I thought you might know how to make it."

"So Ryzek doesn't have your currentgift yet."

"I think he's satisfied with my work thus far."

"You're kidding yourself if you think he'll settle for trusting you over just taking your power for himself," Akos said, quiet. Bracing himself against the counter, because his legs felt so weak. "If it even works that way. And as for your iceflower blend . . . well. I'll never give you something that will make Ryzek Noavek wage war against Thuvhe. I would sooner die."

"Such venom," Vas said. When Akos looked at him, Vas was tapping his fingertip against the point of a knife.

He'd almost forgotten Vas was there, listening. Akos's heart hacked like a scythe in his chest at the sound of his voice. All he could see when he blinked was Vas wiping his dad's blood off on his pants on the way out of their house in Thuvhe.

Vas moved closer to the burner to breathe in the—now fading—yellow fumes. He stayed bent for a tick, then whipped around with his knife drawn and pressed the point to Akos's throat. Akos forced himself to stay still, heart still scythe-like. The point of the blade was cold.

"My cousin was drugged recently," Vas said.

"I don't keep track of your cousins," Akos replied.

"I bet you keep track of this one," Vas said. "Suzao Kuzar. He was there when your father breathed his last."

Akos glanced at Eijeh. Hoping—for what? For his brother to defend him? For a reaction to Vas talking about their dad's death like it was nothing?

"Cyra's an insomniac," Akos said, hands fidgeting at his sides. "It takes a strong potion to make her sleep. That's what I'm making it for."

The knife point dug into Akos's skin, right over the scar Ryzek had given him.

"Vas," Eijeh said, and he sounded a little terse. *Nervous?* Akos thought. But it was a foolish hope. "You can't kill him, Ryzek won't allow it. So stop playing at it."

Vas grunted, and took the knife away.

Akos's body ached as it relaxed. "Is there some kind of Shotet holiday today where you visit the people you hate to make them miserable?" He wiped at the cold sweat on the back of his neck. "Well, I'm not celebrating. Leave me alone."

"No, but your presence has been requested to witness the interrogation of a confessed renegade," Vas said. "Along with Cyra's."

"What use would I be at an interrogation?" Akos said.

Vas tilted his head, a smile creeping across his face. "You were initially brought here to bring relief to Cyra on a regular basis. I assume that is the use you will be put to."

"Right," Akos said. "I'm sure that's the reason."

Vas sheathed his knife—he probably knew as well as Akos did that he wouldn't need it to get Akos to do what he said. After all, they were on a ship. In space.

Akos stuffed his feet into his boots and followed Vas out, Eijeh falling into step behind him. The potion he had made would keep until he got back, stable now that it was cooling. Ornery while heating, though, his mom had liked to say.

People gave Vas a wide berth in the more crowded hallways, not even daring to look his way. They looked at Akos, though. It was almost like being Thuvhesit marked him. It was in his casual chewing of hushflower petals, stowed in his pockets; his careful heel-toe gait, used to slipping on ice; the way he wore his shirts buttoned up to his throat instead of open across his collarbone.

Eijeh's gait was now as heavy as any Shotet's, his shirt unbuttoned under his Adam's apple.

Akos hadn't been to this part of the ship before. The floors turned from hard metal grates to polished wood. He felt like he was back in Noavek manor, swallowed up by dark paneling and shifty fenzu light. Footsteps echoing down the corridor, Vas led them to a tall door, and soldiers parted to let them by.

The room beyond was as dim as the Weapons Hall where he had lost Eijeh to Ryzek's gift. The floors shone, and the far wall was all windows, showing a faint curl of the currentstream as the ship turned away from it. Ryzek stood looking out at it, his hands clasped behind his back. Behind him was a woman bound to a chair. Cyra was nearby, too, and she didn't look at Akos when he went in, which was itself a warning. The door slammed behind him, and he stayed right next to it.

"Clarify for me, Cyra, how it is that you came across this traitor," Ryzek was saying to Cyra.

"When the attack occurred, I recognized the voice that came on over the intercom. I still don't know from where," Cyra said, arms crossed. "Maybe the loading bay. But I knew I could find her by her voice. So I listened. And I found her."

"And you said nothing about this endeavor?" Ryzek frowned, not at his sister, but at the renegade woman, who stared back. "Why?"

"I thought you would laugh at me," Cyra said. "That you would think I was deluding myself."

"Well," Ryzek said, "I probably would have. Yet here we are."

His tone was not what Akos expected from someone who had just gotten what he wanted. He was downright terse.

"Eijeh." Akos shuddered to hear his brother's name in his enemy's mouth. "Does this change the future we discussed?"

Eijeh closed his eyes. His nostrils flared like their mom's sometimes did when she was focusing on a prophecy. Copying her, probably, unless oracles needed to breathe really hard through their noses for some reason. Akos had no idea, but without meaning to, he was pressing toward his brother, right up against Vas's arm, which stayed girder-firm.

"Eijeh," Akos said. After all, he had to try, didn't he? "Eijeh, don't."

But Eijeh was already answering: "The future holds firm."

"Thank you," Ryzek said. He bent over next to the renegade. "Where, Zosita Surukta, have you been all these seasons, exactly?"

"Adrift," Zosita said. "I never found the exiles, if that's what you're really asking."

Still bent, Ryzek looked Cyra over, looked at the inky streaks on her arms. She was hunched, a hand clutching at her head.

"Cyra." Ryzek pointed at Zosita. "Let's figure out if this woman tells the truth."

"No," Cyra said, breathless. "We've talked about this. I won't—I can't—"

"You can't?" Ryzek leaned in closer to her face, stopping just short of touching her. "She defames this family, she weakens our position, she rallies our enemies, and you say you can't? I am your brother and the sovereign of Shotet. You can—and you will—do what I say, do you understand?"

Darkness crowded the gold-brown of her skin. The shadows were like a new system of nerves or veins in her body. She made a choking sound. Akos felt choked, too, but he didn't move, couldn't possibly help her with Vas standing in his path.

"No!" The scream tore from her, and she reached for Ryzek, fingers bent into claws. Ryzek tried to shove her away, but she was too fast, too strong; the currentshadows rushed to her hand like a surge of blood to a wound, and Ryzek screamed. Writhed. Collapsed to his knees.

Vas ran at her, wrenched her away, and threw her to the side.

From the ground, she glared at her brother and spat, "Take my eye, take my fingers, take whatever you want. I won't."

For a while, as Cyra cringed at the pain burned into her body by the current, Ryzek just stood there looking at her. Then he flicked his first two fingers at Akos in a gesture that meant "come." And there wasn't much point in defying him, Akos knew. He'd get what he wanted one way or another. Akos was starting to understand why Cyra had spent so many seasons just following his orders. At a certain point, defying him just seemed like a waste of time.

"I thought you might say that," Ryzek said. "Vas, hold on to my sister, please."

Vas grabbed Cyra by the arms and set her on her feet. Her eyes found Akos's, wide with terror.

"I may have left you to your own devices for a time," Ryzek said. "But I did not stop paying attention, Cyra."

Ryzek went to the side of the room, brushing a wall panel with his fingers. It slid back to reveal a wall of weapons, like the one in Noavek manor, but smaller. *Probably just his favorites*, Akos thought, feeling detached from his own body as Ryzek chose a long, thin rod. At his touch, the current wrapped around the metal, dark streams so like the ones that plagued Cyra.

"You see, I've noticed something peculiar, and I'd like to see if my hypothesis is correct," Ryzek said. "If it is, it will solve a problem before it really even becomes a problem."

He twisted the notches in the rod's handle, and the current got denser. Darker. Not a lethal weapon, Akos noted, but one designed for causing pain.

Cyra's currentshadows flickered and fluttered, like flames caught in a draft. Ryzek laughed.

"It's almost indecent," he said, putting a heavy hand on Akos's shoulder. Akos resisted the urge to shake him off. It would only make things worse. And it was just now dawning on him that the rod was for him. Maybe it was the whole reason he had been brought here—to make Cyra cooperate again. To become Ryzek's new tool of control.

"You may want to just give up now," Ryzek said to him in a low voice. "And get on the ground."

"Eat shit," Akos replied in Thuvhesit.

But of course, Ryzek had an answer to that. He slammed the rod into Akos's back. Pain screeched through him. Acid. Fire. Akos screamed into his teeth.

Stay on your feet, he thought. *Stay—*

Ryzek hit him again, this time over his right side, and he cried out again. Beside him, Cyra sobbed, but Akos was watching Eijeh, passive as he looked out the window. Almost like he didn't know what was going on. Ryzek hit him a third time, and his knees gave out, but he was quiet now. Sweat rolled down the back of his neck, and all around him, everything swayed.

Eijeh had flinched that time.

Another blow, and Akos fell forward onto his hands. He and Cyra moaned at the same time.

"I want to know what she knows about the exiles," Ryzek said to Cyra, breathless. "Before tomorrow's execution."

Cyra wriggled out of Vas's grasp, and went to Zosita, who was still bound to the chair by her wrists. Zosita nodded at Cyra like she was giving permission.

Cyra brought her hands to Zosita's head. Akos saw, through half-focused eyes, the dark webs on the backs of Cyra's hands, and Zosita's contorted face, and Ryzek's satisfied smile. Darkness crowded the corners of his vision, and he tried to breathe through the pain.

Zosita screaming. Cyra screaming. Their voices ran together.

Then he blacked out.

He woke with Cyra at his side.

"Come on." Her arm was across his shoulders. She hoisted him to his feet. "Come on, let's go. Let's go."

He blinked slowly. Zosita was breathing in fits and starts, hair covering her face. Vas was standing nearby, looking bored. Eijeh was crouched in the corner, his head buried in his arms. Nobody stopped them from stumbling out of the room. Ryzek had gotten what he wanted.

They made it to Cyra's room. She dropped Akos at the edge of her bed, then stormed around the room, gathering towels, ice, painkiller. Frantically, tears running down her face. The room still smelled malty from the potion he'd brewed earlier.

"Cyra. Did she tell him anything?"

"No. She's a good liar," she replied as she fought to uncork the vial of painkiller with trembling hands. "You'll never be safe again. You know that? Neither of us will."

She got the stopper out, and touched it to his mouth, though he could easily have grabbed it himself. He didn't point that out, just parted his lips to swallow it.

"I was never safe. You were never safe." He didn't understand why she was so rattled. It wasn't like Ryzek doing something terrible was a new thing. "I don't understand why he made a point to use *me*—"

Her legs brushed his as she came to stand between his knees. They were almost the same height this way, with him perched on her high bed. And she was close, like she sometimes was when they fought, laughing in his face because she'd knocked him down, but that was different. Completely different.

She wasn't laughing. She smelled familiar, like the herbs she burned to clear the room of food smells, like the spray she used in her hair to smooth its tangles. She brought a hand to his shoulder, then trailed trembling fingers along his collarbone, down his sternum. Pressed a gentle hand to his chest. Didn't look at his face.

"You," she whispered, "are the only person he could possibly hold over me now."

She touched his chin to steady it as she kissed him. Her mouth was warm, and wet with tears. Her teeth scored his bottom lip as she pulled away.

Akos didn't breathe. He wasn't sure he could remember how.

"Don't worry," she said softly. "I won't do that again."

She backed away, and shut herself in the bathroom.

CHAPTER 20 | CYRA

I ATTENDED ZOSITA SURUKTA'S execution the next day, as I was supposed to. It was a crowded, loud event, the first celebration that had been allowed since the Sojourn Festival. I stood off to the side, with Vas, Eijeh, and Akos, as Ryzek gave a long speech about loyalty and the strength of Shotet unity, the envy of the galaxy, the tyranny of the Assembly. Yma stood at his side, her hands on the railing, her fingertips tapping out a lilting rhythm.

When Ryzek dragged the knife across Zosita's throat, I felt like crying, but I suppressed my tears. Everyone in the crowd roared as Zosita's body fell, and I closed my eyes.

When I opened them, Yma's hands were trembling on the railing. Ryzek wore a streak of Zosita's blood. And far off, in the crowd that watched, Teka held a hand over her mouth.

As Zosita's blood spread across the floor, as Akos's father's blood had, and so many others, I felt the wrongness of her death like an ill-fitting shirt I could not remove.

It was a relief, to still be able to feel that.

§

All across the loading bay were piles of gray jumpsuits, arranged by size. From where I stood, they looked like a line of boulders. The jumpsuits were waterproof, designed specifically for sojourns to Pitha. There were piles of waterproof masks along the back wall too, to keep the rain from our scavengers' eyes. Old supplies, from some other sojourn, but sufficient.

Ryzek's sojourn craft, with its sleek, golden wings, waited by the release hatch. It would take him, me, Yma, Vas, Eijeh, Akos, and a few others to Pitha's surface to play political games with the Pithar leadership. He wanted to establish "friendly relations"—an alliance. Military assistance, too, surely. Ryzek had a talent for this that my father never had. He must have gotten it from my mother.

"We should go," Akos said, from over my shoulder. He held himself stiffly today, cringing when he had to lift a cup to his lips, crouching rather than bending to pick things up.

I shivered at his voice alone. I thought that when I kissed him, days ago, it would free me from feelings like those, by taking away the mystery of what it would be like, but it had only made things worse. Now I knew what he felt like—what he tasted like—and I ached with want.

"I guess so," I said, and we descended the steps to the loading bay floor, shoulder to shoulder. Ahead of us, the small transport ship gleamed like sunstruck glass under the harsh lights. The polished side bore the Shotet character for *Noavek*.

Despite its ostentatious outsides, the inside of the ship was as simple as any other transport vessel: at the back was an enclosed bathroom stall and a tiny galley; lining the walls were jump seats with seat belts; and up front, in the ship's nose, was navigation.

My father had taught me to fly, one of the only activities we ever did together. I had worn thick gloves so my currentgift wouldn't interfere with the ship's mechanisms. I had been too small for the chair, so he had gotten a cushion for me to sit on. He was not a patient teacher—he screamed at me more than once—but when I got it right, he always said, "Good," with a firm nod, like he was hammering the compliment in place.

He died when I was eleven seasons old, on a sojourn. Only Ryzek and Vas had been with him at the time—they were attacked by a band of pirates and had to fight their way out. Ryzek and Vas returned from the conflict—with the eyes of their vanquished enemies in a jar, no less—but Lazmet Noavek did not.

Vas fell into step beside me as I walked toward the ship. "I have been instructed to remind you to put on a good show for the Pithar."

"What, was I born a Noavek just yesterday?" I snapped. "I know how to handle myself."

"Noavek you may be, but you have become increasingly erratic," Vas said.

"Go away, Vas," I said, too tired to come up with another barb. Thankfully, he heeded me, striding toward the front of the ship, where my cousin Vakrez stood with one of the maintenance workers. A flash of bright hair alerted me to Teka—not working on our ship, of course, but off to the side with her hands buried in a panel of wires. She didn't have any tools in hand—she was just pinching each wire in turn, her eyes closed.

I hesitated for a moment. I could feel myself stirring to action, though I wasn't sure exactly what that action would be. I just knew that I had spent too long standing still while others warred around me, and it was time to move.

"I'll meet you in the ship," I said to Akos. "I want to speak to Zosita's daughter for a moment."

He hesitated with a hand near my elbow, like he was about to comfort me. Then he seemed to change his mind, shoving his hand in his pocket and shuffling toward the ship.

When I drew closer to Teka, she pulled her hand from the tangle of wires, and marked something on the small screen balanced on her knees.

"The wires never shock you?" I said.

"No," she said without looking at me. "Feels like humming, unless they're busted. What do you want?"

"A meeting," I said. "With your friends. You know which ones."

"Listen," she said, finally turning. "You basically forced me to turn in my own mother, and then your brother killed her in front of everyone not two days ago." Her eye was red with tears. "What about that situation makes you think you can ask me for anything?"

"I'm not asking," I said. "I'm telling you what I want, and I think the people you know might want it, too. Do whatever you like, but it's not really about you, is it?"

The patch she wore over her eye was thicker than usual, and the skin that showed above it had a sheen, like she had spent the day sweating. Maybe she had; the quarters of maintenance workers were close to the churning machinery that kept the ship running.

"How are we supposed to trust you?" she said in a low voice.

"You're desperate, and so am I," I said. "Desperate people make stupid decisions all the time."

The hatch on the port side of the transport vessel opened, spotting the floor with light.

"I'll see what I can do," she said. She jerked her chin toward the ship. "Do you even do anything useful in that thing? Or just make nice with politicians?" She shook her head. "Don't suppose you royals go on scavenges, do you?"

"I do, actually," I said, defensive. But it was stupid to pretend, with someone like her, that my life had been anything but privileged by comparison to hers. After all, she was the one-eyed girl with no family left to speak of, who lived in a closet.

Teka grunted a little, then turned back to the wires.

Akos was looking at Vas—sitting across from us—like he was about to lunge at his throat. Two seats down from him was Yma, dressed elegantly as always, her long, dark skirt arranged to cover her ankles. She looked like she was having tea at a sovereign's breakfast rather than strapped into a hard chair on a spaceship. Eijeh was in the seat closest to the toilet, his eyes closed. There were others between Yma and Eijeh: our cousin Vakrez and his husband, Malan, and Suzao Kuzar—his wife was too ill to make the journey, he claimed. And beside the captain, Rel, was Ryzek.

"What was the planet the Examiners actually selected, based on the current's movement?" Yma called out to Ryzek. "Ogra?"

"Yes, Ogra," Ryzek said with a laugh, over his shoulder. "As if that would have done us any good."

"Sometimes the current chooses," Yma said, leaning her head back. "And sometimes we do."

It almost sounded like wisdom.

The engines hummed at the touch of a few buttons, then Rel pulled the lever for the hover mechanism and the ship lifted from the ground, shuddering a little. The loading bay doors opened, displaying the northern hemisphere of the water planet beneath us.

It was covered entirely by clouds, the whole planet embroiled in a storm. The cities—obscured from view now—were buoyant, built to shift with the rising and falling water levels, and to withstand strong winds and rain and lightning. Rel urged the ship forward, and we shot into space, for a moment clutched in the empty embrace of darkness.

It took no time at all for us to enter the atmosphere. The sudden pressure made me feel like my body was collapsing in on itself; I heard someone in the back of the ship retching. I clenched my teeth and forced myself to keep my eyes open. The descent was my favorite part, when huge stretches of land opened up beneath us—or in this case, water, since with the exception of a few soggy landmasses, this place was entirely submerged.

A gasp of pleasure escaped me when we broke through the cloud layer. Rain drummed on the roof, and Rel turned on the visualizer so he didn't have to try to peer through the droplets. But past the drops and visualizer screen, I saw huge, frothy waves, blue-gray-green, and globular glass buildings adrift on the surface, enduring the crash of the water.

I couldn't help it—I glanced at Akos, whose face was frozen in shock.

"At least it's not Trella," I said to him, hoping to bring him back to himself. "The skies are full of birds. Huge mess when they all hit the windshield. Had to scrape them off with a knife."

"You did that yourself, did you?" Yma said to me. "How charming."

"Yes, you'll find I have a high tolerance for disgusting things," I replied. "I employ it regularly. I'm sure you do, too."

Yma closed her eyes rather than answer. But before she did, I thought I saw her glance at Ryzek. One of the disgusting things she tolerated, I was sure.

I had to admire her talent for survival.

We shot over the waves, the ship battered somewhat by the powerful wind, for a long time. From above, the waves looked like wrinkled skin. Most people found Pitha monotonous, but I loved how it mimicked the sprawl of space.

We flew above one of the many floating trash piles the Shotet would soon land on to scavenge. It was larger than I had imagined, the size of a city sector at least, and covered with heaps of metal in all different shades. I wanted more than anything to land on it, to sort through whatever wet artifacts it held for something of value. But we flew on.

The capital city of Pitha, Sector 6—the Pithar were not famous for their poetic names, to say the least—floated on the gray-black seas near the planet's equator. The buildings looked like bubbles adrift, though they were anchored with a vast, submerged support structure that, I had heard, was a miracle of engineering, upheld by the best-salaried maintenance workers in all the galaxy. Rel guided our ship to the landing pad, and through the windows I watched a mechanical structure extend toward us from one of the nearby buildings—a tunnel, it seemed, to keep us from getting soaked through. A shame. I wanted to feel the rain.

Akos and I followed the others—at a distance—from the ship, leaving only Rel in our wake. At the front of our group, Ryzek, Yma at his side, greeted a Pithar dignitary, who gave him a curt bow in return.

"What language would you prefer we conduct our business in?" the Pithar said in Shotet so clumsy I barely understood him. He had a thin white mustache that looked more like mold than hair, and wide, dark eyes.

"We are all fluent in Othyrian," Ryzek said testily. The Shotet had a reputation for only speaking our own language, thanks to my father's—and now my brother's—policy of keeping our people ignorant of the galaxy's true workings, but Ryzek had always been sensitive about the insinuation that he wasn't multilingual, as if it meant people thought he was stupid.

"That is a relief, sir," the dignitary said, now in Othyrian. "I am afraid the subtleties of the Shotet language escape me. Allow me to show you all to your sleeping quarters."

As we passed through the temporary tunnel, beneath the drumming of the rain, I felt a powerful urge to grab a nearby Pithar and beg them to get me out of here, away from Ryzek and his threats and the memory of what he had done to my only friend.

But I couldn't leave Akos here, and Akos's eyes were currently fixed on the back of his brother's head.

There had been four sojourns between this one and the one that had claimed my father's life. The last one had taken us to Othyr, the wealthiest planet in the galaxy, and there, Ryzek had established the new Shotet policy of diplomacy. Formerly, my mother had taken care of that, charming the leaders of each planet we visited while my father led the scavenge. But after her death, Lazmet had discovered he had no talent for charm—surprising no one—and diplomacy had fallen by the wayside, creating tension between us and the rest of the planets in the galaxy. Ryzek sought to ease that tension planet by planet, smile by smile.

Othyr had welcomed us with a dinner, every inch of their chancellor's dining room gilded, from the plates to the paint on the walls to the cloth that covered the table. They had chosen that room, the chancellor's wife had said, for how the color would complement our dark blue formal armor. Graciously, she had also admitted to its ostentatiousness, an elegantly calculated maneuver I had admired even then. The next morning they had treated us all to a session with their personal physician, knowing they possessed the best medical technology in the galaxy. I had declined. I had had enough of doctors for a lifetime.

I knew from the start that Pitha's welcome would not be as frivolous as Othyr's. Every culture worshipped something: Othyr, comfort; Ogra, mystery; Thuvhe, iceflowers; Shotet, the current; Pitha, practicality, and so on. They were relentless in their pursuit of the most durable, flexible, multipurpose materials and structures. The chancellor—Natto was her surname, and I had forgotten her given name, since she was never called by it—lived in a large but utilitarian subterranean building made of glass. She was elected by popular vote on Pitha.

The room I was sharing with Akos—the dignitary had given us a suggestive look when he offered it to me, and I had ignored him—opened up to the water, where shadowy creatures moved just out of sight, and everything looked calm, but that was its only decoration. The walls were otherwise plain, the sheets starched and white. A cot set up in the corner stood on metal legs with rubber feet.

The Pithar had arranged not a fine dinner, but what I would have called a ball if there had been dancing involved. Instead, there were just groups of people standing around in what I assumed was the Pithar version of finery: stiff, waterproof fabrics in surprisingly bright colors—all the better to spot them in the rain, maybe—and not a skirt or dress to be found. I regretted, suddenly, my mother's dress, which fell to my toes, black and high-necked, to disguise most of my currentshadows.

The room was full of murmurs. Moving between each group was a servant with a tray in hand, offering drinks or bites of food. Their synchronized movements were the closest thing to dance here.

"Quiet in here," Akos said softly, his fingers curling around my elbow. I shivered, trying to ignore it. *He's just dulling your pain, that's all it is, nothing has changed, everything is the same as it always was. . . .*

"Pitha isn't known for its dances," I said. "Or any form of combat, either."

"They're not your favorite, then, I take it."

"I like to move."

"I've noticed."

I could feel his breath against the side of my neck, though he wasn't that close—my awareness of him was stronger than it had ever been. I tugged my arm free to take the drink the Pithar servant offered.

"What is this?" I said, suddenly aware of my accent. The servant eyed my shadow-stained arm uneasily.

"Its effects are similar to an iceflower blend," the servant replied. "Dulls the senses, lifts the spirits. Sweet and sour, both."

Akos also took one, smiling at the servant as she walked on.

"If it's not made of iceflowers, what's it made of?" he asked. Thuvhesits worshipped iceflowers, after all. What did he know of other substances?

"I don't know. Salt water? Engine grease?" I said. "Try it; I'm sure it won't hurt you."

We both drank. Across the room, Ryzek and Yma were smiling

politely at Chancellor Natto's husband, Vek. His face had a gray-ish cast, and his skin sagged from his bones like it was half liquid. Maybe gravity was stronger here. I certainly felt heavier than usual, though that was probably due to Vas's constant gaze. Making sure I behaved.

I cringed at my half-empty glass. "Disgusting."

"So, I'm curious," Akos said. "How many languages do you actually speak?"

"Really, it's just Shotet, Thuvhesit, Othyrian, and Trellan," I said. "But I know a little Zoldan, some Pithar, and I was working on Ogran before you arrived and distracted me."

His eyebrows lifted.

"What?" I said. "I don't have any friends. It gives me a lot of free time."

"You think you're so difficult to like."

"I know what I am."

"Oh? And what's that?"

"A knife," I said. "A hot poker. A rusty nail."

"You are more than any of those things." He touched my elbow to turn me toward him. I knew I was giving him a strange look, but I couldn't seem to stop. It was just the way my face wanted to be.

"I mean," he said, removing his hand, "it's not like you're going around . . . boiling the flesh of your enemies."

"Don't be stupid," I said. "If I was going to eat the flesh of my enemies, I would roast it, not boil it. Who wants to eat *boiled* flesh? Disgusting."

He laughed, and everything felt a little better.

"Silly me. I clearly wasn't thinking," he said. "I'm sorry to tell you this, but I think you're being summoned by the sovereign."

Sure enough, when I looked at Ryzek, his eyes were on me. He jerked his chin up.

"You didn't bring any poison, did you?" I said without looking away from my brother. "I could try to slip it in his drink."

"Wouldn't give it to you if I did," Akos said. When I gave him an incredulous look, he explained, "He's still the only one who can restore Eijeh. After he does that, I'll poison him with a song on my lips."

"No one does 'single-minded' quite like you, Kereseth," I said. "Your task while I'm gone is to compose your poisoning song so I can hear it when I get back."

"Easy," he said. "'Here I go a-poisoning . . .'"

Smirking, I swallowed the last of my vile Pithar engine grease, handed the glass to Akos, and crossed the room.

"Ah, there she is! Vek, this is my sister, Cyra." Ryzek was wearing his warmest smile, his arm outstretched toward me like he intended to fold me into his side. He didn't, of course, because it would have hurt him—the currentshadows were there to remind him, staining my cheek and the side of my nose. I nodded to Vek, who stared blank-eyed back without greeting.

"Your brother was just explaining the Shotet rationale behind some of the kidnapping reports associated with Shotet 'scavengers' over the past decade," he said. "He said you could vouch for the policy."

Oh he did, did he?

My anger, then, was like dry kindling, quickly ignited. I couldn't find a path through it; I just stared at Ryzek for a few moments. He smiled back at me, still with that kind look in his eyes. Beside him, Yma was also smiling.

"Because of your familiarity with your servant," Ryzek said lightly. "Of course."

Ah, yes. My familiarity with Akos—Ryzek's new tool of control.

"Right," I said. "Well, we don't consider it kidnapping, obviously. The Shotet call it 'Reclaiming' because everyone brought back to the fold speaks the revelatory tongue, the Shotet language, perfectly. No accent, no gaps in vocabulary. You cannot speak the Shotet language that way, so innately, without having Shotet blood. Without belonging to us, in a more significant way. And I have seen that . . . demonstrated."

"In what way?" Vek asked. As he lifted his glass to his lips, I spotted his rings, one for each finger. Each one smooth and otherwise undecorated. I wondered why he even wore them.

"My servant has shown himself to be a natural Shotet," I said. "A good fighter, with a good eye for what makes our people distinct. His ability to adapt to our culture is . . . shocking."

"Surely a sign of what I was telling you, sir," Yma chimed in. "That there is evidence of a cultural, historical memory in Shotet blood that ensures that all so-called 'kidnapped' people—people with the gift of Shotet language—who make it to our land find true belonging there."

She was so good at pretending to be devoted.

"Well," Vek said. "That is an interesting theory."

"We must also account for the past crimes of one of the . . . shall we say, more *influential* planets in the galaxy . . . against our people. Invasion of our territory, kidnapping of our children, violence toward—sometimes even the murder of—our citizens." Ryzek's brow furrowed as if the mere thought pained him. "Certainly this is not the fault of Pitha, to which we have always been kindly disposed. But reparations are certainly in order. From Thuvhe, particularly."

"Yet I have heard rumors that the Shotet are responsible for the death of one of Thuvhe's oracles, and the kidnapping of another," Vek replied, tapping his rings together as he spoke.

"Unfounded," Ryzek replied. "As to the reason the oldest Thuvhesit oracle took her own life, we can't know it. We don't know the reasons for anything the oracles do, do we?"

He was appealing to Vek's Pithar practicality. The oracles held no importance here; they were just madmen shouting over the waves.

Vek tapped his fingers against the glass in his other hand.

"Yes, perhaps we *can* discuss your proposition further," Vek said reluctantly. "There may be room for cooperation between our planet and your . . . nation."

"Nation," Ryzek said with a smile. "Yes, that is all we ask to be called. An independent nation, capable of determining its own future."

"Excuse me," I said, touching Ryzek's arm lightly. I hoped it stung. "I'm going to find another drink."

"Of course," Ryzek said to me. As I turned away, I heard him say to Vek, "Her currentgift gives her constant pain, you know— we are always looking for solutions to improve her functioning. Some days are better than others—"

Gritting my teeth, I kept marching until I was too far away to hear him. I felt like I might be sick. We had come to Pithar because of their advanced weaponry, because Ryzek wanted an alliance. I had just, in some way, helped him make one. And I knew what Ryzek wanted weapons for—to use against Thuvhe, not to "become an independent nation," as he would have Vek believe. How could I face Akos now, knowing I had helped my brother move toward war against his home? I didn't look for him.

I heard a deep rumble, like thunder. First I thought we were—impossibly—hearing the sounds of the storm through the stretch of water that separated us from the surface. Then I saw, through gaps in the crowd, a line of musicians at the front of the room. The overhead lights dimmed everywhere but above their heads. Each of them sat behind a low table, and on each table was one of the intricate instruments I had pointed out to Akos at the Shotet market. But these were much larger and more complex than the one we had seen. They glinted in the low light, waist-high, their iridescent panes half as wide as my palm.

A harsh crack followed the rumble of thunder, a lightning strike. With that, the other musicians began to play, bringing in the tinkling sounds of light rain, the deeper thrum of thicker droplets. The others played the crashing waves, the lapping of water against a nonexistent shore. All around us were the sounds of water, dripping from faucets, gushing from waterfalls. A Pithar woman with black hair standing to my right closed her eyes, swaying on the spot.

Without meaning to, I found Akos in the crowd, still holding two glasses, both now empty. He smiled a little.

I have to get you out of here, I thought, as if he could hear me. *And I will.*

CHAPTER 21 | AKOS

IN A COLD, BLANK room in Pitha's capital, Akos gave up on sleep. He and Cyra had never slept without a door between them before, so Akos hadn't known that she ground her teeth, or that she dreamt all the time, moaning and muttering. He'd spent most of the night with eyes open, waiting for her to settle, only it never happened. He was still too sore to get comfortable anyway.

He had never been in a room so bare. Gray floors gave way to pale walls. The beds had white sheets and no frames. At least there was a window. In the early morning hours, as light came back to the world, he could just barely make out a maze of scaffolding underwater, green slime and supple yellow vines wrapped around it. Holding up the city.

Well, that was something the Pithar and the Thuvhesit had in common, he thought—they lived in places that ought not to exist.

In those early hours, Akos was swallowed up in the question that wouldn't leave him be: Why hadn't he pulled away when Cyra kissed him? It wasn't like she had surprised him—she had leaned in, slow, her hand warm on his chest and pressing, almost like she was pushing him away. But he hadn't moved a muscle. He'd gone over it in his mind again and again.

Maybe, he thought, as he stuck his head under the bathroom faucet to wet his hair, *I even liked it.*

But he was scared to even entertain the notion. It meant the fate that worried at him, the fate that tugged at the strings connecting his heart to Thuvhe and home, was suddenly izits away from his face.

"You're quiet," Cyra said as they made their way to the landing bay side by side. "Did that engine grease you drank last night get to you?"

"No," he said. Somehow it felt wrong to tease her about talking in her sleep, when he knew the kinds of things that likely haunted her. No trifles there. "Just . . . new place, that's all."

"Right, well, I keep burping up sour, so." She pulled a face. "I am not enamored with Pitha, I have to say."

"Except—" he started, about to add something about the concert the night before.

She interrupted him with, "The music. Yes."

His knuckles brushed hers. He jerked away. He was too aware of every touch, now, even though Cyra had promised she wouldn't make another move, and hadn't talked about it since.

They reached the breezeway—not the word Akos would have picked, but there was a sign over the doorway saying what it was—where some of the others were putting on waterproof jumpsuits and boots. Ryzek, Yma, Vas, Suzao, and Eijeh weren't there, but Vakrez and Malan were, Malan sorting through boots to find the right size. He was a small, thin man, with a beard that was just a shadow under his jaw, and bright eyes. An unequal match for Vakrez, the cold military commander who had seen to Akos's Shotet education.

"Cyra," Malan said, nodding as Vakrez eyed Akos. Akos stood up straighter, lifting his chin. He could still hear Vakrez's relentless voice scolding him for slouching, for dragging his feet, for uttering so much as a curse in Thuvhesit.

"Kereseth," Vakrez said. "You look bigger."

"That's because I actually feed him, unlike your barracks kitchen." Cyra thrust a bright green jumpsuit into Akos's arms that was marked *L*. When he unfolded it, it looked nearly as wide as it was tall, but no reason to complain, as long as he didn't get water in his boots.

"Right you are," Malan said in his reedy voice.

"You used to eat there without complaining," Vakrez said, elbowing him.

"Only because I was trying to get you to notice me," Malan said. "Notice I haven't been back there since."

Akos watched Cyra put on her suit to see how she did it. It looked so easy for her that he wondered if she'd been to Pitha before, but he felt odd, asking her questions—acting at all normal—with Vakrez right there. She stepped into the suit and pulled straps he hadn't noticed before tight around her ankles, binding the fabric to her body. She did the same with hidden straps at her wrists, then fastened the suit up to her throat. Hers was as shapeless as his own, built for a person not made spare by the hard life of a Shotet.

"We were planning to join one of the platoons for the scavenge," Vakrez said to Cyra. "But if you prefer that we go out on a separate vessel—"

"No," Cyra said. "I'd rather try to blend in with your soldiers."
No "thank you," no niceties. It was Cyra's way.

Once they were all in suits and strapped into their boots, they
walked the covered tunnel to a ship. Not the one they'd flown in
the day before, but a smaller floater, round, with a domed roof so
the water would slide off as it flew.

Soon enough they were drifting above the waves, which
looked like snowdrifts to Akos, at a squint. They had the same captain they'd had yesterday—Rel was his name—and he pointed out
where they were headed: a huge island, about the size of a city
sector, piled up high with scrap. The Pithar kept their refuse afloat.

At a distance the trash pile looked like a brown-gray lump,
but once they got closer he saw the pieces that made it up: huge
sheets of twisted metal, old rusty girders with pins and screws still
stuck in them, soaked fabric of all different colors, cracked glass
as thick as his hand. Clustered between some of the larger piles
was Vakrez's platoon, all wearing the same color suits they had on.

They touched down behind the platoon, and filed out of the
floater one by one, Rel at the back. The drum of the rain on the
roof gave way to its splatter on the ground. The drops were heavy,
each one a hard tap on Akos's head and shoulders and arms. He
could feel only their temperature on his cheeks. Warm, which was
unexpected.

Someone at the head of the platoon was talking:

"Your job is to spot things that are actually valuable. Newer
current motors and engines, intact scrap metal, broken or discarded weapons. Do not cause trouble, and if you see any native
observers, be courteous and show them to either me or Commander Noavek, who has just joined us. Welcome, sir."

Vakrez nodded to him, and added, "Remember, the reputation of your sovereign, and of Shotet itself, is at stake here. They see us as barbaric and ignorant. You must behave as if that is not the case."

A few of the soldiers laughed, like they weren't sure they ought to, since Vakrez wasn't smiling even a little. Akos wasn't sure the commander's face remembered how to do it.

"Get to it!"

A few soldiers surged ahead to climb the pile right in front of them, made up of floater parts. Akos searched the ones who dawdled behind for faces he knew from training, but it was hard to tell—they wore head-coverings that looked almost like helmets, and visors to protect their eyes from the rain. He and Cyra didn't have them—he kept blinking raindrops into his eyes.

"Helmets," Malan said. "I knew we forgot something. Would you like me to request that one of the soldiers give you theirs, Cyra?"

"No," Cyra said, almost snapping. "I mean . . . no, thank you."

"You Noaveks," Malan said. "How is it that simple words like 'please' and 'thank you' sound so unnatural coming from you?"

"Must be in the blood," Cyra said. "Come on, Akos. I think I see something useful."

She put her hand in his like it was natural. And maybe it should have been, just him relieving her pain, like he was supposed to. But after the way she had touched him in her room on the sojourn ship, fervently, reverently—after that, how could he possibly lay a casual hand on her again? All he could think about was how hard he was squeezing—too hard? Not hard enough?

They walked between two piles of floater pieces, toward a stretch of scrap metal, some of it warm in color, like sun-kissed skin. Akos walked to the edge of the island, where huge girders kept the shape of the man-made land. He wasn't looking for weapons, or scrap, or machines. He was looking for small things that would tell stories: broken toys, old shoes, kitchen utensils.

Cyra crouched next to a bent pole, scraped at the base like it had been the casualty of a collision. When she tugged at it, it just kept coming, knocking over empty cans and cracked pipes. At the end of the pole—now twice as long as Akos was tall—was a tattered flag with a gray background and a circle of symbols in its center.

"Look at this," she said to him, smiling. "This is their old flag, before their acceptance into the Assembly of Nine Planets. It's at least thirty seasons old."

"How has it not disintegrated in the rain?" he asked, pinching the frayed corner.

"Pitha specializes in durable materials—glass that doesn't erode, metal that doesn't rust, fabric that doesn't tear," she said. "Buoyant platforms that can carry whole cities."

"Not fishing line?"

She shook her head. "Not many fish near enough to the surface for traditional fishing. Deep-sea crafts do some of the work—one fish can feed an entire town, I've heard."

"Do you always make a point to know so much about places you hate?"

"As I told you yesterday," she said, "no friends. Too much time. Let's find more slimy relics of the past, shall we?"

He hunted along the edge of the island, searching for . . . well, nothing in particular, really. After a while everything started to look the same, the dull metal just as useful as the shiny stuff, all the fabric blurring into the same color. Near the far edge he saw a half-rotten bird skeleton. It had webbed feet—a swimmer, then— and a beak with a wicked curve.

He heard a shout behind him, and whipped around to make sure Cyra was okay, his bruised ribs protesting. He saw a flash of teeth—she was grinning, calling for one of the others. When he went back to her, he expected to see something shiny, something useful-looking. But it was just more metal. Gray in color. Dull.

"What the—Commander Noavek!" said the soldier who had come to Cyra's side first, her eyes wide behind her rain-streaked visor. Vakrez jogged over.

"I saw a corner of it peeking out, and dug deeper," Cyra said excitedly. "It's a big piece, I think."

He could tell what she meant—the corner of whatever she had found was thick, and back in the pile of junk were glints of the same shade. It looked like the sheet was as tall as the flagpole had been. He didn't understand why they were so excited about it.

"Cy—er, Miss Noavek?" he said to her.

"It's Pitha's most valuable substance," she said in response, tugging wet fabric away from the metal. "Agneto. Strong enough to withstand heavy hits from things like asteroids, holds up well when we pass through the currentstream. For the past ten seasons, it's the only thing we've been using to repair the sojourn ship, but it's a rare find."

Half the platoon had come running, and now everyone was helping Cyra unearth the sheet, most grinning just like she was. Akos stood back as they dug deeper, finally loosing enough of the sheet to get a good grip. Together they dragged it from the rub- ble, then carried it back to the transport vessel, which had a hold under it big enough to carry the agneto.

He didn't know what to make of seeing them all work together, Cyra and Vakrez Noavek right there with common soldiers, like they weren't royalty. Cyra with that look she sometimes wore when they made iceflower blends together and she got something right at last. A kind of pride, he thought, in doing something useful.

It was a good look for her.

As a kid, he'd dreamt of going off-planet. All the kids in Hessa had, because Hessa kids were mostly too poor to ever leave. The Kereseth family was richer than most in Hessa, but they had nothing compared to farm owners in Shissa or Osoc, up north. Still, his dad had promised him that someday he would take him into space, and they could visit another planet. Akos's choice.

The water planet hadn't been his first choice, or even his second. Nobody in Thuvhe knew how to swim, because pretty much all the water they had came in the form of ice. But now he had been to Pitha. He had been in earshot of the pounding waves, had seen the frothy surface from above, had felt his own smallness as he stood on the landing pad with water in every direction, warm rain pounding on his head.

Then almost as soon as he was starting to get used to it, they were gone. He was dripping water on the floor of the floater, holding a vial of rainwater. Cyra had given it to him as they loaded the agneto into the transport—"You may as well have a memento of your first time on another planet," she'd said with a shrug, like it meant nothing. Only there wasn't much that meant nothing to Cyra, Akos was finding.

At first he hadn't seen the point of a memento, because who

would he show it to? He wouldn't be seeing his family again. He was going to die among the Shotet.

But he had to have hope for his brother, at least. Maybe Eijeh could take it back home with him, after Jorek got him out.

Cyra had two fistfuls of old flag in her lap, and though she wasn't smiling, she had a fierce energy in her face, from finding the agneto.

"I take it you did a good thing," Akos said, when he was sure Vakrez and Malan weren't listening.

"Yeah." She nodded, once. "Yeah, I did." After a tick, she added, "I guess it was bound to happen eventually. I was due."

"Your currentshadows aren't as dark," he said, leaning his head back. She was quiet then. Staring at the streaks of darkness—now more gray than black—that coursed over her palm, all the way back to the sojourn ship.

They made it back in good time, all of them soaked through. Some of the other ships had come back from the scavenge early, so there were people in wet clothes milling around everywhere, trading stories. Everybody peeled the—supposedly—waterproof suits off their bodies and dumped them in piles to be cleaned.

"So the Shotet just have a bunch of waterproof clothes lying around?" he said to Cyra as they walked back to her quarters.

"We've been to Pitha before," she said. "Every sovereign has researchers who prepare for every planet in advance, but any-one over a certain age knows how to survive in any environment, essentially. Desert, mountain, ocean, marsh . . ."

"Desert," he said. "I can't even imagine walking on hot sand."

"Maybe someday you will," she said.

His smile fell away. She was right, probably. How many sojourns would he go on before he died for her family? Two, three? Twenty? How many worlds would he walk on?

"That's not what I . . ." she started. She paused. "Life is long, Akos."

"But the fates are certain," he said, echoing his mother. Few fates seemed more certain than his, either. Death. Service. The family Noavek. It was clear enough.

Cyra stopped. They were near the public training room, where the air smelled like old shoes and sweat. She wrapped her hand around his wrist and held tight.

"If I helped you get out right now," she said, "would you go?"

His heart pounded hard. "What are you talking about?"

"The loading bay is chaos," Cyra said, leaning closer. Her eyes were very dark, he realized. Almost black. And lively, too, like the pain that racked her body also gave her energy to spare. "The doors open every few minutes to let a new ship in. You think they'd be able to stop you if you stole a floater right now? You could be home in days."

Home in days. Akos took in the memory of the place like it was a familiar smell. Cisi, soothing with her smile alone. His mom, teasing them with prophetic riddles. Their little warm kitchen with the red burnstone lamp. The sea of feathergrass that grew right up against the house, the tufts brushing the windows. The creaky staircase that went up to the room he shared with . . .

"No," he said, shaking his head. "Not without Eijeh."

"That's what I thought," Cyra said sadly as she let go of him. She gnawed on her lip, trouble in her eyes. They went all the way to her quarters without talking, and when she got there, she went right into the bathroom to change into dry clothes. Akos parked himself in front of the news feed, out of habit.

Usually Thuvhe was only mentioned in the stream of words at the bottom of the feed, and even then, Cyra told him, the news was only about iceflower output. Iceflowers were the only thing the other planets really cared about, when it came to their cold planet, since they were used in so many medicines. But today the live footage showed a giant snowdrift.

He knew the place. Osoc, the northernmost city of Thuvhe, frozen and white. The buildings there floated in the sky like clouds made of glass, held up by some technology from Othyr he didn't understand. They were shaped like raindrops, like wilting petals, coming to points at either end. They had gone there to see his cousins one year, wrapped up in their warmest clothes, and stayed in their apartment building, which hung in the sky like ripe fruit that would never fall. Iceflowers still grew that far north, but they were far, far below, just colored smudges from that distance.

Akos sat on the edge of Cyra's bed, wetting the sheets with his damp clothes. It was hard for him to breathe. *Osoc, Osoc, Osoc* was the chant in his mind. White flakes on the wind. Frost patterns on the windows. Iceflower stems brittle enough to break at a touch.

"What is it?" Cyra was braiding her hair away from her face. Her hands fell when she saw the screen.

She read the subtitle aloud: "Fated Chancellor of Thuvhe Steps Forward."

Akos tapped the screen to turn up the volume. In Othyrian, the voice muttered, " . . . she promises a strong stand against Ryzek Noavek on behalf of the oracles of Thuvhe, lost two seasons ago, allegedly in a Shotet invasion on Thuvhesit soil."

"Your chancellor isn't elected?" Cyra asked. "Isn't that why they use the word 'chancellor' instead of 'sovereign,' because the position is elected rather than inherited?"

"Thuvhesit chancellors are fated. Elected by the current, they say. We say," he said. If she noticed his slip from "we" to "they," she didn't mention it. "Some generations there is no chancellor, and we just have regional representatives—those are elected."

"Ah." Cyra turned toward the screen, watching beside him.

There was a crowd on the landing platform, bundled though it was covered. A ship was perched at the edge, and the hatch was opening. As a dark-clothed woman stepped down, the crowd burst into cheers. The sights swooped in close, showing her face, wrapped in a scarf that covered her nose and mouth. But her eyes were dark, with a hint of lighter gray around the pupil—the sights were *very* close, buzzing like flies across her face—and gently sloped, and he knew her.

He *knew* her.

"Ori," he said, breathless.

Right behind her was another woman, just as tall, just as slim, and just as covered. When the sights shifted to her, Akos saw that the women were the same, practically down to the eyelash. Not just sisters, but twins.

Ori had a sister.

Ori had a double.

Akos searched their faces for a hint of difference, and found none.

"You know them?" Cyra said softly.

For a tick all he could do was nod. Then he wondered if he ought to have. Ori had only gone by "Orieve Rednalis"—not a name that was supposed to belong to a fate-favored child—because her real identity was dangerous. Which meant it would be better to keep it to himself.

But, he thought as he looked up at Cyra, and he didn't finish the thought, he just let the words tumble out:

"She was a friend of our family when I was a child. When she was a child. She went by an alias. I didn't know she had a . . . sister."

"Isae and Orieve Benesit," Cyra said, reading the names from the screen.

The twins were walking into a building. They both looked graceful with the breeze from inside the building pressing their coats—buttoned at the side, at the shoulder—tight to their bodies. He didn't recognize the fur of their scarves or the fabric of the coats themselves, black and clear of snow even now. An off-world material, to be sure.

"Rednalis is the name she used," he said. "A Hessa name. The day the fates were announced was the last time I saw her."

Isae and Orieve stopped to greet people on the way in, but as they walked away, and the sights peered after them, he saw a flash of movement. The second sister hooked her arm around the first sister's neck, drawing her head in close. The same way Ori had done with Eijeh when she wanted to whisper something in his ear.

Then Akos couldn't see much anymore, because his eyes were full of tears. That was Ori, who had a space at his family table, who had known him before he became . . . *this*. This armored, vengeful, life-taking thing.

"My country has a chancellor," he said.

"Congratulations," Cyra said. Hesitantly, she asked, "Why did

you tell me all that? It's probably not something you should broadcast here. Her alias, how you know her, all that."

Akos blinked his eyes clear. "I don't know. Maybe I trust you."

She lifted her hand, and hesitated with it over his shoulder.
Then she lowered it, touching him lightly. They watched the screen
side by side.

"I would never keep you here. You know that, right?" She was
so quiet. He'd never heard her that quiet. "Not anymore. If you
wanted to go, I would help you go."

Akos covered her hand with his own. Just a light touch, but it
was charged with new energy. Like an ache he didn't quite mind.

"If—when, *when* I get Eijeh out," he said, "would you ever go
with me?"

"You know, I think I would." She sighed. "But only if Ryzek was
dead."

As the ship turned back toward home, news of Ryzek's success on
Pitha came toward them in pieces. Otega was the source of most
of Cyra's gossip, Akos found, and she had a good read on things
before they were even announced.

"The sovereign is pleased," Otega said, dropping off a pot of
soup one night. "I think he made an alliance. Between a histori-
cally fate-faithful nation like Shotet and a secular planet like Pitha,
that's no small feat." Then she had given Akos a curious look.

"Kereseth, I presume. Cyra didn't say you were so . . ." She
paused.

Cyra's eyebrows popped up like they were on springs. She was
leaning against the wall, arms folded, chewing on a lock of hair.
Sometimes she stuck it in her mouth without noticing. Then she'd

spit it out, with a look of surprise, like it had crept into her mouth on its own.

". . . tall," Otega finished. Akos wondered what word she would have chosen, if she felt comfortable being honest.

"Not sure why she would have mentioned that," Akos replied. It was easy to be comfortable around Otega; he slid into it without thinking much about it. "She's tall, too, after all."

"Yes. Quite tall, the lot of you," Otega said, distantly. "Well. Enjoy that soup."

When she left, Cyra went straight to the news feed to translate the Shotet subtitles for him. This time it was startling how different they were. The Shotet words apparently said, "Pithar chancellor opens up friendly support negotiations in light of Shotet visit to Pithar capital." But the Othyrian voice said, "Thuvhesit chancellor Benesit threatens iceflower trade embargoes against Pitha in wake of their tentative aid discussions with Shotet leadership."

"Apparently your chancellor isn't pleased that Ryzek charmed the Pithar," Cyra remarked. "Threatening trade embargoes, and all."

"Well," Akos said, "Ryzek *is* trying to conquer her."

Cyra grunted. "That translation doesn't have Malan's flair; they must have used someone else. Malan likes to spin information, not leave it out entirely."

Akos almost laughed. "You can tell who it is by the translation?"

"There is an art to Noavek bullshit," Cyra said as she muted the feed. "We're taught it from birth."

Their quarters—Akos had started to think of them that way, much as it unsettled him—were the eye of a storm, quiet and settled in the midst of chaos. Everybody was getting everything in order for landing. He couldn't believe the sojourn was coming to a close; he felt like they had just taken off.

And then, on the day the currentstream lost its last blue streaks, he knew it was time to make good on his promise to Jorek.

"You sure he won't just turn me in to Ryzek for drugging him?" Akos said to Cyra.

"Suzao is a soldier at heart," Cyra said, for what had to be the hundredth time. She turned the page in her book. "He prefers to settle things himself. Turning you in would be the maneuver of a coward."

With that, Akos set out for the cafeteria. He was aware of his hurried heartbeat, his twitchy fingers. This time of week Suzao ate in one of the lower cafeterias—he was one of the lowest-ranked of Ryzek's close supporters, which meant he was the least import-ant person most places he went. But in the lower cafeterias, near the ship's chugging machinery, he got to be superior for once. It was the perfect place to provoke him—he couldn't very well be shamed by a servant in front of his inferiors, could he?

Jorek had promised to help with the last move. He was ahead of his father in line when Akos walked into the cafeteria, a big, dank room on one of the lowest decks of the ship. It was cramped and smoky, but the smell on the air was spiced and rich and made his mouth water.

At a nearby table, a group of Shotet younger than him had pushed their trays aside and were playing a game with machines small enough to fit in Akos's palm. They were collections of gears and wires balanced on wheels, one with a big set of pincers fixed to its nose, another with a blade, a third with a thumb-size hammer. They had drawn a circle on the table with chalk, and inside it, the machines stalked each other, controlled by remotes.

As they collided, bystanders shouted advice: "Go for the right wheel!" "Use the pincers, what else are they for?" They wore odd clothes in blue, green, and purple, bare arms wrapped in cords of different colors, hair shaved and braided and piled high. A sweep of feeling overtook him as he watched, an image of himself as a Shotet child, holding a remote, or just braced against the table, watching.

It had never been, would never be. But for just a tick, it seemed like it could have been possible.

He turned to the pile of trays near the food line and picked one up. He had a small vial buried in his fist, and he slipped ahead in line, edging closer to Suzao so he could dose the other man's cup. Right on time, Jorek stumbled into the person ahead of him, dropping his tray with a clatter. Soup hit the woman ahead of him right between the shoulders, and she swore. In the commotion Akos dumped the elixir in Suzao's cup without anyone noticing.

He passed Jorek while he was helping the soup-stained woman clean up. She was elbowing him away, cursing.

When Suzao sat down at his usual table and drank from his tainted cup, Akos stopped to take a breath.

Suzao had barged into his house along with the others. He'd stood there and watched as Vas murdered Akos's father. His fingerprints were on the walls of Akos's home, his footprints on the floors, Akos's safest place marked up and down with violence. The memories, as crisp as ever, steeled Akos for what he needed to do.

He put his tray down across from Suzao, whose eyes ran up his arm like a skimming hand, counting the kill marks there.

"Remember me?" Akos said.

Suzao was smaller than him, now, but so broad through the

shoulders it didn't seem that way when he was sitting. His nose was spotted with freckles. He didn't look much like Jorek, who took after his mother. Good thing, too.

"The pathetic child I dragged across the Divide?" Suzao said, biting down on the tines of his fork. "And then beat to a pulp before we even made it to the transport vessels? Yeah. I remember. Now get your tray off my table."

Akos sat, folding his hands in front of him. A rush of adrenaline had given him pinhole vision, and Suzao was in the very center.

"How are you feeling? A little sleepy?" he said as he slammed the vial down in front of him.

The glass cracked, but the vial stayed in one piece, still wet from the sleeping potion he had poured in Suzao's cup. Silence spread through the cafeteria, starting at their table.

Suzao stared at the vial. His face got blotchier with every second. His eyes were glassy with rage.

Akos leaned closer, smiling. "Your living quarters aren't as secure as you'd probably like. What is this, the third time you've been drugged in the past month? Not very vigilant, are you?"

Suzao lunged. Grabbed him by the throat, lifted, and slammed him hard into the table, right on top of his tray of food. Soup burned Akos through his shirt. Suzao drew his knife and held the point over Akos's head like he was going to shove it in Akos's eye.

Akos saw spots.

"I should kill you," Suzao snarled, flecks of spit dotting his lips.

"Go ahead," he said, straining. "But maybe you should wait until you're not about to fall over."

Sure enough, Suzao looked a little unfocused. He let go of Akos's throat.

"Fine," he said. "Then I challenge you to the arena. Blades. To the death."

The man didn't disappoint.

Akos sat up, slowly, making a show of his trembling hands, his food-stained shirt. Cyra had told him to make sure Suzao underestimated him before they made it to the arena, if he could. He wiped the spit flecks from his cheek, and nodded.

"I accept," Akos said, and drawn by some kind of magnetism, his eyes found Jorek. Who looked relieved.

CHAPTER 22 | CYRA

THE RENEGADES DIDN'T PASS me a message in the cafeteria, or whisper one in my ear as I walked across the sojourn ship. They didn't hack into my personal screens or cause a disruption and kidnap me. A few days after the scavenge, I was walking back to my quarters and I saw blond hair swinging ahead of me—Teka, holding a dirty rag in grease-streaked fingers. She glanced back at me, beckoning me with a curled finger, and I followed her.

She led me not to a secret room or passageway, but to the loading bay. It was dark there, and the silhouettes of transport vessels looked like huge creatures huddled in sleep. In a far corner, someone had left a light on, attached to the wing of one of the biggest transport vessels.

If rain and thunder were music to the Pithar, the churn of machinery was music to the Shotet. It was the sound of the sojourn ship, the sound of our movement side by side with the current-stream. So it made sense that in this part of the ship, where their conversation would be buried by the hum and thrum of machinery on the level below us, was a small, shabby gathering of renegades.

They were all dressed in the jumpsuits that maintenance workers wore—maybe they were all actually maintenance workers, now that I thought about it—and they had covered their faces with the same black mask Teka had worn when she attacked me in the hallway.

Teka drew a knife, and held the blade against my throat. It was cold, and smelled sweet, not unlike some of Akos's mixtures.

"Move any closer to them and I will knock you out cold," Teka said.

"Tell me this isn't your whole membership." In my mind I ran through what I could do to free myself, beginning with stomping on her toes.

"Would we risk you exposing our entire membership to your brother?" Teka said. "No."

The light clipped to the wing of the transport ship lost one of its metal bindings, and swayed on its cord, dangling now from only one fastener.

"You're the one who wanted to meet," one of the others said. He sounded older, gruffer. He was a boulder of a man, with a beard thick enough for things to get lost in. "What did you want, exactly?"

I forced myself to swallow. Teka's knife was still at my throat, but that wasn't what was making it hard to speak. It was finally articulating what I had been thinking for months. It was finally *doing* something instead of just thinking about it, for the first time in my life.

"I want safe transport out of Shotet for someone," I said. "Someone who doesn't exactly want to leave."

"For *someone*," the one who had spoken earlier said. "Who?"

"Akos Kereseth," I said.

There were mutters.

"He doesn't want to leave? Then why do you want to get him out?" the man said.

"It's . . . complicated," I said. "His brother is here. His brother is also lost. Beyond hope of recovery." I paused. "Some people are fools for love."

"Ah," Teka whispered. "I see how it is."

I felt like they were all laughing at me, smiling under their dark masks. I didn't like it. I grabbed Teka's wrist and twisted, hard, so she couldn't point the knife at me. She groaned at my touch, and I pinched the flat of the blade between my fingers, pulling it free. I flipped it in one hand so I was gripping the handle, my fingers slippery with whatever had been painted on the blade.

Before Teka could recover, I lunged, pinning her against my chest by the arm and pointing the knife at her side. I tried to keep as much of the currentgift pain to myself as I could, gritting my teeth so I wouldn't scream. I was breathing hard right next to her ear. She was still.

"I may be a fool, too," I said. "But I am not stupid. You think I can't identify you by the way you stand, the way you walk, the way you speak? If I'm going to betray you, I will do it whether you wear masks and hold me at knifepoint or not. And we all know that I can't betray you without betraying myself. So." I blew a strand of Teka's hair away from my mouth. "Are we going to have this discussion with mutual trust, or not?"

I released Teka, and offered her the knife. She was glaring at me, clutching her wrist, but she took it.

"All right," the man said.

He undid the covering that shielded his mouth. Beneath it, his thick beard crept down to his throat. Some of the others followed suit. Jorek was one of them, standing off to my right with his arms crossed. Unsurprising, since he had so baldly requested his Noavek-loyal father's death in the arena.

Others didn't bother, but it didn't matter—it was their spokesman I had cared about.

"I'm Tos, and I think we can do what you ask," the man said. "And I think you're aware that we would require something else in return."

"What is it you'd like me to do?" I said.

"We need your help getting into Noavek manor." Tos crossed his thick arms. His clothes were made of off-planet fabrics, too lightweight for the Shotet cold. "In Voa. After the sojourn."

"Are you an exile?" I said, frowning at him. "That's off-worlder garb you're wearing."

Were the renegades in contact with the exiles, who had sought safety from the Noavek regime on another planet? It made sense, but I hadn't considered the ramifications before. The exiles were undoubtedly a more powerful force than the rebellious Shotet who had turned against my brother—and more dangerous to me, personally.

"For our intents and purposes, there is no difference between exile and renegade. We both want the same thing: to unseat your brother and restore Shotet society to what it was before your family soiled it with inequity," Tos replied.

"'Soiled it with inequity,'" I repeated. "An elegant turn of phrase."

"I wasn't the one who devised it," Tos said humorlessly.

"To put it less elegantly," Teka said, "you're starving us and hoarding medicine. Not to mention carving out our eyeballs or whatever else gets Ryzek's blood pumping these days."

I was about to protest that *I* had never starved anyone or kept them from adequate medical care, but suddenly it didn't seem worth arguing. I didn't truly believe it, anyway.

"Right. So . . . Noavek manor. What do you intend to do there?" It was the only building that I, specifically, could help someone access. I knew all the codes Ryzek liked to use, and beyond that, the most secure doors were locked with a gene code—part of the system Ryzek had installed after our parents died. I was the only one left who shared Ryzek's genes. My blood could get them wherever they wanted to go.

"I don't think you need to know that information."

I furrowed my brow. There were only a few things a group of renegades—or exiles—could want inside Noavek manor. I decided to make an assumption.

"Let's be clear," I said. "You're asking me to participate in the assassination of my brother."

"Does that bother you?" Tos said.

"No," I replied. "Not anymore."

Despite all that Ryzek had done to me, I was surprised by how easily the answer came to me. He was my brother, my very blood. He was also the only guarantee of safety I currently had—any renegades who overthrew him would not care to spare the life of his sister, the murderer. But somewhere between ordering me to participate in Zosita's interrogation and threatening Akos, Ryzek had finally lost any loyalty I had left.

"Good," Tos said. "Then we'll be in touch."

§

Rearranging my skirt around my crossed legs, I searched the crowded hall that evening for Suzao Kuzar's regiment. They were all there, lined up along the balcony, exchanging giddy looks. *Good*, I thought. They were overconfident, which meant Suzao was also overconfident, and more easily defeated.

The room was humming with chatter, not quite as full as it had been when I fought Lety a few months before, but a much larger crowd than most Reclaimed challengers would ever hope to attract. That was also good. Winning an arena challenge could always give someone higher social status technically, but for it to really matter, everyone in Shotet society had to mutually agree on it. The more people who watched Akos defeat Suzao, the better his perceived status would be, which made it easier for him to get Eijeh out. Power in one place tended to transfer to power elsewhere—power over the right people.

Ryzek had stayed away from tonight's challenge, but Vas joined me on the platform reserved for high-ranking Shotet officials. I sat on one side of it and he sat on the other. In dark spaces it was easier for me to avoid stares, with my currentgift buried in shadow. But I couldn't hide it from Vas, who was close enough to see my skin flush with dark tendrils every time I heard Akos's name spoken in the crowd.

"You know, I didn't tell Ryzek about how you spoke to Zosita's daughter on the loading bay before the scavenge," Vas said to me, in the moments before Suzao entered the arena.

My heart began to pound. I felt like the renegade meeting was marked on me, visible to anyone who looked carefully enough. But I tried to stay calm as I replied, "Last time I checked, it wasn't against Ryzek's rules to speak to maintenance workers."

"Maybe he wouldn't have cared before, but he certainly does now."

"Am I supposed to thank you for your discretion?"

"No. You're supposed to treat this like a second chance. Make sure all this foolishness has just been a momentary lapse, Cyra."

I turned back to the arena. The lights lowered, and the speakers squealed as someone turned on the enhancers that dangled over the fighters, amplifying sound. Suzao entered first, to the screams and cheers of the crowd. He lifted his arms to inspire more screaming, and the gesture did its job: everyone erupted.

"Arrogant," I muttered. Not because of what he had done, but because of what he was wearing: He had left his Shotet armor behind, so he was in just a shirt. He didn't believe he needed armor. But he hadn't seen Akos fight in a long time.

Akos entered the arena a moment later, wearing the armor he had earned and the boots he had worn on Pitha, which were sturdy. He was greeted with jeers and obscene gestures, but they didn't seem to reach him, wherever he really was. Even the wariness that was always in his eyes was gone.

Suzao drew his knife, and Akos's stare suddenly hardened, like he had made a decision. He drew his own knife. I knew which one it was—it was the blade I had given him, the plain knife from Zold.

At his touch, no current tendrils wrapped around the blade. To the crowd, so used to seeing people fight with currentblades instead of plain knives, I was sure it was as if the knife was wrapped in the hand of a corpse. All the whispers about him—about his resistance to the current—were now confirmed. All the better, for his gift to frighten them—fearsomeness gave a person a different kind of power. I would know.

Suzao tossed his knife back and forth, spinning it on his

palms as he did. It was a trick he had to have learned from his zivatahak-trained friends, because he was clearly a student of altetahak, his muscles bulging beneath the fabric of his shirt.

"You seem nervous,"Vas said. "Need a hand to hold?"

"I'm only nervous for your man," I said. "Keep your hand to yourself; I'm sure you'll need it later."

Vas laughed. "I guess you don't need me anymore, now that you've found someone else who can touch you."

"What's that supposed to mean?"

"You know exactly what I mean." Vas's eyes glittered with anger. "Better keep your eyes on your little Thuvhesit pet. He's about to die."

Suzao had struck first, lunging at Akos, who sidestepped the lazy move without batting an eye.

"Oh, you're quick," Suzao said, his voice echoing through the amplifiers. "Just like your sister. She almost got away from me, too. She'd almost opened the front door when I caught her."

He snatched at Akos's throat again, and tried to lift him up to press him against the arena wall. But Akos brought the inside of his wrist to Suzao's, hard, breaking the hold and slipping away. I could hear the rules of elmetahak strategy, telling him to keep his distance from a larger opponent.

Akos spun the knife once on his palm, the move dazzling with its speed—light reflected off the blade, scattering across the floor, and Suzao followed it with his eyes. Akos took advantage of the momentary distraction, and punched him hard with his left hand.

Suzao stumbled back, blood streaming from his nostrils. He hadn't realized that Akos was left-handed. Or that I had been making him do push-ups for as long as I had known him.

Akos pursued him, bending his arm and thrusting up with his elbow, hitting Suzao again in the nose. Suzao's yell echoed in the space. He lashed out blindly, grabbing the front of Akos's armor and hurling him sideways. Akos's balance faltered, and Suzao pressed him to the ground with a knee and punched him hard in the jaw.

I winced. Akos, looking dazed, pulled his knee up to his face like he was going to try to throw Suzao off. Instead, he drew a knife from the side of his boot, and drove the blade into Suzao's side, right between two of his ribs.

Suzao, stunned, fell over, staring at the handle protruding from his side. Akos swiped with his other knife. There was a flash of red on Suzao's throat when he collapsed.

I hadn't even realized how tense I was until the fight was done and my muscles relaxed.

All around me was noise. Akos bent over Suzao's body and yanked his second knife free. He wiped the blade on his pants, and sheathed it again in his boot. I could hear his shaking breaths amplified by the enhancers.

Don't panic, I thought toward him, like he could hear.

He wiped sweat from his forehead with his sleeve, and lifted his eyes to the people sitting around the arena. He turned in a slow circle, as if he was staring every one of them down. Then he sheathed his knife, and stepped over Suzao's body to walk down the aisle toward the exit.

I waited a few seconds, then walked off the platform and into the crowd. My heavy clothes billowed away from my body as I went. I held up my skirts with both hands and tried to catch up to Akos, but he had too much of a lead; I didn't see him as I marched through the corridors toward our quarters.

Once I reached the door, I paused with my hand near the sensor, listening.

At first, all I heard were heavy breaths that turned into sobs. Then Akos screamed, and there was a loud crash, followed by another one. He screamed again, and I pressed my ear to the door to listen, my lower lip trapped between my teeth. I bit down so hard I tasted blood when Akos's screams turned to sobs.

I touched the sensor, opening the door.

He was sitting on the floor in the bathroom. There were pieces of shattered mirror all around him. He had ripped the shower curtain from the ceiling and the towel rack from the wall. He didn't look up at me when I came in, or even when I walked carefully across the fragments of glass to reach him.

I knelt among the shards, and reached over his shoulder to turn the shower on. I waited until the water warmed up, then tugged him by his arm toward the spray.

I stood in the shower with him, fully clothed. His breaths came in sharp bursts against my cheek. I put my hand on the back of his neck and pulled his face toward the water. He closed his eyes and let it hit his cheeks. His trembling fingers sought mine, and he clutched my hand against his chest, against his armor.

We stood together for a long time, until his tears subsided. Then I turned the water off, and led him into the kitchen, scattering mirror pieces with my toes as I walked.

He was staring into middle distance. I wasn't sure that he knew where he was, or what was happening to him. I undid the straps of his armor and guided it over his head; I pinched the hem of his shirt and peeled the wet fabric away from his body; I unbuttoned his pants and let them drop to the floor in a soaking-wet heap.

I had daydreamed about seeing him this way, and even about one day undressing him, taking away some of the layers that separated us, but this was not a daydream. He was in pain. I wanted to help him.

I wasn't aware of my own pain, but as I helped him dry off, I saw the currentshadows moving, faster than they had in a long time. It was like someone had injected them into my veins, so they traveled alongside my blood. Dr. Fadlan had said that my currentgift was stronger when I was emotional. Well, he was right. I didn't care about Suzao—in fact, I was planning to spit on his funeral pyre just to hear it sizzle—but I cared about Akos, more than anyone.

By then he had returned to his body, and he was responsive enough to help me bandage his arm and to walk into his bedroom on his own. I made sure he was under the covers, then put a pot on one of the burners at the apothecary counter. He had made a potion to keep me from having dreams, once. Now it was my turn.

CHAPTER 23 | AKOS

EVERYTHING WAS SLIDING AWAY from Akos, silk on silk, oil beading on water. Losing time, sometimes, a few ticks passing in an hour in the shower—he got out with pruny fingers and bright skin—or a night of sleep lasting all the way until the next afternoon. Losing space, other times, and he was standing in the challenge arena, streaked with another man's blood, or he was in the feathergrass, stumbling over the skeletons of those who had gotten lost there.

Losing hushflower petals to the inside of his cheek, so he could stay calm. Or the steadiness of his hands when they wouldn't stop shaking. Or words on the way to his mouth.

Cyra let him go on that way for a few days. But the day before they were supposed to land in Voa again, when he had skipped a few meals in a row, she came into his room and said, "Get up. Now."

He just looked at her, confused, like she was speaking a language he didn't know.

She rolled her eyes, grabbed his arm, and pulled. Her touch stung. He winced.

"Shit," she said, letting go. "See what's happening? You're starting to feel my currentgift, because you're so weak *your* currentgift is faltering. That's why you need to get up and eat something."

"So you can have your servant back, is that it?" he snapped. Losing patience, too. "Well, I'm done. I'm ready to die for your family, whatever that means."

She bent over, so their faces were on the same level, and said, "I know what it is to become something you hate. I know how it hurts. But life is full of hurt." Shadows pooled in her eye sockets like they were proving her point. "And your capacity for bearing it is much greater than you believe."

Her eyes held his for a few seconds, and then he said, "What kind of a rousing speech is that, 'Life is full of hurt'?"

"The last time I checked, your brother was still here," she said. "So you should keep yourself alive to get him out, if nothing else."

"Eijeh." He snorted. "Like that's what this is about."

He hadn't been thinking about Eijeh when he took Suzao's life. He'd been thinking about how badly he wanted Suzao dead.

"Then what is it about, exactly?" She folded her arms.

"How should I know?" He threw out his arms, emphatic, and smacked his hand against the wall. He ignored the ache in his knuckles. "You're the one who made me this way, why don't you tell me? Honor has no place in survival, remember?"

Whatever spark there had been behind her eyes fizzled at the recollection. He was about to try to snatch the words back, when a knock came at the door. He watched her open it from the edge of his bed. The guard with the most boring job imaginable was standing there, with Jorek behind him.

Akos leaned his face into his hand. "Don't let him in."

"I think you're forgetting whose quarters these actually are," Cyra said, sharp, and she stepped back so Jorek could come in.

"Damn it, Cyra!" He came to his feet. His vision went black for a few ticks, and he stumbled into the door frame. Maybe she was right—he did need to eat something.

Jorek's eyes widened at the sight of him.

"Good luck," Cyra said to him, and she shut herself in the bathroom.

Jorek looked anywhere else, at the wall decorated with armor and the plants dangling from the ceiling and the bright pots and pans stacked on the rickety stove. He scratched his neck, leaving pink lines on his skin, his nervous habit. Akos moved toward him, every part of his body heavy. He was breathless by the time he got to a chair and sat.

"What are you doing here?" he said, feeling savage. He wanted to dig in his nails, refuse to let anything else slide away. Even if it meant hurting Jorek, who had already seen more than his fair share of hurt. "You got what you wanted, didn't you?"

"Yes, I did," Jorek said, quiet. He sat down next to Akos. "I came to thank you."

"This wasn't a favor, it was a transaction. I kill Suzao, you get Eijeh out."

"Which will be easier to do when we land in Voa," Jorek said, still in that horrible quiet voice, like he was trying to soothe an animal. Maybe, Akos thought, that was exactly what he was trying to do. "Listen, I . . ." He furrowed his brows. "I didn't really know what I was asking you to do. I thought . . . I thought it would be easy for you. You seemed like the sort of person it would be easy for."

"I don't want to talk about this." Akos cradled his head in his hands. He couldn't stand to think of how easy it had been. Suzao hadn't had a chance, hadn't known what he was walking into. Akos felt more like a murderer now than he had after his first kill. At least that—Kalmev's death—had been wild and mad, almost a dream. Not like this.

Jorek set a hand on his shoulder. Akos tried to shrug him off, but he wouldn't be shrugged, not until Akos looked at him.

"My mother sent me with this," Jorek said. He drew a long chain from his pocket, with a ring dangling from it. It was made of a bright metal, orange pink in color, and stamped with a symbol. "This ring bears the seal of her family. She wanted you to have it."

Akos ran shaking fingers over the links of the chain, delicate but doubled over for strength. He gathered the ring into his fist, so the symbol of Jorek's mother's family would imprint on his palm.

"Your mother," he said, "*thanks* me?"

His voice broke. He let his head rest on the table. No tears came.

"My family is safe now," Jorek said. "Come and see us some-time, if you can. We live on the edge of Voa, between the Divide and the training camp. Little village right off the road. You'll be welcome among us, for what you've done."

Akos felt heat on the back of his head, Jorek's hand pressing gently. It was more comforting than he would have thought.

"Oh. And . . . don't forget to put my father's mark on your arm. Please."

The door closed. Akos wrapped his arms around his head, the ring still in his fist. His knuckles were split from the fight; he felt the scabs tug when he bent his fingers. The bathroom door squealed as Cyra opened it. She rustled around in the kitchen for a little while, then set a hunk of bread in front of him. He ate it so fast he almost choked on it, then dropped his left arm and turned it so the kill marks faced her.

"Carve the mark," he said. He was so hoarse the words almost didn't come out.

"It can wait." Cyra ran her hand over his short hair. He shivered at the light touch. Her currentgift wasn't hurting him anymore. Maybe Jorek had given him some relief after all. Or it was just the bread.

"Please." He lifted his head. "Just . . . do it now."

Cyra reached for her knife, and Akos watched her arm muscles contract. She was solid muscle, Cyra Noavek, with not much to spare. But inside, growing softer all the time, a fist learning to unclench.

She picked up his wrist. His fingers rested on her skin, dimming the shadows that flowed through her. It was easier, without them, to see that she was beautiful, her hair in long, loose curls, shining in the shifting light, her eyes so dark they looked black. Her aquiline nose, with its fine bones, and the splotch next to her windpipe, a birthmark, its shape somehow elegant.

She placed the tip of the knife against his arm, beside his second mark, with the hash through it.

"Ready?" she said. "One, two . . ."

On "two," she dug in, merciless, with the tip of the blade. Then she found the little bottle in the drawer, with its brush. He watched her touch the dark liquid to his fresh wound with all the finesse of a painter at an easel. Sharp pain went down his arm. A rush of energy followed it—adrenaline—pushing out the aching, throbbing mess of the rest of him.

She whispered the name across his skin: "Suzao Kuzar."

And he felt it, felt the loss and the weight and the permanence, just as he was supposed to. He allowed himself to find relief in the Shotet ritual.

"I'm sorry," he said, not sure what he was apologizing for— being mean to her earlier, or everything that had happened since the challenge, or something else. He'd woken the day after the challenge to her sweeping up broken glass in the bathroom, and later, to her screwing the towel rack back into the wall. He didn't remember ripping it off. Beyond that, he was startled to learn that she knew how to use tools, like a commoner. But that was Cyra, stuffed full of random knowledge.

"I'm not so jaded I don't remember," she said, eyes shifting away from his. "That feeling, like everything is broken. Breaking."

She placed a hand in his, and lifted the other to touch his neck, lightly. He twitched at first, then relaxed. He still had a mark there where Suzao had choked him in the cafeteria.

Then she was moving her fingers back toward his ear, along the scar Ryzek had cut into his neck, and he was leaning into her touch. He was warm, too warm. They never touched like this. He never thought he wanted them to.

"You make no sense to me," she said.

Her palm was on his face, then, her fingers curled behind his ear. Long, thin fingers with tendons and veins always standing at attention. Knuckles so dry the skin was peeling in places.

"All that has happened to you would make another person hard and hopeless," she said. "So how . . . how are you even possible?"

He closed his eyes. Aching.

"Still, Akos, this is a war." She brought her forehead to his. Her fingers were firm, fitted to his bones. "A war between you and the people who destroyed your life. Don't be ashamed of fighting it."

And then a different kind of ache. A pang of longing, deep in his gut.

He *wanted* her.

Wanted to run his fingers along her strict cheekbone. Wanted to taste the elegant birthmark on her throat, and to feel her breaths against his mouth, and to wind her hair around his fingers until they were trapped.

He turned his head, and pressed his lips to her cheek, hard enough that it wasn't quite a kiss. They shared a breath. Then he pulled back, stood up, turned away. Wiped his mouth. Wondered what the hell was wrong with him.

She stood right behind him, so he could feel her body's warmth at his back. She touched the space between his shoulders. Was it her currentgift that made his skin prickle at the contact, even through his shirt?

"There's something I have to do," she said. "I'll be back soon."

Just like that, she was gone.

CHAPTER 24 | CYRA

I WALKED THE MAINTENANCE tunnels, my face pulsing. The memory of his lips against my cheek played over and over in my mind. I tried to stomp it down like a stray ember. I couldn't kindle it and still do what needed to be done.

The path to Teka's narrow closet of a room was complicated, and led me deep into the belly of the ship.

She answered my light knock in seconds. She wore loose clothing, and her feet were bare. She had tied a length of cloth over her missing eye instead of covering it with an eyepatch. Over her shoulder I saw her lofted bed with the makeshift desk under it, now clear of all screws and tools and wires, ready for her to move back to Voa.

"What the hell?" she said, and she dragged me into the room. Her eye was wide with alarm. "You can't just come here without warning—are you crazy?"

"Tomorrow," I said. "Whatever you're going to do to my brother, you should do it tomorrow."

"Tomorrow," she repeated. "As in, the day after today."

"Last time I checked, that was the official definition of 'tomorrow,' yes," I said.

She sat on the rickety stool by her desk, and set her elbows on her knees. I saw a flash of skin as her shirt fell forward—she wasn't wearing a chest binder. It was strange to see her comfortable and in her own space. We didn't know each other well enough to see each other this way.

"Why?" she said.

"Everything is disorganized the day we land," I said. "The security system in the house will be vulnerable, everyone will be exhausted, it's the perfect time to slip in."

Teka frowned. "Do you have a plan?"

"Back gate, back door, hidden tunnels—those are all easy enough to get through, because I know the codes," I said. "It's only when we get to his personal rooms that the sensors require my blood. If you can get to the back gate at midnight, I can help with the rest."

"And you're sure you're ready for this?"

A picture of Zosita was taped to the wall above Teka's head, right over her pillow. Another picture was beside it, a boy who looked like her brother. My throat felt tight. In one way or another, my family was responsible for every loss she had suffered.

"What kind of a stupid question is that?" I said, scowling at her. "Of course I'm ready. But are you ready for your part of our agreement?"

"Kereseth? Yeah," she said. "You get us in, we'll get him out."

"I want it done simultaneously—I don't want to risk him getting hurt because of what I'm doing," I said. "He's hushflower-resistant, so it will require quite a bit to knock him out. And he's a skilled fighter, so don't underestimate him."

Teka nodded, slowly. And stared, chewing the inside of her cheek.

"What happened? You look all . . . frantic, or something," she said. "You guys have a fight?"

I didn't answer.

"I don't get it," she said. "You're obviously in love with him, why do you want him gone?"

I considered not answering that, either. The feeling of his rough chin scratching my cheek, and his mouth, warm against my skin, haunted me still. He had kissed me. Without prompting, without cunning. I should have been happy, hopeful. But it wasn't that easy, was it?

I had dozens of reasons to give her. Akos was in danger, now that Ryzek had realized he could use him as leverage over me. Eijeh was lost, and maybe Akos would be able to accept that once he was home, with his mother and sister. Akos and I would never be equals, as long as he was Ryzek's prisoner here, so I had to make sure he was freed. But the one closest to my heart was the reason that came tumbling out.

"Being here, it's . . . breaking him," I said. I shifted my weight from one foot to the other, uncomfortable. "I can't watch any-more. I won't."

"Yeah." Her voice was soft. "Win or lose—you get us in, we'll get him out. Okay?"

"Okay," I said. "Thank you."

I had always hated going back home.

Many of the Shotet went to the observation deck to cheer as our white planet came back into view. The energy on the ship was frantic and joyful as everyone packed their belongings and prepared to reunite with the young and old who had to stay behind. But I was mournful.

And nervous.

I didn't pack very much. Some clothes, some weapons. I threw out the perishable food, and stripped my bed of its sheets and blankets. Akos helped in silence, his arm still wrapped in a bandage. His bag of possessions was already on the table. I had watched him pack some clothes and some of the books I had given him, his favorite pages folded over. Though I had already read all those books, I wanted to open them again just to search out the parts he most treasured; I wanted to read them as if immersed in his mind.

"You're acting weird," he said once we were finished, and all there was left to do was wait.

"I don't like going home," I said. It was true, at least.

Akos looked around, and shrugged. "Seems like *this* is your home. There's more of you in here than anywhere in Voa."

He was right, of course. I was happy that he knew what "more of me" really was—that he might know as much about me, from observation, as I knew about him.

And I did know him. I could pick him out in a crowd from his gait alone. I knew the shade of the veins that showed on the backs of his hands. And his favorite knife for chopping iceflowers. And the way his breath always smelled spiced, like hushflower and sendes leaf mixed together.

"Maybe next time I'll do more to my room," he said.

You won't be back next time, I thought.

"Yeah." I forced a smile. "You should."

§

My mother had told me, once, that I had a gift for pretending. My father had not liked to see pain, so I had hidden mine from him as a child—my face passive, even as my fingernails bit my palm. And every time she took me to a specialist or a doctor about my current gift, the lies about where we had gone came to me as easily as the truth. Pretending, in the Noavek family, was survival.

I used that gift as I went through the motions of landing and returning home: going to the loading bay after we reentered the atmosphere, piling into a transport floater, making the public walk back to Noavek manor in Ryzek's wake. That evening I ate dinner with my brother and Yma Zetsyvis, pretending not to see her hand on his knee, fingers tapping, or the frantic look in her eyes whenever he didn't laugh at one of her jokes.

Later, she seemed to relax, and they left all pretense behind them, curled together on one side of the table, elbows bumping as they cut their food. I had killed her family and now she was my brother's lover. I would have been disgusted by it had I not understood, so well, what it was like to want to live. To *need* it, no matter the cost.

I still understood it. But now I needed something else more: for Akos to be safe.

Afterward, I pretended to be patient as Akos taught me how to predict how strong a poison would be without tasting it. I tried to seal every moment in my memory. I needed to know how to brew these concoctions on my own, because soon he would be gone. If the renegades and I were caught in our attempt tonight, I would probably lose my life. If we succeeded, Akos would be home, and Shotet would be in chaos, without its leader. Either way, it was unlikely that I would see him again.

"No, no," Akos said. "Don't hack at it—slice. Slice!"

"I am slicing," I said. "Maybe if your knives weren't so dull—"

"Dull? I could cut your fingertip off with this knife!"

I spun the knife in my hand and caught it by the handle. "Oh? Could you?"

He laughed, and put his arm across my shoulders. I felt my heartbeat in my throat. "Don't pretend you're not capable of delicacy; I've seen it myself."

I scowled, and tried to focus on "slicing." My hands were trembling a little. "See me dancing in the training room and you think you know everything about me."

"I know enough. Look, slices! Told you so."

He lifted his arm, but kept his hand against my back, right under my shoulder blade. I carried the feeling with me for the rest of the night, as we finished the elixir and got ready for bed and he shut the door between us.

I closed my eyes as I locked him in, went down the hallway to my bathroom, and poured my sleeping potion into the sink.

I changed into the same clothes I wore for training, loose and flexible, and shoes that would be silent on the floorboards. I braided my hair tightly so it wouldn't get in my way, then pinned it under so no one could grab and pull it in a fight. I strapped the knife to the small of my back, sideways, so I could grab the handle easily. I likely wouldn't use it; I preferred my bare hands in a crisis.

Then I slipped behind the wall panel in my room and crept through the passages toward the back door. I knew the way by heart, but I felt for the notches at every corner anyway, to make sure I was in the right place. I paused by the circle carved into the wall near the kitchens, the sign of the secret exit.

I was really doing it. Helping a group of renegades murder my brother.

Ryzek had lived his life in a daze of cruelty, obeying the instructions of our long-dead father like the man was standing over him, and relishing none of it. Men like Ryzek Noavek were not born; they were made. But time could not move backward. Just as he had been made, he had to be unmade.

I pushed through the hidden door and walked straight through the feathergrass stalks to the gate. I saw pale faces in the grass— Lety's, Uzul's, my mother's—beckoning me toward them. They whispered my name, and it sounded like the shuffle of the grass in the wind. Shivering, I typed my mother's birthday into the box by the gate, and the door sprang open.

Waiting a few feet away, in the dark, were Teka, Tos, and Jorek, faces covered. I jerked my head to the side, and they filed past me, into the feathergrass. I closed the gate behind them, then overtook Teka to show them the back door.

It seemed to me, as I led them down the passageways to my brother's wing, that such a monumental thing shouldn't take place in complete silence. But maybe the reverent quiet was an acknowledgment of what we were doing. I touched the corners, feeling for the deep grooves that suggested upcoming staircases. I traveled by memory, sidestepping protruding nails and cracked floorboards.

At the place where the passageways split, the left leading to my part of the house, and the right leading to Ryzek's, I turned to Tos.

"Go left, third door," I said. I handed him the key to Akos's room. "This will unlock the door. You may have to be a little forceful with him before you drug him."

"I'm not worried," Tos said. I wasn't, either—Tos was big as a boulder, no matter how skilled Akos had become at defending himself. I watched as Tos clasped hands with Teka and Jorek, in turn, and disappeared down the left passage.

When we drew closer to Ryzek's part of the house, I moved more slowly, remembering what Ryzek had said to Akos about the advanced security near his rooms. Teka touched my shoulder, and slipped past me. She crouched, and pressed her palms flat to the floor. Her eyes closed, she took deep breaths through her nose.

Then she stood, nodding.

"Nothing in this hallway," she said softly.

We walked that way for a little while, stopping at each corner or turn so that Teka could use her currentgift to sense the security system. Ryzek would never have anticipated that a girl who lived slathered in grease and crowded by wires could bring about his undoing.

Then the passageway came to an abrupt halt. Boarded up. Of course—Ryzek had probably ordered the little hallways closed after Akos nearly escaped.

My stomach lurched, but I didn't panic. I slid the wall panel back, and stepped into the empty sitting room beyond it. We were only a few rooms away from Ryzek's bedroom and office. Between us and him, there were at least three guards and the lock that only my Noavek blood could open. We wouldn't be able to get past the guards without causing a disruption that would draw the others to us.

I tapped Teka's shoulder and leaned in to whisper in her ear, "How long do you need?"

She held up two fingers.

I nodded, and drew my knife. I held it near my leg, my muscles twitching in anticipation of sharp movement. We walked out of the sitting room, and the first guard was there, pacing the hallway. I walked in his footsteps for a few seconds, matching my gait to his. Then I clapped my left hand over his mouth and stabbed with my right, sliding the blade under his armor and driving it between his ribs.

He screamed into my hand, which was only good enough to muffle, not to silence. I let him fall, and sprinted toward Ryzek's quarters. The others followed me, no longer bothering to be quiet. I heard shouts up ahead. Jorek ran past me and barreled into another guard, knocking him off his feet with sheer force alone.

I took the next one, seizing him by the throat, currentshadows pooled in my palm, and hurling him into the wall to my left. Then I stumbled to a stop in front of Ryzek's door, sweat curling around the back of my ear. The blood sensor was a slot in the wall, just wide enough and high enough to accommodate a hand.

I guided my hand toward it, Teka breathing heavily over my shoulder. All around us was shouting and running, but no one had reached us yet. I felt a pinch as the sensor drew my blood, and I waited for Ryzek's door to spring open.

It didn't.

I withdrew my hand and tried again with my left.

The door still didn't open.

"You can't open it?" I said to her. "With your gift?"

"If I could, we wouldn't have needed *you!*" she cried. "I can turn it on and off, not unlock it—"

"It's not working. Let's go!"

I grabbed Teka's arm, too frantic to care about the pain my touch caused, and dragged her down the hallway. She screamed,

"Run!" and Jorek bashed the guard he was fighting with the handle of his currentblade. He sliced another guard's armor, then chased us into the sitting room. We ran through the passages again.

"They're in the walls!" I heard. Lights burned through the cracks in every secret door and panel. The whole house was awake. My lungs burned from the effort of sprinting. I heard scraping behind us as one of the panels opened.

"Teka! Go find Tos and Akos!" I said. "Turn left, then right, go down the stairs, turn right again. The code for the back door is 0503. Say it back to me."

"Left, right, down, right—0503," Teka repeated. "Cyra—"

"Go!" I screamed, shoving her back. "I get you in, you get him out, remember? Well, you can't get him out if you're dead! So go!"

Slowly, Teka nodded.

I planted myself in the middle of the passage. I heard, rather than saw, Teka and Jorek run away. Guards stormed into the narrow passage, and I let the pain build inside me until I could hardly see. My body was so flush with shadows that I was darkness manifest, I was a sliver of night, utterly empty.

I screamed, and threw myself at the first guard. The burst of pain hit him as my hand did, and he yelled, collapsing at my touch. Tears streamed down my face as I ran toward the next one.

And the next one.

And the next one.

All I needed to do was buy the renegades some time. But it was too late for me.

CHAPTER 25 | CYRA

"I SEE YOU'VE MADE some updates to the prison," I said to Ryzek.

My mother and father had taken me here, to the row of cells beneath the amphitheater, when I was young. It wasn't the official Voa prison, but a special, hidden compound in the city's center, made only for enemies of the Noavek family. It had been stone and metal, like something out of a history textbook, the last time I saw it.

Now the floors were dark, made of a material like glass, but harder. There was no furniture in my cell except for a metal bench and a toilet and sink, hidden behind a screen. The wall that separated me from my brother was made of thick glass, with a slot for food, now open so we could hear each other speak.

I was on the bench now, wedged in the corner with my legs sprawled in front of me. I was heavy with exhaustion and dark with pain, bruised from where Vas had grabbed me in the hidden hallways, to stop me from hurting more of his guards. A lump on the back of my head—from where he had slammed me into the wall to knock me out—throbbed.

"When did you turn traitor?" Ryzek was in the hallway, dressed in his armor. The pale overhead lights tinted his skin blue. He put his arm against the glass that separated us, and leaned in.

It was an interesting question. I didn't feel like I had "turned" so much as finally moved in the direction I had already been facing. I stood, and my head pounded, but it was nothing compared to the pain of the currentshadows, which had gone haywire, moving so fast I couldn't keep track of them. Ryzek's eyes followed them over my arms and legs and face like they were all he could see. They were all he had ever been able to see.

"You know, you never actually had my loyalty to begin with," I said, walking toward the glass. We were just feet apart, but I felt untouchable, for the moment. Finally, I could say whatever I wanted to him. "But I probably wouldn't have acted against you if you had just left us alone, like I told you to. When you went after Akos, just to control me, though . . . well. It was more than I could accept."

"You are a fool."

"I'm not nearly as foolish as you believe."

"Yes, you've certainly proved that." He laughed, gesturing wide, to the prison all around us. "This is clearly the result of your brilliant mind."

He leaned into the barrier again, and hunched so he was closer to my face, his breath fogging the glass.

"Did you know," Ryzek said, "that your beloved Kereseth knows the Thuvhesit chancellor?"

I felt a pang of fear. I did know. Akos had told me about Orieve Benesit when we watched the footage of the chancellor declaring herself. Ryzek didn't know that, of course, but he also wouldn't have brought it up to begin with if Akos had made it out of Noavek manor with the renegades. So what had happened to him? Where was he now?

"No," I said, my throat dry.

"Yes, it's very inconvenient that the Benesit sisters are twins— it means I don't know which one to strike at first, and Eijeh's visions have made it very clear that I must kill them in a particular order for the most desirable outcome," Ryzek said, smiling. "His visions have also made it clear that Akos knows the information I need to accomplish my goal."

"So you still haven't taken Eijeh's currentgift," I said, hoping to stall him. I didn't know what there was to gain from stalling him, just that I wanted time, as much time as I could get before I had to face what had happened to Akos and the renegades.

"I will remedy that soon enough," Ryzek said, smiling. "I have been proceeding with caution, a concept you have never quite understood."

Well, he had me there.

"Why didn't my blood work in the gene lock?" I said.

Ryzek only continued to smile.

Then he said, "I should have mentioned this earlier, but we caught one of your renegade friends, Tos. He told us, with some encouragement, that you were participating in an attempt on my life. He's dead now. I'm afraid I got a little carried away." Ryzek smiled still wider, but his eyes were a little unfocused, like he was on hushflower. As much as Ryzek acted like he was callous, I knew what had really happened: He had killed Tos because he believed it was necessary, but he had not been able to stand it. He had taken hushflower to calm himself down afterward.

"What," I said flatly, finding it difficult to breathe, "have you done with Akos?"

"You don't seem to have any regret," Ryzek continued, as if I hadn't spoken. "Perhaps if you had begged for forgiveness, I would have been lenient with you. Or with him, if you chose. And yet . . . here we are."

He straightened as the door at the end of the cell block opened. Vas marched in first, his cheek bruised from where I had struck him with my elbow. Eijeh came in next, hoisting a sagging man at his side. I recognized the hanging head, the long, lean body that tripped beside him. Eijeh dropped Akos to the floor in the hallway, and he went down easily, spitting blood on the ground.

I thought I saw a flicker of sympathy on Eijeh's face as he looked down at his brother, but a moment later, it was gone.

"Ryzek." I felt wild. Desperate. "Ryzek, he didn't have anything to do with it. Please don't bring him into this—he didn't know, he didn't know anything—"

Ryzek laughed. "I know he doesn't know anything about the renegades, Cyra. Haven't we been over this? It is what he knows about his chancellor that I am interested in."

Both of my hands pressed to the glass, I sank to my knees. Ryzek crouched in front of me.

"This," he said, "is why you should avoid entanglements. I can use you to find out what he knows about the chancellor, and him to find out what you know about the renegades. Very neat, very simple, don't you think?"

I backed up, body pulsing with my heartbeat, until my spine touched the far wall. I couldn't run, I couldn't escape, but I didn't have to make this easy for them.

"Get her out," Ryzek said, typing in the code so the cell door opened. "Let's see if Kereseth is weak enough for this to work yet."

I pushed off the wall, throwing myself as hard as I could at Vas as soon as he entered the cell. I slammed my shoulder into his gut, knocking him flat. He had grabbed my shoulders, but my arms were still mobile enough for me to claw at his face, drawing blood from the skin just under his eye. Ryzek stepped in, hitting me in the jaw, and I fell to the side, dizzy.

Vas dragged me over to Akos, so we knelt across from each other, barely an arm's length of space between us.

"I'm sorry" was all I could think to say to him. That he was here was my fault, after all. If I hadn't fallen in with the renegades . . . but it was too late for thoughts like that.

Everything inside me slowed as his eyes met mine, like I had stopped time. I looked him over carefully, like a caress, his tousled brown hair, the dusting of freckles on his nose, and his gray eyes, unguarded for the first time I could remember. I didn't see the bruises or the blood that marked him. I listened to his breaths. I had heard them in my ear just after I kissed him, every exhale bursting a little, like he didn't want to let it go.

"I always thought my fate meant I would die a traitor to my country." Akos's voice was rough, like he had worn away at it by screaming. "But you made it so I won't."

He gave me a small, wild smile.

I knew, then, that Akos wouldn't give up information about his chancellor no matter what happened. I had never realized how deeply he felt his fate. Dying for the Noavek family had been a curse to him, as surely as falling to the Benesit family was to Ryzek. But because I had sided against my brother, if Akos died for me now, it meant he had never betrayed his home. So maybe it was all right that I had cost us both our lives by helping the renegades. Maybe it still meant something.

With that thought, it was very simple. We would be in pain, and then we would die. I settled into the inevitability of it.

"Let me be clear about what I want to happen here." Ryzek crouched beside us, balancing his elbows on his knees. His shoes were polished—he had taken time to polish his shoes before torturing his sister?

I swallowed a weird little laugh.

"Both of you are going to suffer. If you give in first, Kereseth, you will tell me what you know about the fated chancellor of Thuvhe. And if you give in first, Cyra, you will tell me what you know about the renegades, and their connections to the exile colony." Ryzek glanced at Vas. "Go ahead."

I braced myself for a blow, but it didn't come. Instead, Vas grabbed my wrist, and forced my hand toward Akos. At first I let it happen, sure my touch wouldn't affect him. But then I remembered—Ryzek had said to see if Akos was "weak enough." That meant they had been starving him for the days I had been in the prison; they had weakened his body, and his gift.

I strained against Vas's vise-hand, but I wasn't strong enough. My knuckles brushed Akos's face. The shadows crept toward him, even as I silently begged them not to move. But I was not their master. I never had been. Akos moaned, his own brother holding him in place as he tried to flinch away.

"Excellent. It worked," Ryzek said, coming to his feet. "The chancellor of Thuvhe, Kereseth. Tell me about her."

I pulled my elbow back as hard as I could, twisting and thrashing in Vas's grip. The shadows grew richer and more numerous the more I struggled, like they were mocking me. Vas was strong, and there was nothing I could do to him now; he held me steady with one hand and pushed my palm forward with the other, so it lay flat against Akos's throat.

I could imagine nothing more horrible than this, Ryzek's Scourge turned against Akos Kereseth.

I felt the heat of him. The pain inside me was desperate to be shared; it moved into him, but instead of diminishing in my own body the way it usually did, it only multiplied in us both. My arm shook from the effort of trying to pull away. Akos screamed, and so did I, so did I. I was dark with the current, the center of a black hole, a shred of the starless fringe of the galaxy. Every inch of me burned, ached, begged for relief.

Akos's voice and mine met like two clasped hands. I closed my eyes.

In front of me was a wooden desk, marked with circles from water glasses. A pile of notebooks was scattered across it, and all of them bore my name, Cyra Noavek, Cyra Noavek, Cyra Noavek. I recognized this place. It was Dr. Fadlan's office.

"The current flows through every one of us. And like liquid metal flowing into a mold, it takes a different shape in each of us," he was say-ing. My mother sat at my right, her posture straight and her hands folded in her lap. My memory of her was detailed and perfect, down to the loose strand of hair behind her ear and the faint blemish on her chin, covered with makeup.

"That your daughter's gift causes her to invite pain into herself, and project pain into others, suggests something about what's going on inside

her," he said. "A cursory assessment says that on some level, she feels she deserves it. And she feels others deserve it as well."

Instead of erupting the way she had at the time, my mother tilted her head. I could still see her pulse in her throat. She turned to me in the chair. She was more beautiful than I had dared to remember; even the lines at the corners of her eyes were graceful, gentle.

"What do you think, Cyra?" she said, and as she spoke, she became a dancer of Ogra, her eyes lined with chalk and her bones glowing so brightly beneath her skin I could see even the faint spaces at their joints. "Do you think this is how it works?"

"I don't know," I replied in my adult voice. It was my adult body sitting in the chair, too, though I had only been here as a child. "All I know is that the pain wants to be shared."

"Does it?" The dancer smiled a little. "Even with Akos?"

"The pain isn't me; it doesn't discriminate," I said. "The pain is my curse."

"No, no," the dancer said, her dark eyes locked on mine. But they weren't brown anymore, as they had been when I saw her perform in the dining room; they were gray, and wary. Akos's eyes, familiar to me even in a dream.

He had taken her place, perched at the edge of the seat as if ready to take flight, his long body dwarfing the chair.

"Every currentgift carries a curse," he said. "But no gift is only a curse."

"The gift part of it is that no one can hurt me," I said.

But even as I said it, I knew it wasn't true. People could still hurt me. They didn't need to touch me to do it—they didn't even need to torture me to do it. As long as I cared about my life, as long as I cared about Akos's life, or the lives of renegades I barely knew, I was as vulnerable as everyone else was to hurt.

I blinked at him as a different answer came to me.

"You told me I was more than a knife, more than a weapon," I said. "Maybe you're right."

He smiled that small, familiar smile that creased his cheek.

"The gift," I said, "is the strength the curse has given me." The new answer was like a blooming hushflower, petals unfurling. "I can bear it. I can bear pain. I can bear anything."

He reached for my cheek. He became the dancer, and my mother, and Otega, in turn.

And then I was in the prison, arm outstretched, fingers on Akos's cheek, Vas's hand strong around my wrist, holding me fast. Akos's teeth were gritted. And the shadows that were usually confined beneath my skin were all around us, like smoke. So dark I couldn't see Ryzek or Eijeh or the prison with its glass walls.

Akos's eyes—full of tears, full of pain—found mine. Pushing the shadow toward him would have been easy. I had done it many times before, each time a mark on my left arm. All I had to do was let the connection form, let the pain pass between us like a breath, like a kiss. Let all of it flow out of me, bringing relief for us both, in death.

But he did not deserve it.

This time, I broke the connection, like slamming a door between us. I pulled the pain back, into myself, willing my body to grow darker and darker, like a bottle of ink. I shuddered with the force of that power, that agony.

I didn't scream. I wasn't afraid. I knew I was strong enough to survive it all.

CHAPTER 26 | AKOS

IN THE PLACE BETWEEN sleeping and waking, he thought he saw feathergrass, tilting in the wind. He imagined he was home and could taste snow on the air, smell cold earth. He let longing pierce him all the way through, and then fell asleep again.

Oil beading on water.

He had been on his knees on the floor of the prison, watching currentshadows pull away from Cyra's skin like smoke. The haze tinted the hand on his shoulder—Eijeh's hand—dark gray. He saw Cyra through it only faintly, her chin tipped up, eyes closed like she was sleeping.

And now, lying on a thin mattress with a heater over his bare feet. A needle in his arm. His wrist cuffed to a bed frame.

The pain, and the memory of it, slipping away into numbness.

He twitched his fingers, and the IV needle shifted, sharp, under his skin. He frowned. This place was a dream; it had to be, because he was still in that tomb under Voa's amphitheater, and Ryzek was ordering him to talk about Ori Rednalis. Orieve Benesit. Whatever her name was now.

"Akos?" The woman's voice sounded real enough. Maybe it wasn't a dream after all.

She stood over him, stick-straight hair framing her face. He'd know those eyes anywhere. They had stared at him across the dinner table, crinkled at the corners when Eijeh made a joke. Her left eyelid sometimes twitched when she got nervous. She was here, like thinking about her had brought her. His own name settled him into himself, no more slipping and sliding.

"Ori?" he croaked.

A tear dropped from her eye to the bedsheets. She put her hand on his, covering the tube from the IV needle. Her sleeve, made of thick black wool, was draped over her palm, and the garment pulled tight around her throat. Signs of Thuvhe, where a person would near strangle herself to death to keep any warmth from escaping.

"Cisi's coming," Ori said. "I called her, and she's on her way. I called your mother, too, but she's across the galaxy; it will take her some time."

He was so tired.

"Don't go," he said as his eyes closed.

"I won't." Her voice was husky, but reassuring. "I won't go."

He dreamt he was between the glass prison cells, his knees digging into the black floor, his guts rumbling with hunger.

And he woke in the hospital, with Ori slumped over at his side, her arm sprawled across his legs. Through the window behind her he saw floaters whizzing past and big buildings hanging in the sky like ripe fruit.

"Where are we?" he said.

She blinked sleep from her eyes and said, "Shissa hospital."

"Shissa? Why?"

"Because that's where you got dropped," she said. "You don't remember?"

When she first spoke to him, she had sounded different, careful with every word. But the longer she talked, the more she lapsed into their lazy Hessa rhythms, every syllable sliding into the next one. He found himself doing the same thing.

"Dropped? By who?"

"We don't know. Thought you would."

He strained for the memory, but couldn't quite reach it.

"Don't worry." She put her hand on his again. "There was so much hushflower in your system you probably should have been dead. No one expects you to remember." She smiled. So familiar, slanted mouth into curved cheek. "They must not have known you that well, to dump you in Shissa like some kind of city-dwelling snot."

He'd almost forgotten their jokes about this place. Shissa kids with their heads in the skies, couldn't even recognize an iceflower on sight because they were used to seeing them from a long ways up. Couldn't even fasten a proper coat closed. Useless glass-dwellers, all.

"'City-dwelling snot,' says the fated chancellor of Thuvhe," he said, suddenly remembering. "Or is that your twin? Which one of you is the older one, anyway?"

"I'm not the chancellor, I'm the other one. Fated to raise her sister to the throne or . . . whatever," she said. "But if I *was* her, you would definitely not be addressing me with the 'respect appropriate for my position.'"

"Snob," Akos said.

"Hessa trash."

"I am from the family Kereseth, you know. We're not exactly trash."

"Yes, I know." Her smile softened a little, like she was saying, *How could I forget?* And then Akos remembered the cuff fixing his wrist to the hospital bed. He decided not to bring it up yet.

"Ori," he said. "Am I really in Thuvhe?"

"Yeah."

He closed his eyes. There was a fire in his throat.

"Missed you, Orieve Benesit," he said. "Or whatever your name is."

Ori laughed. She was crying now. "Then what took you so long?"

The next time he woke, he didn't feel quite so numb, and though he ached, certain enough, the sharp agony that had carried him from Voa to Shissa was gone. Cyra's lingering gift had been sent away by iceflowers, no doubt.

Just thinking Cyra's name made his insides twist with fear. Where was she now? Had the people who had brought him here rescued her, too, or had they just left her with Ryzek to die?

He tasted bile, and opened his eyes.

A woman stood at the foot of his bed. Dark curly hair framed her face. Her eyes were wide. There was a little spot at the bottom of one where her pupil bled into her iris—a defect she'd had since birth. His sister, Cisi.

"Hello," she said. Her voice was all softness and light. He'd held the memory of it tight in his mind, like it was the last seed left for planting.

It was too easy to cry right now, all laid out and warm as he was. "Cisi," he croaked, blinking the tears away.

"How do you feel?"

That, he thought, *is a question*. He knew she was just asking after his pain, though, so he said, "Fine. I've been worse."

She moved fluidly in sturdy Hessa boots, stopping by the side of the bed and tapping something near his head. The bed moved, tilting up at his waist so he could sit up.

He winced. His ribs were hurt. He was so numb he'd almost forgotten.

She had been so careful before then, so controlled, that it startled him when she threw herself across him, hands clutching at his shoulder, his side. At first he didn't—couldn't—move. But then he brought his arms around her, and held her tight. They'd never hugged much as kids—except for their dad, they weren't an affectionate family, as a rule—but her embrace was brief. She was here, alive. And they were together again.

"I can't believe . . ." She sighed. And she started to mutter a prayer. He hadn't heard a Thuvhesit prayer in a long time. The ones for gratitude were briefest, but he couldn't bring himself to say it with her. There were too many worries crowding his head.

"Neither can I," he said, once she had finished. She pulled away, still holding one of his hands and smiling down at him. No, frowning now, staring at their joined hands. Touching her cheek, where a tear had fallen.

"I'm crying," she said. "What—I haven't been able to cry since . . . since my currentgift."

"Your currentgift keeps you from crying?"

"You didn't notice it?" She sniffed, wiping her cheeks. "I make people feel . . . at ease. But I also can't seem to do or say anything that makes them uneasy, like . . ."

"Crying," he supplied. That she had a gift with ease didn't surprise him. But the way she described it, it was more like a hand around her throat, squeezing. He couldn't see the gift in that.

"Well, mine stops yours. Stops everybody's," he said.

"Handy."

"Sometimes."

"Did you go on the sojourn?" she said suddenly, holding tight to his hand. He wondered if she was just going to start firing questions at him, now that she could. She added, "Sorry, I just . . . I wondered, when I saw the reports. Because you can't swim. I was worried."

He couldn't help it. He laughed.

"I was surrounded by Shotet, in close proximity with Ryzek Noavek, and you were worried because I can't swim?" He laughed again.

"I can worry about two things at once. Several things, in fact," she said, with a bite. Not a hard one, though.

"Cee," he said. "Why am I cuffed to this bed?"

"You were wearing Shotet armor when you were dropped off. The chancellor's instructions are for you to be treated with caution."

For some reason, her cheeks went pink.

"Ori didn't vouch for me?"

"She did, and I did," Cisi said. She didn't explain why she would be in a position to vouch for him with the chancellor of Thuvhe, and he didn't ask. Not yet, anyway. "But the chancellor is . . . difficult to win over."

She didn't sound critical, but then, Cisi never had. She could sympathize with damn near everybody. Compassion made it hard to maneuver, but she seemed to him to have managed all right in the seasons they had been apart. She looked almost the same, but thinner, with a sharper jaw and cheekbones. Those were from their mom, of course, but the rest of her—too-broad smile, dark brow, delicate nose—was their dad.

Last time she had seen him, he had been a child, soft in the face, shorter than all the other kids. Always quiet, always poised to blush. And now, taller than most men, hard-featured and muscled and marked with kills. Did he even look like the same person to her?

"I'm not going to hurt anyone," he said, in case she wasn't sure.

"I know." It was easy to see Cisi as this soft, gentle thing, but there was a kind of steel in her eyes, and lines around her mouth, early wrinkles from a life of heartache. She was grown.

"You're different," he said.

"You're one to talk," she said. "Listen, I wanted to ask you . . ." She gnawed on a fingernail as she found the words. "I wanted to ask you about Eijeh."

Eijeh's hand had been heavy on his shoulder as he steered his brother into the prison, though Akos whispered his name and begged him for help. Food. Mercy.

He could still feel Eijeh's hand there.

"Is he alive?" she said weakly.

"That depends on your definition of 'alive,'" he said. Sharp, the way Cyra would have said it.

"I saw a hacked Shotet feed last year where he was at Ryzek's side." She paused like she was giving him room to say something, only he didn't know what to say. "And you were at Cyra's," she added, again with that pause.

His throat was as dry as dust. "Have you seen that feed lately?"

"No. Hard to access. Why?"

He needed to know if Cyra was okay. He needed it like dry earth needed water, scrabbling for whatever drops it could find. But if he was in Thuvhe, there was no Shotet feed playing on the screens in every home, no way to check if she was dead or alive, until he went back.

Which was a given. He would go back. He would help Cyra. He would drag Eijeh home if he had to poison him first. He wasn't finished, not yet.

"That's why Isae—I mean, the chancellor—has you cuffed to the bed," Cisi said. "If you could just explain why you were with her—"

"I won't explain." She looked as shocked by the anger in his voice as he was. "I stayed alive, and now this is what I am. Nothing I say to you is going to change what you've already assumed."

He was fourteen and irritable again. Coming home was like walking backward.

"I haven't assumed anything." She looked down. "It's just that I wanted to warn you. The chancellor wants to know for sure you aren't . . . well. A traitor, I suppose."

His hands trembled. "Know 'for sure'? What does that mean?"

She was about to answer when the door to the hospital room opened. A Thuvhesit soldier came in first, dressed in his indoor uniform, dark red slacks with a dark gray jacket. He stood off to the side, and Ori's twin walked in after him.

He knew it wasn't Ori right away, though her eyes were the same and the rest of her was covered in fabric: a hooded gown, sleeves tight at the wrist, buttoned from waist to throat, long enough to brush the toes of her shoes. The shoes themselves were polished, also black, and snapped on the tile with each step. She stood at the foot of the bed, facing him, hands folded. Clean fingernails. A perfect black line on each of her eyelids to mark the path of her lashes. A veil covered the rest of her face, from nose to jaw.

Isae Benesit. Chancellor of Thuvhe.

Akos's Hessa manners hadn't taught him to handle something this grand. Somehow he managed to say, "Chancellor."

"I see you had no trouble distinguishing me from my sister," she said. She had an odd accent, like one from the outer rim of the galaxy, not a fancy one from the planets closest to Assembly Headquarters, as he'd expected.

"It's the shoes," he said, his nerves driving him toward honesty. "A Hessa girl would never wear those."

Ori, following her in, laughed. Seeing them side by side, it was even more obvious how different they were. Ori was slouching, leaning, her face mobile. Isae was carved from rock.

The chancellor said, "Can I ask why you compromised a layer of protection by revealing your face to him earlier, Ori?"

"He's basically my brother," Ori said, firm. "I'm not going to hide my face from him."

"Why does it matter?" I said. "You're twins, right? So I know what you both look like."

In response, Isae clawed at the corner of her veil with her clean fingernails. When the covering fell away, Akos stared. Baldly.

Isae's face was crossed with two scars, one that went through her eyebrow and forehead, and the other that went from jaw to nose. Scars just like Kalmev had, like Akos himself had; they came from sharpened currentblades—a rarity, since the current's flow was weapon enough. Shotet blades, probably.

That explained why she and Ori both covered their faces. Being twins kept everybody confused about who was chancellor. But with their faces bare . . . well.

"Let's not dwell on pleasantries," Isae said, even sharper than before, if that was possible. "I believe your sister was about to tell you what I can do with my currentgift."

"I was," Cisi replied. "Isae—Her Highness, I mean—can summon your memories with a touch. It helps her to verify the testimony of people she feels unable to trust, for whatever reason."

There were a lot of memories Akos didn't want summoned. Cyra's face, with veins of shadow cradling her cheeks, drifted into his mind. He pawed at the back of his head, eyes skipping away from Cisi's.

"It won't work," he said. "Currentgifts don't work on me."

"Really," Isae said.

"Yeah. Go ahead, try me."

Isae came closer, shoes snapping. She stopped at his left side, right across from Cisi. Up close he could see how the scars puckered at the edges. Only a few seasons old, if he had to guess. Their color was dark still.

She touched his cuffed arm, right where metal met wrist.

"You're right," she said. "I see—and feel—nothing."

"Guess you're just going to have to take me at my word," he said, a little terse.

"We'll see" was Isae's answer, as she went back to the foot of the bed.

"Did Ryzek Noavek, or anyone associated with him, ever ask you for information about me?" she said. "We know that you possessed information, since you saw Ori the day the fates were revealed."

"You did?" Cisi said breathlessly.

"Yes." His voice wavered a little. "Yes, he asked me."

"And what did you tell him?"

He pulled his knees up to his chest like a kid scared of a storm, and looked out the window. Shissa was bright at the end of the day, every room glowing with lines of light in all different shades, however you liked it. The building next to theirs was purple.

"I knew not to say anything." He wavered more than before. The memory was inching toward him bit by bit. Cyra's face, the glass floor, Eijeh's hand on him. "I know how to bear pain, I'm not weak, I . . ." Even he knew he sounded crazy, babbling this way. Had he said anything, in the middle of all that pain? "He has . . . *access* to Eijeh's memories of Ori, so it would only have taken him making the connection between Ori and her fate for him to know what you look like, aliases, origins . . . so I tried not to say anything. He wants to know which one of you is which, which one is older. He knows . . . an oracle told him going after one of you was better than going after the other, so anything that distinguishes you from each other is a danger to you. But—he asked again and again, and—I don't think I said anything, but I can't remember—"

Ori moved impulsively toward him, gripping his ankle hard. Squeezing his bones. The pressure helped him hold his head together.

"If you did tell him something useful, such as where Ori grew up, or who raised her . . . would he come for us himself?" Isae asked, apparently unmoved.

"No." He tried to steady himself. "No, I think he's afraid of you."

Ryzek never came himself, did he? Not even for his oracle, not even to kidnap Akos. He didn't want to set foot in Thuvhe.

Isae's eyes had seemed familiar to him, when he watched the footage of the twins in Osoc. But the look in them now wasn't something Ori could have mustered. It was downright murderous.

"He ought to be," Isae said. "This conversation isn't over. I want to know everything you know about Ryzek Noavek. I will be back."

She fastened her veil, and after a tick, Ori did the same. Before she left, though, Ori set her hand on the door and said, "Akos. It's all right. It'll be all right."

He wasn't all that convinced.

CHAPTER 27 | AKOS

A DREAM:

His knees met the floor in the underground prison. Cyra's currentgift crept over him like sharpworms around the roots of iceflowers. And then, her harsh exhale, and the shadows burst into dark clouds around them. He had never seen them do that before, separate from her skin. Something had changed.

She fell sideways, after that, into a pool of blood. Her hands clutched at her stomach, the way his father's had when Vas killed him in front of his children. Her fingers, bent and red, held her insides in.

The blood turned to hushflower petals, and he woke up.

He was tired of the cuff. Or more specifically, of his arm at this particular angle, and the metal-on-skin feeling, and this game where he pretended he was trapped when he wasn't. He twisted his hand around to touch the wrist cuff's lock. The current held cuffs like these shut, so if he pressed his skin into the cracks, he could open them. He'd first discovered the talent on the way to Shotet, right before he killed Kalmev Radix. *In order to* kill Kalmev Radix.

The cuff clicked as it came undone. He yanked the needle out of his other arm, and got up. His body ached, but he was steady enough, so he walked to the window, watching the Thuvhesit floater lights zipping past. Lurid pink and vibrant red and gray green, they wrapped around the squat ships like belts, not bright enough to light the way, just enough to show they were there.

He stood there for a long time, as night got deeper and deeper and traffic died down and Shissa itself went to sleep. Then a dark shape passed over the purple glow of the building across from the hospital. Another one drifted above the iceflower fields far below. A third rushed past the hospital itself, making the glass shudder under his hands. He recognized the patched-together metals. The Shotet ships were filling Shissa like a cup.

An alarm screeched in the corner of the room, and just a tick later, the door opened. Isae Benesit—shoes shining—tossed a canvas bag on the floor at his feet.

"Good to know our handcuffs don't work on you," she said. "Come on. You're going to get me out of here."

He didn't budge. The bag bulged in weird places from stiff armor—his, he assumed. It probably held his weapons and poisons, too; if whoever had dumped him in Shissa like a sack of trash had bothered to outfit him with one thing, they had probably thrown in the whole lot.

"You know, I'd really like to be the kind of person people just *listen* to," Isae said, her formal manner falling away in her frustration. "You think I should carry around a big stick, or something?"

He bent over the canvas bag and pulled his armor over his head. With one hand, he pulled the tough straps tight over his ribs, and with the other, he sorted through the bag for his knife. It was the one Cyra had given him on the street during the festival. He'd given it back to her once, in apology, but she had left it on the table on the sojourn ship before they left, and he had taken it with him.

"My sister?" he said.

"Right here." Cisi spoke from the hallway. "You're so tall, Akos."

Isae grabbed his arm. He let her move him around like a puppet. For someone who asked him to get her out, she sure was acting like she was getting *him* out.

When they were in the hallway, all the lights went off at once, leaving just some strips of emergency light on the left edge of the tile. Isae's hand was tight as she steered him down the hallway and around the corner. From deep in the building, he heard screams.

He reached back for Cisi's hand, and they all started to run, skidding around a corner toward the emergency exit. But at the end of the hallway were two dark figures dressed in Shotet armor.

His steps faltered. He wrenched his arm from Isae's grasp, and stepped back into the shadows.

"Akos!" Cisi sounded horrified.

Around the corner, Isae drew the weapon at her hip. Currentblade, not sharp, but set to a deadly density. The soldiers were moving toward her, slow, like you moved when you didn't want to startle an animal.

"Where do you think you are going?" one of them said. In Shotet, of course—he likely couldn't speak any other languages.

He was shorter than Isae, and sturdy—to put it kindly. His tongue flicked out to wet his lips, which were swollen from the cold. Shotet soldiers had never been this far north before, as far as

Akos could remember. They probably weren't ready for the temperature drop.

"I am leaving this hospital," Isae said in clumsy Shotet.

Both soldiers laughed. The second one was younger, his voice cracking.

"Nice accent," the older one said. "Where did you learn our language, from brim planet scum?"

Isae lunged, and Akos couldn't see much, but he heard her moan when she got hit. That was when he stood, best knife in hand, armor fastened tight.

"Stop," he said, walking around the corner again.

"What do you want?" the older soldier said.

Akos moved into the light. "I want you to leave her to me. Now."

When neither of the soldiers budged, he said, "I am a steward of the family Noavek—" It was technically true, and technically a lie. No one had ever given him a title, after all. "I was sent here by Ryzek Noavek to collect her. That will be much more challenging if I let you kill her."

Everybody went still, even Akos. They would have a clear shot at the emergency stairs, and all they had to do was get past these two . . . obstacles. The older Shotet ran his tongue over his lips again. "And what if I kill you and complete your mission for you? How well will I be rewarded by the sovereign of Shotet?"

"Don't." The younger soldier was wide-eyed. "I recognize him, he—"

The older Shotet swiped with his blade, but he was big and slow, obviously low-ranking. Akos jumped back, hunching to get his gut out of harm's way. When he swung his own knife, he struck only armor, sending sparks flying. But his other hand, his right hand, was already drawing another knife from the side of his boot. That one found flesh.

The soldier fell against him, spilling warm blood on his hands. Akos bore his weight, stunned, not by what he had done, but by the ease with which he had done it.

"You have a choice," he said to the young soldier who was left. His voice was ragged and not quite his own. "Stay and die. Run and live."

The young soldier with the squeaky laugh bolted down the hallway. He almost slipped as he turned the corner. Cisi was shaking, eyes shining from unshed tears. And Isae was pointing her knife at him.

He lowered the soldier to the ground. *Don't throw up*, he told himself. *Don't, don't throw up.*

"Steward of the family Noavek?" Isae said.

"Not exactly," he said.

"I still don't trust you," she said, but she put her knife down. "Let's go."

They hustled to the roof and ran into the wild, frozen air. By the time they made it to the floater—a black one, close to the edge of the landing pad—his teeth were chattering. The door opened at Cisi's touch, and they climbed in.

The floater's controls lit up when Cisi sat in the driver's seat, the night-vision screen expanding in front of her in green and the nav system glowing with a welcome. She reached under the control board and switched off the floater's outer lights, then typed in their home address and set the ship on autonav. High-speed.

It lifted from the landing pad and jerked forward, throwing Akos against the control panel. He'd forgotten to buckle himself in.

He twisted around to watch Shissa shrink behind them. Every building was lit up a different color: purple for the library, yellow for the hospital, green for the grocery. They hung—impossibly— like suspended raindrops. He watched them as the floater sped away, until the buildings were just a cluster of lights. When everything was near dark, he turned back to Cisi.

"You . . ." She gulped. Whatever it was she wanted to say, she couldn't say it, currentgift be damned. He reached for her, setting a clean finger—the others were red and sticky—on her arm.

The words came spilling out. "You killed him."

He cycled through a few different responses in his mind, ranging from *And he wasn't the first* to *I'm sorry*. None of them seemed right. He didn't want her to hate him, but he didn't want her to think he had come away from Shotet innocent. He didn't want to talk about it, but he didn't want to lie.

"He saved us both," Isae said sharply as she switched on the news scroll. A little holoscreen popped up above the autonav map, and Akos read the headlines as they spun in a circle.

Shotet invasion begins in Shissa, two hours after sunset.

Shotet invaders witnessed at Shissa hospital, eight Thuvhesit deaths reported.

"I sent Orieve away right after we left your room," Isae said. "She should have made it out all right. I can't send her a message now, it could be intercepted."

He held his hands against his legs, wishing like hell that he could wash them.

§

A news break appeared on the holoscreen when they descended into Hessa, a few hours before dawn.

Shissa police reporting two Thuvhesit captives taken by Shotet. Footage from the invasion shows a woman dragged from Shissa hospital by Shotet soldiers. Preliminary identification efforts suggest the woman is either Isae or Orieve Benesit.

Something big and fierce shredded his insides.

Orieve Benesit. Ori. Gone.

He tried not to look at Isae, to give her a tick to react on her own, but there wasn't much to watch. Cisi's hand snaked out to touch Isae's, but Isae just flicked a switch to turn the news feed off, and stared out the window.

"Well," Isae said at last. "I'll just have to go get her, then."

CHAPTER 28 | AKOS

WHEN THEY GOT TO Hessa, the floater moved in a wide arc around the mountain and drifted toward the feathergrass. It sank to the ground in front of his family's house, crushing stems and tufts under it. The blood had dried on Akos's hands.

Isae got out of the floater first, and Cisi followed. When Akos jumped out, the doors closed behind him. The feathergrass was flattened in a circle around it.

Cisi led the way to the house, which was good, because Akos didn't have the strength. All the windows were dark reminders of the last time he'd been there. When Cisi opened the door, and the smell of spices and chopped saltfruit wafted over him, he half expected his dad's body to be on the floor in the living room, soaked through.

Akos paused. Breathed. Kept walking.

He skimmed the wood paneling with his knuckles on the way to the kitchen. Past the wall where all the family pictures used to hang. Blank now. The living room wasn't at all the same—it was more a study, with two desks and bookcases and not a squashy cushion in sight. But the kitchen, with its scraped-up table and rough-hewn bench, was the same.

Cisi shook the chandelier over the kitchen table to light the burnstones. Their light was still tinted red.

"Where's Mom?" he said as an image of her popped into his mind: she was standing on a creaky stool, dusting the chandelier with hushflower.

"Oracle meeting," Cisi said. "They meet all the time now. It'll take her a few days."

"Days" would be too late. He would be long gone by then.

The desire to wash his hands became a need. He went to the sink. A lump of homemade soap sat near the faucet, with little purity petals pressed inside it to pretty it up. He worked it into a lather, then rinsed his hands once, twice, three times. Dragged his fingernails along the lines in his palm. Scrubbed beneath them. By the time he was done his palms were bright pink and Cisi was setting out mugs for tea.

He hesitated with his hand over the knife drawer. He wanted to mark the loss of the Shotet soldier on his arm. There was a vial of feathergrass extract beside the other vials he carried to stain the wound. But had he really just let something so Shotet become an instinct? Clean hands, clean blade, new mark?

He closed his eyes like darkness was all he needed to clear his head. Somewhere out there, the nameless soldier he had killed had some family, some friends, who were counting on his loss to be recorded. Akos knew—though it disturbed him to know—that he wasn't about to pretend the death hadn't happened.

So he took out a carving knife and shoved it into the furnace flames, turning the blade to sterilize it. Crouched there by the heat, he carved a straight line into his arm with the hot blade, next to the other marks. Then he poured feathergrass extract on the tines of a fork and dragged it in a straight line down the cut. It was clumsy, but it would have to do.

Then he sat right there on the floor, holding his head. Riding out the pain. Blood ran down his arm and pooled in the crook of his elbow.

"The invaders might come to Hessa," Isae said. "Looking for me. We should leave as soon as possible and find Ori."

"'We'?" he said. "I'm not taking the chancellor of Thuvhe to Ryzek Noavek, not with my fate as it is. That would really make me a traitor."

She eyed his marked arm. "If you aren't already."

"Oh, shut up," he snapped. She raised her eyebrows, but he went on. "You think you know exactly how I'll meet my fate? You think you know what it means, better than I do?"

"You claim to be loyal to Thuvhe, but you tell its chancellor to 'shut up'?" There was a note of humor in her voice.

"No, I told the woman in my kitchen asking for one hell of a favor to shut up," he said. "I would never disrespect my chancellor that way. Your Highness."

She leaned toward him. "Then take the woman in your kitchen to Shotet." Leaned back. "I'm not an idiot; I know I'll need your help to get me there."

"You don't trust me."

"Again. Not an idiot," she said. "You help me get my sister out, and I'll help you get your brother out. No guarantees, of course."

Akos almost swore. Why was it, he wondered, that everyone seemed to know exactly what to offer him to make him agree to things? Not that he was convinced she could help him, but he had been teetering on the edge of agreeing anyway.

"Akos," Isae said, and the use of his name, without malice, startled him a little. "If someone told you that you couldn't go save your brother, that your life was too important to risk for theirs, would you listen?"

Her face was washed out and dotted with sweat, her cheek red from where the soldier had hit her. She didn't look much like a chancellor. The scars on her face said something different about her, too—that she, like Cyra, knew what she was risking when she risked her life.

"All right," he said. "I'll help you."

There was a loud crack as Cisi brought her mug down hard on the table, splashing hot tea over her hand. She grimaced, wiping her hand on her shirt and thrusting it out for him to take. Isae looked confused, but Akos understood—Cisi had something to say, and much as he was afraid to hear it, he couldn't very well say no.

He clasped her hand.

"I hope you both realize that I'm coming with you," she said hotly.

"No," he said. "You can't be in that kind of danger, absolutely not."

"You don't want me to be in danger?" Her voice was rougher than it ever had been before; she was rigid as a crossbeam. "How do you think I feel about *you* going back there? This family has been through enough uncertainty, enough loss." She was scowling. Isae looked like she had just been smacked, and no wonder—she had probably never seen Cisi like this, free to say whatever she wanted, free to cry and yell and make everyone uncomfortable. "If we all get killed in Shotet, we'll get killed together, but—"

"Don't talk about death that way, like it's nothing!"

"I don't think you get it." A tremor went through her arm, her hand, her voice. Her eyes found his, and he focused on the spot on her iris, the place where the pupil broke open. "After you were taken, and Mom came back, she was . . . insensible. So *I* dragged Dad's body out to the field to burn. *I* cleaned up the living room."

He couldn't imagine, couldn't imagine the horror of scrubbing your own father's blood out of the floor. Better to set the whole house on fire, better to leave and never come back.

"Don't you dare tell me I don't know what death is," she said. "I know."

Alarmed, he lifted a hand to her cheek, pressed her face into his shoulder. Her curly hair itched his chin.

"Fine" was all he said. It was agreement enough.

They agreed to sleep for a few hours before they left, and Akos went upstairs alone. Without thinking, he skipped the sixth step, some part of him remembering that it groaned louder than the others. The hallway upstairs was a little crooked; it listed to the right just after the bathroom, the curve *wrong* somehow. The room he'd shared with Eijeh was at the end. He opened the door with his fingertips.

The sheets on Eijeh's bed were curled like they were around a still-sleeping body, and there was a pair of dirty socks in the corner, stained brown at the heels from his shoes. On Akos's side of the room, the sheets were taut around the mattress, a pillow wedged between bed and wall. Akos had never been able to last long with a pillow.

Through the big round window he saw feathergrass rippling in the dark, and stars.

He held his pillow in his lap when he sat. The pair of shoes lined up with the bed frame were so much smaller than the pair he was wearing that he smiled. Smiled, and then cried, shoving his face in the pillow to stifle himself. It wasn't happening. He wasn't here. He wasn't about to leave home when he'd only just found it again.

The tears subsided eventually, and he fell asleep with his shoes still on.

A while later, when he woke, he stood under the spray in the hall bathroom for just a little longer than usual, hoping it would relax him. No use.

When he got out, though, there was a stack of clothes just outside the door. His dad's old clothes. The shirt was too loose through the shoulders and waist, but tight across the chest—he and Aoseh were completely different shapes. The pants were long enough, but just barely, tucked into the top of Akos's boots.

When he took his towel back to the bathroom to hang it—that was what his mom would return to, a wet towel and rumpled sheets and no children—Isae was there, already dressed in some of his mom's clothes, the black pants bunching around her waist under the belt. She prodded one of her scars in the mirror, and met his eyes.

"If you try to say something meaningful and profound about scars, I'll punch you in the head," she said.

He shrugged, and turned his left arm so the kill marks faced her. "I guarantee you yours aren't as ugly as mine."

"At least you chose yours."

Well, she had a point.

"How did you come to be marked by a Shotet blade?" he said.

He'd heard some of the soldiers trading scar stories before. Not kill-mark stories, but other scars, a white line on a kneecap from a childhood accident, a swipe from a kitchen knife during an invasion of Hessa, a drunken accident involving a head and a door frame. They'd all been in stitches over each other's stories. That wasn't going to happen now, he was sure.

"The scavenge isn't always as peaceful as they might have you believe," Isae said. "During the last one, my ship had to land on Othyr for repairs, and while we were there, one of the crew got really sick. While we were parked at the hospital, we were attacked by Shotet soldiers who were raiding the medicine stores. One of them cut my face and left me for dead."

"I'm sorry," he said automatically. For some reason, he wanted to tell her about where Othyrian medical aid went—to Ryzek's supporters only—and how few people knew about it. But it really wasn't a good time to explain Shotet to her, especially not if she would think he was excusing the soldier for stealing medicine and scarring her face.

"I'm not sorry." Isae seized the soap bar next to the sink like she wanted to break it in half, and started washing her hands. "Hard to forget who your enemies are when you have scars like mine." She cleared her throat. "Hope you don't mind, I borrowed some of your mother's clothes."

"I'm wearing a dead man's underwear," he said. "Why would I mind?"

She smiled a little, which Akos felt was progress enough.

None of them wanted to wait any longer than they had to, Akos in particular. He knew the more time he spent there, the harder it would be to leave. Better, he thought, to reopen the wound fast, get it over with, so he could bandage it up again.

They packed supplies, food, clothes, and iceflowers, and piled into the spare floater. It had just enough fuel in it to get them across the feathergrass, and that was all they needed. At Cisi's touch it lifted off the ground, and Akos set the autonav for a spot in what looked like the middle of nowhere. They would go to Jorek's house first. It was the only relatively safe place he knew outside of Voa.

As they flew, he watched the feathergrass below them, showing the wind's pattern as it tilted and turned.

"What do the Shotet say about the feathergrass?" Isae said suddenly. "I mean, we say early Thuvhesit settlers planted it to keep the Shotet at bay, but obviously they have a different perspective, right?"

"The Shotet say they planted it," Akos said. "To keep out Thuvhesit outsiders. But it's native to Ogra."

"I can still hear them from up here," Cisi said. "The voices in the grasses."

"Whose voices?" The sharpness left Isae's voice when she spoke to Cisi.

"My father's, mostly," Cisi said.

"I hear my mother," Isae said. "Wonder if we only hear the dead."

"How long has it been since she died?"

"Couple seasons. Same time I got cut." Isae had lapsed into some other, more casual diction. Even her posture had changed, spine bent.

They kept talking, and Akos stayed quiet, his thoughts drifting back to Cyra.

If she had died, he was sure he would have felt it now, like something stabbing him right through the sternum. It wasn't possible to lose a friend like her without knowing, was it? Though the current didn't flow through him, her life force surely did. She had kept him alive for too long. Maybe if he held on tight enough now, he could do the same for her, from far away.

In late afternoon, when the sun was swollen with what was left of the day, they started to run out of fuel. The floater shuddered. Under them the feathergrass was thinning, and between it there was low, gray-brown grass that moved like hair in the wind.

Cisi guided the ship to a place near some wildflowers. It got frosty here, closer to the equator, but warm swells of air came from the sea and filled the valley of Voa. Other kinds of plants could grow, not just iceflowers.

They climbed out, and started walking. Along the horizon was the purple swell of the currentstream, a little cluster of buildings, and the glint of Shotet ships. Jorek had told him how to get to his family's house, but the last time Akos had been out here was right after he had killed Kalmev Radix, and Vas and the others had just beaten the snot out of him, so he didn't remember it too well. The land was so flat there weren't many places for a small village to hide—lucky.

He heard shifting in the grass ahead of them, and between stalks, he saw something dark and massive. He grabbed Isae's hand, on his left, and Cisi's, on his right, holding them both still.

Up ahead the creature was gliding. The clicking of its pincers came from all directions. It was big—as wide as he was tall, easily— and its body was covered with dark blue plates. It had more legs than he could count, and he could see its head only because of the teeth glistening in its wide, curved mouth. They were as long as his fingers.

An Armored One.

His face was izits from its hard-plated side. It exhaled—like sighing—and its eyes, beady and black, almost hidden under a plate, closed. Beside him, Cisi shuddered with fear.

"The current drives Armored Ones into mad rages," he whispered right against the creature, which had gone to sleep, much as it defied logic. He took a slow step back. "That's why they attack people, because we're such good channels for the current."

His hands squeaked against theirs, his palms were so sweaty.

"But," Isae said, sounding strained, "you don't channel the current, so."

"So they hardly know I'm there," he replied. "Come on."

He led them away from the sleepy animal, checking over his shoulder to make sure it wasn't following. It stayed put.

"I guess we know how you earned your armor," Isae said.

"*That's* where the armor comes from?" Cisi said. "I thought all that stuff about slaying beasts was just stupid Thuvhesit rumor."

"It's not rumor," he said. "It's not really some story of triumph, in my case. It fell asleep and I killed it. I felt so bad about it afterward I marked it on my arm."

"Why did you do it?" Isae said. "If you didn't want to, I mean."

"I wanted armor," he said. "Not every Shotet earns that kind of armor, so it's a kind of . . . status symbol. I wanted them to see me as an equal, and shut up about me having thin Thuvhesit skin."

Cisi snorted. "They clearly have never weathered a Hessa winter."

He led them toward the distant buildings, through patches of wildflowers so fragile they came apart under his boots.

"So are you going to tell us where we're going, or do you expect us to just march right into those buildings up ahead?" Isae said, once they were close enough to see what the houses were made of—blue-gray stone, with small glass windows stained in all different colors. It was just a few buildings, hardly enough to be called a village. With the setting sun glinting off the glass, and the wildflowers growing right up against the stone, the place was downright pretty.

He was taking a chance, coming here, but then, no matter what he did they were in trouble, so it was as good an option as any.

He was twitchy with nerves. These houses would be connected to the Shotet news feed. They would know what happened to Cyra here. He kept his left hand up by his right shoulder as he walked, so he could draw his knife if he needed to. He didn't know what waited for them behind those bright windows. He drew his weapon when he saw a flash of movement, one of the doors opening. A small, sly-looking woman stepped out, her hands dripping water. She was holding a cloth. He knew her—Ara Kuzar. The late Suzao's wife, and Jorek's mother.

Well, at least they were in the right place.

"Hello," Ara said. Her voice was lower than he'd expected. He'd only ever seen her once—as he walked out of the amphitheater after killing her husband. Her hand had been clutched in Jorek's.

"Hello," he replied. "I'm—"

"I know who you are, Akos," she said. "My name is Ara, but I'm sure you already know that, too."

No point in denying it. He nodded.

"Why don't you come inside?" she said. "Your friends can come, too, as long as they don't cause trouble."

Isae arched an eyebrow at him as she took the lead, climbing the steps. Her hands hovered over her legs, moving to grasp fabric that wasn't there to hold. She was used to fine clothing, probably, and still moved like an upper-class woman now, head high and shoulders back. She'd never weathered a Hessa winter, either, but there were harder things to weather.

They followed Ara down a narrow, creaky staircase to a kitchen. The floors were blue tile, the stain uneven, and the white paint flaked off the walls. But it was warm, and there was a big steady table with all the chairs pushed back, like there had been a lot of people there not long ago. A screen played the news feed on the far wall—it was jarring to see the synthetic light buried in the flaky wall, new and old married, as they were all over Shotet.

"I sent a signal to Jorek, so he should return soon," Ara said. "Do your friends speak Shotet?"

"One of us," Isae said. "I only learned a few seasons ago, so . . . go slowly."

"No, we can carry on in Thuvhesit," Ara said. Her Thuvhesit was stilted, but understandable.

"This is my sister, Cisi," he said, gesturing to Cisi. "And my friend—"

"Badha," Isae said easily.

"A pleasure to meet you both," Ara said. "I have to confess, Akos, I am a little offended you didn't accept my gift to you. The ring?"

She was looking at his hands, which were shaking a little.

CARVE THE MARK

"Oh," he said. He stuck a thumb under the collar of his shirt and brought the chain out. From the end dangled the ring she'd sent him through her son. Really, he'd wanted to toss it in the garbage rather than wear it—Suzao's death wasn't something he wanted to remind himself of. But it was something he *needed* to remind himself of.

Ara nodded her approval.

"How do you two know each other?" Cisi asked. He wondered if her softened voice was intended to make this situation comfortable. *Not worth the effort*, he thought.

"That," Ara said, "is a story for another time."

Akos couldn't stand it anymore. "I don't want to be rude," he said, "but I need to know about Cyra."

Ara folded her hands over her stomach. "What about Miss Noavek?"

"Is she . . . ?" He couldn't quite say the word.

"She is alive."

He closed his eyes, just for a tick letting himself think about her again. She was lively in his memories, fighting in the training room like war was a dance, searching windows into black space like they were paintings. She made ugly things beautiful, somehow, and he would never understand it. But she was alive.

"I wouldn't celebrate just yet," spoke a voice from behind him. He turned to see a slight girl with white-blond hair and a pink eye patch over one eye. He recognized her from the sojourn ship, but didn't remember her name.

Jorek was behind her, his mop of curly hair falling in his eyes, the shadow of a beard along his jaw.

"Akos?" he said. "What are you . . . ?"

He trailed off as he spotted Cisi and Isae.

"Cisi, Badha," Akos said. "This is Jorek, and . . . ?"

"Teka," the familiar girl said. That was right—she was the daughter of that renegade who had been executed before the sojourn. Cyra had gone over to talk to her before they set out for Pitha.

"Right," Akos said. "Well, Cisi is my sister, and Badha is my . . . friend. From Thuvhe. Cisi doesn't speak Shotet." He waited a beat. "What did you mean by 'don't celebrate'?"

Teka sat in one of the empty chairs. Slung her body across it, really, her knees spread wide and her arm dangling over the back of the chair.

"By the look of it, little Noavek won't last much longer," she said. "We're trying to figure out a way to break her loose. Now that you've come here—stupid move, I should add—maybe you can help us."

"Break her loose?" Akos turned to Jorek. "Why would *you* want to do that?"

Jorek hoisted himself onto the counter across from Cisi. He flashed a smile at her, his eyes going sleepy, the way people's often did when they were around his sister. Akos recognized, then, the gift of it. Not just a force that strangled Cisi, kept her from crying, but also one that gave her power over other people.

"Well," Jorek said, "this is a renegade stronghold. As you may have gathered."

Akos hadn't really thought about it. Jorek seemed to know things other people didn't, but that didn't mean he was a renegade. And Teka was missing an eye, which meant she was no friend of Ryzek's, but that wasn't a guarantee, either.

"So?" Akos said.

"Well." Jorek looked confused. "She didn't tell you?"

"Tell me what?" Akos demanded.

"Cyra was working with us," Teka said. "During the attack on the sojourn ship, I was supposed to take her out—take out Ryzek's Scourge while announcing his fate on the intercom, see?"

"Don't call her that," Akos said. He felt Isae's eyes on him, and his cheeks went hot.

"Yeah, yeah." Teka waved him off. "Well, she bested me, and she let me go. And then she found me, requested a meeting. She offered to give us whatever we wanted—information, help, whatever—if we did something for her in exchange: get you out of Shotet." Teka looked at Jorek. "That's why she didn't tell him. Because she wanted to get him out, but he wouldn't leave without his brother."

Jorek clicked his tongue.

Those weeks after Ryzek had threatened him, after Cyra tortured Zosita and kept up appearances on Pitha, she had let him think she was just doing whatever Ryzek said. Let Akos believe the worst of her. And all that time she was out working with renegades, giving whatever she could to get him out. It was like she had become someone new and he hadn't even noticed.

"She was helping us assassinate Ryzek when she got caught. She got us out, but it was too late for her," Teka said. "But we followed through on our end. Snuck back in, and she was gone—we don't know where they put her—but you were there, incapacitated, locked up in your room again. Half-starved, might I add. So we got you out. We thought you might be useful in keeping her on our side."

"I also wanted to help you," Jorek supplied.

"Yeah, you're a hero. Noted," Teka said.

"Why . . ." Akos shook his head. "Why would Cyra do this?"

"You know why," Teka said. "What's the only thing more important to her than her fear of her brother?" When he didn't answer, she sighed. Exasperated, clearly. "*You*, of course, have that singular honor."

Isae and Cisi were staring, one with suspicion and the other, confusion. He didn't even know how to start explaining it. Cyra Noavek was a name every Thuvhesit knew, a monster story they told to scare each other. What did you say, when you found out the monster wasn't worthy of the name?

Nothing. You said nothing.

"What did Ryzek do to her?" he said darkly.

"Show him," Teka said to Jorek.

Jorek touched the screen on the far wall, flicking the news feed out of the way. A few swipes of his fingers and there was footage playing on the screen.

The sights moved in from far away, showing an amphitheater with a cage of white light across its gaping top. The seats in the amphitheater were full, the lower rows on stone benches and the higher rows on metal ones, but it was clear from the somber faces that this wasn't a celebration day.

The sights narrowed around a platform, suspended over the seats in wood and metal. Ryzek stood on top of it, polished from his black shoes to the armor that covered his chest. His hair was freshly clipped, showing off the bones in his head, the sheen of his scalp. Cisi and Isae sat back at the sight of him, both at once. Akos was past fear of Ryzek, now. Had long since moved into pure revulsion.

Standing at Ryzek's left was Vas, and at his right . . .

"Eijeh," Cisi breathed. "Why?"

"He's been . . . brainwashed. Sort of," Akos said, careful, and Jorek snorted.

The sights panned left, to the edge of the platform, where soldiers surrounded a kneeling woman. Cyra. She wore the same clothes he'd seen her in days ago, but they were torn in places now, and dark with blood. Her thick hair covered her face, so for a tick he wasn't sure if Ryzek had taken out one of her eyes. He did that when a person was disgraced, sometimes, so they couldn't hide it.

Cyra lifted her head, showing off a few purple-blue bruises and a dull—two-eyed—stare.

Then Ryzek spoke: "Today I bring difficult news. Someone we thought to be one of our most faithful—my sister, Cyra Noavek— has revealed herself to be the worst kind of traitor. She has been collaborating with our enemies across the Divide, providing them with information about our strategy, military, and movements."

"He doesn't want to admit that there's a real renegade group out there," Jorek said, over the roar of disgust from the crowd. "Better to say she's collaborating with Thuvhesits."

"He chooses his lies well," Isae said, and it didn't quite sound like a compliment.

Ryzek continued, "I have also recently uncovered proof that this woman"—he pointed at his sister, conveniently showing off the line of kill marks that went from his wrist all the way up to his elbow—"is responsible for the death of my mother, Ylira Noavek."

Akos covered his face. There was no worse blow Ryzek could have dealt Cyra than this. She'd always known that.

"I confess that my familial attachment has obscured my judgment in this matter, but now that I have learned of her betrayal and her"—Ryzek paused—"her vicious murder of our mother, my vision is clear. I have determined that the appropriate level of punishment for this enemy of Shotet is execution by way of nemhalzak."

When the footage shifted back to Cyra, Akos saw that her shoulders were shaking, but there weren't any tears in her eyes. She was laughing. And as she laughed, the currentshadows danced, not under her skin like blood running through veins, but on *top* of it, like smoke around a thurible. They had done the same thing the night Ryzek forced her to hurt Akos, floated away from her body in a haze.

Her currentgift had changed.

Ryzek nodded to Vas. Vas crossed the platform, drawing the knife at his back. The soldiers around Cyra stepped aside for him. Cyra smirked at him, and said something inaudible. Ryzek said something inaudible back, stepped close, and leaned in, his lips moving fast over words no one else could hear. Vas grabbed her by the hair, forcing her head back and to the side. Her throat was exposed; Vas angled the blade over it, and as the knife dug in, Akos gritted his teeth, and looked away.

"You get the idea," Jorek said. There was silence as the footage stopped.

"What did he do?" Akos said roughly.

"He . . . scarred her," Teka said. "Took all the skin from throat to skull. Not sure why. All the rite requires is flesh. Mutilator's choice."

She drew a line from the side of her neck up to the middle of her scalp. Akos felt like he might throw up.

"That word he used, I don't know it," Isae said. "Nem—nemhalzet?"

"Nemhalzak," Jorek said. "It's the elimination of someone's status, perceived or actual. It means anyone can challenge her to the arena, to fight to the death, and it means she's no longer formally considered Shotet. With all the people she's hurt at his behest, and all the people who loved her mother, well . . . there are plenty of people who want to challenge her. Ryzek will let as many of them do it as it takes to kill her."

"And with that wound in her head, she's losing blood fast," Teka said. "They put a bandage on it, but obviously that's not enough for what he did to her."

"She'll fight all those challenges in that amphitheater?" Akos said.

"Most likely," Teka said. "This is supposed to be a very public event. But that force field will fry anything that touches it—"

Akos talked over her. "Obviously you have a ship, or you wouldn't have been able to dump me on that hospital landing pad."

"Yeah," Jorek said. "A fast, stealthy one, too."

"Then I know how to get her," Akos said.

"I don't remember agreeing to some detour rescue mission," Isae snapped. "Particularly not for Ryzek Noavek's little terror. You think I don't know the things she's done, Kereseth? The rest of the galaxy hears plenty of Shotet rumors."

"I don't care what you think you know," Akos said. "You want my help getting any further? You'll wait for me to do this first."

Isae crossed her arms. But Akos had her, and she seemed to know it.

§

Ara offered Cisi and Isae a spare room upstairs, and a cot on the floor in Jorek's room for Akos. But judging by the look Cisi gave her brother as they reached the top of the staircase, she wasn't about to just let him leave. So he followed her into a little bedroom with a big, bulgy mattress in it, and a furnace in the corner. Multicolored light spotted the floor, sunset burning through the windows.

He took off his armor there, but left the knife in his boot. There was no telling what would happen here. Akos felt like Vas and Ryzek were around every corner.

"Is—Badha," Cisi said. "Why don't you clean up first? I need to talk to Akos."

Isae's head bobbed, and she left, nudging the door shut with her heel. Akos sat down on the bed next to Cisi, blue and green and purple dots of light marking his shoes. She put her hand on his wrist.

"Eijeh" was all she said.

So he told her. About all the memories Ryzek had poured into Eijeh, and all the memories he had drained. About the new words Eijeh used and the way he spun a knife on his palm just like Ryzek did. He didn't tell her how Eijeh had watched while Ryzek hurt Akos, not once, but twice, and he didn't talk about how Eijeh had used his visions to help Ryzek. There was no reason for her to lose hope.

"That's why you didn't try to escape," Cisi said softly. "Because you needed to kidnap him to do it, and that's . . . harder."

Near impossible is what it is, Akos thought.

"That," he said, "and what kind of future do I have in Thuvhe, Cisi? You think I get to be the first one in the galaxy to defy his fate?" He shook his head. "Maybe it's better if we just see the truth. We don't get to be a family anymore."

"No." She was very firm. "You didn't think you'd ever see me again, but here I am, right? You don't know how fate finds you, and neither do I. But until it does, we get to be whatever we can be."

She put her hand in his and squeezed. He saw a little of their dad in her arched, sympathetic eyebrows and the dimple in her cheek. They sat there for a little while, their shoulders touching, listening to the splatter of water coming from the bathroom across the hall.

"What's Cyra Noavek like?" she asked him.

"She's . . ." He shook his head. How could he describe a whole person like that? She was tough as dried meat. She loved space. She knew how to dance. She was too good at hurting people. She had gotten some renegades to dump him in Thuvhe without Eijeh because she hadn't respected his goddamn decisions, and he was stupidly grateful for it. She . . . well, she was *Cyra*.

Cisi was smiling. "You know her well. People are harder to sum up when you know them well."

"Yeah, I guess I do."

"If you think she's worth saving, I guess we all just have to trust you on that," Cisi said. "Hard as it is."

Isae came out of the bathroom, her hair wet but pulled back in a tight knot, like it was lacquered to her head. She wore a different shirt, another one of their mom's, embroidered at the collar with little flowers. She shook out the other one—wet, like she'd washed it by hand—and hung it over a chair near the furnace.

"You've got grass in your hair," Isae said to Cisi, with a grin.

"It's a new look I'm trying," Cisi said in response.

"It works for you," Isae said. "Then again, everything does, doesn't it?"

Cisi flushed. Isae avoided Akos's eyes, turning toward the furnace to warm her hands.

There were a couple more people crammed in the low, dim room with the flaking walls when Cisi, Isae, and Akos went downstairs again. Jorek introduced them to Sovy, one of his mother's friends, who lived just down the road and wore an embroidered scarf in her hair, and Jyo, who wasn't much older than them, with eyes that looked a lot like Isae's, suggesting some common ancestor. He was playing an instrument that lay flat on his lap, pressing buttons and plucking strings faster than Akos could follow. There was food on the big table, half-eaten.

He sat next to Cisi and shoveled some food on his plate. There wasn't much meat—it was hard to come by out here, outside of Voa—but plenty of saltfruit, which was filling enough. Jyo offered Isae a fried feathergrass stalk with a big smile, but Akos snatched it before she could take it.

"You don't want to eat that," he said. "Unless you want to spend the next six hours hallucinating."

"Last time Jyo slipped someone one of those, they wandered around this house talking about giant dancing babies," Jorek said.

"Yeah, yeah," Teka said. "Laugh all you want, but you would be scared too if you hallucinated giant babies."

"It was worth it, whether I will ever be forgiven or not," Jyo said, winking. He had a soft, slippery way of talking.

"Do they work on you?" Cisi asked Akos, nodding to the stalk in his hand.

In answer, Akos bit into the stalk, which tasted like earth and salt and sour.

"Your gift is odd," Cisi said. "I'm sure Mom would have some kind of vague, wise thing to say about that."

"Ooh. What was he like as a child?" Jorek said, folding his hands and leaning close to Akos's sister. "Was he actually a child, or did he just sort of appear one day as a fully grown adult, full of angst?"

Akos glared at him.

"He was short and chubby," Cisi said. "Irritable. Very particular about his socks."

"My socks?" Akos said.

"Yeah!" she said. "Eijeh told me you always arranged them in order of preference from left to right. Your favorite ones were yellow."

He remembered them. Mustard yellow, with big woven fibers that made them look lumpy when they weren't on. His warmest pair.

"How do you all know each other?" Cisi asked. The delicate question was enough to dispel the tension that had come up at Eijeh's name.

"Sovy used to make candy for all the village kids when I was little," Jorek said. "Unfortunately, she doesn't speak Thuvhesit very well, or she'd tell you about my misdeeds herself."

"And I first met Jorek in a public bathroom. I was whistling while I"—Jyo paused—"relieved myself, and Jorek decided it would be amusing to harmonize with me."

"He did not find that charming," Jorek said.

"My mother was a kind of . . . leader of the revolt. One of them, anyway," said Teka. "She came back to us from the colony of exiles from the Noavek regime about a season ago, to help us strategize. The exiles support our efforts to end Ryzek's life."

Isae's brow was furrowed—it was furrowed a lot of the time, actually, like she didn't like the space between her two eyebrows and wanted to hide it—and this time, Akos understood why. The difference between exiles and renegades, and the connection between them, wasn't of much interest to him—all he wanted was to make sure Cyra was safe, and to get Eijeh out of Shotet; he didn't care what else happened there. But to Isae, chancellor of Thuvhe, it was clearly important to know there was a swelling of dissent against Ryzek, both inside Shotet and outside.

"How many of you—renegades—are there?" Isae asked.

"Am I likely to answer that question?" was Teka's reply. The answer was clearly no, so Isae moved on.

"Is your involvement in the revolt why . . ." Isae waved a hand over her face. "The eye?"

"This? Oh, I have two eyes, I just like the patch," Teka said.

"Really?" Cisi asked.

"No," Teka said, and everyone laughed.

The food was plain, almost bland, but Akos didn't mind it. It was a little more like home, a little less like Noavek finery. Teka started humming along to Jyo's song, and Sovy drummed on the tabletop with her fingers, so hard Akos's fork rattled against his plate whenever he set it down.

Then Teka and Jorek got up and danced. Isae leaned over to Jyo while he was playing and asked, "So, if this particular group of renegades is working to rescue Cyra . . . what are the other rene-gade groups doing? Hypothetically, I mean."

Jyo narrowed one eye at her, but answered anyway. "Hypotheti-cally, those of us Shotet who are low in status need things they can't get. And they need someone to smuggle it in for them."

"As in . . . hypothetical weapons?" Isae said.

"Possibly, but that's not top priority." Jyo plucked a few wrong strings, swore, and got himself on the right ones again. "Top priority would be food and medicine. Lots of runs to Othyr and back. Gotta feed people before they can fight for you, right? And the farther out of the center of Voa you get, the more diseased and starved people are."

Isae's face tightened, but she nodded.

Akos didn't think about it much, what was going on outside the tangle of Noaveks he'd gotten himself into. But he thought about what Cyra had said about Ryzek keeping supplies to himself, doling them out to his people or hoarding them for later, and he felt a little bit sick.

Teka and Jorek spun around each other, and swayed, Jorek surprisingly graceful, given his gangliness. Cisi and Isae sat shoulder to shoulder, leaned back against the wall. Every so often Isae gave a tired smile. It didn't quite look right on her face—it wasn't one of Ori's smiles, and she wore Ori's face, scarred though it was. But Akos figured he would have to get used to her.

Sovy sang a few bars of Jyo's song, and they ate until they were warm and full and tired.

CHAPTER 29 | CYRA

IT WAS DIFFICULT TO sleep after someone had peeled one's skin off with a knife, but I gave it my best effort.

My pillowcase was soaked with blood that morning when I awoke, though I had of course lain on the side Vas had not flayed from throat to skull. The only reason I hadn't bled to death yet was that the gaping wound was covered with stitching cloth, a medical innovation from Othyr that kept wounds closed and dissolved as they healed. It was not meant for wounds as severe as mine.

I stripped the case from the pillow and tossed it in the corner. The shadows danced over my arm, pricking me. For most of my life, they had run alongside my veins, visible through my skin. When I woke up after the interrogation—a soldier had told me my heart stopped, then started again of its own accord—the shadows were traveling over the surface of my body instead. They still caused me pain, but it was more bearable. I didn't understand why.

But then Ryzek had declared nemhalzak, and had Vas cut my skin away from my body like the rind from a fruit, and forced me to fight in the arena, so I was in just as much pain as usual.

He had asked me where I wanted it, the scar. If it could even be called that—scars were dark lines on a person's skin, not . . . *patches*. But nemhalzak had to be paid for with flesh, and it had to be on *display*, readily visible. With my mind addled by rage, I had told him to scar me the same way he had scarred Akos, when the Kereseth brothers first arrived. Ear to jaw.

And when Vas had accomplished that much, Ryzek told him to keep going.

Get some of her hair, too.

I breathed through my nose. I didn't want to throw up. I couldn't afford to throw up, in fact—I needed all the strength I had left.

As he had every day since I self-revived, Eijeh Kereseth came to watch me eat breakfast. He set a tray of food at my feet and leaned against the wall across from me, hunched, his posture bad as ever. Today his jaw bore the bruise I had given him the day before, when I tried to escape on the way to the arena and managed to get a few hits in before the guards in the hallway dragged me away from him.

"I didn't think you would be back, after yesterday," I said to him.

"I'm not afraid of you. You won't kill me," Eijeh replied. He had drawn his weapon, and he was spinning the blade on his palm, catching it when it made a full rotation. He did it without looking at it.

I snorted. "I'll kill just about anyone, haven't you heard the rumors?"

"You won't kill me," Eijeh repeated. "Because you love my delusional brother far too much for your own good."

I had to laugh at that. I hadn't realized that silky-voiced Eijeh Kereseth read me so well.

"I feel like I know you," Eijeh said suddenly. "I suppose I *do* know you, don't I? I do now."

"I'm not really in the mood for a philosophical discussion about what makes a person who they are," I said. "But even if you are more Ryzek than Eijeh at this point, you still don't know me. You—whoever you are—never bothered to."

Eijeh rolled his eyes a little. "Poor misunderstood daughter of privilege."

"Says the walking garbage can for all the things Ryzek wants to forget," I snapped. "Why doesn't he just kill me, anyway? All this drama beforehand is very elaborate, even for him."

Eijeh didn't answer, which was an answer in itself. Ryzek hadn't killed me yet because he needed to do it this way, in public. Maybe word had spread that I had helped with an assassination attempt, and now he needed to destroy my reputation before he let me die. Or maybe he just wanted to watch me suffer.

Somehow I didn't believe that.

"Is giving me useless cutlery really necessary?" I said, stabbing my toast with the knife instead of slicing it.

"The sovereign is concerned that you will try to end your life before the appropriate time," Eijeh said.

The appropriate time. I wondered if Eijeh had chosen my manner of death, then. The oracle, plucking the ideal future from an array of options.

"End my life with *this* thing? My fingernails are sharper." I brought the knife down, point first, on the mattress. I slammed it so hard the bed frame shuddered, and let go. The knife fell over, not even sharp enough to penetrate fabric. I winced, not even sure what part of my body hurt.

"I suppose he thinks you're creative enough to find a way," Eijeh said softly.

I stuffed the last bite of toast into my mouth and sat back against the wall, my arms folded. We were in one of the polished, glossy cells in the belly of the amphitheater, beneath the stadium seats that were already filling with people hungry to watch me die. I had won the last challenge, but I was running out of strength. This morning walking to the toilet had been a feat.

"How sweet," I said, spreading my arms wide to display my bruises. "See how my brother loves me?"

"You're making jokes," Ryzek said from just outside the cell. I could hear him, muffled, through the glass wall that separated us. "You must be getting desperate."

"No, desperate is playing this stupid game before you kill me, just to make me look bad," I said. "Are you that afraid that the people of Shotet will rally behind me? How pathetic."

"Try to get to your feet, and we'll all see 'pathetic,'" Ryzek said. "Come on. Time to go."

"Are you at least going to tell me who I'm facing today?" I said. I placed my hands on the bed frame, gritted my teeth, and pushed myself up.

It took all my strength to swallow the cry of pain that swelled in my throat. But I did it.

"You'll see," Ryzek said. "I am eager—and I'm sure you agree—to end this at last. So I have arranged for a special contest this morning."

He was dressed in synthetic armor today—it was matte black, and more flexible than the traditional Shotet variety—and polished black boots that made him appear even taller than he was. His shirt, collared and white, was buttoned up to his throat, showing over the vest of armor. It was almost the same outfit he had worn to our mother's funeral. Fitting, since he intended for me to die today.

"It's a shame your beloved couldn't be here to watch," Ryzek said. "I'm sure he would have enjoyed it."

I replayed it all the time now, what Zosita, Teka's mother, had told me before she walked to her execution. I had asked her if it was worth it to lose her life challenging Ryzek, and she had told me yes. I wished I could tell her that I understood now.

I tipped my chin up. "You know, I'm having trouble figuring out how much of you is actually my brother these days." When I walked past Ryzek on my way out of the cell, I leaned closer and said, "But you would be in a much better mood if your little plan to steal Eijeh's currentgift had worked."

For a moment I was sure I could see Ryzek's focus falter. His eyes touched Eijeh's.

"I see," I said. "Whatever you tried to do didn't work. You still didn't get his gift."

"Take her away," Ryzek said to Eijeh. "She has some dying to do."

Eijeh prodded me forward. He was wearing thick gloves, like he was training a bird of prey.

If I focused, I could walk in a straight line, but it was difficult, with all the throbbing in my head and throat. A trickle of blood—well, I hoped it was blood, anyway—ran over my collarbone.

Eijeh pushed me through the door to the arena floor, and I stumbled out. The light outside was blinding, the sky cloudless and pale around the sun. The amphitheater was packed with observers, all of them shouting and cheering, but I couldn't make out what any of them were saying.

Across from me waited Vas Kuzar. He smiled at me, then bit

his chapped lips. He would make himself bleed if he kept that up.

"Vas Kuzar!" Ryzek announced, his voice amplified by the tiny devices that hovered over the arena. Just above the lip of the amphitheater wall, I could see the buildings of Voa, stone patched over with metal and glass, winking in the sun. One, outfitted with a blue glass spire, almost blended into the sky. Covering the arena was a force field that protected the place from harsh weather—and escape. The Shotet didn't like our war games to be interrupted by storms and cold and runaway prisoners.

"You have challenged the traitor Cyra Noavek to fight with currentblades to the death!" As if on cue, everyone roared at the words *traitor Cyra Noavek*, and I rolled my eyes, though my heart was beating fast. "This is in reaction to her betrayal of the people of Shotet. Are you ready to proceed?"

"I am," Vas said in his usual monotone.

"Your weapon, Cyra," Ryzek said. He drew a currentblade from the sheath at his back, and flipped it in his hand so I could take the handle. His sleeve was rolled up.

I approached him, willing the currentshadows to build within me, beckoning the pain that came along with them. My skin was dusted with dark lines. I moved like I was going to take the knife's handle, but instead, I clamped my hand around Ryzek's arm.

I wanted to show these people who he really was. And pain always did that, took the insides out.

Ryzek screamed into his teeth, and thrashed, trying to throw me off. With all the others, I had simply let my currentgift go where it wanted to, and it always wanted to be shared. With Akos, I had pulled it back, almost ending my own life in the process. But with Ryzek, I pressed it toward him with all the force I could muster.

It was a shame, really, that Eijeh was there so soon, grabbing me and dragging me away.

Still, the damage was done. Everyone in this arena had heard my brother scream at my touch. They were quiet, watching.

Eijeh held me back as Ryzek gathered himself, straightening and sheathing the knife. He set a hand on Vas's shoulder, and said, only loud enough so Eijeh, Vas, and I could hear: "Kill her."

"What a shame, Cyra," Eijeh said softly in my ear. "I didn't want it to come to this."

I twisted free as Eijeh walked out, and backed away, breathing hard. I had no weapon. But it was better to go out this way. By not giving me a currentblade, Ryzek had just shown everyone in this arena that he wasn't giving me a fair chance. In his anger, he had shown fear, and that was enough for me.

Vas started toward me, his movements confident, predatory. He had always disgusted me, since I was a child, and I wasn't sure why. He was as tall and well built as any other man I had ever found appealing. A good fighter, too, and his eyes, at least, were a rare, beautiful color. But he was also covered with accidental bruises and scratches. His hands were so dry the thin flesh between his fingers was cracking. And I had never met a person so . . . empty. Unfortunately, that was also what made him so frightening in the arena.

Strategy, now, I thought. I remembered the footage from Tepes I had watched in the training room. I had learned the lurching, unsteady movements of their combat when my mind was sharp. The key to maintaining control of my body was to keep my center strong. When Vas stepped to lunge, I turned and tripped to the side, my limbs swinging. One of my flailing arms hit him in the ear, hard. The impact shuddered through me, sending a wave of pain through my rib cage and back.

I winced, and in the time it took me to recover, Vas had swiped. His sharpened blade carved a line in my arm. Blood spilled on the arena floor, and the crowd cheered.

I tried to ignore the blood, the stinging, the aching. My body pulsed with pain and fear and rage. I held my arm against my chest. I had to grab Vas. He couldn't feel pain, but if I channeled enough of my currentgift, I could kill him.

A cloud passed over the sun, and Vas lunged again. This time I ducked, and reached out with one hand, skimming the inside of his wrist with my fingers. The shadows danced over to him, not potent enough to affect him. He swung his knife again, and the point of the blade dug into my side.

I moaned, and fell against the wall of the arena.

Then I heard someone shout, "Cyra!"

A dark figure hoisted itself over the arena wall from the first row of seats, and dropped to the ground, knees bent. Darkness crowded the edges of my vision, but I knew who he was, just by watching him run.

A long, dark rope had dropped into the center of the arena. I looked up to see, not a cloud covering the sun, but an old transport vessel, made of an array of metals, honeyed and rusty and as bright as the sun, hovering right above the force field. Vas grabbed Akos with both hands and slammed him up, into the arena wall. Akos gritted his teeth and covered Vas's hands with his own.

Then something strange happened: Vas *flinched*, and dropped him.

Akos sprinted to my side, bent over me, and wrapped an arm around my waist. Together we ran toward the rope. He grabbed it with one hand, and it jerked up, fast. Too fast for Vas to grab.

Everyone around us was roaring. He shouted into my ear, "I'm going to need you to hold on by yourself!"

I cursed at him. I tried not to look down at the crowded seats below us, the frenzy we had left behind, the distant ground, but it was hard not to. I focused instead on Akos's armor. I wrapped my arms around his chest and clamped my hands around the collar of it. When he released me, I gritted my teeth—I was too weak to hold on like this, too weak to support my own weight.

Akos reached up with the hand he had been using to hold me, and his fingers approached the force field that blanketed the amphitheater. It lit up brighter when his fingers touched it, then flickered, and went out. The rope jerked up, hard, making me whimper as I almost lost my grip, but then we were inside the transport vessel.

We were inside, and it was deadly quiet.

"You made Vas feel pain," I said, breathless. I touched his face, ran a fingertip down his nose, over his upper lip.

He wasn't as bruised as he had been the last time I saw him, cowering on the floor at my touch.

"I did," he replied.

"Eijeh was in the amphitheater, he was *right there*. You could have grabbed him. Why didn't you—"

His mouth—still under my fingers—twitched into a smile. "Because I came for you, you idiot."

I laughed and fell against him, not strong enough to stand anymore.

CHAPTER 30 | AKOS

FOR A TICK THERE was only her weight, her warmth, and relief.

And then everything came back: the crush of people in the transport vessel, their silence as they stared, Isae and Cisi strapped in near the nav deck. Cisi gave Akos a smile as he caught Cyra around the waist and picked her up. Cyra was tall, and far from dainty, but he could still carry her. For a while, anyway.

"Where are your medical supplies?" Akos asked Teka and Jyo, who were coming toward them.

"Jyo has medical training; he can take care of her," Teka said.

But Akos didn't like how Jyo was looking at her, like she was something valuable he could buy or trade. These renegades hadn't rescued her out of the goodness of their hearts; they wanted something in return, and he wasn't about to just hand her over.

Cyra's fingers curled around the armor strap on his rib cage, and he shivered a little.

"She doesn't go anywhere without me," he said.

Teka's eyebrow lifted above the eye patch. Before she could

snap at him—which he got the sense she was about to—Cisi
unbuckled herself and made her way over.

"I can do it. I have the training," she said. "And Akos will help
me."

Teka eyed her for a beat, then gestured to the galley. "By all
means, Miss Kereseth."

Akos carried Cyra into the galley. She wasn't completely out
of it—her eyes were still open—but she didn't seem *there*, either,
and he didn't like it.

"Come on, Noavek, get it together," he said to her as he turned
sideways to get her in the door. It wasn't quite steady on the vessel; he stumbled. "My Cyra would have made at least two snide
remarks by now."

"Hmm." She smiled a little. "Your Cyra."

The galley was narrow and dirty, used plates and cups piled
around the sink, jostling each other whenever the ship turned, lit
by strips of white light that kept fluttering like they were about
to go out; everything made of the same dull metal, dotted with
bolts. He waited as Cisi scrubbed the little table between the two
countertops, and dried it with a clean rag. His arms ached by the
time he put Cyra down.

"Akos, I can't read Shotet characters."

"Um . . . neither can I, really." The supply cabinet was
organized, all the individually packaged items in neat rows. Alpha-
betical. He knew a few of them by sight, but not enough.

"You'd think after all that time in Shotet you'd have learned
something," Cyra said from her place on the table, slurring the
words a little. Her arm flopped to the side, and she pointed. "Silverskin is there. Antiseptic on the left. Make me a painkiller."

"Hey, I learned a few things," he said to her, squeezing her hand before he got to work. "The most challenging lesson was how to deal with you."

He had a vial of painkiller in his bag, so he went out to the main deck again and hunted for it under the jump seats, glaring at Jyo when he didn't move his legs right away. He found his roll of leather—made of treated Armored One skin, so it was still hard, not exactly a "roll"—where he kept his spare vials, and found the purplish one that would help Cyra's pain. When he went back to the galley, Cisi was wearing gloves and ripping packages open.

"How steady are your hands, Akos?" Cisi asked.

"Steady enough. Why?"

"I know how to do the procedures, of course, but I can't really touch her, because of the pain, remember? At least, not as steadily as she needs me to; this is delicate work," she said. "So I'm just going to tell you what to do."

Dark streaks still traveled up and down Cyra's arms and around her head, though they were different from the last time Akos had seen them, dancing on top of her in jagged lines.

Cyra croaked from the table, "Akos, is this . . . ?"

"My sister?" Akos said. "Yeah, it is. Cyra, meet Cisi."

"It's a pleasure to meet you," Cyra said, searching Cisi's face. For resemblance, if Akos knew anything. She wouldn't find it—he and Cisi had never looked much alike.

"You too," Cisi said, smiling at Cyra. If she was scared of the woman beneath her—the woman she had heard so many rumors about, all her life—she didn't show it.

Akos carried the painkiller to Cyra and touched the vial to her lips. It was hard to look at her. The stitching cloth that covered the left side of her throat and head was deep red and crusted over. She was bruise-stained and worn through.

"Remind me," Cyra said as the painkiller kicked in, "to yell at you for coming back."

"Whatever you say," Akos said.

But he was relieved, because there was his Cyra, jagged as a serrated blade, strong as Deadened ice.

"She fell asleep. Well, that's good," Cisi said. "Step back, please."

He gave her some room. She was dextrous, to be sure; she pinched the stitching cloth with all the delicacy of someone threading a needle, careful not to brush Cyra's skin, and pulled it back. It came away from the wound easily, wet as it was with blood and pus. She dropped it, one soaked strip at a time, on a tray near Cyra's head.

"So you've been training to be a doctor," Akos said as he watched her.

"It seemed like a good fit for my gift," Cisi said. Ease was her gift—always had been, even before her currentgift came around—but it wasn't her only one, he could see that. She had steady hands and an even temper and a sharp mind. More than just a sweet person with a good disposition, as if anyone was just that.

When the whole wound was clear of the useless stitching cloth, she poured antiseptic all over it, dabbing at the edges to get rid of dried blood.

"I think it's time to apply the silverskin," Cisi said, straightening. "It acts like a living creature; you just have to place it properly and it adheres permanently to the flesh. You'll be fine as long as you can keep your hands steady. Okay? I'll cut the strips now."

Silverskin was another innovation from Othyr, a sterile,

synthetic substance that, as Cisi said, almost seemed to be alive. It was used to replace skin that had been damaged beyond repair, mostly burns. It got its name because of its color and texture—it was smooth and had a silver sheen to it. Once put in place, it was permanent.

Cisi cut the strips with care, one for the section of skin just above Cyra's ear, one for behind it, and one for her throat. After a beat or two of thought, she went back to make the edges of silverskin curved. Like wind through snow, like iceflower petals.

Akos put on gloves, so the silverskin wouldn't stick to his hands instead of her, and Cisi handed the first strip to him. It was heavy, and cold to the touch, not as slippery as he'd imagined it to be. She helped him position his hands over Cyra's head.

"Lower it straight down," she said, and he did. He didn't have to press it in place; the silverskin rippled like water and buried itself in Cyra's scalp the moment it found flesh.

With Cisi's clear voice coaching him, Akos placed the rest of the silverskin. Each piece grew together right away, no seams to speak of between the different strips.

He acted as Cisi's hands for the rest of Cyra's wounds, too, the gashes on her arm and side covered with stitching cloth, the bruises treated with a healing salve. It didn't take long. Mostly they would heal on their own, and the real trick for her would be forgetting how she got them. There was no stitching cloth for the mind's wounds, real though they were.

"That's it," Cisi said, stripping the gloves from her small hands. "Now you just wait for her to wake up. She'll need to rest, but she should be fine now that she's not losing any more blood."

"Thank you," Akos said.

"Never thought I would be trying to *heal* Cyra Noavek," Cisi said. "On a transport vessel full of Shotet, no less." She glanced at him. "I can see why you like her, you know."

"I feel like . . ." Akos sighed, and sat down at the table next to Cyra's head. "Like I just walked right into my fate without meaning to."

"Well," Cisi said, "if you *are* destined to serve the Noavek family, I think you could do worse than the woman who was willing to endure all this just to get you home."

"So you don't think I'm a traitor?"

"That sort of depends on what she stands for, doesn't it?" Cisi said. She touched his shoulder. "I'm going to find Isae, okay?"

"Sure."

"What's *that* look for?"

He was suppressing a smile. "Nothing."

Akos's memories of the interrogation were hazy, and the edges of them, creeping into his mind, were bad enough on their own, without any of the details to make them more real. Still, he let the memory of Cyra in.

She had looked like a corpse, with the currentshadows making her face look pitted and rotted away. And she had been screaming so loud, every izit of her resisting; she didn't want to hurt him. If he hadn't told Ryzek what he knew about Isae and Ori, maybe she had, just to keep from killing Akos. Not like he would have blamed her.

She woke up on the galley table with a twitch and a moan. Then reached for him, touching his jaw with her fingertips.

"Am I sealed in your memory now?" she said, sluggish. "As

someone who hurt you?" The words caught in her throat like she was gagging on them. "The sounds you made, I can't forget—"

She was crying. Half-drunk, too, from the painkiller, but still, crying.

He didn't remember the sounds he'd made when she touched him—when Vas *forced* her to touch him, that was, torturing them both. But he knew she had felt everything he had felt. That was how her gift worked, sending pain both ways.

"No, no," Akos said. "What he did, he did to both of us."

Her hand came to rest against his sternum, like she was going to push him away, and then she didn't. She brushed her fingers over his collarbone, and even through his shirt he felt how warm she was.

"But now you know what I've done," she said, staring at her hand, at his chest, anywhere but his face. "Before, you had only seen me do it to other people, but now you know the kind of pain I have caused people, so many people, just because I was too much of a coward to stand up to him." She scowled, and lifted her hand. "Getting you out was the one good thing I've ever done, and now it's not even worth anything, because here you are again, you . . . you idiot!"

She clutched at her side, wincing. She was crying again.

Akos touched her face. When he first met her, he thought she was this fearsome thing, this monster he needed to escape. But she had unfurled bit by bit, showing him her wicked humor by waking him with a knife to his throat, talking about herself with unflinching honesty, for better or for worse, and loving—so deeply—every little bit of this galaxy, even the parts she was supposed to hate.

She was not a rusty nail, as she had once told him, or a hot poker, or a blade in Ryzek's hand. She was a hushflower, all power and possibility. Capable of doing good and harm in equal measure.

"It is not the only good thing you've ever done," Akos said, in plain Thuvhesit. It felt like the right language for this moment, the language of his home, which Cyra understood but didn't really speak when he was around, like she was afraid it would hurt his feelings.

"It's worth everything to me, what you did," he said, still in Thuvhesit. "It changes everything."

He touched his forehead to hers, so they shared the same air.

"I like how you sound in your own language," she said softly.

"Can I kiss you?" he said. "Or will it hurt?"

Her eyes went wide. Then she said breathlessly, "And if it hurts?" And smiled a little. "Life is full of hurt anyway."

Akos's breaths shuddered as he pressed his mouth to hers. He wasn't sure what it would be like, kissing her this way, not because she surprised him and he didn't think to pull away, but because he just wanted to. She tasted malty and spiced from the painkiller she had swallowed, and she was a little hesitant, like she was afraid to hurt him. But kissing her was touching match to kindling. He burned for her.

The ship jerked, making all the bowls and cups clatter against each other. They were landing.

CHAPTER 31 | CYRA

I FINALLY LET MYSELF think it: he was beautiful. His gray eyes reminded me of the stormy waters of Pitha. When he reached for my cheek, there was a crease along his arm where one wiry muscle met another. His deft, sensitive fingers moved over my cheekbone. His fingernails were stained with yellow powder—from jealousy flowers, I was sure. I was breathless to think of him touching me just because he wanted to.

I sat up, slowly, bringing a hand to the silverskin behind my ear. Soon it would adhere to the nerves in what was left of my scalp, and I would be able to feel it like it was my own skin, though it would never grow hair again. I wondered how I looked now, with a little more than half a head of hair. It didn't really matter.

He wanted to touch me.

"What?" he said. "You're giving me a weird look."

"Nothing," I said. "You just . . . look nice."

It was a silly thing to say. He was dusty, sweaty, and smeared with my blood. His hair and clothes were mussed. *Nice* wasn't exactly the word for it, but the other ones I thought of were too much, too soon.

Still, he smiled as if he understood. "You do, too."

"I look filthy," I said. "But thank you for lying about it."

I braced myself on the edge of the table, and pushed to standing. At first I teetered, unsure of my footing.

"Need me to carry you again?" he said.

"That was humiliating and will never happen again."

"Humiliating? Some people might use another word," he said. "Like . . . gallant."

"Tell you what," I said. "Someday I'll carry you around like a baby in front of people whose respect you're trying to earn, and you can let me know how much you like it."

He grinned. "Deal."

"I'll consent to let you help me walk," I said. "And don't think I didn't notice the chancellor of Thuvhe standing in the next room." I shook my head. "I'd love to know the principle of elmetahak that sanctions bringing your chancellor to the country of her enemies."

"I think it falls under 'hulyetahak,'" he said with a sigh. "School of the stupid."

I held tight to his arm and walked—shuffled, really—into the main deck. The transport vessel was small, with a wide observation window at one end. Through it I saw Voa from above, surrounded on three sides by sheer cliffs and on one by the ocean, forests spread over the distant hills as far as I could see. Trains, powered largely by wind coming off the water, wrapped around the city's circumference and traveled into its center like spokes in a wheel. I had never ridden in one.

"How has Ryzek not found us?" I asked.

"Hologram cloak," Teka said from the captain's chair. "Makes us look like just another Shotet army transport. I designed it myself."

The ship dipped down, sinking through a hole in the rotten roof of some building on the fringes of Voa. Ryzek didn't know this part of the city—no one bothered to, really. It was clear that this building in particular had once been an apartment complex, hollowed out by some kind of destructive event, maybe a near demolition, abandoned halfway through. As the ship sank, I saw into half a dozen lives: a bed with mismatched pillowcases in a ripped-apart bedroom; half a kitchen counter dangling from a precipice; red cushions coated in dust and bits of rubble from a destroyed living room.

We touched down, and some of the others used a rope rigged to a pulley near the ceiling to cover the hole there with a huge piece of fabric. Light still came through it—making the ship almost glow, from the warmth of its patchwork metals—but it was harder, now, to see into the apartments that had been. The space we were in was half packed dirt, half dust-streaked tile. Growing in the cracks of the broken floor were fragile Shotet flowers in gray, blue, and purple.

And at the bottom of the steps that had unfolded from the ship's hold, with the angular eyes I remembered from the footage Akos and I had watched together, was Isae Benesit. She was scarred in a way I hadn't imagined, scarred by a Shotet blade.

"Hello," I said to her. "I've heard a lot about you."

She said, "Likewise."

I was certain of that. She had heard of how I brought pain and death to all that I touched. And maybe she had heard of my supposed madness, too, that I was too insane to speak, like a diseased animal.

Making sure that Akos's hand was still on my arm, I stretched out a hand for her to take, curious to see if she would. She did.

Her hand looked delicate, but it felt callused, and I wondered how it had gotten that way.

"I think we should trade stories," I said, careful. If the renegades didn't already know who she was, it was better not to tell them, for her safety. "Somewhere private."

Teka approached us. I almost laughed at the bright eye patch she wore; though I didn't know her well, it seemed just like her to call attention to the missing eye instead of disguising it.

"Cyra," she said to me. "Good to see you're feeling better."

I stepped away from Akos's steadying hand, so the current-shadows spread over my body again. They were so different now, winding around my fingers like tendrils of hair instead of coursing through them like veins. My shirt was stained with blood and sliced open where they had applied the stitching cloth, and I was bruised in more places than I could count. Still, I tried to pretend I had some dignity.

"Thank you for coming to get me," I said to Teka. "I assume, based on our past interactions, that there's something you'd like in return."

"We can get to that later," Teka said, lip curling. "I think it's safe to say our interests align, though. If you want to clean up, there's running water in this building. Hot water. Pick an apartment, any apartment."

"Luxury of luxuries," I said. I looked to Isae. "Maybe you should come with us. We have a lot to catch up on."

I did the best I could to pretend I was all right until we reached one of the stairwells, out of sight. Then I stopped to lean into one of the walls, breathless. My skin pulsed around the silverskin. Akos's touch was taking away the pain of my currentgift, but there was nothing he could do to save me from the rest, the carving of my flesh, the battles I had fought for my own life.

"Okay, this is just ridiculous," Akos said. He put a hand behind my knees and swung me into his arms, not quite as gently as I would have liked. But I was too tired to object. The toes of my shoes skimmed the walls as he carried me up the stairs.

We found an apartment on the second floor that seemed relatively intact. It was dusty, and the half of the living room that remained overlooked the hollowed-out area where the ship was parked, so we could see what the renegades were doing, rolling out sleeping pallets, sorting through supplies, building a fire in the small furnace they had probably dragged from one of the apartments.

The bathroom, next to the living room, was comfortable and expansive, with a bathtub in the center of the room and a sink at the side. The floor was made of blue glass tiles. Akos tested the faucets, which sputtered at first, but still worked, as Teka had promised.

I was torn, for a moment, between cleaning myself up and talking to Isae Benesit.

"I can wait," Isae said, when she noticed my indecision. "I would be too distracted to have a meaningful conversation with you while you're covered in blood anyway."

"Yes, I'm hardly fit for a chancellor's company," I said, a little edge in my voice. As if it was my fault that I was covered in blood. As if I needed the reminder.

"I spent most of my life in a little cruiser vessel that smelled like feet," she replied. "I'm hardly fit for my own company, by the usual definitions."

She picked up one of the large cushions in the living room and smacked it with the flat of her hand, sending a cloud of dust into the air. After brushing it off, she set it down and sat on top of it, somehow managing to look elegant while she found her balance. Cisi took a seat beside her, though with less ceremony, giving me a warm smile. I was puzzled by her gift, how it slowed my turbulent thoughts and made my worst memories feel further away. I sensed that being around her could become addictive, if you had enough discomfort.

Akos was still in the bathroom. He had plugged the bathtub drain and turned on the faucets. Now he was undoing the straps of his armor with quick, nimble fingers.

"Don't tell me you don't need my help," he said to me. "I won't believe you."

I stepped out of sight of the living room and tried to lift my shirt over my head. I only made it up to my stomach before I had to stop for breath. Akos set his armor down and took the hem of my shirt from me. I laughed, softly, as he guided it over my head and down my arms and said, "This is awkward."

"Yes it is," he said. He kept his eyes on my face. He was blushing.

I had not allowed myself to imagine a situation like this, his fingers brushing my arms, the memory of his mouth on mine so close I could still feel it.

"I think I can handle the pants on my own," I said.

I didn't mind showing skin. I was far from frail, with thick thighs and a small chest, and it didn't concern me. This body had carried me through a hard life. It looked exactly the way it was supposed to. Still, when his eyes dropped—just for a moment—I stifled a nervous giggle.

He helped me into the bathtub, where I sat, letting my underwear get soaked. He searched the cabinet under the sink, scattering a straight razor, an empty bottle with a worn label, and a comb with broken teeth before he found a lump of soap, and offered it to me.

He was quiet, setting his hand on me to suppress the current-shadows while I scrubbed streaks of red from my body. The worst part was probing the edges of the silverskin to wash away a few days' worth of gore, so I did it first, biting down hard on my lip to keep from crying out. Then his thumb was pressing, working a knot from my shoulder, from my neck. Goose bumps spread up and down my arms.

His fingers fluttered over my shoulders, finding places to soothe. His eyes, when they found mine, were soft and almost shy, and I wanted to kiss him until he blushed again.

Later.

With a glance at the living room, to make sure Cisi and Isae couldn't see me, I loosened the armor around my left arm, and peeled it from my skin.

"I have a few more to carve," I said softly to Akos.

"Those losses can wait," Akos said. "You've bled enough for this."

He took the soap from me, and turned it in his hand to capture its lather. Then he ran his fingers up and down my scarred arm, gentle. It was, in some ways, even better than being kissed by him. He had no fragile illusions about my goodness, destined to shatter when he found out the truth. But he accepted me anyway. Cared about me anyway.

"Okay," I said. "I'm done, I think."

Akos stood, holding my hands, and lifted me as I came to my feet. Water ran down my legs and back. As I fastened the armor around my forearm again, he found a towel in one of the cabinets, then pieced together clothes for me—the pants from Isae, underwear from Cisi, one of his own shirts and a pair of his socks, my still-intact boots. I looked at the pile of clothes with some dismay. It was one thing for him to see me in my underwear, but to help me take it off . . .

Well. If that was going to happen, I wanted it to be under different circumstances.

"Cisi," Akos said. He was also staring at the pile of clothes. "Maybe you should help with this part."

"Thank you," I said to him.

He smiled. "It's getting *really* hard to keep my eyes on your face."

I made a face at him as he left.

Cisi came in, and peace came with her. She helped me undo the chest binder. It was, as far as I knew, a uniquely Shotet design, made not to enhance my shape but to hold my chest steady beneath rigid armor. The replacement she handed me was more like a shirt, made for warmth and comfort, the fabric soft. The Thuvhesit version. It was too big for me, but it would have to do.

"That gift of yours," I said as she helped me fasten it. "Does it make it difficult to trust people?"

"What do you mean?" She held up the towel so I could change underwear with some privacy.

"I mean . . ." After pulling on the underwear, I stepped into the first leg of the pants. "You don't really ever know if it's you they want to be around, or your gift."

"The gift comes from me," Cisi said. "It's an expression of my personality. So I guess I don't see a difference."

It was, essentially, what Dr. Fadlan had said to my mother in his office, that my gift unfolded from the deeper parts of me, and it would only change as I changed. Watching the shadows wrap around my wrist like a bracelet, I wondered if their shift meant that I had awoken a different woman from that interrogation. Maybe even a better one, a stronger one.

I asked, "So you think causing people pain is a part of my personality?"

She frowned as she helped me guide my head and arms into the clean shirt. The short sleeves were far too baggy for me, so I rolled them up, leaving my arms bare.

"You want to keep people away," Cisi said finally. "I'm not sure why pain is the way your gift accomplishes that. I don't know you." Her frown deepened. "It's strange. Usually I can't speak this freely with anyone, let alone someone I just met."

She and I traded a smile.

In the living room, where Isae still sat with her legs folded to one side, her ankles crossed, there was a small stack of cushions already ready for me. I sank into it, relieved, and pulled my wet hair over one shoulder. Though the table between us was broken—it had once been made of glass, so glass pebbles covered the wood floor around us—and the cushions were dirty and low to the ground, Isae looked at me like she was holding court, and I was a subject. Now that was a skill.

"How's your Thuvhesit?" Isae said.

"Very good," I said, switching languages. Akos jerked to attention at the sound of his native tongue coming from my mouth. He had heard me speak it before, but it seemed to startle him anyway.

"So," I said to her. "You came here for your sister."

"Yes," Isae said. "Have you seen her?"

"No," I said. "I don't know where she's being kept. But eventually, he'll have to move her. That's what you should plan for."

Akos set a hand on my shoulder again, this time standing behind me. I hadn't even noticed the currentshadows beginning their movement again, I was so distracted by all the other pain.

"Will he hurt her?" Cisi said softly, taking a seat at Isae's side.

"My brother doesn't inflict pain for no reason," I said.

Isae snorted.

"I'm serious," I said. "He is a peculiar kind of monster. He fears pain, and has never enjoyed watching it. It reminds him that he can feel it, I think. You can take comfort in that—he's not likely to hurt her senselessly, without cause."

Cisi wrapped her hand around Isae's and held tightly, without looking at her. Their clasped hands rested on the floor between them, fingers interlaced so I could tell Cisi's skin from Isae's only by its darker shade.

"My guess is that whatever he intends to do with her—which we can reasonably assume is execution—it will be public, and it will be intended to lure you to him," I said. "He wants to kill *you*, even more than her, and he wants it to be on his terms. Trust me, you don't want to fight him on his terms."

"We could use your help," Akos said.

"My help is already yours," I replied.

I set my hand on top of his, and squeezed. Like a reassurance.

"The trick will be persuading the renegades," Akos said. "They don't care about rescuing a Benesit child."

"Let me handle them," I said. "I have an idea."

"How many of the stories I've heard about you are true?" Isae said. "I see how you cover your arm. I see what you can do with your gift. So I know that some of what I've been told must be true. How can I trust you, if that's the case?"

I got the feeling, looking at her, that she wanted the world around her to be simple, including the people in it. Maybe she had to feel that way, carrying the fate of a nation-planet on her shoulders. But I had learned that the world did not become something just because you needed it to.

"You want to see people as extremes. Bad or good, trustworthy or not," I said. "I understand. It's easier that way. But that isn't how people work."

She looked at me for a long time. Long enough for even Cisi to fidget where she sat.

"Besides, whether you trust me or not makes no difference to me," I said, at last. "I am going to rip my brother to pieces either way."

At the bottom of the stairs, when we were all still cloaked in the darkness of the stairwell, I pinched Akos's sleeve to hold him back. It wasn't so dark that I couldn't see his look of confusion. I waited until Isae and Cisi were out of hearing distance before I stepped back, releasing him, letting the currentshadows build between us like smoke.

"Something wrong?" he said.

"No," I said. "Just . . . give me a moment."

I closed my eyes. Ever since I had woken up after the interrogation with shadow on top of my skin instead of beneath it, I had been thinking of Dr. Fadlan's office, of how my gift came to be. It seemed, like most things in my life, tied to Ryzek. Ryzek feared pain, so the current had given me a gift he would fear, maybe the only gift that could truly protect me from him.

The current had not given me a curse. And I had become strong under its teaching. But there was no denying another thing Dr. Fadlan had said—that on some level, I felt like I, and everyone else, deserved pain. One thing I knew, deep in my bones, was that Akos Kereseth did not deserve it. Holding on to that thought, I reached for him, and touched my hand to his chest, feeling fabric.

I opened my eyes. The shadows were still traveling over my body, since I wasn't touching his skin, but my entire left arm, from shoulder to the fingertips that touched him, was bare. Even if he had been able to feel my currentgift, I still would not have been hurting him.

Akos's eyes, usually so wary, were wide with wonder.

"When I kill people with a touch, it's because I decide to give them all the pain and keep none of it for myself. It's because I get so tired of bearing it that all I want to do is set it down for a while," I said. "But during the interrogation, it occurred to me that maybe I was strong enough to bear it all myself. That maybe no one else but me could. And I never would have thought of that without you."

I blinked tears from my eyes.

"You saw me as someone better than I was," I said. "You told me that I could choose to be different than I had been, that my condition was not permanent. And I began to believe you. Taking in all the pain nearly killed me, but when I woke up again, the gift was different. It doesn't hurt as much. Sometimes I can control it."

I took my hand away.

"I don't know what you want to call it, what we are to each other now," I said. "But I wanted you to know that your friendship has . . . quite literally altered me."

For a few long seconds, he just stared at me. There were new things to discover in his face still, even after so long spent in close company. Faint shadows under his cheekbones. The scar that ran through his eyebrow.

"You don't know what to call it?" he said, when he finally spoke again.

His armor hit the ground with a clatter, and he reached for me. Wrapped an arm around my waist. Pulled me against him. Whispered against my mouth: "Sivbarat. Zethetet."

One Shotet word, one Thuvhesit. *Sivbarat* referred to a person's dearest friend, someone so close that to lose them would be like losing a limb. And the Thuvhesit word, I had never heard before.

We didn't quite know how to fit together, lips too wet, teeth where they didn't belong. But that was all right; we tried again, and this time it was like the spark that came from friction, a jolt of energy through my body.

He clutched at my sides, pulled my shirt into his fists. His hands were deft from handling carving knives and powders, and he smelled like it, too, like herbs and potions and vapor.

I pressed into him, feeling the rough stairwell wall against my hands, and his quick, hot breaths against my neck. I had wondered, I had wondered what it was like to go through life without feeling pain, but this was not the absence of pain I had always craved, it was the opposite, it was pure sensation. Soft, warm, aching, heavy, everything, everything.

I heard, echoing through the safe house, a kind of commotion. But before I let myself pull away so we could see what it was, I asked him quietly, "What does it mean, 'zethetet'?"

He looked away, like he was embarrassed. I caught sight of that creeping blush around the collar of his shirt.

"Beloved," he said softly. He kissed me again, then picked up his armor and led the way toward the renegades.

I couldn't stop smiling.

The commotion was that someone was landing a floater in our safe house, ripping right through the fabric that shielded us. The band of light around its middle was dark purple, and it was splattered with mud.

I froze, terrified of the dark shape descending, but then I saw unfamiliar words on the underside of the rotund ship: *Passenger Craft #6734.*

Written in Thuvhesit.

CHAPTER 32 | AKOS

THE SHIP THAT HAD busted through the roof covering was a fat passenger floater, only big enough to hold a couple of people. Tattered bits of the fabric it had torn through floated down after it, catching the breeze. The now-visible sky was dark blue, starless, and the currentstream, rippling across it, was purple red.

The renegades surrounded the floater, weapons drawn. The hatch on its side opened, and a woman descended, showing her palms. She was older, with streaks of gray in her hair, and the look in her eye was anything but surrender.

"Mom?" Cisi said.

Cisi ran at her, wrapping her in a hug. Their mom hugged her back, but scanned the renegades over Cisi's shoulder. Then her stare fixed on Akos.

He felt shifty in his skin. He had thought maybe, if he ever got to see her again, she would make him feel like a kid. But it was just the opposite—he felt old. And huge. Holding his Shotet armor in front of him like it would protect him from her, then wishing, desperately, that he wasn't holding it, so she wouldn't know he'd earned it. He didn't want to shock her, or disappoint her, or be anything other than what she expected, only he didn't know what that was.

"Who are you?" Teka demanded. "How did you find us?"

His mom let go of Cisi. "I am Sifa Kereseth. I'm sorry to alarm you; I mean no harm."

"You didn't answer my question."

"I knew where to find you because I'm the oracle of Thuvhe," his mom said, and all at once, like it was rehearsed, the renegades put down their currentblades. Even those Shotet who didn't worship the current wouldn't dare to threaten an oracle, their religious history was so strong. Awe of her, of what she could do and see, was practically in their bones, running right alongside the marrow.

"Akos," his mom said, almost like it was a question. And in Thuvhesit, "Son?"

He had thought about seeing her again dozens of times. What he would say, what he would do, how he would feel. And mostly, now, all he felt was angry. She hadn't come for him the day of the kidnapping. Hadn't even warned them about the horror that would come to their doorstep, or said a too-meaningful good-bye that morning when they went to school. Nothing.

She reached for him, putting her rough hands on his shoulders. The worn shirt she wore, patched at the elbows, was one of their dad's shirts. She smelled like sendes leaf and saltfruit, like home. The last time he'd stood in front of her, he'd only come up to her shoulder; now he was a head taller.

Her eyes sparkled.

"I wish I could explain," she whispered.

So did he. Wished, more than that, that she could let go of the mad faith that she had in the fates, the convictions she held higher even than her own children. But it wasn't that simple.

"Have I lost you, then?" Her voice cracked a little over the question, and it was that easy for his anger to break.

He bent, and pulled her into his arms, lifting her to her toes without really noticing.

She felt like bones to him. Had she always been this thin, or had he only thought of her as strong because he was a kid and she was his mom? He felt like it would be too easy to crush her.

She rocked from side to side, a little. She'd always done that, like the hug wasn't over until she had tested it for stability.

"Hello," he said, because it was all he could think of.

"You're grown," his mom said as she pulled away. "I've seen half a dozen versions of this moment and still had no idea you'd be so tall."

"Never thought I'd see you surprised."

She laughed a little.

All wasn't forgiven, not by half. But if this was one of the last times he would get to see her, he wasn't going to spend it angry. She smoothed a hand over his hair, and he let her, though he knew his hair didn't need smoothing.

Isae's voice broke the silence. "Hello, Sifa."

The oracle bobbed her head at Isae. Akos didn't need to warn her not to tell the renegades who Isae was; she already knew, as always.

"Hello," she said to Isae. "I'm glad to see you, too. We've been worried about you, back at home. Your sister, too."

Guarded words, full of subtext. Thuvhe was probably in chaos, searching for its lost chancellor. Akos wondered, then, if Isae had even told anybody where she was going, or that she was still alive. Maybe she didn't care enough to. After all, she hadn't grown up in Thuvhe, had she? How much loyalty to their icy country did she actually have?

"Well," Jorek said, warm as ever, "we're honored by your presence, Oracle. Please join us for a meal."

"I will, but I must warn you, I came armed with visions," Sifa said. "I think they will interest you all."

Someone was muttering, translating the Thuvhesit words for the renegades who didn't speak the language. Akos still struggled to hear the difference between the two languages unless he really paid attention. That was the thing about knowing something in your blood instead of your brain, he supposed. It was just *there*.

He spotted Cyra at the back of the crowd, halfway between the renegades and the stairwell they'd just come out of. She looked . . . well, she looked scared. Of meeting the oracle? No—of meeting his mother. Had to be.

Ask the girl to assassinate her own brother, or fight someone to the death, and she didn't even blink. But she was afraid of meeting his mother. He smiled.

The others were moving back to the low stove where the renegades had set up a fire to keep them all warm. In the time Akos had been upstairs helping Cyra, they had dragged a few tables in from some of the apartments, and half a dozen different styles were represented: one square and metal, one narrow and wooden, another glass, another carved. There was some food on them, cooked saltfruit and dried strips of meat, a loaf of bread toasting on a spit, and burnt fenzu shells, a delicacy he'd never tried. Next to the food were little bowls of iceflowers, waiting to be blended and brewed.

Probably by Akos, if he knew Jorek half as well as he thought. It wasn't as elaborate as what they had eaten the night before, but it was enough.

He didn't have to guide his mom toward Cyra. She saw her and walked straight at her. It didn't make Cyra look any less scared.

"Miss Noavek," his mom said. There was a little catch in her throat. She tilted her head to see the silverskin on Cyra's neck.

"Oracle," Cyra said, inclining her head. He'd never seen Cyra bow to anyone like she meant it before.

One of the shadows bloomed over Cyra's cheek and then spread into three lines of inky dark that ran down her throat like a swallow. He set his fingers on her elbow so she could shake his mother's hand when she offered it, and his mom watched the light touch with interest.

"Mom, Cyra made sure I got home last week," he said. He wasn't sure what else to say about her. Or what else to say, period. The blush that had chased him through childhood came creeping back; he felt it behind his ears, and tried to stifle it. "At great cost to herself, as you can see."

His mom looked Cyra over again. "Thank you, Miss Noavek, for what you've done for my son. I look forward, later, to finding out why."

With a strange smile, Sifa turned away, linking arms with Cisi. Cyra hung back with Akos, eyebrows raised.

"That's my mother," he said.

"I realize that," she said. "You're . . ." She brushed her fingers over the back of his ear, where his skin was heating. "You're blushing."

So much for trying to stifle it. The heat spread to Akos's face, and he was sure he was bright red. Shouldn't he have grown out of this by now?

"You don't know how to explain me. You only flush when you don't know what words to use, I've noticed," she said, her finger moving down to his jaw. "It's all right. I wouldn't know how to explain me to your mother, either."

He didn't know what he'd expected. Teasing, maybe? Cyra wasn't above teasing him, but she seemed to know, somehow, that this was off-limits. The simple, quiet understanding softened his insides. He covered her hand. Hooked his finger around hers, so they were linked.

"Maybe now isn't the time to tell you that I'm probably not going to be any good at charming her," she said.

"So don't be charming," he said. "She certainly isn't."

"Careful. You don't know how not-charming I can be." Cyra brought their joined fingers to her mouth, and bit down, lightly.

Akos settled into a place at the metal table next to Sifa. If there was a Hessa uniform, she was wearing it: her pants were a sturdy material, probably lined with something to keep her warm, and her boots had small hooks in the soles to grip ice. Her hair was tied back with red ribbon. Cisi's, he was sure. There were new lines in her forehead, and around her eyes, like the seasons had taken something from her. And of course, they had.

All around them the renegades sat, passing bowls of food and empty plates and utensils. Across from them were Teka, with a floral-patterned eye patch this time, Jorek, his curly hair damp from a bath, and Jyo, with his lap instrument on its head, his chin resting on top of it.

"Food first," Sifa said, when she realized the renegades were waiting for her. "Prophecy later."

"Of course," Jorek said with a smile. "Akos, I wonder if you can make us all some tea to loosen us up a little?"

As predicted. Akos didn't even bother to act annoyed at being given a job when his mom had just burst through the ceiling in a Thuvhesit floater. He wanted something to do with his hands.

"I can."

He filled the water kettle and hung it from a hook in the little stove, then stood at the other end of the patchwork of tables, mixing tea blends for as many mugs as he could find. Most were the standard inhibition-releasing formulas, meant to raise spirits and ease conversation. But he made a painkiller for Cyra, and something calming for himself. As he stood with his fingers in the iceflower bowls, he heard his mom and Cyra talking.

"My son was eager for me to meet you, I could tell," his mom said. "You must be a good friend."

"Um . . . yes," Cyra said. "I think so, yes."

You think *so*, Akos thought, resisting the urge to roll his eyes. He'd given her clear enough labels, back in the stairwell, but she still couldn't quite believe it. That was the problem with being so convinced of your own awfulness—you thought other people were lying when they didn't agree with you.

"I have heard that you have a talent for death," his mom said. At least Akos had warned Cyra about Sifa's lack of charm.

He glanced at Cyra. She held her armored wrist against her gut.

"I suppose I do," she said. "But I don't have a passion for it."

Vapor slipped from the nose of the water kettle, not yet thick enough for Akos to pour. Water had never boiled so slowly.

"You two have spent a lot of time together," his mom said.

"Yes."

"Are you to blame for his survival these past few seasons?"

"No," Cyra said. "Your son survives because of his own will."

His mom smiled. "You sound defensive."

"I don't take credit for other people's strength," Cyra said. "Only my own."

His mom's smile got even bigger. "And a little cocky."

"I've been called worse."

The vapor was thick enough. Akos grabbed the hook with the wooden handle that hung next to the stove, and attached it to the kettle. It caught, and locked in place as he poured water in each of the mugs. Isae came forward for one, standing on tiptoe so she could whisper in his ear.

"If it hasn't already, it should be dawning on you right about now that your girl and your mother are very similar people," she said. "I will pause as that irrefutable fact chills you to the core."

Akos eyed her. "Was that *humor*, Chancellor?"

"On occasion, I have been known to make a humorous remark." She sipped her tea, though it was still boiling hot. It didn't seem to hurt her. She cradled the mug against her chest. "You knew my sister well, when you were children?"

"Not as well as Eijeh did," Akos said. "I was a little harder to talk to."

"She talked about him a lot," Isae said. "It broke her heart when he was taken. She left Thuvhe for a while, to help me recover from *the incident*." She waved her hand over her face, the scars. "Couldn't have done it without her. Those fools at Assembly Headquarters didn't know what to do with me."

Assembly Headquarters was a place Akos had only heard about in passing. A giant ship in orbit around their sun, holding a bunch of drifting ambassadors and politicians.

"Seems like you'd fit in with them all right," he said. Not exactly a compliment, and she didn't seem to take it as one.

"I'm not all I seem," she said with a shrug. She had worn shiny shoes at the hospital in Shissa, sure, he thought, but she also hadn't complained this whole time about her own comfort. If she really had spent most of her life on a cruiser vessel coasting through space, she hadn't lived like royalty, that much was clear. But it was hard to get a read on her. It was like she belonged to no one, and nowhere.

"Well, no matter how well you knew her," she said, "I'm . . . grateful for your help. And Cyra's. It's not what I expected." She glanced up at the hole in the ceiling. "None of this is."

"I know the feeling."

She made a little sound in her throat. "If you get Eijeh out, and don't die in the process, will you come home with us?" she asked. "I could use your insights on Shotet culture. My experience with them has been somewhat one-sided, as you might imagine."

"You think you can just have a fated traitor in your service without raising any eyebrows?" he said.

"You could go by another name."

"I can't hide who I am," he said. "And I can't run away from the fact that my fate lies across the Divide. Not anymore."

She sipped her tea again. She looked almost . . . sad.

"You call it 'the Divide,'" she said. "Like they do."

He had done it without meaning to, without even thinking about it. Thuvhesits just called it feathergrass. Up until a little while ago, so had he.

She set her hand on the side of Akos's head, lightly. It was odd for her to touch him—her skin was cold.

"Just remember," she said. "These people don't care about Thuvhesit lives. And whether you have the last vestiges of Shotet ancestry in your blood or not, you are Thuvhesit. You are one of *my* people, not theirs."

He'd never expected anyone from Thuvhe to claim him. More the opposite, actually.

She let her hand fall, and carried her mug back to her seat next to Cisi. Jyo was playing Cisi a song, with that sleepy look in his eyes that was becoming familiar to Akos. Too bad for Jyo; anyone with a pair of eyes could see Cisi only wanted Isae. And he was pretty sure it went both ways.

Akos carried the painkiller to Cyra. She and his mother had moved on to another topic. His mom was mopping up the juice from some saltfruit with a chunk of bread made from ground-up seeds, harvested in the fields outside Voa. It wasn't so different from what they'd eaten in Hessa—one of the few things Shotet and Thuvhe had in common.

"My mother took us there once," Cyra was saying. "That's where I learned to swim, in a special suit that protected against the cold. It might have come in handy on the last sojourn."

"Yes, you went to Pitha, didn't you?" Sifa said. "You were there, weren't you, Akos?"

"Yes," he said. "Spent most of my time there on an island of trash."

"You've seen the galaxy," she said with an odd smile. She slid her hand under his left sleeve, touching each kill mark. Her smile faded as she counted them.

"Who were they?" she asked softly.

"Two of the men who attacked our house," he said in a low voice. "And the Armored One who gave me its skin."

Her eyes flicked to Cyra's. "Do they know him, here?"

"As I understand it, he is the subject of quite a few rumors, most of them untrue," Cyra said. "They know he can touch me, that he can brew strong poisons, and that he is a Thuvhesit captive who somehow managed to earn armor."

Sifa had that look in her eyes, the one she got when she saw prophecies coming to life. It scared him.

"I have always known what you would become, remember?" Sifa said quietly. "Someone who would always be stared at. You are what you need to be. Regardless, I love the person you were, the one you are, the one you will become. Understand?"

He was caught up in her stare, in her voice. Like he was standing in the temple with dried iceflowers burning around him, staring at her through the smoke. Like he was sitting on the floor of the Storyteller's home, watching him weave the past out of vapor. It was easy to fall into this fervor, but Akos had spent too long suffering under the weight of his own fate to let that happen.

"Give me a straight answer, just this once," he said to her. "Do I save Eijeh or not?"

"I have seen futures where you do, and futures where you don't," she said. And, smiling, she added, "But you always, always try."

The renegades sat at attention, their plates stacked at one end of the big wooden table, and their mugs mostly empty. Teka was wrapped up in a blanket Sovy had embroidered for her, Akos heard her say, and Jyo had put away his instrument. Even Jorek hid his fidgeting fingers under the table while the oracle described her visions. Akos had been watching people get respectful around his mom since he was young, but it felt different here. Like another reason not to belong, as if he needed more.

"Three visions," Sifa began. "In the first, we depart this place before daybreak, so no one sees us through that hole in the roof."

"But . . . *you* made that hole," Teka interrupted. It figured she would reach the limits of her reverence so quickly, Akos thought. Teka didn't seem to like nonsense. "If you knew we would have to leave because of it, you could have avoided making it in the first place."

"So glad you're keeping up," Sifa said, serene.

Akos swallowed a laugh. A few seats down, Cisi seemed to be doing the same.

"In the second vision, Ryzek Noavek stands before an immense crowd while the sun is high." She pointed straight up. A noon sun, in Voa, which was closer to the planet's equator. "In an amphitheater. There are sights and amplifiers everywhere. Very public—a ceremony, maybe."

"They're honoring a platoon of soldiers tomorrow," Jorek said. "Could be that—otherwise there are no upcoming ceremonies until the next Sojourn Festival."

"Possibly," Sifa said. "In the third vision, I see Orieve Benesit struggling against Vas Kuzar's grip. She is in a cell. Large, made of glass. There are no windows. The smell is . . ." She sniffed, like it was still in the air. "Musty. Underground, I think."

"Struggling," Isae repeated. "Is she hurt? Is she—okay?"

"There is quite a bit of life in her," Sifa said. "Or appears to be."

"The cell made of glass—that's a cell beneath the amphitheater," Cyra said dully. "That's where I was held, before—" She stopped herself, fingers fluttering over her neck. "The second and third visions happen in the same place. Do they happen at the same time?"

"It is my sense," Sifa said, "that they are layered over each other. But my sense of placement in time is not always accurate."

Her hands fell to her lap, slipped into her pocket. Akos watched her take something out, a small object. It shone, catching his eye—it was a button from a jacket. It was tinted yellow at the edges where the finish had worn away from frequent buttoning. He could almost see his dad's fingers fumbling with it as he groaned about having to go to one of his sister's military dinners in Shissa, representing Hessa's iceflower flats. *Like this jacket is going to fool anyone*, he had said to their mother once, as they both got ready in the hall bathroom. *They'll take one look at the ice scrapes on my boots and know I'm an iceflower farm kid.* Their mom had only laughed.

Maybe in another future, Aoseh Kereseth would have been sitting next to Sifa at this strange circle of people, giving Akos a steadiness his mom never could foster, twitchy prophet that she was. Maybe she had brought that button to remind him that his dad wasn't where he should be, because of Vas. As he thought of it, he knew he was right, knew that was exactly why she had taken out that button.

"You're manipulating me with that," he snapped, interrupting something Teka was saying. He didn't care. Sifa was only looking at him. "Put it away. I remember him well enough on my own."

After all, he thought, *I'm the one who watched him die, not you.*

Something fierce flickered in his mom's eyes, almost like she was listening to his thoughts. But she put the button back into her pocket.

The button was a good reminder, not of his father, but of how manipulative his mother could be. If she was sharing visions, it wasn't because they were absolute, fixed in time like a fate was. It was because she had chosen a version of the future *she* wanted, and she was trying to push them all toward it. As a kid, he might have trusted her judgment, trusted that whatever future she had picked was the best one. Now, on the other side of his kidnapping and everything else that he'd lived through, he wasn't so sure.

"As Teka was saying," Jorek said, into the strange silence. "Forgive me, I know she's the sister of your chancellor, but the fate of Orieve Benesit isn't particularly relevant to our interests. We are interested only in unseating Ryzek Noavek."

"By killing him," Teka added. "In case that wasn't clear."

"You have no interest in rescuing the sister of a chancellor?" Isae said, flinty.

"She's not *our* chancellor," Teka said. "And we're not a band of heroes, or something. We're not about to risk our lives and safety for Thuvhesit strangers."

Isae's mouth puckered.

"It's relevant to your interests because it's an opportunity," Cyra said, lifting her head. "Since when does Ryzek Noavek call official ceremonies for platoons of sojourning soldiers? He's just doing it so he has a captive audience when he murders Orieve Benesit, to prove he can defy his fate. He will ensure that all of Shotet is watching. If you want to move against him, do it then. Do it when everyone is watching, and take away his moment of triumph."

Akos's eyes swept over the row of women beside him. Isae, startled, and maybe a little bit grateful to Cyra for arguing on Ori's behalf, her fingers loose around her mug. Cisi, wrapping a lock of hair around her finger, like she wasn't even listening. And then Cyra, the low lights reflecting off the sheen on the side of her head, her voice rough.

Teka spoke up. "Ryzek will be in a huge crowd of people, many of whom are his most ardent supporters and fiercest soldiers. What kind of 'move' do you suggest we make?"

Cyra replied, "You said it yourself, didn't you? *Kill him*."

"Oh, right!" Teka smacked the table, obviously annoyed. "Why didn't I think of *killing him*? How simple!"

Cyra rolled her eyes. "This time you won't have to sneak into his house while he's asleep. This time, I'll challenge him to the arena."

Everybody got quiet again. For different reasons, Akos was sure. Cyra was a good fighter, everybody knew that, but no one knew how good Ryzek was—they hadn't seen him in action. And then there was the matter of getting to a place where Cyra could actually challenge him. And getting him to do it instead of just arresting her.

"Cyra," Akos said.

"He declared nemhalzak—he erased your status, your citizenship," Teka said, talking over him. "He has no reason to honor your challenge."

"Of course he does." Isae was frowning. "He could have gotten rid of her quietly when he learned she was a renegade, but he didn't. He wanted her disgrace, and her death, to be public. That means he's afraid of her, afraid she has power over Shotet. If she challenges him in front of everyone, he won't be able to back down. He'll look like a coward."

"Cyra," Akos said again, quiet this time.

"Akos," Cyra answered, with just a touch of the gentleness he had seen in the stairwell. "He is no match for me."

The first time Akos ever saw Cyra fight—*really* fight—was in the training room in Noavek manor. She had gotten frustrated with him—she wasn't a patient teacher, after all—and she had let loose more than usual, knocking him flat. Only fifteen seasons old at the time, but she had moved like an adult. And she only got better from there. In all his time training with her, he had never bested her. Not once.

"I know," he said. "But just in case, let's distract him."

"Distract him," Cyra repeated.

"You'll go into the amphitheater. You'll challenge him," Akos said. "And I'll go to the prison. Badha and I, I mean. We'll rescue Orieve Benesit—we'll take away his triumph. And you'll take away his life."

It sounded almost poetic, which was why he'd put it that way. But it was hard to think of poetry when Cyra's fingers crept to her covered arm, like she was imagining the mark Ryzek would make there. Not that she would hesitate. But Cyra knew what those marks cost; she knew as well as anybody.

"It's settled, then," Isae said, her voice cutting through the quiet. "Ryzek dies. Orieve lives. Justice is done."

Justice, revenge. It was too late to figure out the difference.

CHAPTER 33 | CYRA

AS SOON AS I offered myself to fight my brother in the arena, I tasted the dusty amphitheater air in my mouth. I could still smell it: the crowded bodies, sweating; the chemical odor of the disinfected prison beneath; the tang from the force field that hummed above. I had tried to push it away as I spoke to the renegades, playacting at self-assuredness, but it was there, lingering.

The blood splatter. The screaming.

Akos's mother watched my armored arm, covered now by a blanket from one of the renegades. She was probably wondering how many scars there were beneath it.

What a match for her son I was. Him, aching with each life he had taken. Me, forgetting the number of marks on my arm.

When most of the burnstones in the stove had turned chalky, I slipped away, past the shadow of Sifa's floater, up the stairwell to the broken place where I had washed the blood from my skin. Below, I could hear Jorek and Jyo singing in harmony—sometimes not well—and the others breaking into a chorus of laughter. In the dimly lit bathroom, I approached the mirror, first finding just a dark silhouette in the glass, and then . . .

This is not a crisis, I told myself. *You are alive.*

I probed the silverskin on my head and throat. It tingled where it had begun to grow into my nerves. My hair was piled on one side of my head, the silverskin flat against the other side, the skin around it red and swollen as it adjusted to the new material. A woman on one side and a machine on the other.

I braced myself against the sink, and sobbed. My ribs ached, but there was no stopping the tears now. They came, heedless of pain, and I stopped resisting them.

Ryzek had mutilated me. My own brother.

"Cyra," Akos said, and it was the only time I had ever wished he wasn't there. He touched my shoulders, lightly, sending the shadows away. He had cold hands. A light touch.

"I'm fine," I said, running my fingers over my silver throat.

"You don't have to be fine right now."

The silverskin reflected the muted light that had crept into this half-destroyed place.

In a small, quiet voice, I asked the question that was buried deep inside me. "Am I ugly now?"

"What do you think?" he asked, and not like it was a rhetorical question. More like he knew I didn't want him to placate me, so he was asking me to think about it. I lifted my eyes to the mirror again.

My head did look strange with only half my hair, but some people in Shotet wore their hair this way, shaved on one side and long on the other. And the silverskin looked like a piece from the armor that my mother had collected in her seasons of sojourning. Like the armor on my wrist, I would always wear it, and it would make me feel strong.

I found my own eyes in the glass.

"No," I said. "I'm not."

I didn't quite mean it yet, but I thought maybe, over time, I might start to.

"I agree," he said. "In case that wasn't clear from all the kissing we've been doing."

I smiled, and turned, perching on the edge of the sink. There was worry tugging at the corners of Akos's eyes, though he was smiling. He had looked that way since the discussion with the renegades about our plan.

"What's going on, Akos?" I said. "Are you really that concerned that I can't beat Ryzek?"

"No, it's not that." Akos looked as uneasy as I felt. "It's just . . . you're really going to kill him?"

That wasn't quite what I expected him to ask.

"Yes. I'm going to kill him," I said. The words tasted rusty, like blood. "I thought that was clear."

He nodded. He looked over his shoulder at the renegades, gathered on the first floor still. I followed his gaze to his mother, who was having a close conversation with Teka, a mug of tea clutched in both hands. Cisi wasn't far away from them, staring blankly at the furnace. She hadn't spoken or stirred since the planning session. Many of the others were next to the transport vessel, tucking themselves under blankets, using the bags they had carried here as pillows. We would be up with the sun.

"I need to ask you for something," he said, returning his focus to me again. He took my face in his hands, gently. "It's not fair to ask this of you. But I want to ask you to spare Ryzek's life."

I paused, certain for a moment that he was joking. I even laughed. But it didn't look like he was joking.

"Why would you ask me that?"

"You know why," Akos said, letting his hands fall.

"Eijeh," I said.

Always Eijeh.

He said, "If you kill Ryzek tomorrow, you'll be sealing Eijeh forever with Ryzek's worst memories. His condition will be permanent."

I had told him, once, that the only restoration possible for Eijeh rested in Ryzek. If my brother could trade memories at will, surely he could return all of Eijeh's memories to their rightful place, and take back his own. I could imagine a way to make him do that. Or two.

And for Akos, Eijeh had been a faint glow in the distance for as long as he could likely remember, a tiny flicker of hope. I knew it was impossible for him to let go of that. But I couldn't risk everything for it, either.

"No," I said, my voice steady. "First of all, we don't know how all the memory trading has affected either of their currentgifts. We don't even know if he can set Eijeh right anymore."

"If there's even a chance," Akos said, "a chance to restore my brother, I have to—"

"No!" I pushed him back. "Look at what he did to me. Look at me!"

"Cyra—"

"This—!" I pointed to the side of my head. "All my marks—! Seasons of torture and trails of bodies and you want me to *spare* him? Are you insane?"

"You don't understand," he said urgently. He touched his forehead to mine and said, "I'm the reason Eijeh is the way he is. If I hadn't tried to escape Voa . . . if I had just surrendered to my fate earlier . . ."

I ached.

Somehow it had never occurred to me that Akos held himself responsible for Ryzek unloading his memories on Eijeh. It had been clear to me that Ryzek would have found a reason to do that to Eijeh at one point or another. But all Akos knew was that Ryzek had inflicted that particular harm on Eijeh as a result of his failed escape.

"Ryzek was always going to do what he did to Eijeh, whether you tried to escape or not," I said. "Eijeh is not your responsibility. Everything that has happened to him is Ryzek's fault, not yours."

"It's not just that," Akos said. "When we were taken from our house—it was because of me that they knew which kid to take, him or Cisi. Because I told him to run. It was *me*. So I promised my father, I *promised*—"

"Again," I said, angrier this time, "Ryzek's responsibility! Not yours! Surely your father would understand that."

"I can't give up on him," Akos said, his voice breaking. "I *can't*."

"And I can't participate in this ridiculous quest you're on, not anymore," I snapped. "I can't watch you destroy yourself, destroy your life, to save someone who doesn't want to be saved. Someone who is *gone*, and will never come back!"

"Gone?" Akos's eyes were wild. "What if I had told you that *you* were beyond hope, huh?"

I knew the answer to that. I would never have fallen for him. I would never have turned to the renegades for help. My currentgift would never have changed.

"Listen," I said. "I have to do this. I know you understand that, even if you can't admit it right now. I need . . . I *need* Ryzek to be gone. I don't know what else I can say."

He shut his eyes for a moment, then turned away.

All the others were asleep. Even Akos, lying a few feet away from me on the ground near the ships. I, however, was wide awake with only my racing thoughts as company. I propped myself up on my elbow, and looked out at the bumps of renegades under blankets, the dying light from the furnace. Jorek was curled in a tight ball, his blankets drawn over his head. Teka was in a beam of moonlight that turned her blond hair silver-white.

I frowned. Just as a few memories began to surface, I saw Sifa Kereseth crossing the room. She slipped out the back door, and before I knew what I was doing—or why—I had shoved my feet into my boots and followed her.

She was standing just outside, her clasped hands resting on the small of her back.

"Hello," she said.

We were in a rough part of Voa. All around us were low buildings with flaking paint, windows with bars twisted into decorative patterns to distract from their true purpose, doors hanging off their hinges. The streets were packed dirt instead of stone. Floating among the buildings, though, were dozens of wild fenzu, glowing with Shotet blue. The other colors had been bred out of existence decades ago.

"Of all the many futures I have seen, this is one of the stranger ones," Sifa said. "And the one with the most potential for good and evil in equal measure."

"You know," I said, "it might help if you would just tell me what to do."

"I can't, because I honestly don't know. We are at a murky place," she said. "Full of confusing visions. Hundreds of murky futures spread out as far as I can see. So to speak. Only the fates are clear."

"What's the difference?" I said. "Fates, futures . . ."

"A fate is something that happens no matter what version of the future I see," she said. "Your brother would not have wasted his time in trying to evade his fate if he had known that to be true, undoubtedly. But we prefer to keep our work mysterious, at the risk of it being too rigorously controlled."

I tried to picture it. Hundreds of twisting paths unfolding in front of me, the same destination at the end of each one. It made my own fate seem even stranger—no matter where I went, and no matter what I did, I would cross the Divide. So what? What did it matter?

I didn't ask her. Even if I thought she would tell me—she wouldn't—I didn't want to know.

"The oracles of the planets meet yearly to discuss our visions," Sifa said. "We mutually agree on what future is most crucial for each planet. For this planet, my job—my only job, aside from recording visions—is to ensure that Ryzek leads Shotet for as little time as possible."

I said, "Even at the expense of your son?"

I wasn't sure which son I was referring to: Akos or Eijeh. Maybe both.

"I am a servant of fate," she said. "I do not have the luxury of partiality."

The thought brought a chill to my bones. I understood doing things for "the greater good" in theory, but in practice, I didn't have any interest in it. I had always protected myself, and now I protected Akos, when I could. Beyond that, there weren't many I wasn't willing to cast out of my path. And maybe it meant I was evil, but it was true regardless.

"It is not easy to be a mother and an oracle, or a wife and an oracle," she said, not sounding quite as steady now as she had before. "I have been . . . tempted many times. To protect my family at the expense of the greater good. But . . ." She shook her head. "I must stay the course. I must have faith."

Or what? I wanted to ask. What was so bad about snatching up your loved ones and fleeing, refusing to shoulder a responsibility you never wanted?

"I have a question you might be able to answer," I said. "Do you know the name Yma Zetsyvis?"

Sifa tilted her head so her thick hair spilled over one shoulder. "I do."

"Do you know what her name was before she married Uzul Zetsyvis?" I said. "Was her fate favored?"

"No," Sifa said. She took a breath of the cool night air. "Their marriage was a kind of aberration, unlikely enough to register in the oracles' visions of Shotet. Uzul married far beneath himself, for love, apparently. A common woman, with a common name. Yma Surukta."

Surukta. It was Teka's name, and Zosita's. Women of pale hair and bright eyes.

"That's what I thought," I said. "I would stay and talk, but I have something I need to do."

Sifa shook her head. "It's strange for me not to know what someone is deciding."

"Embrace the uncertainty," I said.

§

If Voa was a wheel, I was walking its circumference. The Zetsyvis family lived across the city, their house on a cliff overlooking Voa. I could see the light glittering inside their estate from far off, when the streets were still broken under my feet.

The currentstream, winding around the sky above me, was deep purple, transitioning to red. It almost looked like blood. Fitting, given our plans for tomorrow.

I felt comfortable in the poor, discarded district where the renegades had chosen their safe house. More often than not, the windows were dark, but sometimes I saw shadowed figures hunched over small lanterns. In one house I spotted a family of four crowded around playing cards scavenged from Zold. They were laughing. There had been a time when I would not have dared to walk these streets, as Ryzek's sister, but now I was disgraced, and no friend of the regime. I was as safe as I could be, here.

I was less comfortable when I crossed into wealthier territory. Everyone in Voa professed loyalty to the Noavek regime—it wasn't optional—but Ryzek kept the oldest and most trusted families in Shotet in a ring around him. I could tell I was in that ring by the buildings alone: they were newer, or patched over and repaired and repainted. The street had turned to stone beneath my feet. There were lights along the way. I saw inside most of the windows, where people in clean, crisp clothes read their screens at the kitchen table, or watched the news feed.

As soon as I could, I turned toward the cliffs, to one of the paths that would take me up the face. Long ago, the Shotet had carved steps into these cliff walls. They were steep and narrow and poorly maintained, so they weren't for the faint of heart. But I had never once been accused of having that kind of heart.

Aching from both yesterday's injuries and my currentgift, I kept one hand on the wall to my left, pressing close. I hadn't realized when I left how sore and exhausted my body still was, how every step throbbed in my still-healing throat and scalp. I paused, and took out the packet of vials I had taken from Akos's belongings before I left.

A line of vials in different colors confronted me. I knew most of them by sight—a sleeping potion, a painkiller, and at the far end, its cork sealed twice with melted wax, the pure red of hush-flower extract. In this quantity, at this potency, it was enough to kill a man.

I swallowed half a vial of the painkiller, then tucked the packet away in my small satchel.

It took an hour of climbing to reach the top. I had to stop several times along the way to rest. The city was smaller every time, its lit windows just blinking lights up here. I could always find Noavek manor, glowing white near the city's center, and the amphitheater, even now protected by a web of light. Somewhere beneath that amphitheater was Orieve Benesit, waiting to die.

When I reached the top, I backed away from the edge as quickly as I could. Just because I wasn't faint of heart didn't mean I enjoyed taunting death.

I followed the road to the Zetsyvis house, into the forests where they bred fenzu for export. The path I walked was guarded by metal grates, to keep people from stealing the valuable insects. Draped over the trees were nets to prevent the fenzu from escaping, more a precaution than anything. Fenzu built their nests around the delicate branches nearest to the sky. The trees themselves were tall and thin, their trunks so dark they looked black, adorned with wiry, dark green clusters instead of the floppy leaves I had seen on other planets.

Finally the Zetsyvis house came into view. There was a guard at the gate, but by the time I punched him in the jaw, it was already too late for him to defend himself. I used his limp hand to unlock the gate. I paused there, remembering how my hand hadn't unlocked Ryzek's room in Noavek manor. How my blood, my *genes*, hadn't unlocked it. And I still didn't know why.

Now is not the time. I shook myself out of the daze, continuing on. I didn't think I would encounter any other security; only Yma lived here now.

I had made sure of that, hadn't I?

The house was modern, recently renovated from the drafty stone castle that had been there before. Large sections of wall had been replaced with glass, and little orbs full of blue-glowing insects were draped across the trees in front, creating a bright canopy that reflected in the windows. Strange plants twisted together in front of the house, some of them creeping up the remaining stone. Some were blooming, too, huge flowers from different worlds in colors I rarely saw on ours: pink as a tongue, rich blue green, black as space.

When I reached the front door, I drew the small currentblade sheathed at my hip, just in case. I was almost afraid to break the silence that surrounded me. But then I pounded, hard, with the handle of the knife, until Yma Zetsyvis answered.

"Miss Noavek," Yma said. She wasn't smiling, for once. She was staring at the weapon in my right hand.

"Hello," I said. "Mind if I come in?"

I didn't wait for an answer. I stepped into the foyer. The floor was made of wood, likely from the dark trees that surrounded the Zetsyvis estate, the same wood used so liberally in Noavek manor. There were few walls here, the whole first floor bare for me to see, and all the furniture stark white.

Yma wore a robe with a pale sheen, and her hair was loose around her shoulders.

"Have you come to kill me?" she said, her face placid. "I suppose it's only fitting that you finish what you started. First my husband, then my daughter . . ."

I thought about telling her that I had not wanted to kill either of them, that their deaths still haunted me in my dreams. That I heard Uzul's heartbeat before I woke, and saw Lety in corners where she had never stood. But there was no reason to say any of those things.

"I just came to talk to you," I said. "The knife is for my protection."

"I didn't think you needed knives," Yma said.

"Sometimes they're more efficient," I said. "Subtle intimidation, and all that."

"Ah." Yma turned away. "Come on, then, let's sit."

She led the way to the sitting area, which I could see from where I stood, the low couches arranged in a square. She turned on a few lights with a gentle touch, so the couches glowed from beneath, and fenzu swarmed in a lantern on the low glass table. I didn't sit down until she did, arranging her robe over her legs so they weren't exposed. She was an elegant woman.

"You're looking better than you were last time I saw you," she said. "I can't say I didn't enjoy watching you bleed."

"Yes, I'm sure that was entertaining for quite a few people,"

I said tartly. "A little harder for you to claim moral superiority when you're thirsting for someone else's blood, though, isn't it?"

"Your crime came first."

"I've never argued that I'm on some kind of high ground with you," I said. "Just that you might be on the low ground with me."

Yma laughed, and she was about to aim another insult at me, I was sure, but I spoke over her.

"I know my brother disgusts you just as much as I do. I've known for a long time," I said. "And I used to feel bad for you, for having to stay close to him to survive. I used to think you were just desperate and doing what you had to."

Yma's face twitched. She looked out one of the expansive windows at Voa, the ocean beyond it visible from this height, though it just looked like emptiness, like the edges of space.

"Used to?" she finally replied.

"Today I began to understand that you're not desperate—at least not in the way I thought. Everything is perfectly in your control, isn't it?"

She jerked her head back toward me, suddenly stern. I had gotten her attention.

"You've lost far more than I realized. You lost them before I ever laid a hand on your husband. Surukta is your name," I said. "Your sister was Zosita Surukta, who fled the planet after she was caught teaching other languages to her neighbors, and later executed for participating in the revolt. Before she was caught, though, your nephew was killed for her crimes, and your niece, Teka, lost an eye to my brother."

"The misdeeds of my family are behind me," Yma said, her voice wavering a little. "You can hardly hold me responsible for them."

"I'm not," I said with a short laugh. "I'm telling you how I know that you are part of the revolt, and have been for quite some time."

"My, you certainly have cooked up a theory, haven't you?" Yma said, and her strange smile returned. "I am on the verge of marrying your brother and solidifying my place as one of the most powerful people in Shotet. I married Uzul Zetsyvis as a means to an end, *this* end. Social advancement. I have a skill for it. Something you would not understand, since you were born into privilege."

"Do you want to know what ultimately gave you away?" I said, ignoring her explanation. "First of all, you were the one who turned Uzul in. You knew what my brother would do to him. People who act out of desperation don't make calculated moves like that."

"You—" She tried to interrupt, but I spoke over her.

"Second, you warned me that they were going to frame an innocent person for the renegade attack, knowing that I would do something about it."

She scowled. "First you tell me about the people I've lost, and then you accuse me of bringing about my own sister's execution? How does that make sense?"

"And last," I continued, "all the *tapping* you do. What is it with you and Teka and the tapping? It's not even a particularly good pattern."

Yma's eyes skirted mine.

"You're a renegade," I said. "That's why, after all that he took from you, you're still able to stand at my brother's side. Because you know you need to be close to him in order to take your revenge."

She stood, robe rippling behind her as she moved toward the window. For a long time she was still, a white pillar in the moonlight. Then, at her side, she tapped her first finger against her thumb. One, three, one. One, three, one.

"The tapping is a message," she said without turning around. "Once, my sister and I taught ourselves a song to remember the fates of the family Noavek. She taught it to her daughter, Teka, as well." She sang it, her voice creaking. *"The first child of the family Noavek will fall to the family Benesit."* I followed her fingers as they found the rhythm again, and her body swayed. "The rhythm was one, three, one, three. . . ."

Like a dance.

"I do it," she said, slowly, "when I need strength for the task at hand. I sing that song in my head, and I tap out its rhythm."

Like at her sister's execution, her fingers on the railing. Like at dinner with my brother, her hand on his knee.

She turned to me.

"So, what? Have you come to get leverage? Do you intend to trade me for your freedom? What?"

"I have to admire your commitment to this game of pretend," I said. "You gave over your husband—"

"Uzul was sick with Q900X. Several ingredients in the treatment protocol are a violation of our religious principles," Yma snapped. "So he sacrificed himself for the cause. I assure you, it was not what I wanted, but as a result of his selflessness— something you clearly know nothing about—I won my place at Ryzek's side."

My currentshadows moved faster, still spurred on by shifts in my emotions.

"I take it you haven't spoken much to the other renegades," I said. "You know they're responsible for saving my life? I've been working with them for a while now."

"Have you," Yma said, flat, frowning at me.

"You didn't really think whatever excuse Ryzek gave for carving up my face was true, did you?" I said. "I helped renegades sneak into Noavek manor to assassinate him, and after the plan failed, I got them out safely. That's how I got arrested. Teka, your niece, was there."

Yma's frown deepened. In this light the creases in her face were more pronounced. She was lined, not from age—she was still too young for that, prematurely white haired though she was—but from grief. Now I knew how to account for her constant smile. It was just a mask.

"Most of the others . . ." Yma sighed. "They don't know what I am. Zosita and Teka are—were—the only ones. This close to my mission's completion, it would have been too much of a risk for me to have any contact with anyone anyway."

I stood, joining her at the window. The currentstream had already turned a deeper red.

"Tomorrow the renegades are moving against Ryzek," I said. "Right before he executes Orieve Benesit, I will challenge him to the arena in such a way that he can't refuse."

"What?" she demanded, sharp. "Tomorrow?"

I nodded.

She gave a short laugh, her arms crossed. "You foolish child. You think you'll be able to defeat Ryzek Noavek in the arena? You really only do think one way. Like a trained killer."

"No," I said. "I came to you with a plan. Your role in it would be simple." I reached into the satchel at my side and took a vial from the packet I had brought with me. "All you have to do is pour this vial into Ryzek's calming tonic in the morning. I assume you'll be at his side when he drinks it."

Yma frowned at the vial.

"How do you know he'll be drinking calming tonic?"

"He always does before he kills someone," I said. "So that he can stomach it."

She snorted a little.

"Believe what you want about his character, I don't really care," I said. "But he drank it the day he ordered me cut to pieces for the public's enjoyment, and I promise you he will drink it in anticipation of killing Orieve Benesit. And all I'm asking is that you pour this in, nothing else. If I fail, then your place at his side will still be secure. He has no reason to suspect you. But if you do this, and I succeed in my plan, I'll never even have to lay a hand on him, and you will be able to take your vengeance without having to marry him first."

She took the vial, examining it. It was sealed with wax that Akos had taken from my desk; I used it to stamp envelopes with the Noavek symbol, just as my mother and father had.

"I'll do it," Yma said.

"Good," I said. "I trust you'll be careful. I can't afford for you to get caught."

"I have been careful with every word and glance since you were a mere child," Yma said. "I sincerely hope, Miss Noavek, that you are not doing this for atonement, because you will not get it. Not from me. Not after all that you have done."

"Oh, I'm not nearly noble enough for that," I said. "For me it's all about petty revenge, I promise you."

Yma sneered at my reflection in the window. I let myself out of her house. I had to move quickly if I wanted to be back at the safe house before the others woke.

CHAPTER 34 | AKOS

CYRA WAS AHEAD OF Akos, standing in the sun, a hood up to shield her face. She wore a heavy cloak to disguise the currentshadows, her hands buried in long sleeves. Behind her was the amphitheater where she'd almost lost her life, but to watch her walk, with that straight spine, it was like nobody had ever tried to peel her apart.

A group of Shotet soldiers stood by the big double doors that led straight to the amphitheater floor. Word on the street—collected by Sovy, who, according to Jorek, "knew *everyone*"—was that the soldiers called to appear in the amphitheater today were being rewarded for a good scavenge. Akos didn't know what they were supposed to have brought back that was so worthy of this honor, but it didn't really matter—they were just a ruse anyway. Ryzek wanted a crowd to witness Ori's execution.

The big double doors opened. Akos squinted into bright light, and the roar of a huge crowd filled his ears. There were so many faces inside that he felt like the entire city was there, though it was more like a fifth of it—and the other four-fifths would watch the live feed on screens around Voa. If they bothered to watch at all.

Cyra turned back with a glimmer of silver, the sun hitting her now-healed throat. Her chin bobbed up and down in a nod, and then the tide of the crowd carried her away from him. Time to go.

"So." Isae had come to stand at his shoulder. "We never actually determined how we were going to get through the *first* door."

"Honestly, I had pretty much decided to just . . . smash the guard's head into the wall," Akos replied.

"I'm sure that won't draw any attention at all," Isae replied. "There's Eye Patch. Let's go."

Isae had taken to calling the renegades by nicknames instead of learning their real names. "Eye Patch" was obviously Teka, Jorek was "Fidget," Jyo was "The Flirt," and Sovy was "The One Who Doesn't Speak Thuvhesit," which was long, but she hadn't used it much. It went both ways, though—Akos had caught Teka referring to Isae as "The Haughty One" that morning as they all shoved food in their mouths, eyeing the hole Akos's mom had made in the ceiling with her floater.

Akos spotted Teka and Cisi standing near the amphitheater doors, and made his way over, keeping Isae in his periphery. They had all been surprised when Teka offered herself up to help them get into the underground prison. It was clear she didn't care about saving Ori's life. But maybe Cyra's point about taking away Ryzek's moment of triumph over his fate had struck her.

"What's your read on the guard?" Teka asked him when he was close enough to hear her. She was wrapped in gray fabric, her hair combed over her missing eye in a sweep of gold. He looked over her shoulder at the guard stationed outside the door Cyra had told them to use. It was the same color as the wall, with an old-fashioned lock that took a metal key. Probably buried in one of the guard's pockets.

But Akos wasn't supposed to be figuring out the door, he was supposed to be figuring out the man. He was no more than five seasons Akos's senior, broad-shouldered and wearing earned armor. The heel of his hand was balanced on the handle of his currentblade, which was sheathed at his hip. Capable, Akos guessed, and not easy to knock senseless.

"I could take him down, but not quietly," Akos said. "I'd probably get myself arrested."

"Well, we'll call that our backup plan," Isae said. "What about distraction?"

"Yeah, sure." Teka folded her arms. "The man was hired to guard a secure door that leads to Ryzek Noavek's secret underground prison, and his failure to do so will probably result in his execution, but he will definitely abandon his post just because you wave something shiny at him."

"Say 'secret underground prison' a little louder, why don't you?" Isae said.

Teka snapped a reply, but Akos wasn't paying attention. Cisi was tugging his sleeve.

"Let me see your vials," she said. "I have an idea."

Akos kept a few vials with him wherever he went—sleep elixir, calming tonic, and a blend for fortitude among them. He wasn't sure what Cisi needed, but he undid the strap holding the vials against his arm and handed the hard little packet to her. All the glass clinked together as she sorted through it, choosing the sleep elixir. She uncorked it, sniffed it.

"That's *strong*," she said. Isae and Teka were still bickering.

About what, he didn't know, but he wasn't going to get between them unless they started throwing punches.

"It's useful for certain situations," Akos replied vaguely.

"Go buy me something to drink from that cart over there, would you?" Cisi said, nodding to the big shaded cart across the square. She sounded confident enough, so he didn't ask questions. He slipped through the crowd, sweat curling over the back of his neck. Like Teka, he wore a gray robe over his armor, which didn't exactly make him inconspicuous—he was still the tallest person in sight—but made him look a little less like the person who had rescued Cyra Noavek from the amphitheater the day before.

The cart was sagging into its wheels, and so lopsided Akos wondered how all the mugs—full of some kind of rich, spicy drink from Othyr that lifted a person's spirits, if the shouts of the seller were to be believed—didn't just slide off and break on the street. The Othyrian man named a price in broken Shotet, and Akos tossed him a coin. Cyra had left a stash of money in their quarters on the sojourn ship, opening it to him without ceremony one morning as she was cleaning her teeth, and he'd kept some of it, just in case.

He carried the hot mug, which was tiny in his hand, over to Cisi, who dumped the vial of sleep elixir in it and sauntered over to the guard. Without a word of explanation.

"I doubt he speaks Thuvhesit," Teka said.

Cisi's posture relaxed, and a smile spread over her face as she greeted the guard. At first the man looked like he would yell at her, but then he got that sleepy look, the same one both Jorek and Jyo had given Cisi yesterday.

"She could be speaking Ogran," he said. "It wouldn't matter."

He'd seen the effects of Cisi's gift before, but only when she wasn't really *trying*. He had no idea how potent the effect would be when she actually put effort into it. The guard was leaning back against the amphitheater wall, a little smile curling his lips, and when she offered him the mug, he cradled it in both hands. And sipped.

Akos hustled through the crowd, quick. If the guard was going to topple, he wanted it to happen as discreetly as possible. And sure enough, by the time he made it to his sister's side, the guard was swaying on his feet, the rest of the Othyrian drink splashing on the packed dirt. Akos caught him by the shoulders and lowered him to the ground, slow. Teka was already crouched over the man's body, searching his pockets. She turned up the key quickly, checked over her shoulder, and crammed it into the lock.

"Okay," Isae said to Cisi. "That was downright alarming."

Cisi just grinned.

Akos dragged the sleeping guard over to the side, next to the building, then ran to join the others in the open doorway. The maintenance tunnel beyond smelled like hot trash and mildew, and the odor sent a sharp feeling into his gut, like a needle, for some reason. The air felt thick, like there was too much moisture in it. Teka locked the door behind her and pocketed the key.

Now that they were in, there was no bickering, no joking, no improvising. It was quiet in the maintenance tunnel except for a faraway dripping sound, and it was worse, not being able to hear the crowd outside or the cheers from the arena above. Not knowing if Cyra had made it in, if she had made her challenge already, or if they would ever get out with Ori in tow. This tunnel felt less like a basement now, and more like a tomb.

"Cyra said to move toward the center," Isae said softly. "She didn't remember the path exactly. Said she was out of it when she was taken here last."

But Cyra wasn't the only person who had been here. Akos closed his eyes, thinking back to the night when Vas had wrestled him from his bed after a few days' starvation—he didn't know how long exactly, just that his door was locked and nobody would explain to him what was going on, and his stomach had *ached* for hours on end. And then stopped aching, like it had given up.

Vas had gotten a few good hits in in the hallway, then tossed him in a floater and flew him *here*. To this tunnel, to this mildew-trash smell and this particular darkness.

"I remember," he said, and he slipped past Isae so he could take the lead.

He was still sweating, so he unfastened the heavy fabric covering his armor and tossed it aside. This path was hazy in his memories, and the last thing he wanted to do was go back to that time, when everything had ached and he had felt so weak he could hardly stand. Eijeh had met him and Vas at the back door, and he had curled his fingers around the armor that covered Akos's shoulder. For a tick it had felt comforting, like his brother was trying to steady him. And then Eijeh had dragged him to the prison. To be tortured.

Akos gritted his teeth, squeezed his knife, and kept going. When he rounded the first corner, saw the first guard in his path, he didn't even think, he just erupted. Slammed the shorter, broader man into the wall, using his chin to drive his skull into the stone. A knife scraped Akos's armor, and a tongue of fire issued from the palm of the guard's hand, put out immediately by Akos's touch.

Akos slammed the guard's head back again, and again, until his eyes rolled back and he slumped. A chill passed over Akos, his hair standing on end. He didn't check if the man was dead. He didn't want to know.

He did glance at Cisi. Her mouth was twisted with disgust.

"Well," Isae said—*chirped*, really. "That was effective."

"Yep," Teka said, and she stepped right on the guard's leg as she kept walking down the next hallway. "Whoever we run into here is a Noavek loyalist, Kereseth. Not worth crying over."

"Do you see tears on my face?" he said, trying for some of Cyra's bravado and falling short when his voice cracked a little. Still, he kept walking. He couldn't worry about Cisi's opinion of him. Not down here.

A few more turns, and Akos wasn't sweating anymore; he was shivering. The hallways all looked the same: uneven stone floor, dusty stone wall, low stone ceiling. Whenever they stepped down, Akos had to duck so he wouldn't scrape his head. The smell of trash was gone, but the mildew was back in force, choking him. He remembered staring at the side of Eijeh's head as his brother yanked him forward through these passages. Noticing that Eijeh had cut his hair short, just like Ryzek.

I can't watch you destroy yourself for someone who doesn't want to be saved, Cyra had said the night before. He had shown her just how deep his insanity ran, and she had refused to go along with it. It was hard to hold it against her. Except he did. Had to.

The door up ahead didn't look right in its stone-and-wood frame. It was made of black glass, opaque, and the locking mechanism was on the side. A keypad. Cyra had given them a list of combination options—all of them, she said, related to her mother in some way. Birthday, death day, anniversary, lucky numbers. Akos still couldn't see Ryzek as a person who cared about his mother enough to lock his doors with her birthday.

But instead of trying even one of the combinations, Teka just started unscrewing the plate that covered the keypad. Her screwdriver was as delicate as a needle, polished and clean. She moved it like it was a sixth finger. Popped the cover off the keypad and set it down, then pinched one of the wires under it, eyes shut.

"Um . . . Teka?" There were footsteps coming from behind them somewhere.

"Shut up," she snapped, pinching a different wire. She smiled a little. "Ah," she said, and it was clear she wasn't talking to them. "I see. Okay then, come along—"

All the lights went out except the emergency light above, which shone down on them from the corner, so bright it left spots on Akos's eyelids. The glass door sprang open, revealing the glass floor that Akos remembered from his very worst memory: his brother forcing him to his knees in front of Cyra Noavek. The pale emergency lights glowed in the floor in the prison hallway, dividing it into grids.

Isae sprinted through the doorway, and ran right down the middle of the hallway, looking left and right every time she reached a new cell. Akos went in after her, scanning the space, but feeling separate from it at the same time. Isae was running back now, and he knew what she was going to say before she said it.

Somehow he felt like he'd known it all along, since he watched his mother flip that button in her fingers, since he realized how easy it would be for Sifa to manipulate them into the future *she* wanted, no matter the cost.

"She's not here," Isae said. Since he'd known her, she'd always been in total control, hadn't even broken down when she found out Ori was kidnapped. Had never faltered, not even once. And now she was almost shrieking. Frantic. "She's not here, Ori's not here!"

He blinked, slow, like all the air around his head had turned to syrup. All the cells were empty. Ori was gone.

CHAPTER 35 | CYRA

AFTER THE DOUBLE DOORS to the amphitheater opened, I knew it was time for me to move. I looked at Akos one last time, noting the red stain on his fingertips from preparing hushflower blends the night before, and the white line along his jaw where he had been scarred, and the natural gathering between his eyebrows that gave him an expression of perpetual concern. Then I slipped between the two people standing in front of me and stepped into the pack of soldiers who were about to receive their honor from my brother.

By the time one of them noticed me walking among them, we were inside the yawning tunnel to the amphitheater floor. But I had drawn my currentblade, so I wasn't concerned.

"Hey!" one of the soldiers snapped. "You're not supposed to—"

I seized him by the elbow and drew him close, touching the point of my knife to the bottom edge of his armor, right above his hip. I pressed it just enough for him to feel the sting of the point.

"Let me walk in," I told him, loud enough for the others to hear. "I'll let him go as soon as we're inside."

"Is that . . . ?" one of the others asked, leaning close to see my face.

I didn't answer. Keeping my hand on his armor, not his skin, I pressed my captive soldier toward the end of the tunnel. None of the others moved to help him, and I credited my reputation for that—my reputation, and the ropes of shadow currently wrapped around my throat and wrists.

I squinted into the bright light at the end of the passageway, and the roar of a huge crowd filled my ears. The big, heavy doors closed behind me and locked, leaving only my hostage and me on the arena floor. The other soldiers had stayed back. Above us, the force field buzzed. It smelled sour as saltfruit, and familiar as the dust that rose into the air with every footstep I took.

I had bled here. I had made others bleed here.

Ryzek was on a wide platform, halfway up the stadium's side. An amplifier swooped over his head and hovered. His mouth was open, like he had been ready to speak, but now all he could do was stare at me.

I shoved my hostage soldier aside, sheathed my currentblade, and pushed away the hood that shaded my face.

It took Ryzek only a moment to put on a mocking smile. "Well. Look at this. Cyra Noavek, back so soon? Did you miss us? Or is this how disgraced Shotet commit suicide?"

A chorus of laughter came from the crowd. The stadium was full of his most loyal supporters, the healthiest and wealthiest and best-fed people in Shotet. They would laugh at anything that resembled a joke.

One of the amplifiers—controlled by remote by someone in the amphitheater—floated over my head to catch my response. I watched it bob up and down like a swallow. I didn't have much time before he sent someone after me; I had to be direct.

I removed each of my gloves, in turn, and unbuttoned the heavy cloak that made me sweat. Beneath it I wore my armor. My arms were bare, and a layer of makeup—applied by Teka that morning—disguised the bruises on my face, making it look like I had healed overnight. The silverskin on my throat and head shone. It itched in earnest now as it knitted together with my scalp.

If my body ached, it didn't mention it. I was on Akos's painkiller, but it was adrenaline that really made me separate from my pain now.

"I'm here to challenge you to the arena," I said.

There was a smattering of laughter from the crowd, like they weren't sure if it was expected of them. Ryzek was certainly not laughing.

"I never knew you to be so theatrical," Ryzek said at last. His face was sweaty; he wiped his upper lip with the back of his hand. "Marching in here with a hostage to make an attempt on your brother's life is . . . well, just as cruel as we have come to expect from you, I suppose."

"No crueler than having your sister beaten to death and recording it so everyone can watch," I said.

"You are not my sister," Ryzek said. "You're my mother's murderer."

"Then come down here and avenge her," I said hotly.

The amphitheater was full of mutters again, noise poured back into it like water into a glass.

"You don't deny killing her?" Ryzek said.

I couldn't even pretend to deny it. Even after all this time, the memory was close to me. I had been yelling at her at the time, throwing a tantrum. *"I don't want to go to another doctor! I won't!"* I had grabbed her arm, and shoved the pain at her like a child thrusting a plate of unwanted food away. But I had pushed too hard, and she had fallen at my feet. What I most remembered were her hands, folded over her stomach. So elegant, so perfect. Even in death.

"I am not here to trade accusations with you," I said. "I am here to do what I should have done seasons ago. Fight me in the arena." I drew my knife and held it out from my side. "And before you tell me that I don't have the rank to make such a challenge, let me point out how convenient that is."

Ryzek's jaw was set. When we were young, he had lost a tooth because he ground them in his sleep. It had fractured from the force, and its replacement was capped with metal. Sometimes I saw it glinting when he spoke, a reminder of the pressure that had created the man standing in front of me.

I went on, "You stripped me of my rank so no one could ever see for themselves that I am stronger than you. Now you hide behind your throne like a cowering child, and call it law." I tilted my head. "But no one can quite forget your fate, can they? To fall to the family Benesit?" I smiled. "Refusing to fight me just confirms what everyone suspects about you: that you are weak."

I heard low whispers in the crowd. No one had declared Ryzek's fate so baldly, so publicly, without suffering the consequences. The last one who had tried had been Teka's mother on the sojourn ship's intercom, and now she was dead. The soldiers by the doors shifted, waiting for the order to kill me, but it didn't come.

All that came was Ryzek's smile, showing teeth. It was not the smile of someone who was squirming.

"All right, little Cyra. I'll spar with you," he said. "Since that seems to be the only behavior that makes sense to you."

I couldn't let him unsettle me, but he was doing well. The smile had chilled me. It made the currentshadows race around my arms and throat, my forever adornments. Always denser, faster, when my brother cued them with his voice.

"Yes, I will execute this traitor myself," he said. "Clear a path."

I knew his smile, and what it disguised. He had a plan. But hopefully mine was better.

Ryzek descended to the arena floor slowly and with grace, walking the path the crowd made for him, pausing at the barrier so a servant could check the tension of his armor straps and the sharpness of his currentblades.

In an honest fight, I would beat Ryzek within minutes. My father had taught Ryzek the art of cruelty, and my mother had taught him political scheming, but everyone had always left me alone to my own studies. My isolation had made me his superior in combat. Ryzek knew that, so he would never make this an honest fight. That meant I didn't know what weapon he was really holding.

He was taking his time on his way to the arena, which meant there was likely something he was waiting for. He didn't intend to actually fight me, obviously, just as I didn't intend to fight him.

If all was going according to plan, and Yma had slipped the contents of the vial into the calming tonic he drank with his breakfast, the iceflowers were already swimming through his body. The timing would not be exact; that depended on the person. I would have to be ready for the potion to surprise me, or fail entirely.

"You're dawdling," I said, hoping that calling him out would speed him up. "What is it you're waiting for?"

"I am waiting for the right blade," Ryzek said, and he dropped down to the arena floor. Dust rose up in a cloud around his feet. He rolled up his left sleeve, baring his kill marks. He had run out of space on his arm, and started a second row next to the first, near his elbow. He claimed every kill that he ordered as his own, even if he himself had not brought about the death.

Ryzek drew his currentblade slowly, and as he raised his arm, the crowd around us exploded into cheers. Their roar clouded my thoughts. I couldn't breathe.

He didn't look pale and unfocused, like he had actually consumed the poison. He looked, if anything, more focused than ever.

I wanted to run at him with blade extended, like an arrow released from a bow, a transport vessel breaking through the atmosphere. But I didn't. And neither did he. We both stood in the arena, waiting.

"What are *you* waiting for, sister?" Ryzek said. "Have you lost your nerve?"

"No," I said. "I'm waiting for the poison you swallowed this morning to settle in."

A gasp rattled through the crowd, and for once—for the first time—Ryzek's face went slack with shock. I had finally truly surprised him.

"All my life you've told me I have nothing to offer but the power that lives in my body," I said. "But I am not an instrument of torture and execution; I am the only person who knows the real

Ryzek Noavek." I stepped toward him. "I know how you fear pain more than anything else in this world. I know that you gathered these people here today, not to celebrate a successful scavenge, but to witness the murder of Orieve Benesit."

I sheathed my blade. I held my hands out to my sides so the crowd could see that they were empty. "And the most important thing I know, Ryzek, is that you can't bear to kill someone unless you drug yourself first. Which is why I poisoned your calming tonic this morning."

Ryzek touched his stomach, as if he could feel the hushflower eating away at his guts through his armor.

"You made a mistake, valuing me only for my currentgift and my skill with a knife," I said.

And for once, I believed it.

CHAPTER 36 | AKOS

The air in the underground prison was cool, but Akos knew that wasn't why Isae was trembling as she said, "Your mother said Ori would be here."

"There has to be a mistake," Cisi said softly. "Something she didn't see—"

Akos was pretty sure there was no mistake, but he wasn't about to share that now. They had to find Ori. If she wasn't in the prison, she had to be closer to the amphitheater—maybe above them, in the arena, or on the platform where Ryzek had cut into his own sister.

"We're wasting time. We need to go upstairs and find her," he said, surprised by how forceful his own voice sounded. "Now."

Apparently his voice had broken through Isae's panic. She took a deep breath and turned toward the door, where the distant footsteps of a few ticks ago had resolved into the menacing form of Vas Kuzar.

"Surukta. Kereseth. Ah—*Benesit*," Vas said, looking at Isae with a little tilt to his mouth. "Not as pretty as your twin, I have to say. Is that scar from a *Shotet* blade, by any chance?"

"Benesit?" Teka said, staring at Isae. "As in . . ."

Isae nodded.

Cisi had backed up against the wall of one of the cells, her hands flat against the glass. Akos wondered if his sister felt like she was standing in their living room again, watching Vas Kuzar murder their dad. That was how he had felt the first few times he saw Vas after the kidnapping—like everything was unraveling inside him at once. He didn't feel that way anymore.

Vas was empty-eyed as always. It had been disappointing to figure out that Vas was so empty of wrath, numb inside as well as outside. It was easier to think of him as pure evil, but the truth was, he was just a pet doing his master's bidding.

The memory of Akos's dad's death surfaced: his broken skin, the rich color of his blood, like the currentstream above them; the bloody blade that Vas had wiped on a pant leg as he left the house. The man with the polished Shotet armor and golden-brown eyes who couldn't feel pain. Unless—*unless*.

Unless Akos touched him.

He didn't bother to reason with Vas. It was a waste of time. Akos just started toward him, his boots scraping the grit they had tracked onto the glass floor. Vas's eyes looked even colder, despite being such a warm shade of hazel, because of the lights coming from beneath him.

Akos had the heart of prey; he wanted to run, or at least keep space between them, but he made himself press against that space. Breathed open-mouthed, with flared nose; never breathing enough.

Vas lunged, and Akos let himself be prey, then; he sprang away. Not fast enough. Vas's knife scraped his armor. Akos winced at the sound, turning again to face him.

He would let Vas get a few close calls in, let him get cocky.

Cocky meant sloppy, and sloppy meant Akos might live.

Vas's eyes were like stamped metal, his arms were like twisted rope. He lunged again, but instead of trying to stab Akos, he grabbed his arm with his free hand and slammed him, hard, against the cell wall. Akos's head snapped back, smacking into the glass. He saw bursts of color and the glow of the floor against the flat ceiling. Vas's hand was clamped around him, stern enough to bruise.

And close enough to grab. Akos seized him before he could try to stab again, pressing his knife arm back as hard as he could muster. Vas's eyes went wide, startled by his touch. In pain, maybe. Akos tried to slam his forehead into Vas's nose, but he just tossed Akos aside.

Akos fell. The grit they had tracked in clung to his arms. He watched Teka dragging Isae and Cisi away, one hand on each arm. He felt relief, even as blood or sweat tickled the back of his neck; he wasn't sure which. His head throbbed from the impact with the wall. Vas was *strong*, and he was not.

Vas licked his lips as he stalked toward Akos again. He kicked, hitting Akos's armored side. And again, this time driving the toe of his boot into Akos's jaw. He sprawled flat on his back, covering his face with his hands, and groaned. The pain made it hard to think, hard even to breathe.

Vas laughed. He bent over Akos, grabbed the front of his armor, and pulled him half off the ground. Flecks of his spit hit Akos's face as he spoke.

"In whatever life there is to come, give your father my greetings."

This, Akos realized, was his last chance. He put his hand on Vas's throat. Not even grabbing, just touching, the best he could do. Vas gave him that startled look he'd given before, that pained look. He was bent, leaving a strip of skin exposed beneath his armor, right over the waistband of his pants. And while Akos was touching him—forcing him to feel pain again—he drew the knife he kept in the side of his boot, and stabbed with his left hand. Up, under the armor. Into Vas's gut.

Vas's eyes were so wide Akos saw the whites around his bright irises. Then he screamed. He screamed, and tears came into his eyes. His blood was hot on Akos's hand. They were locked together, Akos's blade in his flesh, his hands on Akos's shoulders, their eyes meeting. Together they sank to the ground, and Vas let out a heavy sob.

It took Akos a long time to let go. He needed to make sure Vas was dead.

He thought of his dad's button in his mom's hand, its sheen worn away by his fingers, and pulled his knife free.

He'd dreamt of killing Vas Kuzar so many times. The need to do it had been a second heartbeat in his body. In his dreams, though, he stood over the body and raised his knife to the sky and let the blood run down his arm like it was a wisp of the currentstream itself. In his dreams, he felt triumph and victory and vengeance, and like he could finally let his dad go.

In his dreams, he didn't huddle near the cell wall, scrubbing at his palm with a handkerchief. Shaking so badly he dropped the cloth on the glowing floor.

Vas's body looked so much smaller now that he was dead. His eyes were still open halfway, and so was his mouth, so Akos could see Vas's crooked teeth. He swallowed down bile at the image, determined not to throw up.

Ori, he thought. So he stumbled toward the door, and started running.

CHAPTER 37 | CYRA

RYZEK TOOK HIS HAND away from his stomach. Beads of sweat dotted his forehead, right by his hairline. His eyes, usually so piercing, were unfocused. But then his mouth drew down in a frown that was unexpectedly . . . vulnerable.

"It's you who made a mistake," he said, in a higher, softer voice than I had ever heard from him. It was a distinct voice, memorable: Eijeh's voice. How could both Ryzek and Eijeh be living in the same body, surfacing at different times? "By forcing his hand."

His hand?

The sound of the crowd around us had changed. No one was even looking at Ryzek anymore. All heads were turned toward the raised platform from which he had just descended, where Eijeh Kereseth now stood alone with a woman in front of him, a knife held at her throat.

I recognized her. Not just from the footage of the kidnapping that had played on screens throughout the city the day she was taken, but from the past day of watching Isae Benesit talk, laugh, eat. This was her double, Orieve Benesit, face unscarred.

"Ah yes, this is the blade I was waiting for," Ryzek said with a laugh, his natural voice returning. "Cyra, I'd like you to meet Orieve Benesit, chancellor of Thuvhe."

Her throat was purple with bruises. There was a deep cut in her forehead. But when our eyes locked across that substantial distance, she didn't look like someone who was afraid for her life. She looked like someone who knew what was coming and intended to meet it with a straight back and a steady look.

Did Ryzek know she wasn't really the chancellor? Or had she convinced him she was? Either way, it was too late. Too late.

"Ori," I said. In Thuvhesit, I added, "She tried to come for you."

I couldn't tell if she heard me, she was so still.

"Thuvhe is just a playground for the Shotet," Ryzek said. "It was easily penetrated, its chancellor effortlessly taken by my faithful servants. Soon, its chancellor will not be the only thing we take from it. This planet is ours to be claimed!"

He was rallying his supporters. Their roar was deafening. Their faces twisted with glee. The mania made the currentshadows wrap around my body, tight as ropes binding a prisoner, and I flinched.

"What do you think, Shotet?" Ryzek said, lifting his head to the crowd. "Should the chancellor die at the hand of one of her former subjects?"

Ori, still looking at me, didn't make a sound, though the amplifier drifted so close to her head it almost hit Eijeh. The one who carried my brother's horrors inside his head.

The chant began immediately. "Die!"

"Die!"

"Die!"

Ryzek spread his arms wide, like he was basking in the sound.

He turned, slowly, beckoning more and more of it, until the thirst for Ori's death felt like a tangible thing, a weight in the air. Then he held up his hands to quiet them, grinning.

"I think it's Cyra who will decide when she dies," he said. He lowered his voice a little. "If I fall—if you don't supply me with an antidote of some kind—she will fall, too."

I said weakly, "There is no antidote."

I could save her. I could tell Ryzek the truth—the truth I had told no one, even Akos, as he begged me to preserve what little hope he had left for his brother—and delay her execution. I opened my mouth to see if the truth would come out, despite my paralysis.

If I told Ryzek the truth—if I saved Ori's life—we would all be trapped in this amphitheater, surrounded by a sea of Ryzek's supporters, with no victory to claim for the renegades.

My mouth was dry. I couldn't swallow. No, it was too late for Orieve Benesit. I couldn't do it. I couldn't save her without sacrificing us all. Including the true chancellor of Thuvhe.

Ryzek swayed, and I stepped forward, weapon outstretched, to meet him as he fell. I thrust the knife, and his weight dragged us both to the ground.

High above us, Eijeh Kereseth—curly haired, wide-eyed, and gaunt—drove the currentblade into Orieve Benesit's gut.

And twisted it.

CHAPTER 38 | AKOS

As Ori collapsed, Akos heard a bloodcurdling scream. Ryzek fell on his side, his arms crossed in front of his body and his head limp against the dirt. Cyra got to her feet, knife in hand. She had done it. She had killed her brother, and the last hope for Eijeh's restoration.

Isae was shoving her way through the crowd as everything turned to chaos. She was clawing, her teeth gritted, fighting her way to the platform. Akos hoisted his body over the arena barrier and sprinted across the dirt, past Cyra and Ryzek, over the other barrier and into the crowd again. People elbowed and kicked and pressed, and his fingernails came away red with somebody else's blood, and he didn't care.

Up on the platform, Ori grabbed Eijeh's arms to hold herself up. Blood sputtered from her lips as she tried to breathe. Eijeh hunched over her, holding her elbows, and together they dropped to the ground. Ori's brow wrinkled, and Akos watched, not wanting to interrupt.

"Bye, Eij," she said, her voice caught by the hovering amplifier.

Akos bent low and barreled into the last of the crowd. Children screamed someplace far away. A woman moaned as someone trod on her—she couldn't get up, so people were just running over her.

When Isae got to Eijeh and Ori, she threw Akos's brother back with a roar. In half a tick she was on top of him, her hands around Eijeh's throat. And he didn't seem to be moving, even though she was choking him to death.

Akos didn't move right away, he just watched her do it. Eijeh had killed Ori. Maybe he deserved to die.

"Isae," Akos said with a croak. "Stop."

Ori was reaching for her sister, fingers straining at the empty space. It was only when Isae saw it that she let go of Eijeh and crouched next to her sister instead. Ori held Isae's hand tight to her chest, and their eyes met.

A small smile. Then gone.

Akos pushed his way onto the platform, where Isae was bent over Ori's body. Ori's dark clothes were wet with blood. Isae didn't cry, or scream, or shake. Behind her, Eijeh was—for some reason—lying still, eyes closed.

A shadow passed over them. The renegade ship, glowing orange, yellow, and red, coming to their rescue, piloted by Jyo and Sifa.

Teka was already crouched over the control panel on the right side of the platform. She was trying to pry the screen away from the rest of the mechanism, but her hand was trembling around the screwdriver, so she kept losing the screws. Finally Akos drew his knife and forced it between screen and mechanism, pressing them apart. Teka nodded her approval, and jammed her fingers inside to disable the force field.

There was a flicker of bright white as the force field winked out. The transport ship sank into the amphitheater, and hovered as low as it could go without crushing the seats. The floor hatch opened over them, and the steps came down.

"Isae!" Akos shouted. "We have to go!"

Isae gave him a look that was like poison. She put her hands under Ori's arms and tried to drag her toward the ship. Akos went to Ori's legs, to help, but Isae snapped, "Hands off her!" so he stepped back. By that time, Cisi had made it to the platform, and Isae didn't yell at her. Together they carried Ori's body up the steps to the ship.

Akos turned to Eijeh, who hadn't moved from where he was when Isae tackled him. When Akos shook his older brother's shoulder, he still didn't move, so Akos touched his fingers to Eijeh's throat to make sure he was still alive. And he was. Strong pulse. Strong breaths.

"Akos!" Cyra shouted from the arena floor. She was still next to Ryzek's body, knife in hand.

"Leave it!" he shouted back. Why not just leave his body to carrion birds and Noavek loyalists?

"No!" Cyra said, her eyes wide, urgent. "I can't!"

She held up the knife. He hadn't looked close before; all he had seen was Ryzek's body, limp, and Cyra standing over it with blade drawn. But when she gestured toward the weapon, he saw that the blade was clean. She hadn't stabbed Ryzek. She hadn't stabbed him, so why had he collapsed?

Akos remembered Suzao's face hitting his soup in the cafeteria, and the guard outside the amphitheater door, going limp, and it was obvious: Cyra had *drugged Ryzek*.

Even though he knew Cyra was more than Ryzek's Scourge, or even Ryzek's Executioner—even though he had seen the better parts of her, getting stronger in the worst environment possible, like the hushflower that bloomed in the Deadening time—somehow, he'd never considered this possibility:

Cyra had spared Ryzek. For him.

CHAPTER 39 | CYRA

THE HATCH DOOR OF the renegade ship closed behind us. I
checked Ryzek's pulse before untying the rope from his chest. It
was weak, but steady, just as it was supposed to be. Given the timing of his fall, and the strength of Akos's sleep blends, it would be
a while before he woke. I hadn't stabbed him, though I had taken
great pains to make it look as if I had, in case anyone was watching
closely on the sights.

Yma Zetsyvis had disappeared in a pale blue flourish in the cha-
otic aftermath of the challenge. I wished I had gotten the chance
to thank her, but then, she hadn't poisoned Ryzek for me; she had
believed it would kill him, as I had led her to believe it would. She
probably would have hated my gratitude. And when she found out
that I had lied to her, she would hate me more than before.

Isae and Cisi crouched on either side of Ori's body. Akos stood
behind his sister. When she snaked her hand back to reach for him,
he was already stretching toward her; they clasped fingers, Akos's
gift freeing Cisi's tears.

"May the current, which flows through and around each and all
of us, living and passed, guide Orieve Benesit to a place of peace,"

Cisi murmured, covering Isae's bloody hands with her own. "May we who live hear its comfort clearly, and strive to match our actions to the path it sets for us."

Isae's hair was stringy and wet with spit, sticking to her lips. Cisi brushed it away from her face, tucking it behind her ears. I felt the warmth and the weight of Cisi's currentgift, settling me into myself.

"May it be so," Isae finally said, apparently closing the prayer. I had never heard Thuvhesit prayers before, though I knew they spoke to the current itself, rather than its alleged master, like the smaller Shotet sects. Shotet prayers were lists of certainties rather than requests, and I liked the honesty of Thuvhesit tentativeness, the implicit acknowledgment that they didn't know if their prayers would be answered.

Isae stood, her hands limp at her sides. The ship lurched, sending us all off balance. I didn't worry that we would be pursued across the skies of Voa; there was no one left to order it.

"You knew," Isae said, looking up at Akos. "You *knew* he had been brainwashed by Ryzek, that he was dangerous—" She gestured to Eijeh, still lying unconscious on the metal floor. "From the very beginning."

"I didn't think he would ever—" Akos choked a little. "He loved her like a sister—"

"Don't you dare say that to me." Isae bent her fingers into fists, her knuckles turning white. "She was *my* sister. She does not belong to him, or to you, or to anyone else!"

I was too distracted by their conversation to stop Teka from kneeling next to Ryzek. She put her hand against his throat, then his chest, sliding it under his armor.

"Cyra," Teka said in a low voice. "Why is he alive?"

Everyone—Isae, Cisi, Akos—turned to Teka, their tense

moment broken. Isae looked from Ryzek's body to me. I stiffened. There was something threatening about the way she was moving, speaking, like she was a coiled creature ready to strike.

"The last hope for Eijeh's restoration lies in Ryzek," I said, as calmly as I could. "I spared him for the time being. After he returns Eijeh's memories I will happily cut out his heart myself."

"Eijeh." Isae laughed. And laughed again, madly, looking at the ceiling. "The drug you gave Ryzek put him to sleep . . . yet you chose not to share this with him when my sister's life was threatened?"

She stepped toward me, crushing Ryzek's fingers under her shoe.

"You chose the dim hope of a traitor's restoration," she said, low and quiet, "over the life of a chancellor's sister."

"If I had told Ryzek about the drug, we would have been trapped in that amphitheater with no leverage and no hope of escape, and he would have killed your sister anyway," I said. "I chose the path that guaranteed our survival."

"Bullshit." Isae leaned close to my face. "You chose Akos. Don't pretend it's any different than it is."

"Fine," I said, just as quiet. "It was Akos or you. I chose him. And I don't regret it."

It wasn't the whole truth, but it was certainly true. If simple hatred was what she craved, I would make it easier for her. I was used to being hated, especially by the Thuvhesit.

Isae nodded.

"Isae . . . ," Cisi began, but Isae was already walking away. She disappeared into the galley, closing the door behind her.

Cisi wiped her cheeks with the back of her hand.

"I can't believe this. Vas is dead, and Ryzek is alive," Teka said.

Vas was dead? I looked at Akos, but he was avoiding my eyes.

"Give me a reason not to kill Ryzek right now, Noavek," Teka said, turning to me. "And if that reason is something about Kereseth, I will hit you."

"If you kill him, you won't have my cooperation in whatever plan the renegades concoct next," I said dully, without looking at her. "If you help me keep him alive, I'll help you conquer Shotet."

"Yeah? And what kind of help would you be, exactly?"

"Oh, I don't know, Teka," I snapped, finally breaking my spell to glare at her. "Yesterday the renegades were just squatting in a safe house in Voa, clueless, and now, because of me, you're standing over the unconscious body of Ryzek Noavek with Voa in utter chaos behind you. I think that suggests my capacity to help the renegade cause is considerable, don't you?"

She chewed on the inside of her cheek for a few seconds, then said, "There's a storage area below deck with a heavy door. I'll toss him in there so he doesn't wake up on us." But she shook her head. "You know, wars have been started over less. You didn't just make her angry, you enraged an entire nation."

My throat tightened.

"You know there was nothing I could have done for Ori, even if I *had* killed Ryzek," I said. "We were all trapped."

"I know that." Teka sighed. "But I'm pretty sure Isae Benesit doesn't believe it."

"I'll talk to her," Cisi said. "I'll help her see it. Right now she just wants people to blame."

She shed the jacket she wore, leaving her arms bare and covered with goose bumps, and draped it over Ori. Akos helped her tuck the edges under Ori's shoulders and hips, so her wound was hidden. Cisi brushed Ori's hair into place with her fingers.

They both left, then, Cisi to the galley and Akos to the hold, with heavy footsteps and trembling hands.

I turned to Teka.

"Let's lock my brother up."

Teka and I dragged Ryzek and Eijeh to separate storage rooms, one by one. I rooted out more sleeping elixir to drug Eijeh. I wasn't sure what was wrong with him—he was still unconscious and unresponsive—but if he woke up as the same warped man who had murdered Ori Benesit, I didn't want to deal with it yet.

Then I went to the nav deck, where Sifa Kereseth sat in the captain's chair, her hands on the controls. Jyo was nearby, using his screen to contact Jorek, who had returned home after Ryzek fell, to get his mother. I sat in the empty chair beside Akos's mother. We were high in the atmosphere, almost past the barrier of blue that separated us from space.

"Where are we going?" I said.

"Into orbit until we make a plan," Sifa said. "We can't go back to Shotet, obviously, and it's not safe to go back to Thuvhe yet."

"Do you know what's wrong with Eijeh?" I said. "He's still catatonic."

"No," Sifa said. "Not yet."

She closed her eyes. I wondered if the future was something she could search, like the stars. Some people had mastery over their gifts, and some were simply servants to them—I had never stopped to wonder, before, which category the oracle of Hessa fell into.

"I think you knew we were going to fail," I said softly. "You told Akos that your visions were layered over each other, that Ori would be in the cell at the same time Ryzek faced me in the arena. But you knew they weren't, didn't you?" I paused. "And you knew

Akos would have to face Vas. You wanted him to have no choice other than to kill him, the man who murdered your husband."

Sifa touched the autonav map so the colors reversed—black for the expanse of space, and white for the route we were taking through it—and sat back in her chair, her hands in her lap. I thought she was just waiting to answer me, at first, but when she didn't say anything for a while, I realized she had no intention of doing so. I didn't press her. My mother had been intractable, too, and I knew when to give up.

So it surprised me a little when she spoke.

"My husband needed to be avenged," she said. "Someday Akos will see that."

"No he won't," I said. "He'll only see that his own mother maneuvered him into doing the thing he most hates."

"Maybe," she said.

The darkness of space wrapped around us like a shroud, and I felt calmer, consoled by the emptiness. This was a different kind of sojourn. Away from the past, instead of away from the place I was supposed to call home. Here, the lines between Shotet and Thuvhesit were harder to see, and I almost felt safe again.

"I should check on Akos," I said.

Before I could get up, her hand had closed over my arm, and she had leaned close enough to me that I could see streaks of warm brown in her dark eyes. She flinched but didn't pull away.

"Thank you," she said. "I'm sure that choosing mercy for my son over revenge against your brother was not easy for you."

I shrugged, uncomfortable. "I couldn't very well free myself from my own nightmares by bringing Akos's to life," I said. "Besides, I can handle a few nightmares."

CHAPTER 40 | AKOS

AFTER THE SHOTET TOOK Akos and Eijeh from their home and dragged them across the Divide; after Akos broke free from his wrist cuffs, stole Kalmev Radix's knife, and stabbed him with it; after they beat Akos so badly he could hardly walk, they took the Kereseth brothers to Voa to present them to Ryzek Noavek. Down the cliff face and through the dusty, winding streets, sure they were both about to die, or worse. Everything had been too loud, too crowded, too little like home.

As they walked down the short tunnel that led to the front gate of Noavek manor, Eijeh had whispered, "I'm so scared."

Their dad's death and their kidnapping had cracked him open like an egg. He was even oozing, his eyes always full of tears. The opposite had happened to Akos.

No one cracked Akos.

"I promised Dad I'd get you out of here," he'd said to Eijeh. "So that's what I'm going to do, understand? You'll make it out. That's a promise to you, this time."

He'd put his arm over his older brother's shoulders, pulled him tight to his side. They walked in together.

Now they were out, but they hadn't walked out together. Akos had had to drag him.

The hold was small and dank, but it had a sink, and that was pretty much all Akos cared about. He stripped to the waist, his shirt too stained to salvage, made the water as hot as he could stand, and worked the greasy soap into lather in his hands. Then he stuck his head under the faucet. Salty water ran into his mouth. As he scrubbed his arms and hands, scraping at the dried blood under his fingernails, he let himself go.

Just sobbed into the stream of water, half horrified and half relieved. Let the splatter sound drown out the strange, heaving noises coming from his own mouth. Let aching muscles shudder in the heat.

He wasn't really upright when Cyra came down the ladder. He was hanging on the edge of the basin by his armpits, his arms limp around his head. She said his name, and he forced himself to his feet, finding her eyes in the cracked mirror above the faucet. Water ran in rivers down his neck and back, soaking the top of his pants. He turned the water off.

She reached over her head to drag her hair to one side. Her eyes, dark as space, went soft as she looked him over. Current-shadows floated over her arms, draped themselves across her collarbone. Their movements were languid.

"Vas?" she said.

He nodded.

In that moment, he liked all the things she didn't say more than the things she did. There was no "Good riddance," or "You did what you had to do," or even a simple "It will be all right." Cyra didn't have the patience for that kind of thing. She fell on the hardest, surest truth, again and again, like a woman determined to crush her own bones, knowing they would heal stronger.

"Come on" was all she said. "Let's find you some clean clothes."

She looked tired, but only in the way a person was tired when they'd had a long day at work. And that was another thing about her, too—because so much of her life had been hard, she was steadier than other people when hard things came. Maybe not in such a good way, sometimes.

He pulled the stopper out of the drain so the reddish water disappeared, izit by izit. He dried off on the towel next to the sink. When he turned toward her, the currentshadows went haywire, dancing up her arms and across her chest. She winced a little, but it was different now, not so all-consuming. This was a Cyra who had a little space between her and the pain.

He followed her up the ladder again, down the narrow hall to the storage closet. It was stuffed full of fabric—sheets, towels, and at the bottom, spare clothes. He pulled on an oversize shirt. It felt better to be wearing something clean.

By that time Cyra was on her way to the nav deck, empty now that the transport ship was set to orbit. Near the exit hatch, his mom and Teka were wrapping Ori's body in white sheets. The galley door was still shut, his sister and Isae inside.

He stood at Cyra's shoulder, at the observation window. She'd always been drawn to sights like these, big and empty. He couldn't stand them, but he did like the winking of the stars, the glow of far-off planets, the dark red-purple of the currentstream.

"There is a Shotet poem I like," she said in clear Thuvhesit. He'd heard her speak just a few Thuvhesit words in all the time they'd spent together. That she spoke it now meant something—they were on equal footing, in a way they couldn't have been before. She had just about died to make them that way.

He frowned as he chewed on that. What a person did when they were in pain said a lot about them. And Cyra, always in pain, had almost given her life to free him from Shotet prison. He would never forget it.

"The translation is difficult," she continued. "But roughly, one of the lines reads, 'The heavy heart knows that justice is done.'"

"Your accent is very good," he said.

"I like the way the words feel." She touched her throat. "It reminds me of you."

Akos took the hand that was on her neck and laced his fingers with hers. The shadows snuffed out. Her brown skin had turned dull, but her eyes were alert as ever. Maybe he could learn to like the big empty of space if he thought of it like her eyes, soft-dark with just a hint of warmth.

"Justice is done," he repeated. "That's one way of looking at it, I guess."

"It's my way," she said. "Judging by your expression, I assume you've chosen the path of guilt and self-loathing instead."

"I wanted to kill him," he said. "I hate that I wanted to do something like that."

He shuddered again, and stared at his hands. All cracked from hitting things, the same way Vas's had been.

Cyra waited awhile before responding.

"It's hard to know what's right in this life," she said. "We do what we can, but what we really need is mercy. Do you know who taught me that?" A grin. "You."

He wasn't sure how he'd taught her about mercy, but he knew

the cost of it, for her. Mercy for Eijeh—and sparing Ryzek's life, for the time being—meant she had to hold on to the worst of her pain for even longer. It meant trading triumph *at last* for Isae's anger and the renegades' disgust. But she seemed at ease with it, still. No one knew how to bear other people's hate like Cyra Noavek. Sometimes she even encouraged it, but that didn't bother him so much. He understood it. She really just thought people were better off staying away from her.

"What?" she said.

"I like you, you know," he said.

"I know."

"No, I mean I like you the way you are, I don't need you to change." He smiled. "I've never thought of you as a monster or a weapon or—what did you call yourself? A rusty—"

She caught the word *nail* in her mouth. Her fingertips were cool, careful as they ran over the scars and bruises he wore, like she was taking them back. She tasted like sendes leaf and hush-flower, like saltfruit and like home.

He put his hands on her, sighing into her skin. They got bolder, fingers laced with fingers, knotted in hair, taking in fistfuls of shirt. Finding soft places nobody else had ever touched, like the bend in her waist, like the underside of his jaw. Their bodies pressed together, hip bone against stomach, knee against thigh . . .

"Hey!" Teka yelled from across the ship. "Not a private place, you two!"

Cyra rocked back on her heels, and glared at Teka.

He knew how she felt. He wanted more. He wanted everything.

CHAPTER 41 | CYRA

I DESCENDED THE STAIRS that led beneath the renegade ship to the hold, where my brother was locked in one of the storage rooms. The doors were solid metal, but each one had a vent near the low ceiling so air could circulate through the ship. I approached his room slowly, running one finger along the smooth wall. The lights flickered above my head as the ship shuddered.

The vent was at eye level, so I could see inside. I expected Ryzek's body to be limp on the floor next to bottles of solvent or cans of oxygen, but it wasn't. At first I didn't see him at all, and I gulped air, frantic, about to scream for help. But then he stepped into my line of sight, his body cut into stripes by the blades of the vent.

Still, I could see his eyes, unfocused but full of contempt.

"You're more of a coward than I thought you were," he said in a low growl.

"It's interesting being on this side of the wall this time," I said. "Be careful, or I will be as unkind to you as you were to me."

I held up my hand, letting smoky current unfurl around it.

Tendrils of ink-darkness wrapped around my fingers like hair. I ran my nails along the vent, lightly, marveling at how easy it would be to hurt him here, with no one to stop me. Just the opening of a door.

"Who did it?" Ryzek said. "Who poisoned me?"

"I already told you," I said. "I did."

Ryzek shook his head. "No, I've been keeping my iceflower blends under lock and key since the first assassination attempt that you participated in." He was almost, but not quite, smiling. "And by 'lock and key,' I mean a gene lock, accessible by Noavek blood alone." He waited a beat. "Locks that we both know you were, and are, unable to open."

My mouth dry, I stared up at him through the narrow space. He had security footage of the first assassination attempt, of course, so he had likely seen me trying to open the lock on his door with no success. But it didn't seem to surprise him.

"What do you mean?" I said, quiet.

"You do not share my blood," he said, pronouncing each word deliberately. "You are not a Noavek. Why do you think I started using those locks? Because I knew only one person would be able to get through them: me."

And I had never tried to get past them before the assassination, because I had always kept my distance from him. Even if I had, I was sure he would have kept a convincing lie ready for the occasion. He was always prepared to lie.

"If I'm not a Noavek, then what am I?" I said sharply.

"How should I know?" He laughed. "I'm glad I was able to see your face when I told you. Emotional, volatile Cyra. When will you learn to control your reactions?"

"I could ask the same of you. Your smiles are getting less and less convincing, Ryz."

"Ryz." He laughed again. "You think you've won, but you haven't. There are things I haven't told you, your true parentage aside."

Within me everything was turbulent. But I stood as still as I could, watching his lips part in that smile, his eyes crinkle at the corners. I searched his face for a sign of shared blood, and found none. We didn't look alike, but that in itself was not strange— sometimes siblings took after different parents, after distant relatives, bringing long-forgotten genes back to life. He was either telling me the truth or he was playing with my mind, but either way, I would not give him the satisfaction of seeing me react any further.

"This desperation," I said in a low voice, "does not become you, Ryzek. It's almost *indecent*."

I reached up, and pressed the vents flat with my fingertips.

But I could still hear him as he said, "Our father . . ." He paused, and corrected himself. "Lazmet Noavek is still alive."

CHAPTER 42 | AKOS

HE LOOKED OUT THE observation window at the dark sky. A strip of Thuvhe showed on the left, white with snow and cloud cover. No wonder the Shotet had named the planet "Urek," which meant "empty." From up here, its blankness was the only thing about it worth noting.

Cisi offered him a mug of tea, yellow green. The blend for fortitude, judging by its shade. He wasn't any good at mixing that one, since he'd spent most of his time working with hushflower, to put people to sleep and to kill their pain. It didn't taste like much—bitter like a new stem, freshly snapped—but it made him steadier like it was supposed to.

"How's Isae?" he asked her.

"Isae is . . ." Cisi frowned. "I think she heard me, on some level beyond her grief. But we'll see."

Akos was sure they would, and probably not what they wanted to see. He'd seen the hate in Isae's face as she glared at Cyra near the hatch door, her sister's body laid out behind her. One talk with Cisi couldn't take away hate like that, no matter how much warmth there was between them.

"I'll keep trying," Cisi said.

"That is the distinct feature of all my children," their mom said, climbing the grate steps to the nav deck. "They are persistent. To the point of delusion, some might say."

She said it with a smile. She had an odd way of complimenting people, their mother. He wondered if she had been counting on his delusional persistence when she arranged for them to get to the prison too late. Or maybe she really hadn't counted on Eijeh interrupting her plans with some oracle maneuvering of his own. He would never know.

"Is Eijeh awake?" he asked her.

"Awake, yes." Sifa sighed. "But just staring blankly, for now. He doesn't appear to hear me. I don't know what Ori did to him, before . . . well."

Akos thought of the two of them, Eijeh and Ori, on the platform, clutched together. The way she had said good-bye like he was the one leaving instead of her. And then he had, slipping away just because she touched him. What could Ori's touch do? He'd never asked her.

Sifa said, "We'll have to give it time, and see if we can use Ryzek to restore him. I think Cyra had a few ideas for that."

"I bet she does," Cisi said, a little darkly.

Akos sipped Cisi's tea, and let himself feel something like relief. Eijeh was out of Shotet, Cisi and Sifa were alive. There was some peace in knowing that all the men who had invaded their house and killed their father were gone now. They were marks on his arm. Or they would be, when he got around to carving Vas there.

Their little ship rotated, showing less of Thuvhe and more of the space beyond it, all dark but for the speckle of stars and the glow of a distant planet. Zold, if he remembered his maps right, which was not a guarantee. He'd never been much of a scholar.

It was Isae who broke the quiet, marching out of the galley at last. She looked better than she had a couple of hours before: She had pulled her hair back tight, and found a shirt to replace her bloody sweater. Her hands were clean, even under the fingernails. She crossed her arms, and took a wide stance at the edge of the nav deck platform.

"Sifa," she said. "Pull us out of orbit and set the autonav for Assembly Headquarters."

Sifa sat in the captain's chair and said—shooting for casual, and winding up at nervous—"Why are we going there?"

"Because they need to see, firsthand, that I am alive." Isae gave her a cold, appraising stare. "And because they will have a cell that can hold both Ryzek and Eijeh until I decide what to do with them both."

"Isae . . ." Akos started. But there was nothing to say that he hadn't already said.

"Don't test my patience; you'll find it has limits." Isae had gone full chancellor. The woman who had touched his head and told him he was Thuvhesit was gone now. "Eijeh is a Thuvhesit citizen. He will be treated like one, just like the rest of you. Unless, Akos, you would like to declare your Shotet citizenship and be treated the same as Miss Noavek."

He was no Shotet citizen, but he knew better than to bicker with her. She was grieving.

"No," he said. "I wouldn't."

"Very well. Is the autonav set?"

Sifa had pulled up the nav screen, which floated in little green letters in front of her, and was typing in coordinates. She sat back in her chair.

"Yes. We'll arrive in several hours."

"Until then, you will make sure that Ryzek Noavek and Eijeh are kept under control," Isae said to Akos. "I have no interest in hearing from either of them, understand?"

He nodded.

"Good. I will be in the galley. Let me know when we begin our approach, Sifa."

Without waiting for an answer, she marched away again. He felt her footsteps vibrating through the floor grate.

"I have seen war in every future," his mom said out of nowhere. "The current guides us there. The players change, but the result is the same."

Cisi took their mom's hand, and then Akos's. "But we're together now."

Sifa's troubled look gave way to a smile. "Yes, we are together now."

Now. For just a breath, he was sure, but it was something. Cisi rested her head on Akos's shoulder, and their mom smiled at him. He could almost hear the feathergrass scratching at their house's windows in the wind. But he still couldn't quite smile back.

The renegade ship arced away from Thuvhe. Up ahead he saw the cloudy pulse of the current making a path through the galaxy. It bound all the planets together, and though it didn't seem to move, every person could feel it singing in their blood. The Shotet even thought it gave them their language, like a tune only they knew, and they had a point. He was proof of that.

But he still felt—heard—only silence, otherwise.

He put his arm across Cisi's shoulders, and caught sight of his marks, turned out toward the light. Maybe they were marks of loss, like Cyra said, but standing there with his family, he realized something else. You could get things back.

ACKNOWLEDGMENTS

THANK YOU, THANK YOU, THANK YOU:

Nelson, husband, friend, for brainstorming with me, reading my early drafts, and sharing this weird, wonderful life with me.

Katherine Tegen, my editor, for your transformative notes, your insistence on getting this book right, your solid instincts, and your kind heart.

Joanna Volpe, my agent, for knowing *this* was the right idea, for being my rudder, and for your well-timed Real Talk. And for exchanging weird gifs with me. I cherish them.

Danielle Barthel, for patiently keeping me responsible, for your feedback, and for our wacky Friday afternoon phone calls. Kathleen Ortiz, for tirelessly and cheerfully working to ensure that this book found its very best home in so many countries. Pouya Shahbazian, for being a good human being, for pictures of adorable children, and for your excellent insight. Everyone else at New Leaf Literary, for your support and your great work in the world of books (and movies).

Rosanne Romanello, for steadying me, planning ahead, and those little pushes that help me grow. Nellie Kurtzman, Cindy

Hamilton, Bess Braswell, Sabrina Abballe, Jenn Shaw, Lauren Flower, Margot Wood, and Patti Rosati, in marketing, for your patience and flexibility (special shout-out to BESS'S GRID!). Josh Weiss, Gwen Morton, Alexandra Rakaczki, Brenna Franzitta, and Valerie Shea, for unparalleled copyediting/proofreading skillz, particularly when it comes to world-building inconsistencies and logic. Andrea Pappenheimer, Kathy Faber, Kerry Moynagh, Heather Doss, Jenn Wygand, Fran Olson, Deb Murphy, Jenny Sheridan, Jessica Abel, Susan Yeager, of sales; Jean McGinley, in sub rights; Randy Rosema and Pam Moore, finance whizzes; Caitlin Garing, audio extraordinaire; Lillian Sun, in production; and Kelsey Horton, in editorial, for all your hard work (!!!), kindness, and support. Joel Tippie, Amy Ryan, Barbara Fitzsimmons, and Jeff Huang, for a truly gorgeous book. I could not have asked for better. And of course, Brian Murray, Suzanne Murphy, and Kate Jackson, for making this Harper house one I'm happy to call home.

Margaret Stohl, Jedi Knight and the woman I want to be when I grow up, for taking good care of my brain. Sarah Enni, for being my buddy, beta reader, and a badass woman. Courtney Summers, Kate Hart, Debra Driza, Somaiya Daud, Kody Keplinger, Amy Lukavics, Phoebe North, Michelle Krys, Lindsey Roth Culli, Maurene Goo, Kara Thomas, Samantha Mabry, Kaitlin Ward, Stephanie Kuehn, Kirsten Hubbard, Laurie Devore, Alexis Bass, Kristin Halbrook, Leila Austin, and Steph Sinkhorn for your endless support, humor, and honesty. Hot damn, I ♥ you guys so much. Tori Hill, for your expertise in the care and feeding of (neurotic) authors. Brendan Reichs, coconspirator in Charleston shenanigans, for keeping it classy. All the YALLpeople, for letting me make crazy spreadsheets for you twice a year. The basket cases in my inbox, for showing me I'm not alone.

Alice, MK, Carly, and all the other nonwriter types in my life who put up with my hermit tendencies and remind me that work is not life and life is not work.

Mom, Frank III, Ingrid, Karl, Frank IV, Candice, Dave; Beth, Roger, Tyler, Rachel, Trevor, Tera, Darby, Andrew, Billie, and Fred: if I obsess over the importance of family in my writing, it's because of you guys.

Katalin, for teaching me how to throw a punch—I write much more accurate training scenes now! Paula, for saying all the brilliant words that got me to take better care of myself.

All the women I know who suffer from chronic pain, for helping me find Cyra.

Teenage girls, because you're amazing, inspiring, and worthy.

GLOSSARY

altetahak – A style of Shotet combat best suited for students who are strong in build, translates to "school of the arm."

Benesit – One of three fated families on the nation-planet of Thuvhe. One of the current generation is destined to be Thuvhe's chancellor.

current – Both natural phenomena and, in some cases, religious symbol, the current is an invisible power that gives people abilities and can be channeled into ships, machines, weapons, etc.

currentgift – Thought to be a result of the current flowing through a person, currentgifts are abilities, unique to each person, that develop during puberty. They are not always benevolent.

currentstream – A visual representation of the current in the sky, the brightly colored currentstream flows between and around each planet in the solar system.

elmetahak – A style of Shotet combat that has fallen out of favor, emphasizing strategic thinking. Translates to "school of the mind."

feathergrass – A powerful plant that originated on Ogra. Causes hallucinations, particularly when ingested.

Hessa – One of three major cities in the nation-planet of Thuvhe, has a reputation for being rougher and poorer than the other two.

hushflower – The most significant iceflower to the Thuvhesit, the bright red hushflower can be poisonous when not diluted. Diluted, it is used both as an analgesic and for recreational purposes.

iceflower – Thuvhe's only crops, iceflowers are hardy, thick-stemmed plants with different-colored blooms, each one uniquely useful in medicines and other substances throughout the solar system.

izit – A unit of measurement, about the width of the average person's pinkie.

Kereseth – One of three fated families on the nation-planet of Thuvhe, residing in Hessa.

Noavek – The only fated family of Shotet, known for their instability and brutality.

Osoc – The coldest of the three major cities of Thuvhe, and the farthest north.

Othyr – A planet near the center of the solar system, known for its wealth and its contribution to technology, particularly in the realm of medicine.

Pitha – Also known as "the water planet," a nation-planet of highly practical people who are prized for their engineering of synthetic materials.

season – A unit of time that has its origins in Pitha, where one revolution around the sun is jokingly referred to as "the rainy season" (since it rains constantly there).

Shissa – The wealthiest of the three cities of Thuvhe. The buildings in Shissa hang high above the ground "like suspended raindrops."

sojourn – A seasonal journey undertaken by the Shotet people in a massive spaceship, involving one revolution around the solar system, and the scavenging of a "current favored" planet's valuable materials.

Tepes – Known also as "the desert planet," it is the closest nation-planet to the sun, known for being highly religious.

Thuvhe – The Assembly-recognized name for both the nation and the planet itself, also known as the "ice planet." It contains both the Thuvhesit and Shotet people.

Urek – The Shotet name for the planet of Thuvhe (though they refer to the nation of Thuvhe by its proper name), meaning "empty."

Voa – The capital city of Shotet, where most of the population is located.

zivatahak – A style of Shotet combat best suited for students who are quick in mind and body. Translates to "school of the heart."

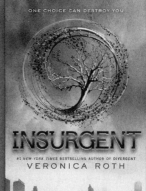